THE BRIGHTEST DAY, THE DARKEST NIGHT

By the same author:

The Whitest Flower
The Element of Fire

BRENDAN GRAHAM

The Brightest Day, The Darkest Night

HarperCollins*Publishers*

Although this book is based on real events of the
American Civil War 1861–1865, the main characters
portrayed are entirely the work of the author's imagination.

HarperCollins*Publishers*
77–85 Fulham Palace Road,
Hammersmith, London W6 8JB

www.harpercollins.co.uk

Published by HarperCollins*Publishers* 2005

1

All lyrics by Brendan Graham © Warner Chappell Music Ltd/
Brendan Graham. Reproduced by permission of
International Music Publications Ltd/
Brendan Graham. Pure Music Ltd.

A catalogue record for this book
is available from the British Library

ISBN 0 00 225978 8

Set in Sabon by
Palimpsest Book Production Limited, Polmont, Stirlingshire

Printed and bound in Great Britain by
Clays Ltd, St Ives plc

ACKNOWLEDGEMENTS

No book is an island. During its course many ships come. Some pass in the night, some anchor for longer. Without them all the book is lost at the many reefs on the voyage.

This book was written at many ports. From America's Deep South to the plains of Pennsylvania; from the shores of Lough Mask to the shores of Lake Annaghmakerrig; from the hills of Dublin to the coastline of New South Wales.

On the journey, Norwegian composer Rolf Lovland sent me a melody which, with lyrics added, became Jared Prudhomme's song to Louisa – 'You Raise Me Up'. American writer Bee Ring sent me a letter – Sullivan Ballou's letter to his wife before the battle of Bull Run. This became the basis for Lavelle's letter to Ellen – and also gave me the title for the book. Singer Cathy Jordan sang 'The Fairhaired Boy' – Ellen's song throughout – and brought Ellen to life. In Dublin's National Concert Hall, I was swept away by Martin Hayes' fiddling of *Port na bPucai*. When I 'returned', the whole scene of the 'Cripple's Waltz', had formed in my mind in its entirety. E. Moore Quinn, Associate Professor of Anthropology at the College of Charleston, sent me a book by Catherine Clinton, which led to many new insights on Civil War women in the South.

From New Orleans and the great plantation houses of Louisiana, through almost every State in between, to Boston, I was facilitated, pointed in the right direction, corrected and redirected, by librarians, archivists, museum directors, battlefield curators and Civil War enthusiasts of every hue of Blue and Grey. I list them in no particular order but to each I am sincerely indebted: The staff of the National Park Service, U.S. Department of the Interior at the National Military Parks and National Battlefield Parks of: Gettysburg; Fredericksburg and Spotsylvania; Antietam; Petersburg; Harpers Ferry; Glendale/Frayser's Farm. Terry Reimer, Director of Research, Ann M. Lee, National Museum of Civil War Medicine, Frederick; D. Scott Hartwig, Supervisory Park Historian, Gettysburg; Randy Cleaver, Historian, Richmond National Battlefield Park; Bob Krick, Historian, Richmond National Park

Service; John M. Coski, Historian/ Library Director, Museum of the Confederacy, Richmond; New Orleans Confederate Museum; Pamplin Historical Park & the National Museum of the Civil War Soldier; Lexington Visitor Centre, Virginia. Kathleen M. Williams, Manager of Circulation Services/ Bibliographer of Irish Studies, Thomas P. O'Neill, Jr, Library, Boston College; Dr Kenneth W. Jones, Librarian, Tarleton State University, Texas; Michael R. Machan, Reference Librarian, Thomas Cooper Library, University of South Carolina; Bernice Bergup, Humanities Reference Librarian, Davis Library, University of North Carolina; Boston Public Library. In Louisiana, staff at Evergreen Plantation; Houmas House Plantation; Oak Alley Plantation. Dr Inge Leipold, MA, Munich. Nicholas Carolan, Traditional Music Archive, Dublin; National Library, Dublin; Director Sheila Pratschke and staff, Tyrone Guthrie Centre, Annaghmakerrig.

To the multitude of authors and historians, who have so passionately and painstakingly kept alive the many facets of this monumental event in their nation's history, I am also indebted. I gratefully acknowledge the part they played in helping me shape both the backdrop to this book as well as some of its thematic threads. For omissions, errors of fact and novelist's licence, I am totally responsible.

I have missed a number of deadlines with this book. Throughout it all my publishers HarperCollins have been stoic in their patience. My editors, Patricia Parkin and Maxine Hitchcock, have borne long-running 'author-displacement activity' with good grace and good humour. Carole Blake, my agent, came on board during the saga that was the writing of this book – and must have wondered why!

My wife Mary and family have fortunately been blessed with endurance and forbearance – and sorely needed it at many stages along the way. Drafts and redrafts were all willingly typed and re-typed at the most inconvenient of times without (mostly) a murmur. Donna made some valuable observations at the final stages. To them, and all who helped keep both author and book afloat, *buiochas om' chroi*.

Brendan Graham, Co. Mayo, September, 2005

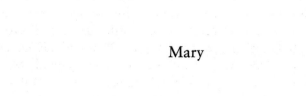

Mary

PROLOGUE

Half Moon Place, Boston, 1861

Ellen O'Malley opened her eyes.

Blinked.

Raised her head.

Waited, watching for the sky.

Soon the sun would come creeping into the corners of Half Moon Place. 'Like a broom,' she thought. Sweeping out the dark.

When the sun brushed along the narrow alleyway towards where she sat, she opened her throat, and began singing,

> 'Praise to the Earth and creation,
> Praise to the dance of the morning sun.'

She sat atop a mound of rubbish, raised from the ground and the sordid effluents that back-washed the alleyway. The mane of red hair that fell from her head to her waist, her only garment. The sailors who frequented the basement dram-houses of Half Moon Place, had rough-handled her, taken her clothes for sport. But no more.

Ellen hadn't even resisted. Instead, offered prayers for their wayward souls, which hurried them off.

The glasses she missed more. The alley children had stolen them, fascinated by the purplish hue that helped her eyes. Years in the cordwaining mills of Massachusetts had taken their toll. But she was blessed more than most. Without them she could still see the sun and the stars and the moon. The shoe-stitching she could no longer do. She couldn't blame Fogarty then, the landlord's middleman, when eventually he put her out for falling behind with the rent. He wasn't the worst; had stretched himself as far as one of his kind could.

Even in her current situation, any passer-by would have still considered Ellen O'Malley a striking woman. Firm of countenance, fine of forehead and with remarkable eyes. 'Speckled emeralds,' she had once been told, 'like islands in a lake.' She smiled at the memory. Tall, she sat unbowed by the circumstances in which she now found herself. Her fortieth year to Heaven behind her, a casual onlooker might have placed Ellen O'Malley at not yet having reached the meridian of life. A flattery from which, once, she would not have demurred.

She had only been out the few nights now and the New England Fall had not been harsh. Biddy Earley, whose voice Ellen heard at night, driving a hard bargain with the men of the sea would, in the daylight hours bring her a cup of buttermilk and a step of bread for dipping in it. Part-proceeds of the previous night. Likewise, Blind Mary, all day on her stoop in nodding talk with herself, would bring her a scrap of this or that, or the offer of a 'gill of gin'. Then, nod her way homewards again, scattering with her stick the street urchins who taunted her.

Still with her song, Ellen reflected on her state. She was, at last, stripped of everything – a perfection of poverty. No possessions, no desires. Life . . . and death came and went along the passageways of Half Moon Place with such a frequent regularity that her situation attracted scant attention. Nor did she seek it.

'Into Thy hands Lord, I commend my Spirit.'

Nothing remained within her own hands, everything in His.

It was a wonderful liberation to at last hand over her life. Not forever seeking to keep the reins tightly gripped on it. Death, when it came, would hold no fears for her. Death was re-unification with the One who created her.

She looked down at her nakedness, unashamed by it, her body now shriven of sin, aglow with the light of Heaven. She had been beautiful once, had fallen from grace, and now, was beautiful again; if less so physically, then spiritually at least.

She thought of her children: Mary, her natural daughter; Louisa, her adopted daughter; Patrick, her son and then, Lavelle, her second husband. How she had betrayed them; her self-exile from their lives; her atonement; and finally, now her redemption.

She had been right all those years ago. To unhinge herself from their lives after her affair . . . keep them free of scandal. Because of her the girls, postulants then, would likely have been driven from the Convent of St Mary Magdalen. With words like 'the very reason the vow of purity is so highly prized among the Sisters is that, in its absence, it is humanity's fatal flaw.' Ellen considered this a moment . . . how very true in her own case.

And clothes? Clothes were the outer manifestation of the inner flaw – something with which to cover it up. Down all the centuries since paradise lost. Now, her paradise regained, she had no earthly need of them.

'I am clothed . . .' she sang in her song, '. . . the sun, the moon and the stars – finer raiment than ever fell from the hands of man.'

Then she prayed.

'Jesus, Mary and Joseph, I give you my
    heart and my soul;
Jesus, Mary and Joseph, assist me in my last agony;
Jesus, Mary and Joseph, may I breathe forth my soul in
peace with you. Amen.'

She followed with the Our Father – in the old tongue *Ár n-Athair atá ar Neamh*. Then finally, she raised to heaven the long-remembered prayers of childhood.

Afterwards she sang again. The songs she had sung to her own children – nonsensical, infant-dandling songs: *aislingí*, the beautiful sung vision-poems; and the *suantraí*, the 'sleep-songs' with which she once lullabyed them. Sang to the sun and the teetering tenements of Half Moon Place.

ELLEN

ONE

Convent of St Mary Magdalen, Boston, 1861

'Half Moon Place . . .' Sister Lazarus warned, '. . . is reeking with perils.' The two younger nuns in her presence looked at each other. Ready for whatever perils the outside world might bring. It was not their first such outing into one of Boston's less fortunate neighbourhoods. Still, Sister Lazarus considered it her bounden duty, as on every previous occasion, to remind them of the 'reeking perils' awaiting them.

'Now, Sister Mary *and* Sister Veronica . . .' the older woman continued, '. . . you must remain together at all times. Inseparable. The fallen . . . those women whom you will find there . . . if they are truly repentant . . . wanting of God's grace . . . wanting to leave . . .' She paused. '. . . wanting to leave behind their . . . *previous lives* . . . then you must bring them here to be in His keeping.'

'Here,' was the Convent of St Mary Magdalen, patron saint of the fallen of their gender. 'Here' the Sisters would care for those women, the leftovers of Boston life. Care for their temporal needs but primarily their spiritual ones.

Sister Lazarus – 'Rise-from-the-Dead' as the two younger nuns referred to her – reminded them again that their sacred mission in life was to 'reclaim the thoughtless and melt the hardened'.

The older nun took in her two charges, still in their early twenties. Sister Mary, tall, serene as the Mother of God for whom she had been named. Blessed with uncommon natural beauty. Most of it now hidden, along with her gold-red tresses, under the winged, white headdress of the Magdalens. And not a semblance of pride in her beauty, Sister Lazarus thought. Oh, what novenas Sister Lazarus would have offered to have been blessed with Sister Mary's eyes – those sparkling, jade-coloured eyes, ever modestly cast downwards – instead of the slate-coloured ones the Lord had seen fit to bless *her* with. The older nun corrected her indecorousness of thought. Envy was a terrible sin. She turned her attention to the other young nun before her.

Sister Veronica's eyes were entirely a different matter.

Sister Veronica did not at all keep her attractive, hazel-brown eyes averted from the world, or anybody in it – including Sister Lazarus. Nor was Sister Veronica at all as demure in her general carriage as Sister Lazarus would have liked. Instead, carried herself with a disconcerting sweep of her long white Magdalen habit. Which always to Sister Lazarus, seemed to be trying to catch up with the younger nun. Unsuccessfully at that!

'Impetuosity, Sister Veronica,' the older nun had frequently admonished, 'will be your undoing. You must guard against it!'

She saw them out the door, a smile momentarily relieving her face. If the hardened were indeed to be melted, these two were, for all such 'meltings', abundantly graced. Though Sister Lazarus would never tell them so. Praise, even if deserved, should always be generously reserved.

Praise could lead to pride.

'There are so many fallen from God's grace, Louisa,' Sister Mary said when once out of earshot of the convent. She used the other nun's former name, the one she had known her adopted sister by for more than a dozen years. Since first they had come out of Ireland.

'God takes care of His own,' Louisa replied.

'And Mother?' Mary asked, the question always on her mind.

Louisa took her sister's arm.

'Yes . . . and Mother too,' Louisa answered. 'We would surely have heard. Somebody would have brought news if something had happened'.

But something *had* happened.

Life had been good once. Their mother had made their way well in America, educating both herself and them. She had re-married – Lavelle – built up a small if successful business with him. Then it had seemed to all go wrong, the business failing. When a move from their home at 29 Pleasant Street to more straitened accommodation had been imminent, Mary and Louisa had both secretly decided to unburden the family of themselves. To follow the nudging, niggling voice they had been hearing.

'It almost broke poor Mother's heart,' Mary said.

'Then, do you remember, Louisa, once in the convent, everything silent – just like you?'

Louisa nodded, remembering. As a child she had been cast to the roads of a famine-ridden Ireland, her parents desperate in the hope she would fall on common charity and survive the black years of the blight. Six months later Louisa had returned to find them, huddled together; their bodies half eaten by dogs, likewise famished. She had gone silent then. All sound, it seemed, trapped beneath the bones that formed her chest. Nor did she retain a memory of any name they had called her by – not even their own names.

A year later Ellen had found her, taken her in. Though some early semblance of speech had returned in the intervening year, her silence had helped Louisa survive. Drawn forth whatever crumbs of charity a famished people could grant. So she had remained silent. Kept her secret. Afraid, lest once revealed, all kindness be cut off and she condemned, like the rest to claw at each other for survival. She had remained 'the silent girl' until they reached America and Ellen had christened her. After the place in which they had found her – Louisburgh, County Mayo – and the place to which they were then bound for, Boston, with its other Louisburgh . . . Square.

Gradually the trapped place beneath Louisa's breast had freed itself. Then, in the safe sanctum of the cathedral at Franklin Street she had whispered out halting prayers of thanksgiving.

At the edge of Boston Common, they stood back to let a group of blue-clad militia double-quick by them. The young men all a-gawk at the wide-winged headdresses of the two nuns.

'Angels from Heaven!' a saucy Irish voice shouted.

'Devils from Hell!' another one piped.

Then they were gone, shuffling in their out-of-time fashion to be mustered for some battlefield in Virginia.

'I pray God that this war between the States will be quickly done with,' Mary said quietly.

'Do you remember anything, Mary – anything at all?' Louisa asked, returning to the topic that, like her sister, always occupied her mind.

'Nothing . . . only, like you, that Mother had once called to the convent, leaving no message . . . and then those messages left by Lavelle and dear brother Patrick that they had not found her. I cannot imagine what . . . unless some fatal misfortune has . . . and I cannot bear to think that.'

Louisa's mind went back over the times she and her adoptive mother had been alone. That time in the cathedral at Holy Cross when Ellen had tried to get her to speak. How troubled her mother had seemed. And the book, the one which Ellen had left on the piano. Louisa had opened it. *Love Elegies* . . . the sinful poetry of a stained English cleric – John Donne. It had shocked Louisa that her mother could read such things – and well-read the book had been.

'Did you ever see a particular book – *Love Elegies* – with Mother?' she asked Mary.

Mary thought for a moment.

'No, I cannot say so, but then Mother was always reading. Why. . . ?'

'Oh, I don't know, Mary, something . . . a nun's intuition.' Louisa laughed it off. Then, more brightly, gazing into her sister's face, 'You are so like her . . . so beautiful . . . her green-speckled eyes, her fiery hair . . .'

'That's if you could see it!' Mary interjected.

'Personally cropped by the stern shears of Sister Lazarus,' she added. 'That little furrow under Mother's nose – you have it too!'

Louisa went to touch her sister's face.

'Oh, stop it, Louisa!' Mary gently chided. 'You are not behaving with the required decorum. If "Rise-from-the-Dead" could only see you!'

Louisa restrained herself. 'I am sorry . . . you are right,' she said, offering up a silent prayer for unbecoming conduct – and that the all-seeing eye of Sister Lazarus might not somehow be watching.

'We are almost there,' was all Mary answered with.

Half Moon Place held all the backwash of Boston life. As far removed from the counting houses of Hub City as was Heaven from Hell. It housed, in ramshackle rookeries, the furthest fringes of Boston society – indolent Irish, fly-by-nights and runaway slaves. None of which recoiled the two nuns. Nor the reeking stench that, long prior to entering them, announced such places. Since Sister Lazarus had first deemed them 'morally sufficient' for such undertakings, many the day had the older nun sent them forth on similar missions of rescue.

11

Them returning always from places like this with some unfortunate in tow, to the Magdalen's sheltering walls.

This was their work, their calling. To snatch from the jaws of iniquity young women who, by default or design, had strayed into them.

'Reclaim the thoughtless and melt the hardened.' Sister Lazarus's words seemed to ring from the very portals of what lay facing them today. Half Moon Place indeed would be a fertile ground for redemption.

'A Tower of Babel,' Louisa said, stepping precariously under its archway into a rabble of tattered urchins who chased after some rotting evil.

'Kick the Reb! Kill the Reb!' they shouted, knocking into them with impunity.

A nodding woman, on her stoop, shook her stick after them.

'I'll scatter ye . . . ye little bastards! God blast ye! D'annoyin' the head of a person, from sun-up to sundown!'

From a basement came the dull sound of a clanging pot colliding with a human skull. A screech of pain . . . a curse . . . it all just melting into the sounds that underlay the stench and woebegone sight of the place.

Further along, a woman singing. The snatches of sound attracted them. 'The soul pining for God,' Mary said, as the woman's keening rose on the vapours of Half Moon Place . . . and was carried to meet them. They rounded the half-moon curve of the alleyway. The singing woman sat amidst a pile of rubbish as if, herself, discarded from life. The long tarnished hair draped over her shoulders her only modesty. But her face was raised to a place far above the teetering tenements, and her song transcended the wretchedness of her state.

'If not in life we'll be as one
Then, in death we'll be,
And there will grow two hawthorn trees
Above my love and me,

12

And they will reach up to the sky –
Intertwined be . . .
And the hawthorn flower will bloom where lie
My fair-haired boy . . . and me.'

It was Louisa who reached her first, hemline abandoned, wildly careering the putrid corridor. Mary then, at her heels, the two of them scrabbling over the off-scourings and excrement. Then, in the miracle of Half Moon Place, breathless with hope, they reached her. As one, they clutched her to themselves.

Praising God. Cradling her nakedness. Wiping the grime and the lost years from her face.

'Mother!' they cried. 'Oh, Mother!'

TWO

They huddled about her, calling out her name, their own names. Begging for her recognition.

'Mother! Mother! It's us . . . Mary and Louisa,' Mary said, stroking her mother's head. 'You'll be all right now. We'll take you back with us.'

'Mary? Louisa? It's . . .' Ellen began.

'Her mind is altered,' a voice rang out, interrupting. 'Too much prayin' and Blind Mary's juniper juice,' the voice continued.

'We are her daughters,' Mary said, turning to face the hard voice of Biddy Earley.

'Daughters – ha!' the woman laughed. 'Well blow me down with a Bishop's fart,' she said, arms akimbo, calloused elbows visible under her rolled-up sleeves. 'Oh, she was a close one, was our Ellie. Daughters? An' us fooled into thinking she had neither chick nor child.'

'What happened to her?' Louisa asked.

'The needle blindness . . . couldn't do the stitchin' no more. But she's not as bad as she makes out . . . can see when she wants to!' the woman answered disparagingly. 'Fogarty, the landlord's man, tumbled her out. Just like back home, 'ceptin' now it's your honest-to-God, Irish landlords here in America, 'stead of the relics of auld English

14

decency. 'Twould put a longing on a person for the bad old days!'

Ellen, struggling to take it all in, again made to say something.

'Sshh now, Mother,' Louisa comforted. 'Talk is for later. We have to get you inside,' she said, looking at Biddy Earley.

Reluctantly, Biddy agreed, cautioning that the 'widow-woman brought all the troubles on herself.'

Mary and Louisa, shepherding Ellen, followed Biddy down into the dank basement where the woman lived.

'I've no clothes for her, mind – 'ceptin' what's on me own back,' she called to them over her shoulder.

Mary would stay with Ellen, Louisa would make the journey back to the convent to get clothes. The Sisters, providential in every respect, always kept some plain homespun, diligently darned against a rainy day – or a novice leaving.

Mary then removed her own undergarment – long white pantaloons tied with a plain-ribboned bow at the ankle. These she pulled onto her mother. Similarly, and aware of the other woman's stare, she removed as modestly as she could, the petticoat from under her habit, fastening it around Ellen. Biddy, for all her talk about 'no clothes', produced a shawl, even if it was threadbare.

'Throw that over her a while,' she ordered Mary.

Ellen again started to say something, prompting the woman to come to her and shake her vigorously.

'Just look at you – full of gibberish . . . same as ever!' she said roughly. 'This is your own flesh and blood come for you, widow-woman! Will you whisht that jabberin'!'

To Mary's amazement, Biddy Earley then drew back her hand and slapped Ellen full across the face.

'You wasn't so backward when you was accusatin' me o' stealin' your book,' she levelled at Ellen.

'What book?' Mary asked, shocked by the woman's action and holding her mother protectively.

'Some English filth she kept recitatin' to herself. Ask Blind

Mary – stuck sittin' on that stoop of hers – about it. That and her niggerology! When, if Lincoln will have his way, the blacks'll be swarmin' all over us . . . and them savages no respecters o' the likes of you neither, *Sister*!' Biddy Earley added for good measure.

Mary didn't know what to make of it all. All of her endless prayers answered and the joy, the unparalleled joy, of finding her mother alive after all these years. But yet, so dishevelled, and living in such a place.

Biddy Earley, settling a streelish curl beneath her headscarf, continued in similar vein. 'Then looking down on the likes o' me for going on me back to the sailors. Sure it's no sin if it's keeping body and soul together, is it, Sister?' she asked boldly, uncaring of the reply. 'No sin if you don't enjoy it?' she added, with a rasp of a laugh.

'Why don't you come with us?' Mary asked the woman, thinking of Sister Lazarus's words. But Biddy Earley, however hardened, was no candidate for 'melting' by nuns.

'I ain't no sinner, Sister – I don't need no forgivin',' she retorted, unyieldingly. 'Now sit quiet till t'other one comes back and then clear off out o' here, the three o' yis!'

Mary sat silently, offering thanks for the all-seeing hand that led herself and Louisa to this place. With her fingers, she stroked her mother's hair, recalling the hundred brush-strokes of childhood each Sunday before Mass. As much as the dimness would allow, she studied her mother, hair all tangled and matted, its once rich lustre dulled. The fine face with that mild *hauteur* of bearing, now pin-tucked with want and neglect. How could her mother so terribly have fallen?

The woman's term for Ellen – 'widow-woman' – what did it mean? And Ellen using her old, first-marriage name of O'Malley, as Mary had also learned from Biddy.

And Lavelle? What of Lavelle – Ellen's husband now? Had he never found her . . . that time he had left the note at the convent . . . gone looking for her in California? The questions came tumbling one after the other through Mary's mind.

She wished Louisa would hurry. It was all too much.

Then Ellen slept, face turned to Mary's bosom, like a child. But it was not the secure sleep of childhood. It was fitful, erratic, full of demons. She awoke, frightened, clutching fretfully at Mary's veil. Then, bolt upright, peered into the near dark.

'Mary! Mary! Is that you Mary, *a stor*?' Ellen said, falling into the old language.

Then, at the comforting answer, fell to weeping.

THREE

It was some hours before Louisa returned.

Ellen, startled by the commotion, awoke and feverishly embraced her. 'Oh, my child! My dear child!' Then she clutched the two of them to her so desperately, as though fearing imminent separation from them again.

Along with the clothing, Louisa had brought some bread and some milk. This they fed to her with their fingers, in small soggy lumps as one would an infant.

Ellen alternated between a near ecstatic state and tears, between sense and insensibility, regularly clasping them to herself.

When they had fed their mother, Mary and Louisa prepared to go, bestowing God's blessing on Biddy for her kindness.

'I don't need no nun's blessing,' was Biddy's response. 'D'you think *He* ever looks down on *me* . . . down here in this hellhole? But the Devil takes care of his own,' she threw after them, to send them on their way.

Out in the alleyway, they took Ellen, one on each side, arms encircling her. As they passed the old blind woman on the stoop, she called out to them. 'Is that you, Ellie? And who's that with you? Did the angels come at last . . . to stop that blasted singing?'

Ellen made them halt.

'They did Blind Mary, they did – the angels came,' she answered lucidly.

'Bring them here to me till I see 'em!' the woman ordered, with a cackle of a laugh.

They approached her.

'Bend down close to me!' the woman said in the same tone.

Mary first, leaned towards her and the woman felt for her face, her nose, the line of Mary's lips.

'She's the spit of you, Ellie. And the hair . . . ?'

'What's this? What's this?' the blind woman said, all agitated now as her fingers travelled higher, feeling the protective headdress on Mary's face.

'A nun?' the woman exclaimed.

'Yes!' Mary replied. 'I am Sister Mary.'

'And the other one? Are you a nun too? Come here to me!'

Louisa approached her. 'I am called Sister Veronica.'

Again the hands travelled over Louisa's face, the crinkled fingers transmitting its contents to behind the blindness.

Louisa saw the old woman's face furrow, felt the fingers retrace, as if the message had been broken.

'Faith, if she's one of yours, Ellie, then the Pope's a nigger,' Blind Mary declared with her wicked laugh.

Louisa flinched momentarily.

The old woman carried on talking, her head nodding vigorously all the while, but with no particular emphasis. 'I'm supposin' too, Ellie – that you never was a widow-woman neither?'

'No, I wasn't – and I'm sorry . . .' Ellen began.

The woman interrupted her, excitedly shaking her stick. 'I knew it! I knew it! Too good to be true! Too good to be true! That's what my Dan said afore he left to *jine the cavalry* . . . for the war,' she explained, still nodding, as if in disagreement with herself . . . or her Dan. 'What was you hiding from, down here, Ellie?' she then asked.

This time however, Ellen made no answer.

*

It was a question that resounded time and again in Mary and Louisa's minds, as they struggled homewards. Out under the arch they went, drawing away from Half Moon Place, the old woman's cries, like the stench, following them.

'The Irish is a perishing class that's what!' Blind Mary shouted after them. 'A perishing class . . . and my poor Dan gone to fight for Lincoln and his niggerology. This war'll be the death of us all.'

FOUR

By the time they had reached the door of the convent, Louisa and Mary were in a perfect quandary.

They could not reveal Ellen's true identity, lest they all be banished. Acceptance into the convent as a novice implied a background and family beyond blemish. There could be no whiff of scandal attached to those who were to be Brides of Christ.

It would be held that they had known all along of their mother's fallen state *and* engaged in the concealment of it.

'It was not a deceit then but it is a deceit now,' Mary said to Louisa, 'to continue not to reveal her identity . . . whatever the consequence.'

'It is a greater good not to reveal her,' Louisa argued. 'Mother is in dire need of corporeal salvation, if not indeed of spiritual salvation!'

'That is the end justifying wrongful means,' Mary argued back, torn between her natural instinct to follow Louisa's reasoning, and the more empirical precepts of religious life.

'We have been led to her for a purpose,' Louisa countered. 'It would not be natural justice to have her now thrown back on the streets. Natural justice supersedes the laws of the Church.'

Mary prayed for guidance. 'Lord not my will, but Thine

be done.' Having passed the question of justice to that of a higher jurisdiction, Mary was somewhat more at ease with Louisa's plan.

'I don't think "Rise-from-the-Dead" will recognise the likeness between you and Mother.' Louisa gave voice to Mary's own fear.

Mary looked at her mother's sunken state. Sister Lazarus would have seen her only the once . . . and that many years ago. Still, little passed unnoticed with 'Rise-from-the-Dead'.

They both impressed upon Ellen the importance of not revealing herself. She was a Penitent, rescued from the streets. Nothing more.

'That I am,' she echoed.

Sister Lazarus received them full of concern.

'Oh, the poor wretch! Divine Providence! Divine Providence that you rescued her, from God knows what fate!'

Mary's heart beat the easier as the older nun bustled them in without any hint of recognition.

'A nice hot tub, then put her to bed in the Penitents' Infirmary,' Sister Lazarus directed. 'You, Sisters, take turn to sit with her, lest she take fright at her unfamiliar surroundings.'

They stripped her then, Louisa supporting her in the tub, while Mary sponged from her mother's body the caked history of Half Moon Place, both of them joyful beyond words at having been her salvation. She, who through famine and pestilence, had long been theirs.

When Louisa spoke, Ellen would turn to look at her, face spread wide in amazement. 'I know, Mother,' Louisa said. 'I was "the silent girl". All those years when you tried to get me to speak, I would not. Like your story, it is for another day.'

Ellen then turned her head from one to the other of her children, eyes brimming with delight, as if the angels of the Lord had come down from on high and tended her.

Shakily then, she pressed the thumb and forefinger of her right hand to her lips and leaned, first to Mary's forehead, then to Louisa's, crossing them in blessing, as she had done, down all the day-long years of childhood.

FIVE

Ellen slept in the Penitents' Dormitory. About her were raised the fitful cries of other Penitents rescued from the jaws of death or, as the Sisters saw it, from a fate far worse – the jaws of Hell. For here were common nightwalkers, bedizened with sin; others sorely under the influence of the bewitching cup. Still others snatched from grace by the manifold snares of the world, the flesh and the devil. These, if truly penitent, the Sisters sought to reclaim to a life of devotion. But for now these tortured souls struggled. Redemption was not for everyone.

Penitents, those who desired it, could be regenerated. Eventually, shed of all worldly folly, their former names would be replaced by those of the saints. These restored Penitents would then be released back to secular society.

Some Penitents, drawn either by love of God, or fear of the Devil, remained, took vows, becoming Contemplatives. Continuing to lead lives of prayer and penance within the community of the Sisters.

Her own sleep no less turbulent than those around her, Ellen's mind roved without bent or boundary. Before her, on a pale and dappled horse, paraded Lavelle. Loyal, handsome Lavelle, all gallant and smiling.

Smiling, as on the day she, with Patrick, Louisa and Mary

24

in tow, had docked at the Long Wharf of Boston. Lavelle, with his golden hair, waiting in the sun, waving to them amid the baubled and bustling hordes on the shore. Patrick, curious about this stranger who would replace his father. Their mother's 'fancy man' in America, as Patrick called Lavelle.

In the dream she saw herself laughing, this time at her doorway, talking with Lavelle. He asking a question, she saying 'yes' and then him high-kicking it, whistling through that first Christmas snow, down the street merrily. Then springtime . . . the wedding . . . she, taking 'Lavelle' for a name, relinquishing her dead husband's name of O'Malley.

Out of the past then a nemesis – Stephen Joyce – who had delivered her first husband Michael to that early death.

Her dream changed colours then. Gone was the brightness of sun and snow . . . of music on merry streets. Now appeared a purpled bed. On it Stephen Joyce, book in hand reading to her. She, naked at the window, her body turned away from him. Singing to the darkly-plummed world outside . . . the night pulping against the window, its purple fruit oozing through the windowpane, over her body . . . staining her. Abruptly again, her dream had changed course. Now Stephen – dark, dangerous Stephen – he, too astride a horse, a coal-black horse, sword in hand and beckoning her. And Patrick – her dear child, Patrick – what was Patrick doing here? Giving her something . . . but beyond her reach. Mary and Louisa, white-winged, holding her back from going to him. Lavelle again, this time madly galloping towards them on the pale horse. Them cowering from its flashing hooves.

Frightened, she bolted upright in the bed, Louisa at her side restraining her, soothing her anxiety.

'There, Mother, there – it's just a bad dream, I'm with you now,' Louisa said tenderly.

Fearfully, Ellen embraced her, afraid her adopted daughter might disappear back into the frightening dreamworld.

Louisa held her mother, until sleep finally took Ellen.

*

Through the New England winter began the long, slow restoration. First the temporal needs of the body. Not a surfeit of food but 'little and often' as Sister Lazarus advised, 'and a decent dollop of buttermilk daily, combined with fruit – and *young* carrots', for the recovery of Ellen's eyes. 'Common luxuries, which no doubt have not passed this poor soul's lips since Our Saviour was a boy,' Sister Lazarus opined.

Mary trimmed the long mane of Ellen's hair, removing the frayed ends and straightening the raggle-taggle of knots that had accumulated there. Gradually, the pallor evaporated from Ellen's face, a hint of rose-pink returning to her lips. Under the Sisters' care, the physical contours of Ellen's body began somewhat to re-establish themselves. It was not long before Louisa and Mary could both begin to see their mother re-emerge, as they had once remembered her.

'It is the buttermilk,' Lazarus was convinced, thankfully still showing no signs of recognition.

With Mary and Louisa's help Ellen could now go to the Oratory for prayer and reflection. There they would leave her a while, to ponder alone. Never once did they ask about her missing years. She was grateful for that . . . was not yet ready to tell them. But that day would come. Perhaps early in the New Year.

Before Christmas, when she was stronger, and at Sister Lazarus's insistence that 'God and Reverend Mother will provide,' Mary and Louisa took Ellen to an oculist. Years of making the Singer machines sing for Boston's shoe bosses, had taken its toll on their mother's eyes.

Dr Thackeray, a kindly, intent man – a Quaker, Ellen had decided, without knowing why – held his hand up at a distance from her, asking her to identify how many digits he had raised. Depending on her answer, he moved either further away or closer to her. At the end of it all he disappeared, returning at length with a stout brown bottle which he declared to contain 'a soothing concoction'.

'This to be poulticed on both eyes for a month of days; to be changed daily – only in darkness,' he instructed. 'Even then both eyes must remain fully shuttered.' She would, he said, 'see no human form until mine, when you return.'

He gave no indication of what improvement, if any, he expected after all of this.

During her month of darkness, Ellen's general state of health continued to incline. She grew steadily stronger, the tone of her skin regained some former suppleness, and from Mary's constant brushing, the once-fine texture of her hair had at last begun to return.

'It is as much the nourishing joy at your presence, as anything Sister Lazarus's buttermilk and young carrots might do,' she said with delight to Mary and Louisa.

Ellen was thankful of Dr Thackeray's poultice. That she would not have to fully face them when, at last, she told her daughters the truth; not have to look into their eyes, they into hers.

Blindness she had long been smitten with, before ever she had put first stitch into leather.

Stephen Joyce, who had ignited such debasing passions in her, was not to blame. Nor Lavelle . . . least of all, her ever-constant Lavelle. The blindness was solely hers – her own corroding influence on herself.

She worried about her dream and its recurrence – that by now she should have exorcised all the old devils about Stephen. Why had he appeared so threatening – sword aloft? Why the black horse and Lavelle the pale one? Good and Evil – and had they at last met? And Patrick – she unable to reach him?

Stephen first had appeared in her life in 1847. There were troubled times in Ireland – blight, starvation, evictions. Like a wraith he had come out of the night to meet with her husband Michael.

She had not interfered as rebellious plots against landlords

27

were hatched but she had sensed tragedy. This dark man who could excite the hearts of other men to follow him, would she knew, one day bring grief under her cabin roof. And so it was. Not a moon had waned before her husband Michael, her beautiful Michael, lay stretched in the receiving clay of Crucán na bPáiste – the burial place high above the Maamtrasna Valley.

Evicted then, during the worst of the famine, and in desperation to save her starving children, she had been forced to enter a devilish pact. Her allegiance to the Big House was bought, her children given shelter. The price – her forced emigration from Ireland – and separation from them. Patrick aged ten years, Mary a mere eight. It was Stephen Joyce, the peasant agitator, scourge of the landlord class, who had come to her to guarantee their safety. Whilst she had blamed him for Michael's death, she had, for the sake of her children, no choice but to accept his offer. Eventually, she had returned to reclaim them.

Now years later, here in America, her children had reclaimed her.

SIX

'Sit still, Mother!' Mary chided, as she unfettered Ellen's eyes.

'Mary . . . I have something . . .' Ellen began, wanting at last to tell her.

Mary, remembering the tone her mother adopted when she had something to say to them, knew it was pointless resisting. She put the used poultices on the small table, fixed her attention on Ellen's closed eyelids . . . and waited.

'I . . . I have . . . something to confess to you . . . a grave wrong,' Ellen began, falteringly.

'Have you confessed it to God?' Mary asked, simply.

'Yes, Mary . . . many times . . . but, in His wisdom, He has directed that you and Louisa should find me – so that I should also confess it to you.'

Mary took her mother's hands, bringing Ellen close to her. 'If God has forgiven you, Mother, then who am I not to?'

'I still must tell you, Mary,' Ellen said, more steadily.

Faces now inclined towards each other, mother and child, priest and penitent, Ellen began. 'I committed . . . the sin of Mary Magdalen . . . with . . . Stephen Joyce,' she said quietly, her long hair forward about her face, shrouding their hands.

Mary uttered no word. Remained waiting, still holding her mother's hands. Ellen, before she continued, opened her eyes and peered into Mary's. Into her own eyes, it seemed.

'I betrayed you all: Lavelle, a good man and a good husband; you, my dear child; Patrick . . . Louisa.' Then, remembering Mary's father, Michael: 'Even those who have gone before!'

Ellen knew how the words now struggling out of her mouth would be at odds with everything for which Mary had held her always in such loving regard. She trembled, awaiting her child's response.

'Mother, you must keep your eyes closed . . . until it is time,' Mary said, without pause, putting a finger to her mother's eyes, blessing her darkness, protecting her from the world.

Mary then fell to anointing the fresh coverlets for Ellen's eyes. She said nothing more while completing the dressing. Then, Mary left the room.

When she returned she pressed a set of rosary beads into Ellen's hands.

'One of the Sisters sculpted these from an old white oak,' Mary explained. 'Louisa and I were saving them for you until the bandages came off . . . but . . .' She didn't finish the sentence, starting instead a new one . . . 'We'll offer up the Rosary – the Five Sorrowful Mysteries.'

Ellen, in reply, said nothing until between them then, they exchanged the Five Mysteries of Christ's Passion and Death.

The Agony in the Garden . . .

The Scourging at the Pillar . . .

The Crowning with Thorns . . .

The Carrying of the Cross . . .

The Crucifixion.

Passing over and back the Our Fathers . . .

'. . . forgive us our trespasses . . . as we forgive those who trespass against us.'

And the Hail Marys, '. . . pray for us sinners . . .' the words taking on the mantle of a continued conversation.

Like a shielding presence between them, Ellen counted out

the freshly-hewn beads, reflecting upon the Fruits of the Mysteries – contrition for sin; mortification of the senses; death to the self.

Afterwards, in unison, they recited the *Salve Regina*. 'To thee do we fly poor banished children of Eve, To thee do we send up our sighs, mourning and weeping . . . and after this, our exile . . . O clement, O loving, O sweet Virgin Mary! Pray for us . . . that we may be made worthy . . .'

When it was done they sat there, unspeaking. Ellen, the great weight partly uplifted from her; Mary, unfaltering in compassion at the enormity of what had passed between them.

'I will tell Louisa myself, Mary,' Ellen said. 'Then I must find Patrick . . . and Lavelle.'

The younger woman stood up, made to go and stopped. Turning, she embraced the shoulders of the other woman, pulling her mother towards her, the fine head within her arms. Gently, she stroked the renewed folds of Ellen's hair. As a mother would a damaged child.

SEVEN

The following evening Louisa came.

With mounting trepidation, Ellen heard the flap of Louisa's habit, the whoosh of air that preceded her adopted daughter. Everything but flesh of flesh, Louisa was to her. How frightened the child must have been all those years to have so stoically maintained her silence. That, if she had spoken, she would again have been shunned. Left to the roads and the hungry grass.

Ellen awaited her moment and when Louisa had removed the poultices, caught her by the wrists.

'Sit for a moment, Louisa!'

Slowly, agonisingly, Ellen fumbled for the words with which to tell Louisa. Almost as soon as she had begun, Louisa stopped her, putting a hand to Ellen's lips.

'Mother, dearest Mother, you needn't suffer this . . . I already know,' she said, causing Ellen to startle. 'I suppose I've always known,' Louisa continued. 'You almost told me once . . . in word and look. That last time I played for you . . . the Bach . . . the loss of Heaven in your face . . .' She paused. '. . . and then, the book.'

'Oh, my dear Louisa . . . you never . . .' Ellen began.

'No, I never said anything.' Louisa answered the unfinished question. She gave a little laugh. 'In my silent state I didn't have to!'

'You never condemned me?' Ellen asked.

'Condemn you, Mother? You who saved me from certain death? Who loved me as her own?' Louisa held her tightly. 'Condemn you?' she repeated. 'I thank God every waking moment that He at last restored you to us.'

The Vespers bell tolled, calling the Sisters to evening prayer. Still embracing, Ellen and Louisa fell silent, each making her own prayer . . . for the other.

Ellen explained what she still must do regarding Patrick and Lavelle.

'You must do as conscience directs,' Louisa answered.

'It would be my dearest wish to first remain here a while, with you and Mary,' Ellen replied.

The prayer bell stopped. Louisa waited a moment for Ellen to continue.

'What restrains me is that by remaining, it may reveal me and so force you and Mary to finish your work here. So, I have decided to take my leave quietly and avoid that possibility.'

'How will you live, what will sustain you?' Louisa worried.

'The Lord will sustain me – as He has up to now.'

Next afternoon Sister Lazarus came to visit Ellen. She could not see how closely the nun studied her, as she complimented Ellen on her wellbeing. 'Doing nicely, are we? Doing nicely! Thanks be to God and His Holy Mother.'

The following day Sister Lazarus again visited her, this time with Louisa and Mary in tow.

'Mrs Lavelle, or Mrs O'Malley or whatever it is we are calling ourselves today . . .' she began. 'You and your daughters, have practised a great deceit upon the Sisterhood of this house.'

Ellen started to speak, but to no avail.

Sister Lazarus, once risen, was not for lying down again. 'It came to me at prayer – the occasion when some six years past you called to the door of this holy house. I would have uncovered you sooner but for your dilapidated state. But God is just. As He has restored you, so has He revealed you,' she said, in the manner of those to whom God regularly reveals things.

She then gave the two younger nuns a dressing down for their concealment. They would first have to go to Reverend Mother, then prostrate themselves before the entire congregation and profess their wickedness.

'You have betrayed the moral rectitude with which our work amongst the fallen is underpinned. Without moral rectitude we are nothing. Nothing but chaff in the wind.'

Sister Lazarus then ordered the young nuns to 'fall on your knees in the Oratory.' She forbade them to attend upon Ellen until 'Reverend Mother shall make known her decision.'

Reverend Mother, a solemn, no-nonsense nun whose singsong Kerry accent long flattened by years in America, spelled it out clearly and succinctly.

Firstly to Ellen.

'When your eyes have been given whatever restoration God may decree, you must leave here . . . and may God grant you forgiveness for in what jeopardy you have placed His holy work.'

A certain sadness creeping into her voice, Reverend Mother then addressed Mary and Louisa; 'Sister Mary and Sister Veronica, you have broken trust with God and with your Sisterhood. That there can be no scandal attached to the work which we do here is the rock on which we are founded. Therefore, can neither of you remain here.'

She paused, letting the import of the banishment sink in. Then raising her Reverend Mother's voice, pronounced the full edict of what this would entail.

'There is now a great calamity upon this, your adopted country – a "Civil" War, they name it. For its duration,

whatever length that be, I charge you to bind up the wounds
of those fallen in battle. You will carry out your duties
without fear or favour to either side. You will at all times
remember that those who oppose each other, irrespective
of uniform, are God's creatures and created in His eternal
likeness.'

Again she paused before making the final pronouncement.

'You will be dispatched South to the battlefields and may
God bestow upon you both the necessary fortitude for that
work – a fortitude which, thus far, you have so inadequately
failed to display.'

Ellen was bereft. What ignominy she had now visited on
Mary and Louisa. To be banished. Better they had never
found her, left her there to die on the dunghill of Half Moon
Place. She could not speak.

They, for their part, stood beside her, heads bowed in shame,
dutifully accepting their banishment.

'Not my will but Thine,' Ellen thought she heard Mary
whisper.

The audience brought to a conclusion, Sister Lazarus ushered them out informing the young nuns that, 'In charity,
Reverend Mother has decided that you both may remain here
until your mother's treatment is complete. In the meantime
you will be restricted to within convent walls and in waking
hours to within the Oratory itself.'

Both Mary and Louisa nodded in silent assent, awaiting
what yet further there was to come. Sister Lazarus did not
hold them in suspense for long.

'You will undertake penance and fasting as directed and
converse with none other than myself, or Reverend Mother
should she require it.' Reverend Mother did not.

When Dr Thackeray's 'month of days' had run its course,
Ellen returned to the oculist, shepherded this time by Sister
Lazarus. Little was exchanged by way of conversation between
them. Sister Lazarus, Ellen guessed, no doubt praying for a

miracle – that the blind might quickly see and be sent forth!

Indeed Sister Lazarus's rigor mortis-like countenance seemed to considerably soften when Dr Thackeray, upon examination of Ellen, professed himself 'cautiously pleased' at her progress. Though her eyes were still impaired, she could now see more and at a greater distance, during each test through which he had put her.

'These will improve you further,' he said, producing a pair of spectacles of a more lightly-shaded hue than those previously stolen.

He re-dressed her eyes, advising her to 'continue the poulticing for a further uninterrupted period of two weeks.'

Behind her, Ellen imagined Sister Lazarus's lips move in supplication to the Almighty – that a more immediate miracle might occur.

On their homewards journey, Sister Lazarus solicitously guided Ellen, thus avoiding any mishap which might befall her . . . and longer extend her time at the convent.

'God is good . . . God is good,' Sister Lazarus regularly repeated to no one in particular. Ellen herself was unsure if this acclamation served purely to acknowledge the restorative powers of the Lord, or was a thanksgiving for her own resulting departure from the convent which the healing itself would precipitate.

Two weeks to the day of her visit to Dr Thackeray, Ellen, along with Mary and Louisa were quietly exited from the grounds of the Convent of St Mary Magdalen and led to Boston's railroad station.

From there the two nuns would travel to Richmond, Virginia, and await further instructions.

At Mary and Louisa's insistence, Ellen accompanied them, her newly constructed spectacles perched snugly on her nose. All the better with which to see the fatal tides of civil war on which they were now cast.

EIGHT

Union Army Military Field Hospital, Virginia, 1862

Manual of Military Surgery for the Surgeons of the Confederate States Army

> '. . . the rule in military surgery is absolute, viz: that the amputating knife should immediately follow the condemnation of the limb. These are operations of the battlefield and should be performed at the field infirmary. When this golden opportunity, before reaction, is lost, it can never be compensated for.'

Wearing Dr Thackeray's spectacles, Ellen read carefully the surgery manual. The spectacles had been such a boon to her, not that she could overdo it, but a world previously closed had now again been opened.

She paused, thinking about her eyes before continuing. They had troubled her less than expected. Not that they were perfect. At times she found herself looking slightly to the right of people, as if they had imperceptibly shifted under her gaze.

Reading was problematic. She laughed to Mary about, 'How childlike my reading skills have become.' But, in general, she found the condition of her eyes to be of little hindrance to her work.

Dr Sawyer had been marvellous, procuring a continuation of Dr Thackeray's soothing balm. He had also today located for her a pair of more recently developed shaded spectacles, an improvement on those given her in Boston.

'Developed alongside those new-fangled rifle sights,' he had told Ellen. He, Dr Shubael Sawyer, rather brusque of manner but an efficient practitioner of his profession, was the operating surgeon in the field hospital in which she, Louisa and Mary now found themselves.

'Maybe this war, after all, will bring some benefit to humanity . . . though such benefits will weigh poorly enough when the balances are writ,' Dr Sawyer had added.

These she now substituted for Dr Thackeray's spectacles and continued with reading the manual . . .

'Amputate with as little delay as possible after the receipt of the injury. In army practice, attempts to save a limb, which might be perfectly successful in civil life, cannot be made. Especially in the case of compound gunshot fractures of the thigh, bullet wounds of the knee joint and similar injuries to the leg, in which, at first sight, amputation may not seem necessary. Under such circumstances attempts to preserve the limb will be followed by extreme local and constitutional disturbance. Conservative surgery is here in error; in order to save life, the limb must be sacrificed.'

So there it was, in black and white. The saw saved lives. In the time she had been here, Ellen had lain hands on everything she could read on medical practise. Not that there was much available. Good fortune had brought her current reading, *The Confederate Manual of Surgery*. A prize of war captured from the enemy. But there was a shortage of nurses for the many hospitals the war had occasioned. They had received some training from a Sister of Mercy who had then been moved to some duty elsewhere. She, like Mary and Louise, had had to learn quickly. It had been trial and error, mistakes made, while assisting at the regular stream of operations and mostly amputations.

'Hips . . . I don't like hips,' Dr Sawyer said plainly to her later that afternoon. 'Too near the trunk. We lose ninety per cent if we have to take the leg from the hip joint . . . and one hundred per cent if we don't!' It was Ellen's first hip joint operation.

Three aides were required for such an operation. 'Fetch the Sisters,' Dr Sawyer ordered her. 'The sight of blood holds no terrors for them.'

The soldier, a wan looking boy from Rhode Island, with freckled face and red hair had lost a lot of blood.

'Pray, ladies,' he said, when Mary and Louisa arrived, 'that I'll be one of the ten per cents! I ain't seen much of life.'

They laid him out on the only available operating table – a diseased-looking church pew.

'I hope it's a good Catholic pew and not a Protestant one, Sister!' the young soldier said to Mary, putting a brave face on it. She held his hand, making the Act of Contrition with him, something of which Mary was aware Dr Sawyer did not approve.

'O my God, I am heartily sorry for having offended Thee . . . and I detest my sins . . . firmly resolve never more to offend . . . but to amend my life . . .'

When he had repeated the words firmly resolving to 'sin no more' Mary administered the chloroform by means of a dampened napkin. This she held cone-shaped over his mouth and nose, telling him to 'inhale deeply', ensuring that he also had an adequate supply of natural air while inhaling. Soon the young Rhode Islander was in a surgical sleep, though still exhibiting the 'state of excitement' they had come to expect in the early stages after administration of the anaesthetic.

'Remove his uniform, Sister,' Dr Sawyer ordered Louisa. Deftly, while Ellen restrained him, Louisa opened the top of the soldier's tunic and with Mary's help slipped it off. Then, she rolled up his flannel shirt to the chest. Next, Louisa unbuttoned his trousers, the left side peppered with shot and clotted with blood. She at one leg, Mary at the other, together pulled the trousers from him. The doctor waited while they addressed the matter of the boy's undergarment. He noted that not once did either woman flinch from the indelicacy of her task.

'Mrs Lavelle!' was all Dr Sawyer then said.

Ellen had assisted him previously on other operations and knew what was required. Quickly, she swabbed away the matted blood from the boy's shattered hip. She looked at the doctor for affirmation that his point of incision was now clearly visible. He nodded. Then Ellen slipped one of her hands under the boy's buttock, the other one meeting it from the top. Her hands, stretched to their limit formed a human tourniquet. Her job, to stop all blood to the site of amputation. Thumbs meeting she pressed hard, clamping the thigh, praying to God for the strength to maintain the pressure. If everything went to plan it would be over in less than three minutes. Dr Sawyer was quick. Time being of the essence.

She closed her eyes thinking of nothing else but the exertion of her hands.

The technique the doctor would use was the *oval* method. This, though similar to the older, *circular* technique, lent itself better to amputation through the joint capsule – the cut made higher on one side of the limb than the other. Using the ebony-handled Lister amputation knife handed him by Louisa, Dr Sawyer made the incision in the Rhode Islander's skin. Mary then retracted the skin to allow the muscle tissue to be cut. 'An ample flap, Sister!' the surgeon warned. An 'ample flap' of skin was critical after the operation, for re-covering the heads of bones exposed by the saw.

'Raspatory!' Shubael Sawyer demanded the bone-scraper, which Louisa was about to hand him. The smashed bone, now exposed, was dissected back with this implement.

Meanwhile, Mary, checking the boy's pulse found it had sunk too low and in a sure voice asked, 'Ammonia?' When the doctor nodded, she applied a quick whiff of liquor of ammonia to revive the patient. Louisa next handed the large rectangular-shaped Capital Saw to the fast-working surgeon.

Ellen turned her head away as the saw bit into the boy's hip socket and then hacked its way through the bone.

'Pressure, Mrs Lavelle! Pressure!' Dr Sawyer rasped at Ellen, and she willed her thumbs and fingers to clamp even tighter around the boy's thigh.

It was over in no time. With the tenaculum, Dr Sawyer then winkled out the main arteries, the blood droppletting from them. Ellen held on for dear life to stem its flow. Working quickly the doctor next ligated the blood vessels with surgical thread. In advance of the operation Ellen had already wound this silken thread around the tenaculum. Now Dr Sawyer slipped it from over the instrument onto each severed vessel, and tied. Only at his command to 'release!' did Ellen slowly uncoil her hands from what was now the remaining stump of the young soldier's hip.

All eyes focused on the ligations – the full flow of blood now released against them. They held fast, no oozing apparent. Next was required the Gnawing Forceps to grind down the stump of bone to an acceptable smoothness. The flaps of skin, which Mary had previously retracted, she now folded back over what was left of the boy's hip. Using curved suture needles, Shubael Sawyer knitted together the skin with surgical thread, but loosely, to allow for post-operative drainage of the severed thigh. Louisa then fanned the patient to purge his lungs of the chloroform and administered another whiff of liquor of ammonia, neither of which served to resuscitate him.

'Brass monkey,' the doctor ordered. Louisa never raised

41

her eyes, immediately understanding the abbreviated form of the expression the men used to describe weather – 'So cold it would freeze the balls off a brass monkey!' She uncorked the chloroform and sprinkled it on the young man's scrotum. The immediate reaction of cold caused a stir in him but not sufficient to bring him to consciousness. Louisa then administered a further, more generous sprinkling. This time the Rhode Island Red bolted upright.

'My balls – they're frozen!' he shouted in disbelief. Then, remembering those present, groggily apologised, 'I'm sorry, ladies . . . Ma'am,' and made to cover his indecency. His severed limb, now on the floor parallel to the pew on which he sat, seemed to trouble him less greatly than his exposed and frozen manhood.

Later they learned that the Rhode Island Red had succumbed to his injuries.

Became one of the ninety per cent failure rate for such operations. Didn't make the ten per cent.

NINE

By 1862, French physicist, Jean Bernard Foucault had made scientific history by measuring the speed of light using revolving mirrors. Foucault's compatriot Victor Hugo, with his classic novel *Les Miserables*, was making a different kind of history. It was left to yet another Frenchman to change forever how Americans would kill Americans.

Captain Claude-Etienne Minié had supplied the world with his own particular brand of French artistry – the minié ball. This was a one-inch-long, leaden slug, the base of which, when fired from the newly-developed rifled musket would expand into the rifle's grooves and spiral through the air as it was projected. The result was deadly accuracy at two hundred and fifty yards. And at half a mile the minié ball could still kill. The Frenchman's invention could travel five times further than the bullet of any other weapon.

The first time Ellen saw Hercules O'Brien he had been struck by not just one minié ball but two. 'Science will kill us all,' he told her, ignoring his smashed arm and the furrowed groove which ran from front to back along the left side of his blocky skull.

'What do you mean, Sergeant O'Brien?' she asked.

'Well, look how Science has lepped into action in this war.'

She waited till he continued.

'Exploding mines that go in the ground, so a man, even if he is safe from battle, cannot take a walk to a leafy glade or a cooling brook for fear he step on one and be blown to smithereens.'

Ellen thought how cruel a mind had human science to invent such an inhuman device.

'. . . and there isn't a sharpshooter but has the new telescope lens. There's no place safe left to hide . . . and the Gatlings, the repeating guns,' he explained for her benefit, 'cut a man in two, they would . . . leave his legs still walking and his body gone.

'The generals are fighting with the old tactics while the men are cut to ribbons with the new weapons. General Meagher is still calling for bayonet charges. "Let them taste steel," he says, but all we get is Rebel lead.'

'Stop talking,' she ordered, 'while I bandage this head of yours!'

Hercules O'Brien paid no heed to her. 'I'm telling you, missus, before the century is out, Science will be the master of mankind. Science will blow up the world!'

Whatever about 'Science blowing up the world', Ellen had already seen the devastating results of the minié ball.

The old round musket ball used early on by the Confederates, would pierce clothing and skin but would bounce off the deeper tissues. The conical minié ball however would bore through all tissue, usually resting near the opposite side of the body to which it had entered. If it did not exit entirely, it left a trail of destruction in its wake.

Now, his head at last bandaged, she gently pushed a probing finger into the sergeant's other wound. The human finger still more sensitive than what Science could produce. And less likely to damage arteries and nervous tissues.

She kept looking at him, talking, feeling the tension rise within him; wondering how this pint-sized man had earned the name of Hercules?

'I'm a great big man in a little man's body,' he said seriously. 'Hercules lived in ancient times and he lifted the world on his back . . . and sure amn't I carrying the whole Union army on mine!'

She looked at him. His visible eye, from where she had just bandaged him, was dancing with mirth. At last her fingertip found something hard and solid.

'I've found it, Sergeant O'Brien!' she said.

'No matter that science will kill us all, you can't beat the human touch.' He winked at her, the eye still working overtime.

'Well, I *will* need the forceps with which to get it out,' she countered.

The thin Moses forceps with the sharp beak soon had her gingerly withdrawing the minié ball. He never complained and when she showed him the bloodied missile, he said, 'Thank you, ma'am. I'd like to keep it as a souvenir 'case I collect no more of them!'

'You were lucky, Sergeant O'Brien,' she said. 'No splintering . . . and that the second one skidded from your head, rather than collided with it.'

'Would have made no differ ma'am,' Hercules O'Brien answered, tapping his skull. 'Not even the damned minié ball could get in there.'

Later, she came back, asked him if he'd come across a soldier named Lavelle O'Malley, thinking by now that both Patrick and Lavelle would have enlisted. Because it seemed as if all the rest of America had.

'No, ma'am,' he answered, watching her. 'Three-quarters of America is out there . . . and half of Ireland. What brigade is he with?'

When she couldn't tell him he enquired, 'Is he your husband, ma'am?'

'He was . . .' she almost said, then corrected herself. 'Yes.'

45

TEN

The hospital was one of many field hospitals dotted all over the countryside, wherever men might fall in battle. A once-schoolhouse, now it had rows of rough bunks lining each wall, an anteroom for amputations and an added-on storeroom for medical supplies and operating implements. A further room was used as a makeshift canteen – for those who could walk to it. A nearby cabin, abandoned to war, provided accommodation for Ellen, the two nuns, and occasionally for those who came temporarily to assist. Dr Sawyer had private accommodation some slight further distance away.

They could comfortably take one hundred patients – at times stretched to two hundred. Three nurses and a doctor were not sufficient . . . but it was all they had to make do with, most of the time.

Although officially a Union hospital for soldiers of the North, Mary and Louisa had impressed on Dr Sawyer that 'all the fallen of whichever side, should fall under our care, if needed.' It was not a philosophy to which the brusque doctor easily subscribed, even with Mary gently reminding him that, 'if your own son were wounded near Confederate lines, you would wish some kind Sister to take him in – or a good Christian doctor, such as you, to save him.'

In the end he had little choice, the two nuns and Ellen

gathering in whomsoever they found needing attention – Union Blue or Confederate Grey.

Regularly, Ellen enquired of those whom she tended from both North and South, of Patrick and Lavelle. But it was ever without success. Most were sympathetic, complimenting her on her son's and husband's valour in serving 'the cause' – whichever cause they considered it to be – and her own womanly duty to the wounded.

From a few, her enquiry evoked a different response – a gruff Georgian officer telling her, 'Lady, chaos rules out there. Nobody knows nobody . . . no more. A quarter of my gallant lads were killed the first day, a quarter more the second. Moving men into battle is like shovelling fleas 'cross a farmyard – not half of them get there.'

She had begun to give up hope of ever seeing them again. This whole bloody business about 'valour' and 'gallant lads' was beginning to weary her. There seemed to be no end to the harvest of wounded and wasted who, day by day, were being shunted into the hospitals. Or the more deadly harvest . . . the hundreds and hundreds of young men being regularly flung two or three deep into earthen pits. A lonely thin board then scrawled with some illegible writing to mark their brief existence in this life. One such makeshift cross she had seen had stated only that: *Here lyes 120 brave men who dyed for there contree.* Not even the loved one's name to comfort those who later would come searching for them.

'Fleas across a farmyard.' Word had come down that over a million men had begun the year massing for war. How in a million could she find but two – Patrick and Lavelle?

She never spoke to Mary or Louisa about her rapidly fading hopes. Nor did they enquire of her. She had asked Dr Sawyer and he had sought for her the list of the dead, wounded and missing from Union Headquarters. When it eventually came, he apologised for its incompleteness. 'It changes hourly – they cannot write quickly enough to keep up with the dead.'

She raced through the names – O'Malley, Bartley; O'Malley, Thomas; O'Malley, John; O'Malley, Peter. She heaved a sigh of relief. No Patrick O'Malley. Nowhere either could she find the name Lavelle, making her think perhaps they had both sided with the South. It was some comfort, this not knowing – if only a crumb. Maybe Patrick had not become embroiled in this war madness after all? She prayed that if he had, he would be with Lavelle. Lavelle would shelter Patrick from harm, as if his own son, because he was hers.

Ellen thought she had witnessed everything in this demonic war but when Private Edward Long was smilingly delivered to her, she had to stop in disbelief.

'How old are you?' she asked the pint-sized patient.

'Nine years, ma'am . . . but squarin' up to ten!' the private proudly replied.

'Nine . . . years . . . of . . . age . . . ?' she drew out the words one by one. 'Nine years of age?'

'Yes, ma'am,' the child confirmed, as if there should be any doubt in her mind.

'Private Edward Long – Illinois – at your service, ma'am,' he added, looking up at her.

'Yes!' she said, 'but what are you doing here?'

'For to get mended . . . again,' he said, with all the innocence of childhood. 'I got clipped by a minié ball.'

'Where?' she asked, and saw him hesitate. There was no obvious sign of injury on him.

He threw his eyes down to the ground.

'I'm not saying, ma'am . . . but another one went in *front* of me and shot my drum.'

Then she understood. He had been grazed by a bullet on his buttocks and manfully wasn't about to reveal that fact to any female. She resisted the urge to pick him up, cradle him in her arms.

'All right, soldier!' she said, 'follow me – we've a special private place here for the brave musicians who lead our boys into battle.'

Off she set, him falling in behind her, trying to keep pace, swinging his arms up and down, all four foot six of him.

'Where's your mother?' she asked, when she got him down to the end of the ward.

'At home!' he said, matter-of-factly.

'Does she know where you are?'

'Yes, ma'am,' he answered, 'she sure does. Me and all my six brothers joined up to fight. Four is dead now. Just me and Jess and Billy-Bob left.'

She looked at him. 'You should go home, Edward,' she said gently, thinking of his mother.

'Oh, but I will, ma'am, when I git my furlough. I'll be going home for a month.'

'Why not stay there . . . with your mother?' she persevered.

'I couldn't do that, ma'am,' he said, his baby blue eyes fixed on hers, 'until we whip the Rebs and send *them* home!'

She gave up. He was the youngest she had seen. Most of the American boys were about eighteen, the foreign soldiers older. Many, though, of the homegrown farm boys who enlisted were much younger.

'A hundred thousand fifteen-year-olds', Dr Sawyer had told her, 'barely out of knee-britches and learning to kill! The fresh flower of manhood, thus brutalised by an old man's war.'

She had seen them come in, stretchered and corpsed, some as young as twelve. But never before a nine-year-old.

She heard Louisa calling her, squeezed both his arms. 'Wait here, soldier, you need the doctor to fix you up,' she said, to spare his blushes.

'What about my drum?' he asked. 'Can he fix my drum too?'

'I'm sure he can,' she smiled, and hurried to where Louisa and the commotion of some new arrivals beckoned.

The little fellow had grit, real Illinois grit. She doubted

there was much the matter with him. They'd see to his bum and his drum. Send him home to his mother. Maybe this time she'd keep her little drummer boy at home in Illinois. If she could afford to feed another mouth as good as the army could.

Later, she sat deep into the night, keeping the last vigil with some frightened soul admitted earlier and for whom nothing could be done. Nights such as these were the darkest hours, when her God would seem to have deserted her and she would pray instead to Science. That it would deliver its yet most infernal machine, and in one hellish blow strike down the massing millions of men. Be so terrible a holocaust that it would stop everything. Then, the pitying cry of some farm boy, or some veteran's curse, demanding her to be present, would draw her back from the abyss.

One such night she could bear it no longer. Stole away from her watch, went into the night. The land was flat here on the plains of Virginia – some rolling hills to break the monotony, the misty Blue Ridge Mountains to the west, behind them. It was a rich land, far better than what she had known in Ireland. No bare acre here but gentle farmlands where wheat could be harvested, peaches plucked, a pig or a rooster raised. Until they were commandeered for hungry marching bellies, by one side or the other . . . or stolen by marauding men, cut adrift from their regiments and the mainstream of battle. She walked to the copse of trees, now bathed in the glimmering moonlight of her adopted land. Sad for all that had been visited upon it. There in the sheltering trees she found a horse, black as Hades, gashed above the foreleg, watching over its fallen master. The man, a captain, was beyond repair. She prayed over him, went deeper into the twining trees, the horse hobbling behind her. Ahead some snuffling sounds.

Following the sounds, her eyes made out the low shapes of hogs, feeding on the ungathered dead.

She ran at them, shouting, the night-horse her ally. Grudgingly they gave ground, snorting and bellowing their way further into the undergrowth.

She scrambled onto the horse's back, fearful they would return before she had raised help. The horse bore her bravely, terrible images assailing her mind. Images of the famished dead back in her own land, Ireland . . . ravenous pigs and dogs. Her own neighbours, every last hope of food gone; the cabin pulled down around them, so no one would witness their last indignity; the dog whose head she had cracked as it defended its food. Somehow, it all – the spectre of famine back again and the Hades horse – decided her. No longer would she remain a spectator, waiting. She would rise herself, go out and find Lavelle and Patrick.

And she would go South. When the time was right.

ELEVEN

'Niggerology! That's what's causing all the trouble!' Jeremiah Finnegan roared. 'That's why all of yous in here is bent and broken. Niggerology!' he roared again.

Ellen ran down the room to where the man was lying, head back, face to the ceiling.

'If I'm going to die, I'm going to die roarin'!' he yelled, before she could reach him.

'Jeremiah! Jeremiah!' she said sternly. 'Stop that! You're not helping any by shouting your head off.'

She caught him by his remaining arm.

'But it's true, Miss Ellie – it's true! Look at me – all I'm fit for is to be roarin'!'

'I know, Jeremiah, I know,' she said more gently, looking at the half-man on the ramshackle cot; over one eye, a wad of cotton wool to cover the blank hole where his eye had been. Taken clean by a minié ball. Then his arm and his leg with cannon fire, as he fell.

'I have only my roarin' so that people can know me. I can't see. I can't walk. I can't hold a lady to dance with. I'm eternally bollixed!' he said defiantly.

She couldn't but help smile at the man's description of himself. With his one good eye he caught her smile – and kept going. 'But I can ring the rafters of Heaven and Hell! Damn their heathen eyes – the niggers – and those what supports them!'

What could she say to him? 'But you're *not* eternally damned and neither are those "niggers", as you call them,' she whispered, rubbing her palm along his remaining arm.

'Ticket' Finnegan – as they called him back home in the County Monaghan hinterland, always wanting to be off, get his ticket to America . . . to anywhere out of the humpbacked hills of Monaghan – calmed to her touch.

'I'm not afraid of dying, Miss Ellie,' he said, still remonstrating with her. 'But I won't die easy, whimperin' me way out like those Rebs over there. I came into the world roarin' and I'm goin' out of it the same way!'

'I'm sure you are,' she answered.

He was a fine block of a man; had a good few years on most of the boys that both armies had gobbled up. Now, like all around him, he had been cut down in his prime. It was a shame, a crying shame.

'Is there anyone you want me to write to?' she asked.

'Divil a one – bar the Divil himself – to say I'm comin'!' he said. 'Just sit a while and talk the old language to me!'

She looked around the room. Everywhere, a chaos of bodies. Most of them incomplete. Most needing care and comforting – before or after the surgeon's saw.

Ticket Finnegan hadn't long left, probably less than most.

'All right!' she decided, and began to talk to him of the old times and the old places.

'*Tír gan teangan, tír gan anam* – A land without a language is a land without a soul,' he whispered as she spoke to him in the ancient soul-language of the Gael.

How true it was, and she thought of the 'niggers', as Ticket – and most of the Irish – called them. Most too, like him, believed the black people had no souls, were just 'heathens'. So what then, if the heathens were also slaves?

Demonisation and colonisation.

The same thinking had demonised and colonised the Irish.

Depicted them as baboons in the London papers; blaming the Almighty for sending down a death-dealing famine on them. When all He had sent was a blight on the potatoes. It was the English who had sent the famine. Stood by. Did nothing. Let a million Irish die. But what harm in that? Sure weren't the Irish peasants only heathens . . . had no souls, only half human, somewhere between a chimpanzee and *Homo sapiens* . . . the missing link? Now she saw those self-same Irish peasants here being blown to Kingdom Come for Uncle Sam and they couldn't see that it was the same old story all over again. Slavery had taken the black people's language, their customs and traditions, their music. It had taken their country away from them – this new one – as well as those previously stolen from them. Slavery had tried to take their souls. Ellen O'Malley hoped it hadn't.

Now she talked to this half a man, in the voice previously reserved for her children – a kind of *suantraí* or lullaby-talk. 'I ain't never been baptised!' he said, surprising her. When she said she would send for a priest, he glared at her. 'I don't want no priest mouthin' that Latin gibberish over me!' Then his look softened. 'Would you do it for me, Miss Ellie – you'd be as good as any of them . . . you and the Sisters?'

She called Mary and Louisa to be witnesses, and fetched a tin-cupful of water. Then, his head in her arm, like a new-born, she sprinkled on it a drop of the water. Having no oils with which then to anoint him, she moistened her thumb against her mouth. With it she made the Sign of the Cross on his forehead, his ears, over his good eye and on his lips saying, 'I baptize you in the name of the Father, the Son and the Holy Ghost . . . There now, you're done . . . ready for any road.'

He was soothed now. His pain must have been intense. A miracle he had survived at all. Better he hadn't. He shook free his hand from hers, reached over to where his other hand would have been. Forgetting.

'I still feel it there, Ellie, but sure it's only the ghost of it

. . . only the ghost of it! If only I could wrap it round a lady's waist,' he said wistfully.

She took his hand again. 'Will you pray with me, Jeremiah?' she asked, still in Irish.

'Sure isn't what we're doin' . . . prayin'?' he replied, the good eye darting wickedly at her.

And she supposed it was.

'I can feel the Divil comin' for me, even after you sprinklin' the water on me,' he said, gripping her hand more tightly. 'He took the one half of me and now the wee bollix is comin' for the other half!'

He raised up his head, as if to see. 'G'way off to fuck, ye wee bollix ye!' he roared, startling her and the whole ward into silence. They were all well used to death by now – in its many guises. The sudden rap, the last rattle of breath, the gentle going – and those who roared!

She said nothing, just gripped his hand.

He raised his head again. 'Who made the world?' he shouted at them all.

'Gawd did,' a Southern voice called back.

'Who made America?'

'Paddy did!' the Irish roared back, as Jeremiah Finnegan handed in his ticket. Leaving both God's world and Paddy's America behind him.

She waited a few moments. Disengaged her hand, shuttered close the one mad eye on him.

'He died roarin', ma'am,' a gangrened youth in the next cot said.

'That he did, son! That he did!' she said, to the frightened boy.

TWELVE

Mary watched Ellen move among the men. The transformation in her mother since first she and Louisa had found her was nothing short of miraculous. Ellen's hair tied back from her face, accentuating her finely chiselled features, seemed to strip away the years. Modesty prevented Mary from ever using a looking glass but now, involuntarily, she put a hand to her face, fingering the high cheekbones, the generous span of mouth, the furrow between lips and nostrils. Upon her own face, Mary found replicated every feature of her mother's. She smiled as she watched Ellen go about her duties with an enthusiasm that further belied her years. In her plain blue calico dress – its only adornment a neat white collar – Mary's mother had a word for everybody.

'God never closes one door but He opens another,' Mary said to Louisa, marvelling how, after their banishment from the convent, the three of them had found such a fulfilment in their work here on the battlefields. Such an all-enveloping joy at being together again after all those years.

'Her heart still longs for Patrick and Lavelle,' Louisa answered. 'She will not remain here forever, Mary.'

'Oh, I know, Louisa . . .' Mary answered, 'but whatever the future holds, I will always hold dear these memories, these beautiful moments, of Mother bending to comfort a departing soul, writing out a letter to a loved one . . . of just being restored to us. I would happily depart this world with such images graven forever on my heart.'

Louisa, too, had witnessed the change in Ellen, the re-blooming; the coming of joy. All of which was a source of similar joy to Louisa herself!

She could not love Ellen more. Their time together here had been restorative for each of them in its own way. It was a privilege to serve those fallen in battle, to bind up their wounds – a rich and rewarding privilege. So, that when word had come down, from the Surgeon-General's office, through Dr Sawyer, asking her to accept the role of matron, Louisa had wholeheartedly accepted.

She now spoke to her sister. 'Well, before you take your leave of us, Mary, we have a St Patrick's Day celebration to organise!'

Not that St Patrick's Day was anywhere near in the offing. Nor that this mattered to those Irish currently under the care of the Sisters. Now, in the midsummer of 1862, the Irish had decided that 'this little skirmish' here in America should not prevent them from celebrating the national saint's feast day . . . even if some three months after the declared date of March 17.

'To show these foreigners, North and South, how to have fun,' Hercules O'Brien put forward to Louisa. 'We had a great St Pat's . . . beggin' your pardon, Sister, St Patrick's Day, during winter camp when there was no fighting . . . but that was only among ourselves . . . and sure it's now we need a diversion.'

After repeated 'spontaneous' entreaties from a number of the men – carefully orchestrated by O'Brien – Louisa had acquiesced. As matron, she warned that any celebration would have to be both 'orderly and circumspect'. She received every assurance it would . . . 'be as quiet as a dormouse dancing'.

Somehow, Louisa felt remarkably unassured by this assurance, as Jared Prudhomme's blue eyes beckoned her to him, for the third time that day.

Jared Prudhomme, proud to be from Baton Rouge, Louisiana, was 'the man side of seventeen', he told Louisa, when three weeks prior, he first came to them. He was tall, possessed of piercing blue eyes and with a beauty of countenance not normally bestowed on mortals. That he was dishevelled from battle, his blond hair unkempt about his face, did not in any sense diminish from his striking appearance. It was, Louisa had decided, because of some inner light of character which shone from the boy, and which was unquenchable.

She went to him. As on the two previous occasions today, she would be polite, not overstay with him, as she had when first he fell under her care. Then, though his shoulder wound had not been serious, due to a delay in getting him to hospital, he had lost a copious amount of blood. She had nursed him back, dressed his shoulder. One day, while leaning over him, their faces close, he had said, 'You have the scent of the South on you . . . it reminds me of so much!' She hadn't answered him and then he was apologetic. 'Did I embarrass you – I know you are not as other ladies?' She had raised her head, looked at him, smiled. He had no guile. 'Thank you,' she had said and left it at that.

Then, one morning, she had arisen, found herself rushing her prayers. At first, she couldn't quite fathom it but something about it bothered her. When she had reached his bedside, he had greeted her with his usual smile and she felt bathed in the light of his company. Leaving him, she realised that her earlier undue haste at prayers was not just to do her rounds but to get to him. When next she tended him, she was conscious of this feeling, her fingers betraying her as she peeled back the dressing from his bare shoulder.

'I am unsettling you,' he said in his quiet, direct way, 'and

58

I would rather fall to the enemy than cause any such emotion in you.'

This had discomfited her further.

'Yes!' she said, continuing her work. 'It is an uncommon feeling . . .' She paused, her words landing soft against his skin, her breath moistening the broken tissue.

Now, today, as she went to him, a faint tremor of apprehension came over her.

'I wanted to ask you before everybody else . . . and maybe I am already too late,' he began. 'Would you dance with me tonight – for St Patrick?' he added in quickly, upon seeing the look come over her face. 'It is my last night, before going out again . . . and I would go more lightly having danced with you,' he pleaded.

She looked at him, mended now, his face aglow at her. She had intended giving him a further talk about how 'All must be included in a Sister's love' or that 'Sisters, in spirit and in substance, must be faithful to their vows as a needle to the Pole.'

He looked so young, so fragile, his blue eyes entreating her, that she had not the heart. Before she had thought it out any further she had said 'yes!', the words of Sister Lazarus pounding in her brain . . . 'Impetuosity, Sister, will be your undoing. You must guard against it!'

The rest of that day Louisa allowed no excuse to bring her within the company of Jared Prudhomme.

Somewhere, somehow, Mary, in her own quiet way, had managed to forage a few gills of whiskey, some for everyone in the hospital. Not that she was in favour of the pleasures – or dangers – of 'the bewitching cup', herself.

'Blessings on ye, Sister – your mother never reared a jibber,' or some other such well-meant phrase, greeted the dispensation of the whiskey. Some had to be helped drink it. One soldier, half his neck torn away, tried to gather up the precious fluid in his hands each time it seeped from his throat.

Being a fruitless endeavour, he finally abandoned it. Instead cupping the amber-coloured liquid directly back into the gaping hole itself.

'A shortcut, ma'am,' he gasped to Mary, the rawness of the whiskey snatching the breath from him.

Another dashed it on the stump of his leg to 'kill the hurtin'.'

Overall, Sister Mary's whiskey produced a tizzy of excitement among the men. Americans, North and South toasted 'the Irish, on whichever side they fight', while the Irish toasted themselves, St Patrick, and the 'good Sisters', in that order.

The day, aided by the whiskey, invoked a kind of nostalgia in all of them. Some dreamed of the South – magnolia-scented days, fair ladies and the Mississippi. Some dreamed of the green lushness of the Shenandoah Valley. Others again sailed to further waters and valleys – the Rhine, the Severn, the Lowlands of Holland.

The Irish dreamed only of Ireland.

Ellen thought of the Reek, St Patrick's holy mountain.

'Do you remember how once we climbed it to look over the sea for a ship to America?' she asked Louisa and Mary.

They both nodded.

'I was afraid you wouldn't take me with you,' Louisa said. 'That after finding me, you would leave me. I prayed so hard to St Patrick.'

Ellen remembered too when she had returned to Ireland to collect them. Her money had been running low, with staying in Westport, waiting for passage to America. She had herself, Patrick and Mary to look out for first. Rescuing the girl from the side of the road had been an impulsive charity, one she had already been beginning to regret. But a ship *had* come before she was forced to take a decision about 'the silent girl', before they had named her 'Louisa'.

'Little did any of us then know what lay before us in this far-off land,' Mary reflected.

'We're still split apart from each other here,' her mother answered, thinking of those not present. Only this time it wasn't the famine, or 'the curse of emigration', or some other external force. This time it had been her own fault; her own fallibility that had scattered them. She was fortunate to have found again Mary and Louisa, or rather to have been found by them. But always her thoughts went to Patrick and Lavelle.

Of them there was no sign.

She knew they were out there somewhere, either with the Union Army of the Potomac, or with the Confederate Army of Northern Virginia.

A chill crossed her. They would have seen combat by now. She looked around the room. She always looked when a new consignment – the flotsam and jetsam of each fresh battle – arrived. Each time she looked, dread was in her eyes and in the back of her throat, and in the petrified pit that was her stomach. Now, as her gaze took in the men about her – a torn-out throat, a hole through a nose, like a third, sunken eye, a lifeless sleeve or trouser leg – she would have been happy to see them there. At least know that they were alive.

In her care.

'I know what you're thinking, Mother.' It was Mary. 'Trust in the Lord!'

'Oh, I do, Mary! Believe me, I do – but sometimes I just wish I could help Him a bit more!'

'You are . . . by helping those whom He has put in your way to help,' Mary answered.

'Mrs Lavelle!' – it was Dr Sawyer.

The mound of amputated limbs had grown so high outside the 'saw-mill' window that they now tumbled from the top and were strewn on the ground like disarrayed matchsticks. The doctor wanted some order – these scattered limbs retrieved and a second mound started beside the first one.

Three months prior she would have fallen faint at the prospect. Now, she never flinched, nor did Mary and Louisa, who came to help her.

Ellen began to gather the legs and the arms. She tried to avoid picking them up by the hand or the foot. Did not want to touch the fingers or toes, have that intimacy. This proved impossible.

At times there was only the bare, half-hand, or the foot, where the surgeon had tried to save most of the arm or leg.

Then she began to recognise them. Couldn't help but remember the stout arm of Jeremiah Finnegan, or the worm-infested leg of that sweet young Iowa boy, now with gangrene set in. Somehow, it wasn't so bad if the rest of the body was alive, back inside the hospital. From some of the limbs, fresh blood still oozed so that they were warm and living to the touch.

It wasn't right. They shouldn't be allowed to accumulate here like heapfuls of strange fruit, burning in the sun until the blowflies and maggots came. Those over which the maggots already crawled, she picked up with her apron, then shook off what worms remained on her, once she had deposited the putrid limb. Other limbs had corroded to the bone, caked by the sun, stripped clean by flesh-eating things.

To distract her mind she recited the Breastplate of St Patrick:

> 'Christ with me,
> Christ before me,
> Christ behind me,
> Christ within me,
> Christ on my right hand,
> Christ on my left hand,
> Christ all around me,
> Christ in the heart of all who think of me,
> Christ in the mouth of all who speak of me,
> Christ in every eye who looks at me,
> Christ in every ear who listens to me.'

Even the words of the prayer seemed to take on an incongruity, far removed from their intended bidding.

'Christ on my right foot,' she prayed while handling a foot, pierced through like a stigmata. She remembered the poor wretch who had, in a state of fear, pulled the trigger of his rifle before raising it to the enemy and shot himself.

'Christ on my left foot.' She had it all out of kilter. But did it matter? She cast the stigmatic foot onto the mound, watched it slide down again in some crucified dance.

'Christ with me,' she intoned, invoking again the protection of the saint's breastplate.

And the stench, the yellow dripping stench: powerful, unavoidable, permeating her clothes, her pores, the follicles of her hair. She thought she would drown in its noisome pool, it oozing over her whole body, closing out air and decency.

She redoubled her prayer but the drenching slime slid into her mouth, over her tongue and down her throat like the melt of Hell.

When they had finished she went straight to Dr Sawyer, gave him her mind about how 'the great Abraham Lincoln couldn't even run a decent abattoir, let alone this war or this country!'

That evening the regular cries for relief and 'Sister! Oh Sister!' were broken by a new sound. That of someone scratching out a tune on an asthmatic fiddle. Where the instrument came from nobody knew or, if they did, would not reveal.

Soon the fiddler, a Donny McLeod late of the Scottish Highlands, via East Tennessee, was madly flaking out the old mountain reels. For Ellen, the tunes recalled better days of sure-footed dancers, the men hob-nailing it out, striking splanks from the floor, while slender-waisted girls swung from their arms. Now, the magic of the wild fiddle music seemed to banish away forever the misfortunes of the waiting war.

It was Hercules O'Brien who started it.

Up he rose, arm in a sling – which he immediately cast off.

'Head bandaged like a Turk, with only the ears out,' as he

63

described himself, he grabbed hold of the remaining arm of a grizzled old veteran.

'C'mon, Alabarmy – let's see if you can dance better than you fight!' the little man challenged.

'Well, I'll be darned, O'Brien, if any o' that Irish nigger-dancin' will best ol' Alabarmy,' the Southron answered back.

And the two faced each other in the middle of the floor, Hercules O'Brien lashing it out heel to toe for all he was worth.

'You's sweatin' like a hawg,' Alabarmy goaded as the blood seeped out through his partner's bandaged head. 'Like a stuck hawg!'

A great roar of laughter arose at this goading of the Irishman.

Not to be outdone, Hercules O'Brien shouted back above the din, 'And if you'd lost a leg 'stead of an arm, you'd be a better dancer,' which raised another bout of laughter. Then the Irishman crooked his own good arm in Alabarmy's one arm and swung him . . . and swung him in a dizzy circle with such a wicked delight. Until they all thought Alabarmy would leave this earth, courtesy of the buck-leppin' O'Brien.

Next, another was up and then another, curtseying to prospective partners, the 'ladies' donning a strip of white bandage on whatever arm or leg they had left to distinguish themselves from the men.

'Could I have the pleasure, Jennie Reb?' Or 'C'mon, Yankee, show us your nigger-jiggin'!'

Ellen stood watching them, the music reeling away the years. Back to the Maamtrasna crossroads, high above the two lakes – Lough Nafooey and Lough Mask. Them gathering in from every one of the four roads, the high bright moon lighting the way. Like souls summoned from sleep the dancers came, filtering out of the night to the gathering. There, under the moon and the great bejewelled sky they would merge out of shadow – a glance, a half-smile, then hand within hand, arm around waist, breath to breath. Then bodies in remembered rhythm would weave their spell, and they would rise above the ground, be lifted; the diamond sky now at their feet – a blanket of stars beneath them.

The priests were right – the devil was in the dancing, in the wicked reels; the way you danced out of your skin, out of yourself. 'Going before themselves,' the old women called it. Leaving sense and the imprisoned self behind. Being lost to the dance.

Remembering wasn't good, Ellen reminded herself. A life could be lost to it . . . wasted, looking backwards. Looking forwards was as bad. She was of late looking too much back-wards, and looking forwards, wondering where, if ever, she would find Lavelle and Patrick. Trapped between the future and the past, no control over either. Helplessly suspended in the now.

Ellen took in the scene in front of her. Was that all that mattered? All there was? The now of these broken men, momentarily lifted above the brutal earth to dance among the stars?

Across the room she saw Foots O'Reilly in conversation with Mary. Then she watched Mary bend, her arms encirc-ling the man's back, lifting him into a sitting position. He was from Cavan 'and a mighty dancer,' he had told Ellen, 'could trip over the water of Lough Sheelin without damp-ening me toes.' Hence, the nickname 'Foots'. Then a Southern shell had ripped one dancing leg from under him.

'That won't hold Foots O'Reilly back none,' he swore. Tomorrow he would undergo the surgeon's saw to save the second leg, gangrened to the knee.

'I could dance with the one, ma'am, but I can't dance with the none. Now I'll lose me name as well as me pegs. "Foots" with no foot at all to put under me.' He had cried in her arms then.

Ellen watched Mary hoist the one-legged dancer, so that he half stood, half leaned against her, arms clasped to her, head draped over her shoulders. She dragged him out to the

65

dancing square. The others witnessing it stopped, even the fiddle boy. Then Mary whispered into his ear, 'Come on now, Mr O'Reilly. Dance with me . . . you show them!'

And she manoeuvred him slowly around in the silence, his gangrenous leg trailing behind them. Then again and again they turned, in grotesque pirouette, she in her white nun's ballgown, he the mighty dancer, until Mary could support his dead weight no longer.

'Thank you, Mr O'Reilly . . . Foots,' Mary said to him. 'I shall always remember this dance . . .' and she sat him gently down again.

Then, all those who could were once more 'footin' it': the wounded and the wasted, the stumped and the stunted. All flailed and flopped and picked themselves up again as the fiddler played his relentless reel. Then, suddenly, he changed into waltz-time.

'I thought he'd kill the lot of them . . .' Ellen said to Mary who had come beside her, '. . . but isn't it wonderful to see?'

Mary smiled back at her.

As the young Tennessean, bow astride his fiddle, led them into the waltz, they watched Hercules O'Brien prop up Alabarmy in front of him, placing the Southerner's shelled-out sleeve over his shoulder. Twins from Arkansas – a crutch apiece – hobbled around in a kind of teetering dance, Ellen ready to catch whichever one of them, who any minute must fall.

Then, someone bowing to Ellen . . . a deep bow. It was Herr Heidelberg, the Dutchman, as the men called the German soldier from the town of the same name. Like all who had come newly to America, Germans as well as the Irish, Poles and a host of other nations had joined in the fray to fight for their 'new country' – the North in Herr Heidelberg's case.

'I better likes dance mit de Frauen den de Herren,' he said shyly.

What Ellen could see of Herr Heidelberg's face was pink with both excitement and embarrassment. The German was the object of much ridicule from the rest of the men due to his manner of speaking, and now could risk further ridicule.

Ellen curtseyed to him.

'Delighted, Herr Heidelberg!' she replied.

It was the only name by which she knew him . . . and though denied his real name, the association with his home-town had always seemed to please him.

Herr Heidelberg swept her around like a Viennese princess, her dress spattered with the earlier work of the day, flouncing about her. The men made space for them, Ellen and her waltz king with half a face, clapping them on to twirl upon twirl, him counting to her under his breath.

'*Ein, zwei, drei, ein, zwei, drei.*' His bulk making her move like a turntable doll, just to keep pace with him. And all the while the young fiddler discoursing sweet music from his violin.

When they had finished, the others all clapped and cheered – and cheered again, more loudly; those who could not clap, clanking their crutches. He turned to her, flushed with delight.

'*Danke schön! Danke schön* . . . I have not so very good time before in America,' and she saw the tears form and spill down his bandaged cheek.

'Thank *you*, Herr Heidelberg. You're a brave dancer.'

He beamed at her and self-consciously retired away from her to the rear of the ward.

Finding herself beside the young fiddler Ellen enquired of him the tune. 'It has no name . . . I picked it up from folk in the foothills.' He smiled at her. 'I could call it "The North and South Waltz".'

'More like "The Cripples' Waltz", ma'am, beggin' your pardon,' Hercules O'Brien chipped in, ''cos that's what it was!'

'If you was a gentleman, Sergeant O'Brien,' the fiddler remonstrated, 'you'd name it for the lady . . . "Mrs Lavelle's", or, with permission, ma'am, "Ellen's Waltz".'

'Waltzes can be trouble . . .' she said, remembering Stephen Joyce, and something about 'the carnal pleasures of the waltz'.

'I am honoured but perhaps there is a young lady in East Tennessee who more greatly deserves the honour,' she said . . . and he struck up another waltz as if in answer.

All of a foam after her own decidedly non-carnal waltz with Herr Heidelberg, Ellen went to the open doorway for some cooling air. She stood there watching the sky, listening to the music, thinking of those whom she most dearly missed. The sky, the everlasting sky. Lavelle out there under it. Dead or alive. Maybe watching that same sky, thinking of her. An old poem-prayer – pagan or Christian, she didn't know – formed on her lips. She had learned it at her father's knee. All those nights of wonder long ago, under the sheltering stars. High on the Maamtrasna hill, above the Mask and Lough Nafooey. Above Finny's singing river. Above the world.

'I am the sky above Maamtrasna,
I am the deep pool of Lough Nafooey;
I am the song of the Finny river,
I am the silent Mask.
I am the low sound of cattle
And the bleating snipe;
I am the deer's cry
And the cricket's dance.
In the lover's eye, am I;
In the beating heart;
I am the unlatched door;
I am the comforting breath.
Now and before, after and evermore,
I am the waiting shore.'

'The waiting shore,' she repeated, the great sky listening. 'I am the waiting shore.'

Music, dancing, always seemed to start her thinking. Too much of it was bad. Thinking led to feelings. High, lonesome feelings like the fiddle-sound behind her. Still, these days she didn't much give into herself. Just kept working with a kind of blind faith. That one day she'd find them, or they'd find her. Looking back on life was as bad as looking back on Ireland. She was done with all that, was now facing the new day – whatever that might bring . . . to wherever it might lead her. Like here . . . a pale 'St Patrick's night' in Virginia – . . . Maryland . . . Carolina. She'd never thought of States as feminine. Then again, men were always naming a thing for their women, as if to protect – or to own – it. Louisiana . . . Georgia . . . the Southern States seemed to have the best of the gender divide. Louisiana – Louisa's Land. Ellen thought of her adopted daughter.

Louise, in many respects, was more like herself than Mary was. If not in looks, then certainly in temperament. Ellen smiled. Louise had some inherent waywardness. Needed always to be holding herself in check; dampening down her natural high spirits. Her passion for this life sometimes outbalancing her preparation for the next.

Ellen looked back through the door, to catch a glimpse of Louisa. There she was, gaily dancing with that young Southern boy Jared Prudhomme. Ellen had noticed them talking together. She would speak to Louisa about it.

The one thing, Ellen knew, which held the Sisters high in the respect and affections of the men, was that they, unlike the lay nurses, divided their care equally among all the men. To move from this understanding would undermine the position of the Sisterhood – and re-instate all the barriers and prejudices they had worked so hard to remove. Louisa's vocation, Ellen knew, was more difficult than Mary's. Louisa would always be torn between the things of the world and her higher calling. More passionate, more reckless than Mary, Louisa went headlong at life. Not always a good thing. In moments

69

left Louisa unguarded against herself. Much as Ellen herself had been.

Ellen looked again. Mary too was caught up with the celebrations. But it was different. This Earth, with all its hollow baubles, was merely a waiting place for Mary. Until she was borne away by an angel band to eternal glory. Even in that, Mary had an unsullied purity of thought. She did not seek everlasting life, as a thing in itself. With her, it was ever the higher ideal – to see His face, to continue her worship of Him in Heaven as she had on Earth. Mary was fallible humanity at its most beautiful. Mary was a saint.

The sound of a galloping horse startled Ellen. Some news of a battle? Surrender? Peace?

Her heart leaped at the thought.

The horse, pale against the rising moon had no rider. It galloped by her, so close she could smell the thick odour of its lathering skin. On it ran until she could hear its distant drumming but see it no more.

'"Behold a pale horse, And his name that sat on him was Death; And Hell followed with him;" Revelations, Chapter Six, Verse eight,' she said, after it.

She remembered the Hades horse in the woods – the memories it had evoked. Black horse, pale horse. It reminded her of something. Out there too champing for battle was the red horse of slaughter, the white horse of conquest. Four horses in all, ever present at the revelation of evil – the Apocalypse. She felt a tremor run over her body.

She walked out a piece into the night, following the sound of the retreating hooves, the horse bringing back her old dream. Lavelle, constant, loving Lavelle, true as the guiding moon. Out there somewhere beneath it. And Stephen, he, who had excited such a temporary madness in her, awaking every reckless passion. She lingered on thoughts of him, their times together, her skin alive with the remembering. Under what moon, what banner, was Stephen Joyce? She dared not think. She and Stephen Joyce could never meet again. She dismissed him from her mind, irritated by her lapse, thinking she long ago had.

When Ellen turned to come back, she saw two figures flit away from the din of the hospital into the glinting night and towards the woods. She hoped they would not arouse the interest of jittery-fingered pickets who lay at every pillar and post between them and the enemy. Especially, as he was a Southern boy.

She would need to speak to Louisa. Urgently.

THIRTEEN

Jared Prudhomme raised his hand to the winged headdress which Louisa wore.

'I am afraid to remove it.'

'As am I,' she said simply.

Reverentially, the boy raised the starched white edifice above Louisa's forehead. If he had been expecting her hair to fall, covering her face – it did not. She was cropped more closely than a boy. He touched her cheek. Her eyes never left his for a moment, as if nothing had been revealed. In the far distance, the odd shot loosed by an edgy picket punctured the night. In the near distance she heard a horse.

Tomorrow, she knew, he would return to it. Be out there in some bare, unsheltering plain, or in some fiery copse. Or moving through some ripening wheat field, his golden head . . . She shivered at the thought. Already he had some fixed premonition regarding tomorrow. She had seen it before in men. Invariably they were right, the death prophecy fulfilling itself. But its foretelling allowed them to prepare. Write the last letter; leave some memento; make final amends with their Maker. The grizzled older campaigners took it all in their stride. They had all 'seen the elephant' before. Death, to them was as inevitable as the sun rising. But he was just a boy – a golden boy – and a boy in love.

'You are more beautiful . . .' he began.

'Sshh!' she said. 'Nothing is required.'

When she left him, returned past the silent, growing mounds of limbs, she crossed herself for the limbless and un-whole who, inside the rickety hospital, awaited her.

She considered her solemn vow of chastity not to have been broken.

FOURTEEN

Inside, the limbless continued dancing unabated, and the un-
whole undeterred. Now, songs were interspersed to allow
some respite to the dancers, most of the songs hurled insults
at the opposite side. The 'Southern Dixie' answered by the
'Union Dixie'.

> Way down South in the land of traitors,
> Rattlesnakes and alligators . . .

Or, another 'Yankee Doodle'.

> Yankee Doodle said he found,
> By all the census figures,
> That he could starve the rebels out,
> If he could steal their niggers.

Answered by

> We do not want your cotton,
> We do not want your slaves,
> But rather than divide the land,
> We'll fill your Southern graves.

Then 'The Irish Volunteer' of the North clashed with 'The Bonnie Blue Flag' of the South. Both, Ellen recognised, sung to the same air of 'The Irish Jaunting Car'!

The dancing resumed and Ellen was aware that Louisa was back in the midst of things. Shortly thereafter Jared Prudhomme re-appeared and Alabarmy called on him.

'Lad, if these Yankees can't whup us with minié balls, they ain't gonna whup us with songs . . . so give us one of yer best, boy!'

Jared Prudhomme stood tall, laughed and started to sing.

'Her brow is like the snowdrift,
Her nape is like the swan,
And her face it is the fairest,
That 'ere the sun shone on.

'. . . And for Bonnie Annie Laurie
I'd lay down my head and die.'

They all liked him Ellen knew, both North and South, as did she. He was truly beautiful, in so far as one could ascribe beauty to a youth. But for all his seventeen youthful years, he had a manly bearing. Looked all straight in the eye, neither seeking favour, nor giving it. Yet with that generosity of youth that the cynicism of older age – and war – had not yet destroyed.

He sang as he looked. Clear voiced. Uninhibited by those present. Sang to 'Annie Laurie', as if she were there in the very room listening to him. And she was, Ellen knew, casting a glance towards Louisa. The girl's white-bonnetted head was fixed on the boy. He did not look at her. He had no need to. The spirit within the song left his lips irrevocably bound for no other place than her.

Ellen stood transfixed. The boy reminded her so much of herself. Before she lost the gift. The gift was not the singing itself – the mere outpouring of notes – but the thing within and above the singing. She could still sing – as a person might. But the gift was lost to her. The gift came with purity – purity of intent, purity of the art itself. Letting go of desire, of ambition for the voice – the instrument – to be admired, the singer to be praised. The voice was not the gift, but the gift could inhabit the voice . . . but not by right or by skill alone.

The boy had the gift. Though he sang for Louisa, he did not sing *to* her. Then he had stopped before he had started it seemed, leaving them there suspended in the moment. The song, at one level, having passed them by. At another, having entered within, transcending them into some knowledge undefined by words or melody alone.

The listeners came back before he did. Clapped loudly, recognising that they had been transported and were now returned. '*Arisht*,' the Irish called. 'One more, lad!' both friend and foe alike, echoed.

The boy just smiled, looked at Louisa, dropped his head slightly to gather himself and then looked at her again. Almost imperceptibly, she motioned her consent, the slightest tilt of her head towards him.

'With your permission, ladies, I will dedicate this song to you all who daily raise us up.'

Acclamation arose from all those assembled. Again he looked at the ground, waiting until the burr of noise had receded.

'When I am down and, oh my soul, so weary;
When troubles come and my heart burdened be;
Then, I am still and wait here in the silence,
Until you come and sit awhile with me.'

At the refrain, this time he looked directly at Louisa. She held his gaze, letting his sung words seep into her.

'You raise me up, so I can stand on mountains;
You raise me up, to walk on stormy seas;

I am strong, when I am on your shoulders;
You raise me up . . . to more than I can be.'

All were hushed as the boy drew breath.

'You raise me up, so I can stand on mountains;
You raise me up to walk on stormy seas;'

This time they all joined in, raising their voices in the redemptive words. A chorus of broken angels but all fear lifted from them.

'I am strong, when I am on your shoulders;
You raise me up . . . to more than I can be.'

At the final line his gaze never removed from Louisa, the rapture on her daughter's face provoking the opposite emotion in Ellen. When he finished there was again the hiatus, no one wanting to break the moment, steal wonder away.

'We'll give you that – you can sing you Rebs!' Hercules O'Brien eventually ventured, nodding his block of a head in approval at the boy. Then looking at Ellen he called for 'A soothing Irish voice to calm the storms of battle'.

She resisted, didn't want to follow the boy, break the spell he wove. Then the boy himself called her, 'It would do us great honour. Mrs Lavelle – a parting song. A song some may not hear again . . . after tomorrow.'

All knew what he meant. Some did not look at her . . . shuffled uneasily. Those that could – those recovered by her healing hands who, tomorrow would go out again – she could not refuse them. For some reason the pale and riderless horse flashed by her mind.

She started falteringly, sang it to the boy. Her own favourite. Favourite of all whom she loved and who in turn had loved her.

'Oh, my fair-haired boy, no more I'll see,
You walk the meadows green;
Or hear your song run through the fields
Like yon mountain stream . . .'

She looked at the boy as she sang, something fiercely ominous in her, some darker shade of meaning she had not noticed before, now present in the words.

'So take my hand and sing me now,
Just one last merry tune . . .'

His clear blue eyes never left hers as she sang her tune in answer to his.

'Let no sad tear now stain your cheek,
As we kiss our last goodbye;
Think not upon when we might meet,
My love my fair-haired boy . . .'

They were all her fair-haired boys, all the crippled, the crutched, the maimed and the motherless. Some called her 'Mother' – and even when they didn't, she knew she was their mother in-situ, the comforting words, the tender touch.

'If not in life we'll be as one,
Then, in death we'll be . . .'

She did not mean to sadden them with thoughts of death but to comfort them. Death indeed would come to many here . . . maybe to Hercules O'Brien . . . maybe by the hand of Ol' Alabarmy, his dancing partner. Perhaps death would dance with the shy Rhinelander. He had danced with her, as if it were the last waltz on this wounded earth. Or death could call time on the young fiddle player from East

78

Tennessee. Or even, Ellen kept her eyes on the beautiful boy, to Jared Prudhomme, in love with her Louisa . . . and she with him.

How, Ellen wondered, could anything other than the boy's death solve Louisa's dilemma?

'And there will grow two hawthorn trees,
Above my love and me,
And they will reach up to the sky Intertwined be . . .'

She was singing not to death . . . but to hope. Hope that after death love might still survive, but hope none the same.

'. . . And the hawthorn flower will bloom where lie,
My fair-haired boy and me.'

The boy came to her, held her arms, looked deep into her eyes. 'Thank you, Mrs Lavelle – Mother! Everything will be all right now – you'll see!'

She didn't know how to reply to him. Just squeezed his arms . . . let him go slowly, a certain sadness creeping over her. Maybe it was the song.

Then the Tennessee fiddle player called for a 'last fling of dancing' – 'I Buried My Wife and Danced on Top of Her'.

Ellen was glad to be shaken out of her thoughts and as well didn't want to send the men to sleep, morose about tomorrow. Though, even jigs and reels sometimes didn't prevent that. She remembered Stephen Joyce wondering to her once about 'how the Irish could be both happy and sad – at the same time!'

She entered joyfully into the spirit of the dance, lilting the tune, swinging and high-steppin' it with her boys; Hercules O'Brien roaring at the top of his voice, reminding them all to 'Dance, dance, dance all you can, Tomorrow you'll be just half-a-man!'

Then a new sound – the stentorian voice of Dr Sawyer

cutting through the din. 'Stop it! Stop it at once!'

He looked the length of the hospital at them, withering them with his gaze, reducing them back to what they previously had been – men of rank, diseased and disabled.

'It's madness, sheer irresponsible madness! Sister, . . . you are in charge here?'

Louisa stepped forward: – 'Yes, Doctor.'

'These men, half of them at death's door and look at them – lungeing about like lunatics . . . limbless lunatics.'

The men huddled back at his onslaught.

'Feckless nuns and jiggers of whiskey – against my better judgement from the start. This won't go unanswered!' And he turned and marched out, killing all joy.

'You won't best us!' Hercules O'Brien shouted after the retreating figure. 'Even if it's our lastest Paddy's Night . . . it was the bestest.' Then he turned, went down to where Ol' one-armed Alabarmy now stood, all crumpled and defeated.

All watched as Hercules O'Brien bowed to his foe.

'Thank you, sir, you're a gallant soldier.'

Then Ellen, Louisa and Mary watched, the splendour rising in them, as each of the lame and the limbless, the Southron and the Northman, bowed to each other, offering gratitude for the frolics now finished and solicitude for whatever the morrow might bring.

In turn then the men thanked Ellen and the Sisters – especially Sister Mary for 'The jiggers of whiskey and one helluva party for a nun!'

Those that could fight would want to be up and bandaged by five o'clock. That meant four for Ellen and the others. If they weren't called on during the night and Ellen suspected they might well be. Dr Sawyer had been right . . . up to a point, and damaged limbs could only take so much. Still, they settled the men down as best they could and changed any dressings, oozing from the evening's exertions.

And it was all worth it. The night's fun was worth it.

*

80

The fiddling was furious, the band of fiddlers flaking it out. Ellen recognised them. There was Hercules O'Brien mummified for death. His head bandaged; blood plinking from his bow.

There too, was Ol' Alabarmy thwacking his bow madly across his instrument. Where was his other hand? Grotesquely, the fiddle stuck out from Alabarmy's neck, there being no other visible form of support. And Herr Heidelberg, atop a giant barrel. Like the others, he held a bow. To it was fixed a bayonet. When, each time, he drew his bow across the strings, it sliced a collop of flesh from his face. She cried out to him, but he seemed not to hear.

Ellen and the boy, Louisa's boy, were in front of the fiddle band, dancing 'The Cripples' Waltz' but the timing was wrong . . . all wrong. The fiddle band played one tune, they danced to a different one, the boy whispering loudly to her to 'Listen! Listen, Mother! D'you hear it – in the floor – the skulls?'

She didn't know what he was talking about. But he persisted at her to 'Listen!' Again calling her 'Mother.'

Then, at last she could hear it. The amplified sound of their feet exploding on the floor, driving up her legs, shivering into her body.

'It's the skulls!' he whispered, with a mad glee that she had at last understood him. 'That's what gives it the sound – the skulls, goat skulls and sheep skulls and . . . and . . . listen to the walls!' he then demanded, pulling her close to the wall, pushing her face against it until she could feel the wild music entering the hollowed-out eyes and ears . . . and the slit of the nose. Coming back louder than when it went in. They did it in Ireland he told her. Buried the skulls of dead animals in the floors and the walls. To catch the sound of the wicked reels and the even wilder women who splanked the floor to them.

The music came thick and furious. She recognised the tunes – 'I Buried My Wife and Danced on Top of Her', then 'Pull the Knife and Stick It'.

81

The only dancers were the boy and her. She wanted to ask him about Louisa . . . about . . . but he kept telling her to 'listen!', like *she* was the child. She obeyed him, the skull sound all the time rapping out its rhythm like a great rattling gun. It got louder and louder, until frightened, she looked at the floor. There, reaching up from beneath, were hands without arms and arms without hands.

If she could only dance fast enough, she could avoid them. Keep one step ahead. She shouted at the Cripple Band to play faster. But the faster they played the more Herr Heidelberg's bayonet slashed his face, the more the bow of Hercules O'Brien splinked blood onto his face, his tunic, and his instrument. Ol' Alabarmy smiled dreamily through it all.

The boy seemed not to notice, not to see. Only to hear. 'Isn't it beautiful?'

She tried to fight him off – make him see. He must be blind, crippled as the rest of them. Now, he caught her roughly by the shoulder, again trying to face her towards the wall.

'No!' she shouted, trying to get away from him. Trying to keep dancing, keep ahead of the jiggling hands.

'No! No!' she shouted, more vehemently, trying to wrest her body free.

'It's time, Mother – four o'clock!' Mary said, gently but firmly shaking her shoulder.

FIFTEEN

When Louisa awoke, the clarion calls of war were already summoning men to be ready for death. Before he would go out today, the boy had last night asked her to 'Place my name, company and regiment on a piece of paper and pin it to my breast.'

She prayed, her daily prayers – the Sign of the Cross, the Morning Invocation of the Light, the Lord's Prayer – for him. Not that death should pass him by, for that alone was the Lord's domain, but that if it came, it should be quick and clean. Not lingering and painful, his youthfulness ebbing away, his beauty distorted.

Louisa knew he would be fearless, be raised in courage because of her. She smiled – boys to men do quickly grow. She rose, dressed, put on her headdress, remembering.

'The White Bonnet Religion', the soldiers called her faith. White bonnet, black bonnet, no bonnet, Louisa wondered what it was religion had to do with what would happen here today? Yet, the vast bulk of those who would line up to kill each other lived by some religious code. The politicians who, from afar, waged this war, also waged it with the absolute conviction that God was on their side. They had spoken with Him – and He had told them!

It had always seemed such an obscenity to her, lining up God in the ranks.

Beside her, Mary also prepared for the long day. In perfect prayer, Mary would be. Not distracted by the thoughts which flitted in and out of Louisa's own head. She loved Mary so. Mary was her window to God. Amongst all the Sisters, all the doctors, the heroes of battle, Mary was the most perfect human being Louisa had ever known. A constant reservoir of love to all who came within her sphere. And Mary's love was infinite.

'I have no right not to dispense it freely,' was how Mary saw it. 'It is not mine not to give. I am His river.'

Mary looked at her adopted sister and smiled. Mary could see beneath, Louisa knew, into her very soul. That was the way with her. Louisa wondered what Mary would find there this morning? Whatever, there would be no judging of it.

Neither spoke. Nor was there need to.

SIXTEEN

The hospital was already alive with movement – an air of excitement. Those who could, mad for action. Mad to fight for America.

'America!' Hercules O'Brien began the day. 'Wide open spaces and narrow minds. If it ain't American it ain't good! In ascending order, Irish, African, German, Jew.'

'But cannon fodder is different, Hercules,' 'Souper' Doyle, a Confederate from Co. Galway, answered. 'The off-scourings of the world is good enough for American buck and ball. Didn't you hear the officers *colloguing* with each other, how "Irish Catholics were a resource of fodder for enemy cannon that couldn't be ignored?" Well it's our America now, whether the Northern Yankees like it or not. We're no longer lodgers in someone else's home!'

Souper Doyle resented how his name had followed him here to America. What harm if his people had 'taken the soup', changed, for a while, to the 'English religion', for food to keep body and soul together during the worst of the Bad Times. Sure hadn't they changed back again, when the winter of Black 'Forty-Seven was over! But the name had stuck . . . the Doyles were 'soupers'. Thomas Patrick Doyle had hoped that when he left Godforsaken Galway behind, he would also leave there all references to soup. So

he had taken a purseful of coin and the passage money to
America from the recruiting officer who had come to Ireland,
seeking 'stout-hearted fighting men'. The man with the
drawling accent had promised them 'Glory' . . . during the
war, and a 'grander life in a free America' . . . after they
had won it!

'Souper!'

He winced now as Hercules O'Brien addressed him.
Souper Doyle wondered, that if he ever got out of this
hellish army in one piece, if he could find some place far
out in the west where there was no damned Irish? Where
he wouldn't be known, and change his name? Hercules!
Now there was a grand name . . . a grand, stout-hearted
name.

'Souper!' the current owner of that name called out again.

'You Rebs will need a flag of truce to get back to your
lines.' Then turning to the nuns asked, 'Is there not a flidgin'
of white among the lot of you Sisters to make a truce flag
for the Rebs?'

Louisa came to the rescue, running to their quarters and
salvaging a well-washed winter petticoat from its out-of-season
hibernation. It wasn't white – a cream-coloured flannel – but
it couldn't be mistaken for what it was.

When he saw her return with it, Jared Prudhomme insisted
he be the flagbearer. Vowing devotion to her faded thrown-
off, he fixed it atop his bayonet.

'May it and the Lord keep you safe,' Louisa whispered to
him.

Mary then, gave the Rebel band her blessing, putting them,
as Alabarmy pronounced it, 'Under the one Sister's protection and the other Sister's petticoat!'

Out they went then, the small band of Johnny Rebs. The
boy, good-as-new from his wound, proudly bearing Louisa's
petticoat aloft, led them. Then Ol' Alabarmy, defiant as ever,
proclaiming his one arm 'good enough to pull a trigger on

nigger-jiggin' Yankees.' With them, the Tennessee fiddle player, his asthmatic fiddle strapped to his knapsack – and Souper Doyle. 'One of our own, misleadin' himself,' Hercules O'Brien bemoaned.

'The mighty great man in a little man's body' as the men called the diminutive sergeant, should not yet have been ready enough for more action but he had seemed hell-bent on returning to the fray. Now he came to Ellen, awkward in his own way.

'Blessings on you, ma'am, for the tender touch – and the mighty *craic*. I hope you find your husband!'

And he pressed into her hand a letter.

'Read it after I'm gone,' he said gravely, 'and tell her I forgive her.'

She started to say something, saw a strong man's tears well up in his eyes, fighting not to fall.

'Better be dead than finished,' he said, and went.

Ellen watched after him, knowing she would not see him again. Something about the small way he carried himself.

Like hedgehogs in March they went, sniffing out if the world had changed during the long sleep into spring.

They waved the Southerners off, the nurses . . . and the nursed who could walk. Then the Union soldiers, Hercules O'Brien among them, went out to their own side.

Two thoughts struck Ellen. The first that what she was witnessing seemed to deny the very essence of the work she was doing – healing. If it was just patching them up to go out again, have another chance at death, what was the weary point of it all?

Her second thought was that their leaving freed up some space. For the inevitable mangled fruit that would be harvested from today's reeking plain.

She had taken no more than a dozen steps inside the hospital when she heard the gunfire. Just a small fusillade. Men jerked up in their beds.

'It's the Rebs!' one whispered – and all knew. 'Our boys got the Rebs!'

She ran to the door, Louisa already ahead of her, turning her head back, a stricken look upon her face. They careered across the short distance to where the crumpled group of grey-clad bodies lay. Ellen saw Louisa's petticoat on the ground, tossed this way and that by the eddying breeze.

It was Louisa who reached them first, pulling his body from under the others. Holding his golden head on her lap, talking to him, calling him 'Mr Prudhomme!' Straining to hold back unSisterly tears. Frantic for any visible sign of life.

There was none.

She sat there. Stunned beyond words. Only, 'Mr Prudhomme! Mr Prudhomme!' Cradling his stilled youth. Then, bent to his ear, whispered words the world could not hear. Words, she hoped the heavens would.

Mary gathered Souper Doyle in her arms, the neck reefed from him, his chest punctured. She tried to stem the hole in his throat with her hand. It was to no avail. He had seemed such a lonely man, didn't mix much with the others. She knew what they said about him. Had spoken quietly to a few of them. That it wasn't Christian to call him that. To judge.

'Thomas,' she said, gently. 'The Lord is waiting. He will not judge you.'

He tried to respond. Made some distressing gurgling sounds in his throat . . . and died.

Mary waited with him, praying for the eternal repose of his soul and asking forgiveness for those whom Souper Doyle could no longer forgive.

Likewise, Ol' Alabarmy – 'long gone' – when Mary reached him was finally home.

The young fiddle player lay on his back, beneath him his instrument . . . smithereened into the last silence. He was still alive, barely. Ellen knelt beside the boy, lifting his head against her breast.

'We'll get you back inside, fiddle player,' she said, more in desperation than in hope. He rolled his eyes up at her.

'No, lady,' he said quietly.

'Rosin' up my bow – I'll be at the crossroads and I hope the Devil don't take me the wrong way!'

'The Devil shouldn't have all the best music,' she answered grimly and got him to listen as she said an Act of Contrition into his ear.

'You never let up with the white bonnet religion?' he smiled.

'Nothing else makes any sense,' she said. 'Are you hurting?'

'Not in that way,' he answered.

'What then?' she asked, anxious of any final comfort she could bring him.

He didn't answer her immediately. Then, in a moment, raised his head to her. 'If my mother were here with *your* son . . .' he said, forming the words so slowly, so deliberately, that she would not mistake them, '. . . she would surely kiss him.'

And he kept his eyes open, fixed on her face, as she leaned down and gave him the tenderest mother-kiss.

Ellen just sat with him then, rocking him to herself, thinking of her own son and a mother in East Tennessee.

Beyond her, Ellen saw Louisa still sheltering the golden head of Jared Prudhomme.

'He is dead – the beautiful youth!' she heard Louisa say, in a far off voice. 'Dead!'

She watched, as Mary went to Louisa, knelt beside her sister, and made the Sign of the Cross on the boy's forehead.

'He is home, Louisa, death exalts his face,' Ellen heard Mary say.

Mary then came to Ellen. 'The Lord is good, He will receive them all,' she comforted and gave thanks that the young fiddle player had died 'in a mother's arms'.

Where Mary saw hope Ellen saw only hopelessness.

'No young man believes he shall ever die,' she said to Mary.

89

America was losing its young to this war . . . and in losing its young was losing its old.

'The young are beautiful,' Mary answered. 'He takes them first to himself.'

'Yes . . .' Ellen said, looking at her daughter. 'The young are truly beautiful.'

She herself felt old, unbeautiful. War killed all that was beautiful. Plucked out singing youth from life. Silenced it. Diseased men's hearts and minds, eating up what measure of goodness there once was there. Poxing the soul as well as the body. The land would wait till it was ready – nurturing below its terrible fruit until the sons of sons had forgotten. Then there would be rivers of blood, seasons of storms, Lucifer rising.

Then would the land wreak its revenge.

With the men, Ellen and the two nuns helped lever the dead bodies onto the rude planks that would be their coffins. Until they were upended again from them – returned to the land.

Louisa's petticoat now lay where she had placed it, on the boy's breast – a mocking testament to safe passage. Ellen put her arm around Louisa's shoulder, trying to salve the frantic heart within.

'God decrees,' Ellen thought, but didn't say it.

Inside, Dr Sawyer summoned them, addressing Louisa.

'It was against my disposition, Sister, that I agreed to Confederate soldiers being sheltered here. Events have proven me correct. We cannot be responsible for any but our own. Let the Rebels gather up their dead and wounded – and we ours!'

Displaying no hint of her private emotions, Louisa answered him. 'It is not the Christian way. All men are brothers. In war, in life . . . and in death. The Lord is neither North nor South. Who are we to dispute with the Lord, to say mercy to this one because he is in blue uniform . . . no mercy to this one because he is in grey?'

'Mercy is one thing, Sister . . .' Dr Sawyer retorted, ignoring her point, '. . . but what I witnessed last night was the worst excesses of your religion. It was cruelty – of the highest order. Men who could barely stand, to have them discard their crutches in riotous carousing. It was not just a physical cruelty but a cruelty of spirit to raise such hope in them. Hope which could not be sustained but, by the very nature of that in which we are all engaged, must be crushed out of them again!'

'Doctor Sawyer!' Louisa said, when he had finished, 'I am not one of those who subscribe to the notion that being a nun is a perversion of womanhood. That, somehow, "convent chastity" is an escape from the responsibility of Christian marriage . . . or from life itself.'

The doctor commenced saying something, but Louisa was not yet finished. 'It may discomfit you that we Sisters are independent women, capable of running our own affairs – "performing the male role" as you so put it. We are also capable of joy, Doctor. Joy and sorrow . . . and modest dancing . . .'

'Modesty!' Dr Sawyer interrupted. 'Ever the companion of what the wise call "plain sense" . . .'

In turn, he was interrupted. 'Leg!' A male voice shouted from the bowels of the saw-mill. Shubael Sawyer turned, rolling his sleeves up, breathing fire about 'public women'.

'I think it is Mr O'Reilly,' Ellen said, following him, 'to lose the second leg.'

And so it went the war between men and women. Most times it settled into an uneasy truce. The dictates of the greater war silencing the battleground of the lesser.

'It is like the steps to Calvary for the good doctor, in accepting us,' Mary said later. 'He has great difficulty in climbing them, but he knows he must and will get there in the end!'

'I should not be so hard on the doctor,' Louisa replied. 'He works tirelessly to save those he can, and America has not seen such change. We have, all of us, stepped outside the feminine ideal, so long sanctified by male and female alike. It will take time and, besides, the doctor fears we are baptising too many!'

SEVENTEEN

That night Ellen took out the letter which Hercules O'Brien had thrust into her hand. It was a beautiful hand, which had written it. Delicate, not too flowered but perfectly formed.

Dear Mr O'Brien,
    We had lost all hope since not hearing from you for such an interim. I was forlorn with grief. Mother comforting me at every moment. What a blessed relief, nay a joy, it was to then learn that you were alive and well, if not wholly whole, and in the care of the good Sisters.
    The weight of the world seemed lifted from our shoulders but I had been so wounded with worry and with grief that all previous feeling has been dulled. Would that it would surface and shine again, as prior to your going it had shone like a glittering prize. Despite all entreaties to myself it is to no avail. I must therefore resign myself with calm regret that I can never be yours.
    Do not think ill of me though I suffer grievously this new state, fearing also that the gallant injuries you have sustained may adversely affect your

prospects in life upon your discharge. This, I pray, the All-Provident in His mercy, will not decree.

Now that the safety of your person is assured and I no longer fear the worst, any future correspondence would be superfluous. Mother sends her solicitations and prays that you and our glorious Union Army, will be victorious over the Rebels.

Respectfully yours,
Arabella

It was such a cruel letter, such an unwomanly letter. But it was not the first such letter Ellen had seen. Some she had read to poor boys on the very cusp of death. Watched them then give up the fight and refuse all ministrations, the life-wish gone. Others about to go on a furlough after injury would, following such a letter, cancel the much anticipated trip home, strap on their gun and go out again, hungering for the enemy bullet that would take them. How war shattered everything . . . flesh and bone . . . and hope. Hercules O'Brien had no hope left. She had seen it in him. Seen that great big man in a little man's body made small again. Be robbed of all hope, except perhaps that a Rebel shell would speedily discharge him of this life.

That the science of war would finally kill him.

She wondered about Lavelle. Where he lay. If he had hope?

PATRICK

EIGHTEEN

West End, Boston, 1856

When Patrick O'Malley had slowly pushed open the door of his modest home in Boston's West End, he was hoping not to find his mother there. She never missed a thing. Would ask him about the bruises on the knuckles of his right hand. Then, give him the usual lecture about 'learning, not fighting'.

Patrick, in his late teens, had the stamp of the 'black Irish' on him. That wayward strain of the Spanish, who had come with their Armada of ships, to Ireland's west coast in the sixteenth century. Patrick didn't care. Just took after his father, Michael. In fact, he was unlike his red-haired mother, Ellen, whom he now wished to avoid, in almost every respect. Of a saturnine complexion, this was complemented by olive-black hair and a lustrous set of eyes, of which any Basque from the Pyrenees would have been proud. However, if Patrick O'Malley's physical attributes had been shipped to Ireland from some far-distant shore, his character was distinctly Irish and carved from the same rock of rebelliousness as his mother.

He unshouldered the sleeve of his coat, gentling it down over his hand. The mere movement made his dark features grimace with pain. He looked at the discoloured swelling then turned the palm upwards. The stripes were still there. Some months previous at Eliot School in Boston's North End from where he had now just come, Patrick's hand had been caned until it bled. The Ten Commandments had cost him dearly but he hadn't cared. Wouldn't give those Nativist bastards the satisfaction of reciting *their* 'Protestant version' of it. Eventually, his rebelliousness had led to Boston's Catholic hierarchy, and even the American Constitution, being invoked. The outcome was that no longer were students of Eliot School required to recite any version, much less the Protestant version, of prayers in public.

It was a victory for the Paddy-Irish – and the predominantly Protestant-Nativist element in the school didn't like it. As evidenced by today's altercation. Eliot School, situated in 'The Little Britain of Boston', prided itself on having 'the best spoken English in the country at large'.

Those who, like Patrick, had any thickness of speech, attracted the odium of the blue-bloods of Beacon Hill. One such was Lemuel Shipley, a product of the *Peter Piper's Practical Principles of Plain and Perfect Pronunciation* school of Boston-speak. Lemuel Shipley was never reticent in venting his perfectly formed contempt for all things Irish and Catholic. Today he had gone too far, again calling Patrick, 'Paddy . . . or is it Mick . . . ?' and 'Is yer Biddy mudder comin' for yeh agin today, Paddy?' Patrick had grabbed the boy and thickened his lip with a right-hander.

'Now we'll see who talks funny, Thicklip Thipley!' Patrick had called after the bloodied blue-blood.

He smiled at the memory, and dashed his hand into the pail of cold water, relieved that his mother wasn't yet at home. He held his hand there until the hot throbbing ache had changed to a cold sharp one. It was then he saw her note.

When Lavelle, Patrick's stepfather, had arrived home Patrick was at the doorstep, his face ashen, his mother's note in his good hand.

'What is it, Patrick?' Lavelle had asked, some instinct in his well-weathered face.

'She's gone!'

Lavelle grabbed the note from his stepson.

My dear ones,
　　It grieves me so to write this letter, but I must leave your lives. I pray forgiveness for the ruin I have brought upon them.
　　Do not seek me.
　　May God take you all in His care.
　　Your dearest Mother and Wife,
　　Ellen

Lavelle looked at the note then to Patrick. Then he read it again. Perplexity heaped upon perplexity, blue eyes clouded in his strong face, one hand unconsciously furrowing the thick, wheaten-coloured hair.

'What . . . ? Why . . . ?' Lavelle fought for some comprehension, some unjumbling of the emotions afflicting him. Dazed with the certainty of what her own hand had written, he walked past Patrick into the house, seeking some sign of her. As if some tangible presence should still be there.

She had taken nothing – no clothes apart from what she stood in. No memento of their lives together. Not even her books.

Lavelle was desolate.

Patrick looked at his stepfather. Lavelle, the surname by which Patrick had always known the other Irishman, did not deserve this. Patrick, at first had resented this tall and handsome man in his late thirties who had replaced his dead father. But then, since first arriving in America, a bond had grown between them. A bond Patrick had never felt with his mother. If she was the family's stormy, mercurial sea, then Lavelle had been the bedrock. Lavelle had allowed Ellen every liberty of enterprise not normally granted a wife and mother – even in liberal Boston. A liberty that for a while, even Patrick had to admit, had worked.

They had grown a small but successful business, importing French wines from Montreal. His mother could turn her hand to everything. Had seen an opening in a well-heeled Boston society. Some difficulty had arisen and she had gone again to Montreal seeking to resolve them. And now this.

For hours they turned it over and over between them.

Montreal must have failed. It must have been that she had been unable to salvage the relationship with their suppliers. Though neither Lavelle nor Patrick could fully understand why Ellen had insisted on blaming herself for the recent downturn of their business and, as a consequence, their continually reducing circumstances.

But as to the reason for her flight? Each explanation seemed more unlikely than the previous one.

'Perhaps before going she went to see Mary and Louisa . . . leave a note at the convent. Maybe *they* know?' Lavelle said, brightening at the possibility.

Together then they set out for the convent of St Mary Magdalen, only to be denied permission to see the two postulants. A Sister Lazarus was summoned. Yes, a woman in a distressed state had called, seeking contact with the two young novices. Lavelle's hopes grew. From the description he gave of Ellen, the nun affirmed, 'I am certain it was she.' Sister Lazarus, having reminded Ellen that the novices 'now had no earthly parents, only their Heavenly Father to cling to,' had offered to 'take a message'.

'What did my mother say?' Patrick asked.

'She said, "It was nothing of importance", and left,' Sister Lazarus flatly replied.

Walking homewards, Patrick and Lavelle were both relieved and worried. Relieved that Ellen was alive. Worried at the apparent distressed state in which she now was. The remainder of that day, and the next, they combed the area surrounding the convent.

No sign of her was to be had, nor any reported sighting.

NINETEEN

Some ill had befallen her, Lavelle knew. Although he did not share this presentiment with Patrick.

She had gone but not returned.

Perhaps he himself had been at fault. Allowed too much responsibility to rest on her shoulders. There was no doubt she was capable but she had stepped far beyond where most of her gender had gone. Far beyond the domestic threshold into the public domain.

Too far . . . perhaps.

Gradually, they widened their search. Traipsed the Common where she had loved to bring the children; the Long Wharf; up along Washington Street, between Milk and Water, with its patchwork of buildings, to the Old South Meeting House. Across from here, Lavelle had asked her to marry him. She had laughed at his impudence . . . and immediately agreed. Quincy Market – she loved to stand in its midst, watch the copper grasshopper spin from side to side atop the domed cupola of Faneuil Hall. Reverently, Lavelle even entered The Old Corner Bookstore, her favourite haunt of all. A discreet enquiry. Mr Proprietor remembered her: 'passionate about the written word', but had not seen Mrs Lavelle for some time . . . believing she had 'exorcised the city from her life and moved to the suburbs – for the inner life. From reading Donne,' Mr Proprietor supposed.

Eventually, they tracked down Harriet Brophy, their one-time neighbour from Pleasant Street and Ellen's companion at those Daughters of the Commonwealth meetings.

The woman flapped and flitted about them. 'My, young Patrick! My, look at you! Still at Eliot School after the commotion you caused over the Protestant prayers. But this news of Mrs Lavelle. Oh, I am frantic to learn about your poor mother! Let me see, I think the last time I saw Mrs Lavelle was at our meeting where that Mr Joyce spoke. *Renaissance or Revolution: the Future for Ireland*? Such a gallant man, Mr Joyce!'

Lavelle tried to track down Stephen Joyce. Last heard of, the poet-revolutionary had returned to Ireland to keep the agitation with England alive. Others said he had since gone South to align himself with the brewing restlessness there. It was the man's wont to traverse continents seeking causes. Lavelle even began to wonder if Ellen herself had taken up some cause? While she seemed to have stripped herself of her old Irish republican ideals, she had put on the new clothes of Bloomerism – the rising women's movement. Whatever cause Ellen might have championed it was, Lavelle concluded, one not clearly visible. No trace of her was anywhere to be seen.

With increasing dismay, Lavelle put a notice in the 'Missing Friends' columns of Boston's *Pilot* newspaper. The *Pilot* was widely read among the city's Irish community. His dismay was yet further increased at the hundreds of similar postings from people wanting to trace female relatives who had come in their thousands ahead of them out of Ireland. Many of those sought, it seemed, meriting a similar description of 'red-haired Irish woman, attractive to the eye'.

As time drifted, first into weeks, then months, Lavelle began to despair of ever seeing Ellen again.

Patrick was more and more filled, not with despair at ever

finding Ellen, but with anger. Anger at the growing conviction that his mother had once more deserted him, as she had in Ireland nine years previously. Patrick knew she'd had little choice then, but the weight of her leaving, the cruelty of that separation, had never left him. True, she had returned but he had still resented her coming to reclaim them, clad, in the gorgeous finery of Boston – and with a man, Lavelle, awaiting her return there. A man to replace his father. She had, Patrick reckoned, on this more recent escapade probably found some new 'fancy man'.

His mother was alive all right.

Alive – and out there. Somewhere.

Of that Patrick was convinced.

TWENTY

Eliot School was not sorry to see the back of Patrick O'Malley. Nor he of the school when, two years later, in 1858, he passed through its portals for the last time. He had concentrated hard on his studies, remembering at least, his mother's advice that if they were to 'up themselves' in America, then education was the only route. However, if Patrick had learned one lesson from his time at Eliot School it was that, no matter how long he was in this country, he would never be 'American'.

The Nativist blue-bloods descended from old-line Puritan stock, and the Scots-Irish would never accept Paddy Catholic as equal. No matter how much education, no matter what laws were passed – and they were the ones passing most of them!

The Nativists had a fear of the 'niggers-turned-inside-out', as they dubbed the Irish, of getting any social or political grip on Boston life. To this fear was added a bilesome loathing.

It wasn't just in Boston either, but in New York and other major cities of the North, like Philadelphia.

'Brotherly love, me arse . . . Oxy!' Patrick pronounced to his friend. 'Those northern Nativists would bite the bollocks off you for dumpling stew!'

The other youth, born in County Roscommon, Ireland and known since birth as 'Oxy', agreed.

That Oxy Moran and Patrick O'Malley were as unlikely

104

a pairing for close friendship, as one could imagine, was conceded by both. 'Polar opposites' was how Oxy described it. 'You are on Jupiter, I on Mars.'

But they were both Irish and both Catholic, thrown together in an antagonistic land. That apart, they had few similarities of character: Patrick was ebullient, defiant, ready to take on the world; Oxy was the antithesis of this – quiet, intellectual, witty, his dark curling hair framing a delicate forehead and thoughtful eyes.

'You should be a writer –' Patrick teased '– you have the look.'

'Oh, but I am,' Oxy had replied, '. . . in my head . . . I just don't write it down.'

'How can you be a writer then?' Patrick started, ready for argument.

Oxy had given him one of those dreamy half-smiles and replied, 'Oh, Patrick, my friend, being a writer is purely a state of mind – like love or unhappiness.'

'That's how my sister Mary would answer,' Patrick observed, 'and there is no arguing with her. Even if she's wrong, she's right . . .'

'Because she's sure,' Oxy added in.

'Yes, that's it, I think,' Patrick answered. 'She is clear on things, even if it is not so patently clear to others. You're like that.'

'I must have learned it from *my* sisters,' Oxy smiled. 'I was one against many "Marys" in our household. Six sisters – and all older – how unfortunate could one boy be?'

'And none of them ever followed you to America?' Patrick asked.

'No,' his friend answered. 'My father's view was that America was a man's calling – and that daughters should stick by the home place, "not be going before themselves out foreign to America". He was keen for me to see the world . . . and prove myself in it.'

'Strange then, how it was your female aunt who took you

in here, in Boston?' Patrick said teasingly.

'Yes, my father's sister – but he didn't see the conflict in that. He could sometimes be blinkered, my father.' Oxy stopped for a moment. 'But a good man, who worked hard and reared us right . . . a brilliant man pinched in by Roscommon. If he'd come to America himself, he would have been a millionaire . . . or a politician.'

'Or both,' Patrick inserted. 'They seem to go together over here.'

Patrick had often wondered about his friend's name – Oxy? It was a strange name in a land riddled with the names of saints – Patrick, Mary, Joseph, Brigid.

Oxy explained. 'My father had his differences with the Catholic Church. When my eldest sister Aurora was born, the local priest refused her baptism, because she had not been given the name of a saint. Thereafter, my father refused to darken the door of the local church, declaring God to be found more in the fields and hedgerows than in the hearts of the peddlers of power, the name he called the clergy. He made up his own rules and when I was born he christened me Oxy . . . said it fitted me well . . . me being a Moran . . . me being a boy after six girls – a bit of a contradiction – an oxymoron. He had his humour, my father. A great man . . .' Oxy paused, his mind far away. 'I always wanted to be what he wanted . . . to be like him.'

'And are you like him?' Patrick asked.

'Yes, I am, as it happens. People should live by their own rules. Not those of others. There are too many rules for everything. Power for the few and prisons for the many . . . that's what rules are.'

And Oxy had defied the rules, stood staunchly by his friend throughout all that Eliot School business, quietly stating the inequality of it all. Patrick had admired him greatly then. Others of the Boston Catholic-Irish had not stood up to be counted but Oxy Moran had.

*

106

The year after leaving Eliot School, despite the school's reputation for scholarship, had been fruitless for Patrick and Oxy. Choices were limited in Boston's strongly Puritan and anti-Catholic businesses. Especially for those Irish who had stood up against the Lord's Prayer.

Patrick had for a while secured a position as a grocer's assistant, but he craved more excitement than shining apples with the cuff of his coat. Adventuring was what fired him, whether war or travel, he cared not. Setting out stalls around which the dandering ladies of Boston could gossip was not to be a lasting post for Patrick O'Malley. It did, however, provide him with a modest store of funds when, disillusioned with life in New England, the following year, 1859, the two had resolved to go 'adventurin' to America's South.

'They don't like the Northern Yankees, no more than us' seemed to Patrick as good a reason as any. 'They want their own republic down there – just like the Irish,' Oxy reflected, in his quiet way. 'But the cotton kings of Boston still want to crack the whip on the South, keep a tight grip on the reins of production.'

'You'd think the Yankees having once been colonised by the British, wouldn't want to do the same to their own people?' Patrick wondered.

'Well they are . . . but they aren't . . . their *own* people,' Oxy reasoned. 'The southerners are French, and worse, in Yankee eyes . . . they're Catholic – and Acadians from Canada – and then they're the whole lot mixed up together – Creole.'

Oxy thought Creole had a wonderful sound to it – 'like the wind through cypress trees – sinuous, musical, exotic. Cree . . . ole, *chroí-ól*,' he repeated. 'The Irish words for *heart* and *drink*. What could be better?'

'Maybe you'll land yourself a pretty young Creole, Oxy?' Patrick laughed.

'Maybe I will . . .' his friend answered. 'They say that, at twelve or thirteen years, the young Creole girls suffer a rib to be taken from them to make their waists more slight . . . more desirable.'

'Less of a handful!' Patrick interrupted.

'Beauty out of pain cometh!' Oxy smiled, in that strangely attractive way Patrick noticed he sometimes did.

The thought of it fascinated Oxy. That one would suffer such surgical de-boning for a more graceful female form.

Regarding his mother, Patrick had these days all but banished her from his mind.

Let Lavelle continue his futile search for her – go west along the railroads. He was for going South and fighting these Boston Yankees . . . if war started up and it came to that.

South – and the Creole girls.

TWENTY-ONE

Not a day had Lavelle not thought of Ellen. Not a night passed had he not wondered again why she had left them and where had she gone. Patrick, he knew, had no doubt that she was still alive. The boy was tired of always 'waiting' for her. Had decided to 'go on an adventure' himself and departed for New Orleans with his friend Oxy Moran. Lavelle was at least pleased about that. Oxy was a steady lad, would steer Patrick straight. Keep him out of scrapes.

'Hard to kill a bad thing!' was Patrick's response, the last time Lavelle had drawn down the subject of Ellen's disappearance. Lavelle, ignoring the barb, was not so sure. He felt that if she were still alive she would have made some contact, sent some sign. Relented her self-banishment.

But, of her, from her, there was no whisper.

He pored through her books for any clue as to where she might have gone: Wordsworth's *Lyrical Ballads*; Blake's *Songs of Innocence*; Whittier's *Legends of New England in Prose and Verse*.

The latter he had given her one Christmas to wean her away from the English poets. But there was no quill mark, no stubbed page anywhere to give any indication of where she might have bound herself. Only then did he notice that the book of Donne's poems was missing. Donne was her very favourite – she must have taken it.

He was at his wits' end, his mind inletting every nook and cranny of their lives together. How he missed the vibrancy of her. With her it was always life at full tilt, he the more passive. It had never bothered him. Resilience, that's what she had, resilience by the bucketful. Up and at things, getting the business going, taking on the Brahmins of Beacon Hill in their own back yard. Then, ferrying Louisa around, to this expert and that, trying to break down the walls that stopped the child from speaking. Then reading, reading, reading, all the time trying to 'up' herself. Reading herself into America, its land and its laws. What had made her give up all of that – banish herself from their lives? It was so unlike her. Unless, with the burden of everything sliding from under them, that her resilience had run out. Seeped away from her without them ever noticing it.

Later that night as he lay awake, the words of one of her songs came back to him.

> Oh, my fair-haired boy,
> No more I'll see
> You walk the meadows green . . .

It could now be *his* song for her, he realised.

> All joy is gone that we once knew,
> All sorrow newly found,
> Soon you'll in California be,
> Or Colorado bound.

He stopped . . . California! They had often talked of California. And, even after the business failed, of him going west. California was another America – a different country. Such a place would spawn a curiosity in her.

Lavelle resolved to go to California. Work his way there. Build the railroads to build America.

The following day he went to the Convent of St Mary Magdalen. No permission would be given, he knew, to see either Mary or Louisa. Instead, he left word for them with the older nun who answered the door . . . and headed west.

TWENTY-TWO

New Orleans, 1860

It took Patrick and Oxy a year of 'adventurin' to reach the 'Jewel of the South' – New Orleans. In that intervening year they'd seen, according to Patrick, 'The whole wide world of America.' Which prompted Oxy's observation on the vast tracts of land they had travelled since leaving Massachusetts, 'It isn't that much bigger than Ireland . . . once you get to know it!'

Patrick laughed, started to list out all the places they had been through, rejoicing in the names and the memories they evoked. 'Maryland, Virginia, the Appalachian Trail, the Carolinas, Georgia, Alabama . . . Louisiana . . . Do you mean Ireland's bigger than all of them together, Oxy – or a corner of one of them?'

'All!' Oxy responded, not giving an inch to Patrick, nor to all the States, even if gathered up together. 'Apart, maybe from that big pond!'

By this diminutive did Oxy refer to the mighty Lake Pontchartrain, between which and the meandering Mississippi to the south of the city, was wedged New Orleans. The Pontchartrain held some strange fascination for Oxy. A song he had once learned about it.

'I always wanted to see it after that song,' he said wistfully to Patrick, and began to sing in a beautiful clear voice.

> "Twas on one bright March morning,
> I bid New Orleans adieu,
> And I took the road to Jackson town . . .

> '. . . All strangers there, no friends to me,
> Till a dark girl towards me came,
> And I fell in love with a Creole girl,
> By the lakes of Pontchartrain.

> '. . . The hair upon her shoulders
> In jet black ringlets fell;
> To try and paint her beauty,
> I'm sure 'twould be in vain . . .

> '. . . I asked her if she'd marry me,
> She said it could never be,
> For she had got another,
> And he was far at sea . . .

> 'So fare thee well my Creole girl,
> I never will see you no more,
> But I'll ne'er forget your kindness,
> In the cottage by the shore;

> '. . . And at each social gathering,
> A flowing glass I'll raise,
> And I'll drink a health to my Creole girl,
> And the lakes of Pontchartrain.'

Patrick listened spellbound, as Oxy, his head lifted to a place above the endless waters, sang of them, to them, in the sweetest of voices. He had never before heard his friend sing. Oxy must have waited for years to get to this place. Somehow

113

fascinated by the love story of the Creole girl that he had heard back in Ireland. How strange now to have realised his dream, sang at its shores.

'Was it that – the song,' he asked Oxy, 'made you want to come here?'

'It was,' Oxy replied. 'The song . . . and other things.' He left it there, giving Patrick one of his enigmatic smiles, of which there was no further question to be asked.

Prior to Patrick's departure Lavelle had gifted him a sum of money. Although it could hardly be called a handsome sum, this, when added to his greengrocer's money, was nevertheless more than sufficient for Patrick's needs, and he had been able to put some by.

Oxy Moran, on the other hand, had that kind of aunt who doted on her nephew and had the wherewithal to indulge her dotage. When Oxy had informed her that he was going South, she had immediately taken him to the First Bank of Boston and showered him with a largesse of funds so that he could be 'a gentleman while on your travels' . . . also warning him to 'be careful of thieves and vagabonds in that southern land!'

The further South they had travelled, the more they both had become aware of the brewing restlessness. And the sometimes distinct lack of southern hospitality that greeted them. Until they identified themselves as Irish, not 'Yankee'!

They had been in New Orleans only a month when, to Patrick's great surprise, he espied the tall figure of Stephen Joyce.

Sartorially elegant, Stephen Joyce was not to be mistaken, either here or anywhere. He was a man who would always stand out, Patrick knew. Tall and angular, sinewed like whipped cord, the man's dark hair swept back from his face to the nape of his neck, a wayward strand or two drooping over the intent forehead. Eyes black as opals – centred with the stone's same burning zeal. But it was not the man's physicality alone that marked him for easy recognition by Patrick.

It was more the air of languid arrogance with which Stephen Joyce joined in conspiratorial-type conversation with his two equally intent companions.

'Mr Joyce!'

The other men broke away at the sound of the interloper.

Unperturbed, Stephen Joyce turned. 'Patrick! Patrick O'Malley!' he exclaimed, the slightly gaunt face coming alive with recognition, Patrick's eyes being drawn to the dark spot – the macula – under the man's left eye.

'Let me look at you! My, how you've grown – you still have your father's dark head but your mother's fair cheek. How is she . . . and my friend Lavelle?' he asked animatedly.

Patrick hesitated. 'My mother has disappeared . . . Lavelle still searches for her!'

'But . . . ?' The granite black eyes seemed perplexed. 'When . . . why?'

Patrick explained the calendar of misfortune that had beset them since they had last seen Mr Joyce.

'It wasn't the first time,' Patrick added.

'But she had no choice the first time, Patrick, you know that,' Stephen Joyce replied. 'Either *she* went or you all would starve. Think what fortitude that demanded of her?'

'She had a choice now,' Patrick retorted.

The older man placed a sympathetic hand to his shoulder. 'I am so sorry to hear of this turn of events and more so of your disaffection. Your mother is a remarkable woman and has suffered much.'

Of his own part in all of the foregoing 'turn of events', Stephen Joyce was careful to reveal nothing.

115

TWENTY-THREE

When as pre-arranged he met them again the following afternoon in the bustling French Quarter, Stephen Joyce had, it appeared, plans that would keep his Patrick and Oxy both gainfully – and at least partially – occupied while in New Orleans.

'Both of you must advance yourselves while you're here,' he stated. 'So I want each of you to compose two letters – one each extolling the righteousness of the Northern cause, the other extolling that of the Southern. When you have done bring them to me.'

Wondering what he had in mind, both did as directed.

In their presence Stephen read and then re-read the letters.

'Well, it is clear!' he announced, at last – it being anything but clear to them. 'Oxy, you have a very fine hand, a fluency with words and an understanding of opposing politics. You will be my pen. Patrick, you have a strong heart, an undivided loyalty to that which you believe – you will be my sword.'

They looked at him.

'I have need at times both for a telling nib and a trusty sword. There are many enemies at large and the watchful eyes of a trusted friend are essential.'

Patrick nodded, well pleased with the responsibility laid on him.

116

'I have also the need to communicate with many – both enemy and friend – and you, Oxy, I believe will be a first-rate scribe in this respect.'

Oxy blushed slightly, looked at Patrick then back to Stephen. 'And the salary, Mr Joyce?'

Stephen laughed at the boy's boldness. 'You both will receive an honorarium – and lodgings.'

When Stephen left them, the two were beside themselves with excitement at this latest turn of events.

'The pen and the sword,' Oxy said, a smile lighting his fineboned features.

'I wonder what it will entail,' Patrick mused.

'It will be everything,' Oxy said, 'a going to the end of the earth.'

And New Orleans itself seemed to them like the end of the earth. It was a world apart from the stuffy and reserved New England they had known. Even the yellow fever epidemic of 1853, when eight thousand of her citizens had died – another thirty thousand fleeing the city – had done nothing to dim the Jewel of the South's lust for life. They secured rooms – a cabildo – in the Vieux Carre, the old quarter of Place d'Armes, near the Mississippi river levee. Towered over by the cathedral of St. Louis, Place d'Armes was the heart of the old city's forty-four blocks of houses. But the fires of the last century had razed the French designed buildings to the ground. Then, under the Spanish, the French Quarter was rebuilt – *briquette entre poteaux* – bricks between posts and covered with plaster. Patrick and Oxy admired the broad windows under graceful arches brought by the Spanish and the now moss-draped gallery, from which they now viewed the seething city life below.

'It's a stew of noise, colour and bustle,' Oxy exclaimed.

'And smell!' Patrick added.

'Ah, but the Creole girls . . .' Oxy replied. 'Look at their undisguised beauty. Their scent rises as oceans of flowers.

They are the jewels of the Jewel.'

While New Orleans boasted of some twenty-five or more slave markets, these Oxy and Patrick avoided, as far as was possible, but they did on Sunday, after Mass in the Cathedral, stroll on to Congo Square. Here the slaves held their own market, 'not selling whites' as Oxy remarked but fruits and vegetables and wares of every description, in the hope of being able to buy back their freedom. They danced, singing their sad songs of home, their war chants, their songs of the Mississippi-land that held them captive. 'It's darkest Africa . . .' Oxy again said to Patrick, '. . . darkest Africa . . . in darkest America.'

In the months that followed this meeting, Stephen Joyce exhibited a great enthusiasm to take them under his wing. They became his protégés. And apt pupils they were too.

Stephen, because of his high educational background at Dublin's Trinity College, had been readily accepted into New Orleans society. Even into the closely-knit bayou, plantation society, which flourished along the levees of the Mississippi. He fitted in so well: he was a gentleman, he spoke French, could discourse on the Classics – and he shared the South's republican ideals. Stephen tutored the boys in the politics of Southern Republicanism and the economics of black bondage. He kept them occupied writing letters in support of or against this or that, making contact with those who mattered in New Orleans society . . . or even in Richmond itself, capital of the South. Those, who one day might return allegiances and take up Ireland's cause.

'I have a horse for you both . . .' their patron one day surprised them with. 'We are going bayou riding.' Stephen waved away Patrick's question. 'To visit Emeritus Labiche and his wife, Lucretia.'

'And . . .' paused their benefactor, 'there also are young men of your own age . . . and young ladies too!'

TWENTY-FOUR

A day's ride brought them to the perimeter of the Labiche plantation. Wearied with circling bayous, traversing swamps and anxious to come to a final rest, Patrick and Oxy nevertheless could not fail to halt and gaze in awe at the sight which now presented itself.

'It is the Garden of Eden,' Oxy proclaimed.

'Pray God there are angels within!' Patrick answered, unable to remove his eyes from the splendour before them.

'Greek Revival . . .' Stephen Joyce explained. '. . . the architectural style.'

This was Manoir Labiche, officially named Le Petit Versailles. Ahead of them lay a long avenue, on either side lined with moss-draped cypress trees. Thirty on one side. Thirty-one on the other. Strangely imbalanced.

'It is a month of trees!' Oxy said, working it out. 'Thirty days hath September, April, June and November – on the left – and all else have thirty-one . . . save February, which one in four, has one day more.' He paused, chin in hand, then pronounced, 'I'll guarantee you the house was completed in a leap year – in February. That's it!' Oxy proclaimed. 'The house itself is February then, all the months are accounted for. How clever!'

'And how clever of you Mr Moran to have worked out so

quickly the conundrum of the cypress trees,' Stephen Joyce added.

Patrick had often wondered how Stephen had entered such society as this. It was, he was sure, down to what his mother had always preached, 'education'. Stephen moved easily at all levels, had many friends among the business classes and in political circles. Due, no doubt, to his earlier involvement with the struggle for Irish independence. Schooled in the classics, Stephen could as freely converse in French as in English. He had about him a confidence – an assured and convincing way of speaking that implied an equality, if not a superiority, with all. Almost bordering on arrogance, Patrick thought, but it got him places.

At the end of the trees the house awaited them. From it a duet of white, half-circular staircases, spiralled outwards to the vast lawns at the end of the cypress avenue. The staircases curved upwards, like welcoming arms, to a verandah supported by an army of Doric columns. The verandah itself, which ran the length of the house, stood out from the house itself by a span of fourteen feet.

'Enough for two carriages to pass,' Oxy said, his face awonder.

Scattered about the house, were its 'dependencies' – smaller houses, *pigeonnaires* and *garçonières* – the boys' houses.

Stephen explained, 'Here in the South they mature quickly. At seventeen, the boys are considered adults. The *garçonières* allow them to come and go as they please.'

'And the girls?' Patrick enquired.

'A father would be worried if his daughter was not married off by sixteen – thirteen or fourteen is not uncommon. At twenty, if a young lady were still unmarried, all hope would be forlorn.'

The moment when Patrick first set eyes upon Emmeline Labiche, all hope was born.

'She is as fair as a summer's day,' Oxy whispered to him

120

as a regular congregation gathered to welcome them at what Patrick thought was the front of the house, but which Oxy delighted in telling him was the back.

'This is the South!' his friend said. 'Everything opposite!'

Emmeline Labiche *was* fair – dark-haired and dark-eyed and blessed with an intoxicating reserve, and at no more than fifteen summers ripe for marrying. Of equal allure, her sister Cordelia was scarcely a twelve-month older.

Emeritus Labiche greeted them effusively in French. To which Stephen responded with equal affection, it seemed to Patrick.

The Creole planter was as sturdy of frame as of temperament. Sturdy, but not a large man, rather low-sized as the Creoles often were, Patrick placed him in his early forties. Eyes dark as his coal-black hair and as striking, he was given to expansive gestures when he spoke; throwing out his arms, patting down his large moustache, laughing. A man used to giving orders.

'Cato, Plato!' the robustly toned master of Le Petit Versailles shouted to two slaves. 'Gather in the horses!'

Plates of freshly cut pineapple, succulent and cooling, magically materialised as Madame Labiche – a funereal lady with a decorous collar – welcomed them with similar though more muted expressions of hospitality. First *en Français*, then in English, for the young gentlemen's benefit.

Later, accompanied by a whistling chorus from the slaves who ferried the fare from the outside kitchen, they were feted sumptuously. When Patrick enquired as to the whistling 'tradition', Emeritus Labiche pooh-poohed the question. 'Tradition . . . pah!' Maybe it will one day become one, but for now while I can hear the heathens whistling, I know they are not eating my food!'

And what food it was. Nut-flavoured hams, large as whole hogs, frilled with white paper, set in crusts of clove-dotted sugar and served with piled-high platters of 'sweet Irish Taters'. Afterwards, a sugared mound of calf's-foot jelly and a berg of vanilla ice cream served over beds of shimmering ice from the Great Lakes.

'Were you aware, Mr Joyce, of a scheme the British once came up with in the Sugar Islands?' Emeritus Labiche asked in a manner which displayed that he thought Mr Joyce was not. Their host paused perfunctorily, before himself supplying the answer. 'It was both revolutionary and evolutionary – interbreeding the Irish with the Blacks!'

He stopped for the effect this remark would have on his guests.

'They did it to improve the stock – of the nigger, of course! But all the British got for their trouble was an even more cussed bunch of niggers than they already had!' He laughed loudly. Stephen Joyce did not.

'Well, then, Emeritus,' the Irishman replied, 'you'd better win this little *contretemps* brewing with the North, else those British Yankees might make similar good use of former slaveholders!'

'*Mon Dieu*, Stephen!' their host exclaimed, 'you are never found wanting. I am glad you will be for us, not against, if the invader comes. Save us from such a fate.'

Again he laughed and this time Stephen Joyce joined with him.

'Whatever the Yankees might do to us men,' Emeritus Labiche continued in more serious tone, 'it is through our womenfolk that the civilisation of the South remains and will remain superior to that of the North.' He inclined his head towards his wife and two daughters.

'The North has erred in its dangerous tendencies. A woman trying to do a man's business is the misfortune of the age. A challenge to marriage and the very hierarchies which sustain us.'

Silently, Patrick agreed. Lavelle had been too lenient with his mother, had given her too much leeway. And where had it landed them all?

It was Stephen who spoke next. 'Come now, Emeritus, you cannot expect me to accept an understanding of the Southern lady that is so rigidly biological.'

'Woman has but one right – and that is a sacred right –

protection,' his host responded. 'And she has but one duty – undiluted allegiance to her protector. Then you have order.'

'What says Madame Labiche?' Stephen asked.

'Oh, I concur with Monsieur Labiche. It is indelicate in the extreme for any woman to relinquish her private life and enter the public sphere,' Lucretia Labiche replied, delicately fingering the rosette ribbon adorning the centre-point of her hair net. 'A lady should always hold herself under scrutiny!'

Noiselessly, as the conversation grew, new courses appeared and disappeared before them. Now a French punch bowl, graved with a grape motif, symbol of abundance, was produced. Whilst the men were served rum, laced with sliced pear, the ladies were permitted to sample only the soaked slices of pear but not imbibe the rum itself. Conversation abated as two female house slaves, Lively and Promptly, and their male counterparts, Caesar and Cicero, served further groaning plates of Southern hospitality.

'The Labiches have been here since before the Louisiana Purchase from the French in 1803,' their host explained. 'The Mississippi was their main street, as today it is ours; the concourse by which they commerced with the world.'

To hold the mighty river in check, he continued, Grandfather Labiche, had with the young Emeritus, built up the once four-, now fifteen-foot-high river embankment, using an army of black labour. It was Emeritus Labiche's proudest boast – 'The best levee in Louisiana.'

Now he stood up.

'Father is going to the levee,' Emmeline said, to no one in particular but nonetheless smiled at Patrick.

It was a tradition of the household that the patriarch of the family would, as a matter of duty after dinner each evening, check the levels of the Mississippi and the steadfastness of the manmade bulwark against the river's might.

'I'll walk down with you, Emeritus,' Stephen Joyce offered, but Madame Labiche was quick to intervene, to request that 'in my husband's absence we should seize the opportunity of encroaching on Mr Joyce's good nature', that he should 'remain and entertain us ladies with stories of the revolutions in Ireland and your banishment to Van Diemen's Land . . . and subsequent escape,' she hastily added.

At this intervention Monsieur Labiche took his intended leave while Mr Joyce, in turn, deferred to Madame Labiche's request and remained.

'Without the high banks of the levee we should be washed away to America,' Emmeline explained to Patrick as they retired to the withdrawing room. In tones that indicated the destination of that misfortune, to be altogether worse than the misfortune itself. Though it did strike Patrick that the Gulf of Mexico was a much more likely journey's end to which fair Emmeline would be washed away rather than perfidious America.

Then, Mr Joyce regaled them with stories of his younger days, and his fight against the English coloniser.

'It is precisely the same here, Mr Joyce,' Lucretia Labiche professed. 'The Northerners seek to control our cotton, our cane and our culture . . . but we shall not have it!' she declared. 'I trust we ladies can count on the protection of such gentlemen as are present, in the event of engagement with the enemy.'

Mr Joyce avowed that she could. Patrick and Oxy likewise pledged themselves to the protection of the younger Labiche ladies. The latter, to repay the compliment of such gallantry, would play some music for their guests. Lively, the female slave produced a duet of matching stools for the Warnum rosewood piano. A pleasant interlude of tunes and sweet-throated songs followed, until Emeritus Labiche returned and the ladies retired.

Patrick later had good reason to remember the piano manufacturer's name. In his room he found tucked under a snuffbox a 'property' bill-of-sale, relating to the piano and other property bought at an auction in New Orleans.

124

Appolonia Creole negress of indeterminate age and having an ugliness of the eye – 700

Lively Creole mulatress – excellent seamstress – 1200

Rosewood piano Robert Warnum (needing tuning) – 600

Socrates a blacksmith negro of confidence – 1500

Jewel (15) Congo (first generation). Strong of back, needing occasional whipping – 800

Cupid (17) Creole (second generation) pleasing to the eye – 1000

A moderately-crippled female with no name good teeth, capable of breeding and non-field work – 300

Duet of rosewood piano stools – 300

Aphrodite a negro girl about nine years old – of potential – 600

Also for sale, one brute negro, a cow and her calf, some sheep and a pair of oxen.

Patrick read through the bill again. This time more slowly. Two piano stools equalled a crippled slave. A piano needing tuning was of a price with a nine-year-old girl 'of potential'. Creole slaves were worth more. These were second-generation, born in bondage so partly broken and less troublesome to train. Worth more as an investment, Patrick supposed. It was nothing special here – the buying and selling of people alongside sheep and a pair of oxen. Just a business transaction on a careless piece of paper.

He thought of the Labiche girls, white and beautiful – a protected species – delicately seated at the rosewood piano, with Lively the other 'bought property', fetching the stools for the 'young misses'. The negroes themselves looked well-cared for. Happy almost, Patrick had to concede. Who was to say that this 'peculiar little arrangement', which worked so well here in the South, should be turned on its head by outsiders?

'If the slaves were freed, it would upset everything, North and South,' Oxy had said to him as they retired from the pleasures of their first day at Plantation Labiche. 'The free slaves will swarm North, tumbling the price of labour and sending German, Pole and Paddy alike back to the disembarking ports.'

'And here,' Patrick added, 'without servants, the ladies will no longer be ladies. Everything will be topsy-turvy!'

'Would you fight, Patrick – if there's a war?' Oxy had asked him, his customary earnestness still present.

'Of course,' he had replied. 'I have sworn it to fair Emmeline . . . and you, Oxy?'

'Yes, but I would not fight to defend slavery, only for the honour of Southern ladies!'

'Would you die for them, Oxy?' Patrick had asked of his friend.

'I would . . . but I'd rather not!' Oxy Moran had squarely replied.

TWENTY-FIVE

The following morning Emeritus Labiche took his guests on a tour of Le Petit Versailles. The two hexagonal-shaped *garçonnières* stood at a discreet distance to the back left and right of the house. 'My twin sons stay in these when they are with us,' Emeritus explained. Adjoining the *garçonnières* on the left was a house for tutors and guests. At a distance in front of the *garçonnières* were the *pigeonnaires* where baby pigeons were raised – a delicacy of the family.

Then, the kitchen, separated from the house in case of fire. Across from it in perfect symmetry the abode of the house slaves. Between house and kitchen stood a massive, cased bell, its bronze rim etched with the heroes of Ancient Greece. 'Cast in Pittsburgh,' he told them.

Green-sprigged boxwood hedges rectangled the whistling walk, from kitchen to house. Nearby a black, life-sized Venus in veined Italian marble, but otherwise unadorned, attracted some side glances from the young men.

The dependency buildings were completed by an ice house and a privy set. Both of these conveniences were well-distanced from each other. Behind the dependencies stretched an avenue, lined each side by twenty-six Virginia oaks, dripping with Spanish moss.

'This is the avenue of the weeks.' Oxy, in his element,

127

continued to unlock the mysteries of Le Petit Versailles.

At the end was the house of the plantation overseer, Bayard Clinch. Manacled to a post outside this house was an exceptionally large dog, its ice-blue eyes coldly registering every human movement. 'A Catahoula – a Spanish war-dog,' their host explained. Beyond the overseer's house sat the field slave cabins. Twenty-two of them – on stilts. Whitewashed inside and out and with blue or red-painted doors. Each cabin was divided in two. Each of the two units housed a family.

'This is the most valuable part of the plantation,' Emeritus Labiche pronounced. Patrick, remembering the piece of paper he had found asked,

'How many slaves do you hold Monsieur Labiche?'

'The plantation owns at any time four hundred working slaves. Mr Clinch and Beauty there, look after the field slaves. Some have been with the family for generations, like old Theophilus and his wife Theophile. Their sons and daughters were born here and their grandchildren. It's a system that works well. Everybody knows where they fit.' Emeritus Labiche talked openly, warmly.

'The names they have – Theophilus and Theophile, Plato and Cato, Caesar and Cicero?' Patrick questioned.

'When each new child is born, the parents will ask that I name it – a name that befits the child's character. The negroes like the classical Greco-Roman names of scholars and philosophers . . .' He paused. 'Usually I try – and Madame Labiche is of great assistance in this – to name them in matching pairs. This naming by the master and the mistress is very important to them. Gives them a sense of belonging.'

'The low-bred with high ideas will always breed. It's what keeps them low,' Oxy asided, quietly to Patrick.

'Their new children are likewise of importance to us – they are the future of the plantation. It is they who will keep the sugar mills grinding,' Emeritus Labiche further explained, not hearing his guest's remark.

In the afternoon, the two Miss Labiches, having spent some

128

morning hours with their tutor, Dr Delarousse, took the young gentlemen to see the gardens. Queen, a matronly house slave in charge of all to do with domestic matters, accompanied them, to ensure that at no time were they left unchaperoned.

Patrick however, was able to engage in some conversation with Emmeline when the girl asked, 'Do you like gardens, Mr O'Malley?'

'Yes . . . if you are in them, Miss Emmeline.'

This caused her to fall silent and he was sorry he had made so bold with his reply.

'The trees . . . the plants here?' he began, in an attempt to restore the conversation.

'Well, the cypress is our great tree,' Emmeline replied. 'Its roots can stay underwater for one hundred years and it never rots – termites don't like it.' She gave the hint of a smile. 'The slave cabins are constructed from it. The Spanish moss, which drapes from its branches, is also put to good use. It is submerged in water for three months, then resurrected and hung out to dry. It turns then into black horsehair – the *bousillage* upon which you lay your head last night!' He smiled and she continued, melodious in speech as she was in song.

'The maples attract wasp nests. But of all trees, my favourite is the magnolia, which flowers throughout April, May and June. It is so scented and bounteous . . . so like the South itself.' She paused, deep in thought.

He watched the soft rise and fall of her neck, where the words were formed. Wished she would talk forever in that rich-whispering way she had.

'Do you think, Mr O'Malley, that there will be war between the States – Father says it is inevitable. That it will come next year, in 1861?'

He stopped. Looked at her standing there, framed by the creamy, darkening pink of magnolia blossoms, a *Fleur du Sud* – 'Flower of the South'.

'Miss Emmeline, I pray there will not but . . .'

'But it will not be your war, Mr O'Malley. You are not an American, much less a Southerner – though we should be glad to have you,' she quickly added, catching his arm. Queen shifted her feet, wanting them to keep walking.

'It is true, I was not born in America, but in every other respect – by education and inclination – I am as American as the magnolia blossom!'

She laughed, 'Oh, I do like you, Mr O'Malley – though a lady should never so openly profess to such a feeling in case she be thought not a lady. But you are able to make a lady laugh. Next to being a gentleman, it is the virtue I most admire in a man.'

Patrick looked at Emmeline scarcely believing she had lived but fifteen short summers.

'I thank the day which brought me here,' was his answer.

Both of them fell into silence and resumed walking.

'May no Northern flags in Southern winds flutter,' she said momentarily, causing him to blurt out, 'I have met no one quite like you, Miss Emmeline. You are so passionate about the South. You speak of it as if it were altogether another country?'

'Oh, but it is! It is!' she repeated. 'Don't you understand, Mr O'Malley, it is *altogether* a different country?'

Patrick could. Life here was timeless, cocooned against change, filled with a great comforting certainty. Here, roles were clearly defined. Patrick liked that. Father, mother, daughters, overseer, slaves – a perfect pyramid of order like the house and its dependencies.

Order preserved things from change. Kept everything intact. Immutable.

The South was not like Boston, brash with commerce, bristling with change and the Nativist hate for all things not American.

Patrick decided there and then that if the call to arms came, he would answer it clad in honest grey and under the Bonnie Blue Flag of the South.

TWENTY-SIX

'Men go to war because they want to,' Emeritus Labiche pronounced later, at table. 'Be it to free the blacks, not to free
the blacks; to save the Republic; to quash the Republic and
save the Union – it is a calling for men.'

Patrick enjoyed these evenings. Emeritus Labiche had a
view on everything. And was steadfast in its constancy. The
master of Manoir Labiche, would not easily be for turning,
it seemed to Patrick. Now he listened as the Southerner continued to hold forth on war.

'Some will go for cotton, commerce, or cash; others for
some disused notion of honour or glory; others because they
are American, more again because they are not. War binds
men together, brings them in from the cold, so to speak –
even if it be as corpses!'

'War is a cod!' Oxy Moran interrupted. 'At the end of
the day every difference has to be patched up. War is all a
cod.'

'A cod it may be, Mr Moran . . . but there is no way of
avoiding it,' Emeritus Labiche responded somewhat testily.
'Men must unfurl their banners to protect their homes and
their way of life.'

'And their ladies!' Madame Labiche deftly reminded him.

*

'God knows how Madame Labiche came by such comely daughters,' Oxy later observed to Patrick. 'Her face would be her fortune if only it were rented out for funerals.'

'A face to die for!'

Oxy laughed out loud.

TWENTY-SEVEN

'Steer well clear of the Irish Channel,' Stephen Joyce advised, reading his young compatriots an article from the *Daily Delta*, about that part of New Orleans, properly named Adele Street.

> 'The inhabitants appear for the most part to be an intemperate and bloodthirsty set, who are never contented unless engaged in brawls, foreign or domestic – such as the breaking of a stranger's pate or the blacking of a loving spouse's eye. These are the ordinary amusements.'

'A shower of bricks is the preferred welcome for strangers,' he went on to inform them, 'so that anyone in the city with a bandaged skull or blackened eye can safely be asked had he "passed through the Channel recently?" These swamp Irish are well used to wrestling alligators, so humans don't trouble them much!' he added.

'Why don't the slaves dig the swamps?' Oxy asked.

'Slaves are too valuable,' Stephen replied. 'To lose a good slave could cost $2000 – a "swamp Paddy" costs nothing.'

'And a strong slave can breed future slaves. Children born to a plantation become its property – like foals and horses,' Patrick added.

133

'It *is* indeed a peculiar institution . . .' Oxy commented. 'A very peculiar institution.'

'Yes, but how could the South survive without it?' Stephen Joyce challenged them. 'Slavery is like the household itself, central to the stability of the Southern state at large.'

Oxy rose to the bait with Stephen. 'That is the very reason the North wishes to crush it. For by crushing slavery, it will subjugate the South and remove that which is the bulwark of the South – the household!'

'But the North itself is wedded to slavery through cotton . . .' Patrick interjected, 'and is why Northern bleating about slavery is so hypocritical.'

'Will you stand with the South, Stephen, if it comes to that?' Patrick asked.

'It is too early to say, Patrick. Word has come that, in the event of war I may be offered a commission in the army of the North.' He paused, noticing Patrick's dismay.

'There is for and against that,' Stephen continued. 'Within the bigger frame of Ireland's struggle with England. The Irish could raise a great army under the mantle of the North but . . .' he reflected, '. . . my heart lies with the South – its republican ideals, its badge of honour.'

TWENTY-EIGHT

'My darling brothers, Lamarr and Lovelace, are returning
from visiting with dear, cheery little cousin Constance.'
Emmeline Labiche announced this with great excitement,
waving a rose-hued envelope. It was the summer of 1860.
Patrick and Oxy had returned to the Labiche Plantation, this
time alone, as Stephen had gone North to 'enquire of matters.' He had told them he would not require their company
. . . but 'that the Labiche ladies might!'

'How I miss the affection of the brotherly touch, in times
when I am dispirited,' Emmeline added, displaying not the
faintest hint of dispiritedness, her dark eyes alight, her delicate complexion betraying an uncharacteristic glow. She was
like a painting, Patrick thought. An exquisite and beautiful
painting, perfectly captured in every detail. Fragile, preserved,
unattainable – except when she smiled. Came alive at some
news or excitement. Like now. Or, even sometimes, he noted,
when he addressed her.

Cordelia, too, evinced a great anticipation at the coming
home of her twin brothers.

'Oh, Mr Moran and Mr O'Malley, you will simply adore
them and they you!'

Patrick and Oxy's introduction to Lamarr and Lovelace
Labiche was in true Southern style. Patrick, fascinated as ever

by the splendour of the architecture, had convinced Oxy to accompany him on a further examination of the house.

They both marvelled at the high open doors to the front and back. These formed a central, air corridor perfectly aligned with the centre-point of the giant embrace of the stairs. All rooms of the house were to the left or right of this central corridor.

'The ceilings are high, the hot air rises, keeping the lower levels cool,' Patrick remarked.

'Cooler!' Oxy corrected.

Like a far-distant drum roll, they heard it first, before feeling the drumming in the ground. Then, whipped up the wild whooping of horsemen charging through the cypresses.

The Labiche boys were home!

Patrick wondered how the riders would halt in time before reaching the house. But it was not the Labiche boys' intention to halt.

In they thundered, passing within the arch of the white staircases. Oxy, the more quick-witted, realising the riders' intent, grabbed Patrick by the collar and bundled the two of them to safety in the library, as neck and neck the two black steeds powered their way through the house.

'They're back! They're back!'

Patrick could hear Emmeline's voice, somehow carrying through the clatter of hooves. He and Oxy, on their feet again, rushed out to see the horsemen storm the garden, one brute's haunch sending the black-veined Venus to her naked eternity. Then a launch into the air over the boxwood hedge, each rider hanging from the saddle, miraculously snatching a green sprig for a beloved sister. Down the oak avenue, past the slave cabins they raced. Eventually, both riders and horses came to a shuddering halt beyond the finishing line of the last cabin.

'Lamarr is the victor!' Emmeline cried out deliriously, running, dress daintily hiked, to welcome her brothers.

'No, Emmy, it is Lovelace. Now it is six to five in his favour!' Cordelia called after her, she too in headlong flight.

'Whoever first gains the majority of thirteen is the winner for the season,' she explained all a-flutter to the guests.

'It is such an excitement to have such gallant brothers!'

Oxy wondered about the statue – were there to be thirteen such shattered Venuses before the racing season ended?

'Oh, Father will not be angry when it was so close a race – something equally agreeable will replace it!' Cordelia explained and dashed on.

As Oxy later remarked to Patrick, of the smithereened Venus, 'And that was that – just as I was forming an attachment to her!'

The nineteen-year-old Labiche twins Lamarr and Lovelace, dark as their mounts, both sported fledgling moustaches. They were of such a similarity that the only thing distinguishing them seemed to be their names. Apart from the small lick of hair that on one forehead – Lamarr's – curled eastwards, and on the forehead of Lovelace, curled westwards.

'Mother, ever-thinking of the good of her family, decided it should be so,' Emmeline explained.

Now the boys sat with their sisters, complimenting them, professing love, caressing soft, sisterly hands. 'Like re-united lovers,' Oxy thought they were. 'It was beautiful to behold, beautiful! To my dying day, I will never forget that picture of contentment,' he said later to Patrick.

Whatever the pool of contentment, the two young bucks were not content to remain still in it for long. The next day, the brothers made plans to take Patrick and Oxy to a quadroon ball in the French Quarter of New Orleans, downtown from Canal Street, the city's dividing line.

The men wore masks, the ladies went without.

'Keep your masks affixed,' Lovelace Labiche cautioned. 'It is then of no concern as to who might recognise you and whom you might recognise in turn.'

Patrick and Oxy were then propelled forward by the brothers. Into a throng of likewise masked gentlemen and the most beautiful creatures of every shade and hue on which eye had ever rested.

Except black.

But all were of black lineage – somewhere along the line. Some, the octoroons, were almost white, the quadroons a quarter less so.

'One could meet one's neighbour, an uncle, even one's own father here . . . and not recognise him!' Oxy exclaimed.

'There are tales – even between brothers and sisters,' Lamarr let it be known in reply.

'The game is in the pretence of not knowing,' Lovelace added.

It was an evening full with music and mystery and conversations spiced with innuendo, as thinly disguised as those engaged in it. Respectable mothers – *femmes de couleur libre* – of mixed descent, would bring their even more creamily complexioned daughters here. Lamarr Labiche explained it to them. 'A mulatto is sprung from white and black; griffe is mulatto and black – see her . . . there . . . dark chocolate! Over there is a quadroon – milk chocolate – mulatto and white, lighter to the taste.'

Patrick and Oxy were fascinated by the classification of caste, as Lovelace took over the explanations. 'But the tastiest to the tongue are the octoroons, from a mixture of quadroon and mulatto stock. They are almost as white as we are . . . apart from their passion,' he added.

Elegant and refined, the *femmes de couleur* were prohibited by law from marrying white men, but not from being their mistresses. Marrying free men of colour was also not countenanced. So, rich white Creoles came to the balls to pay court to the exotically-dressed quadroons.

'The old-style quadroon balls have mostly died out,' Lamarr confided, 'but *placage* still exists. Watch it in action!' he said to them.

They watched as a Creole gentleman was refused permission by a mother to speak to the most beautiful sight Patrick and Oxy had ever seen. No arrangement of *placage* would be made here, the suitor deemed unsuitable to provide a small home and other acceptable financial arrangements for the woman's daughter.

Patrick did not find the place or the evening much to his liking. 'It is an auction room,' he said dismissively, 'a beautifully-costumed auction room!'

Lamarr and Lovelace, on the other hand, relished the high-intrigue atmosphere, cavorting among the *femmes de couleur*, while seeking to 'unmask' what gentlemen suitors they recognised.

And Oxy Moran, from the pinched-in County of Roscommon, met Kizzie Toucoutou from the wide, wide shores of the Pontchartrain.

Kizzie Toucoutou was black, not that her mother Angelique, or indeed Kizzie regarded herself as black. Nor was it considered by either lady an impediment to Kizzie's advancement in this world. More especially to the advancement of Kizzie's children . . . whenever she had them – and she *would* have them and by a white man too!

'Bleaching the line, Kizzie, my dear!' her mother never stopped reminding her. 'Bleaching the line. That is why the good Lord put us here. Eventually, your children, perhaps, but certainly your children's children, will be so well bleached, they will be indistinguishable, as long as the rules are followed,' her mother warned.

Kizzie nodded. She understood the rules. She must never marry beneath her: black; mulatto; or quadroon. By doing so, she would be bleaching *their* line. She must have children but only by a white man . . . as her mother had. One who could provide for Kizzie and her children – a house in New Orleans and a regular income. Most of all her consort must be of unquestionable racial stock who, through breeding and circumstance, could bestow on her children that certain

'Southern White' attitude – as well as its pigmentation. And Kizzie Toucoutou with her fiercely dark eyes carried that attitude so well. From the tilt of her aristocratic forehead, through the flowing lines of her body, to the way she held forward her delicate instep when addressing you. But Kizzie could never marry her white man. He would be already married – and even if not, here in New Orleans it just could not be.

'It is pure economics,' Angelique Toucoutou explained to her daughter. 'Your beauty, your body, your intellect . . .' she paused, 'but not your soul . . . for the white man's seed . . . his capital . . . and our future.'

None of this Kizzie found alarming, or demeaning. It was a proud and strong tradition. She was only a conduit, bridging one generation to the next. The white man unwittingly relinquishing more than she ever would – the future of his race, and children.

As her mother often said to her, 'Look at you, my darling Kizzie – tall, beautiful, graced with such finery of character – you could have been a plantation mistress at any of the houses along the River Road!'

Now tonight, Kizzie was slightly bored with it all, this being on show to men who made no secret that they were inspecting little more than property. Those already with mistresses, their arrogant faces behind those hideous masks, letting it be known they weren't desperate for new flesh . . . only if something exceptional was on offer. And Kizzie was exceptional, she knew that, but Mère Toucoutou would raise her fan, and whisper to her daughter, 'Not him!' or 'Too old' and sometimes 'Without means', even 'Gouted from liquor'. The men always knew. There would be no overt signal from Mère Toucoutou. Then, slightly flushed, the suitors would once more circle the ornate hall, downwardly adjusting their horizons to the lower pecking order in which they now found themselves.

'Those Labiche boys . . .' her mother said. 'Just look at them!' Kizzie discreetly cast her eyes to where the Labiche boys were 'cavorting' as her mother disparagingly put it. There they were, the 'terrible twins', back in New Orleans, fresh from some new escapade or other. Together, they had previously approached her, unintroduced. Then, ignoring her mother, had boldly asked if she was 'taken'. She, in turn had ignored their insulting behaviour, looked beyond them, while her mother despatched them with a flick of her fan. With them she noticed the two other young men. Strangers. One dark-haired and not a Southerner but at home with the likes of the Labiches; the other, slender, less dark-haired and holding a certain grace. She wondered what he was doing in the company of the other three. As if prompted by her thought, the slender one looked up and smiled at her before she could avert her eyes.

Later, again she looked. He seemed apart from the other three – not frequently engaging in their animated talk. Once again he surprised her. She looked down, but momentarily looked up before slightly turning her body away from him. She knew he would approach her whenever the opportunity presented and her mother be otherwise distracted in conversation.

Kizzie Toucoutou then, ever so delicately, took the slightest of half-steps away from the space which her mother now occupied.

TWENTY-NINE

'Goin' fishin' for alligators . . .' Lamarr announced, 'for our city friends.'

'We'll bring Beauty,' Lovelace added.

The Labiche twins had exhorted Patrick and Oxy to return with them after the visit to the French Quarter, citing that 'our sisters will cease to love us!' if they returned alone, now that they had lost the company of Mr Joyce who had returned separately to New Orleans. Patrick was the more easily persuaded of the two. Oxy less so.

As they set out on their fishing expedition Patrick could well understand why almost half of all the wetlands in the United States were in Louisiana. It was the Mississippi. The river, majestic, meandering and muddy, half a mile wide, two hundred feet deep, everywhere enriched the soil and soul of Louisiana. It also brought the paddle-steamers to gawp at the undisguised splendour of the giant plantation houses – not to the displeasure of those who lived in them – whose back doors faced to the river.

'Big Muddy there, all two thousand, three hundred miles of it from Minnesota to the Gulf, drains the land from two Provinces in Canada and thirty-one of the dis-united States,' Lamarr explained.

'Dumps all that down here in Louisiana.'

'Yes – and we're tired of being the piss-pot of America!' Lovelace added, vehemently.

Behind each other the two pirogues moved silently through the swamp. In the lead, Lamarr, Patrick and the alligator bait. Behind them Lovelace, Oxy and the Catahoula.

'What is the difference between a swamp and a bayou?' Oxy, off on another tack, and as curious as ever, asked.

'A swampland is the best kind of land you can get. Food and lumber – two things a man can't do without,' Lamarr answered. 'A bayou is a shallow channel. Runs through a swamp – like a slow-moving road.'

'All of New Orleans was a swamp when the Labiches first came,' Lovelace interjected. 'But "muck is money," Grandfather Labiche would always say . . . and he was right. There are more millionaires from Natchez to New Orleans than in New York, New England and New Mexico all strung together.' A fact, stated with such conviction, that neither Patrick nor even Oxy, felt qualified to disagree with.

Ahead, beneath a drooping blackwood a great blue heron, fresh from a watery dive, fanned out its wings to catch what drying breeze there was. Blue catfish, some three feet in length, contemptuously slunk beyond the arc of the pirogue's pole. Then other colours; the red flash of mullet jumping; a tall great egret, still and white and waiting its long-beaked chance; the poked-out petals of the milky-toned bull-tongue. Everywhere were the swampy greens of Louisiana. The trees with their moss-green veils, and the sliced swamp, water parting before them, wrinkling back on itself like a sash of green slime.

They poled silently on in the twin pirogues, dugouts split from the same cypress tree. From time to time the Labiche boys told them of 'watermouths' and 'cottonmouths' and 'diamondbacks', chuckling to each other at the nervousness their conversation of snakes struck into their 'citified' guests. Then, some fifty feet ahead, something disturbed the surface. Lamarr motioned them towards a sheltering cypress.

'This will do,' he said.

Over a sturdy branch Lamarr cast the noose of a large rope. He then looped the other end through the noose and pulled it firm, securing the rope around the branch. To the free end of the rope, he attached what looked to Patrick like a small anchor.

'The fishing rod,' Lovelace explained.

On this anchor-like hook Lamarr impaled a slab of raw meat which now hung about six feet above the water.

'We only want the big "uns" . . . boots for Lamarr and me and pretty purses for our pretty sisters,' Lovelace explained.

They withdrew and waited.

Eventually, Patrick saw what looked like a broad-snouted pirogue weave its way towards the bait. He thought the bait set too high – the height of a man – but said nothing. Only watched.

The alligator approached in a circular swirling movement, gathering momentum, then propelling itself out of the water. It could not reach the bait. Again and again it tried – only once nipping the bloodied tail-end of the meat. It was big, but not big enough for Lamarr.

'Wait!' was all he said.

They came, drawn by blood, piroguing silently through the muddy water. Others ventured the six-foot jump and failed, then circled and tried again. It was then that Patrick understood the skill of the hunters. They wanted no small fry. They were after the best the swamp could offer.

'Don't they know they're the lucky ones?' Oxy whispered, as the smaller-fry alligators fruitlessly persevered. 'Why don't they go home?' Then, what they had all been waiting for arrived. More a paddleboat than a pirogue. So large that Patrick wondered aloud 'What if it thinks we, not that, are the real bait?'

'Gators are not aggressive unless attacked or nesting,' Lovelace answered, in a manner indicating the question should not have been asked in the first place.

Both Patrick and Oxy felt decidedly uncomforted by his assurance.

At the approach of the giant male the smaller alligators dispersed into the swamp's many-sided corridors. Head out of the water, top teeth overlapping bottom, deadpan eyes, he gathered himself. Then, air and water displacing with the power of the surge, he hung gloriously in the air, great, scaled tail thrusting him upwards.

The giant jaws opened.

Snapped.

Locked over both meat and hook.

'Got him!' Lovelace shouted.

The alligator hung there, a creature helpless between two worlds, unable to sink or swim, or fly. This way and that he flailed, his thrashings awakening the swamps with shrieking and squawking and the scuttling of lesser beasts. Man, the interloper, and *El Lagarto*, giant lizard of the swamps, had engaged.

Patrick was mesmerised by the spectacle of the alligator, its head and upper body now like a pendulum, oscillating from side to side above the water. He wondered if the groaning cypress would hold? Half hoping it wouldn't but rapt by the blood-pleasure of what they had achieved.

'Pole – and pole steady!' Lamarr instructed him, while priming his gun. Gingerly Patrick edged the pirogue towards the alligator, ready to push the pole off the swamp bottom at the slightest hint that the thrashing tail might catch them. Closer and closer they approached. The alligator, a grey and dark olive mixture, unable to bellow, exuded its musky smell at them in a last defiance. Lamarr stood behind Patrick, his eye cocked against the gun and emanating a strange kind of manic calm.

Even after he had shot the gargantuan at close range, it still lashed out at the savageness of the world it was leaving.

'He must be nineteen feet!' was the only eulogy its executioner accorded the beast when, finally its thrashings stopped.

145

Nevertheless, Lamarr Labiche secured its jaws with the killing rope.

Beauty, who had remained in regal silence, eyes capturing the entire set of events, now began to get agitated.

'She doesn't like being so close to the alligator,' Patrick suggested, himself experiencing the same sensation.

'That's not it!' Lovelace declared, a tremble of excitement in his voice. 'Runaways! She can sniff a nigger at half a mile.'

He slipped the collar from the war-dog. She never moved . . . awaited his command.

'Go, Beauty! Get!'

Catapulted by his command, Beauty bounded over the side of the pirogue, the huge hunting haunches untroubled by cypress roots or the draping moss through which she sped. Vainly they paddled after her until she was out of sight. Not long it was till the sounds of close pursuit rang back to them. Then came screams and the curdling cry of the Catahoula.

Patrick, frantic with apprehension asked, 'Will we be in time?'

'They're runaways,' Lovelace Labiche answered, nonchalantly. It was the same as trapping alligators.

When they reached the spot where the hound had run its prey to ground, it turned and snarled at them.

'Heel, Beauty! Heel!' Lamarr ordered. Proudly the beast moved its massive body to sit beside him. On the ground, her upper leg almost torn from its joint, was one of the young field slaves.

'Ah, it's Jewel!' Lamarr said in recognition. 'Silly girl!'

Beside her, unharmed, but cowering in fear was a young male black slave. 'Young Massa . . . don' let dat dog get me!' he implored.

'Don't worry, Cicero,' Lamarr answered in soothing tones. 'Beauty prefers her own gender if she has a choice. Jealousy, I suppose! Besides, you're too valuable to have hobbling about on one good leg. A whipping will do you!'

'Yes, young Massa! Please de whip and I ain't nebber gonna run no more!'

Patrick ran to the girl who was helpless with pain.

'She'll bleed to death!' He tore off his shirt, bound it around her leg. Immediately the blood seeped through it.

'I ain't goin' back!' she moaned. 'Massa gonna kill me!'

Oxy and Patrick between them got her into the pirogue.

'Lamarr! Lovelace! Cut the alligator loose, it's going to slow us down!' Patrick demanded.

'No!' Lovelace retorted sternly. 'We *must* bring it back. Think of the disappointment my sisters will express.'

'Jewel will be fine,' Lamarr added. 'Queen is able to work magic with them.'

Back at Le Petit Versailles, there was already a hullabaloo over the two missing slaves. Clinch was furious over the escape. Furious too that Beauty had been denied him for pursuing the runaways.

'Taken on a hunting jaunt!' the overseer said sneeringly. 'When she had work to do here. You've cost your father dearly,' he said, nodding at the damaged slave.

Patrick wondered at how meekly the brothers took the admonition from the overseer. But good overseers were hard to find and Bayard Clinch knew it. The Labiche plantation had prospered under his tenure. Word would spread, his stock rise among other plantation owners. He could afford to rein in the young massas.

That evening Emeritus Labiche summoned the household and all of the slaves for prayer. Patrick could not but help notice the number of slave children who were of less than full, high colour. The word had long been in New Orleans that slave owners saw it as their duty to improve their stock by introducing superior seed. Masters of plantations were thus *obliged* to breed with strong-backed female slaves to produce a smarter, if paler strain.

Bleaching the line.

The service began, Emeritus Labiche in his hickory-rich, prayer voice, announcing, 'We are gathered here as one family in the sight of God, to ask forgiveness for our brother Cicero and our sister Jewel.' He paused. 'Forgiveness . . . for the betrayal of us all!' He let the words fall, like Heaven's brimstone smiting a sinful earth. 'And the Hound of God has wreaked its vengeance on Sister Jewel . . . and' – a longer pause – 'the mark of the Lord shall purge the sin from Brother Cicero.'

At this, a great wailing arose from the slaves to a vengeful Lord.

Emeritus Labiche moved to comfort his people. '"And God shall wipe away all tears from their eyes; and there shall be no more death, neither sorrow, nor crying, neither shall there be any more pain, for the former things are passed away".

'The Book of Revelation, Chapter Twenty-One, Verse Four,' he added, so that they knew it was not his voice that spoke – but God's. Their black God.

'Bring them here,' he mournfully ordered his overseer. His wife, Lucretia he bade to 'take your daughters inside!'

What was about to be witnessed was not for tender-gazed and womanly, white eyes. Only for the eyes of slaves. Black women and their children.

First was Jewel.

'You, Jewel! You have been justly punished for your crime. Now you will be marked so all will know you have broken a sacred trust. Bayard,' Emeritus Labiche then called, almost gently.

The overseer stepped forward as if summoned to perform a rite of the Church.

'Plato, Cato . . . you know what to do!' Bayard Clinch said. The two male slaves stepped forward and pinned the already prostrate Jewel's arms to her side.

The overseer then held the hissing branding iron aloft so all could see, and yanked the girl's hair so that her right cheek was exposed.

At this a keening cry arose from those gathered.

Quickly, methodically he branded the girl's flesh with the letter 'V'. 'V' for vengeance, 'V' for Versailles.

Patrick was forced to turn away but he could not escape the sizzling sound of the raw-hot metal against Jewel's skin. Nor the agony of her pain which rent the plantation skies.

Next it was 'Brother Cicero'. He, in addition to receiving the brand of Versailles, had the crown of each ear cut away with shears. What remained of his ears was then cauterised so he would not bleed to death.

'Cropping,' Lamarr dutifully explained to Patrick, 'so all will know he was a failed runaway.'

After the 'rites of penance' had been completed, Emeritus Labiche again prayed forgiveness for his errant slaves, asking the Lord to 'charitably guide the hand of my justice.' He concluded with a beseeching prayer.

'Lord, grant that I may always be right for Thou knowest I am hard to turn. Amen.'

'Amen!' the kneeling slaves echoed.

Afterwards there was no further discussion of the incident. Property had been recovered, branded with the mark of ownership, lest it again go astray. The business of Versailles had been attended to. Normality had been restored.

That evening, and for some while thereafter, Monsieur Labiche exhibited a marked disinclination to 'go to the levee'.

Nor was any comment passed on this newfound break with the family tradition.

THIRTY

A number of times during the remaining year did Patrick and Oxy visit Versailles, 'the lesser', as Oxy called it. Stephen Joyce on occasion accompanied them but more often than not had pressing business either in Richmond – the Southern capital, or Washington 'the other capital', as Emeritus Labiche labelled it.

Patrick sometimes accompanied Stephen on these visits to the capitals, on other occasions Oxy also came with them.

If Stephen went alone, the work he left for them was light and invariably Patrick and Oxy would point their mounts towards Versailles. Patrick's 'eyes never tiring of the beauty within.' As Oxy saw it.

The Labiche plantation, with or without Stephen Joyce, always received them in like manner: a generous welcome, sumptuous meals; hunting, fishing. Cousins visiting and evenings spent in bright conversation, rippling with music and young ladies.

While Patrick and Emmeline had formed a deeper attachment, Oxy's interest lay not with Cordelia but with his Creole lass from the Pontchartrain – Kizzie Toucoutou. Nevertheless, he accompanied Patrick on all such visits.

'I am your "Queen" – your chaperone,' he joked, each time Patrick pressed a visit upon him and not wanting to reveal too much of Kizzie to Patrick . . . or anything of her to the Labiches.

Kizzie he had come upon one day, she sauntering from the markets. Since the ball, he had watched the streets from the gallery outside his room, hoping for a glimpse of her. None was to be had. Then they had almost bumped into each other. Try as she did to at first disguise it, he knew she had recognised him. He offered to carry her basket, laden with fruits. She had said nothing. Just handed it to him. Surprised, he blurted out, 'Your colours are beautiful . . . your tignon . . . your dress – vivid like New Orleans itself.' She had smiled then, let him talk – this one was polite, not afraid to graciously compliment . . . unlike those boorish Labiches.

As if he had somehow known what she had been thinking, he had turned and looking directly at her, asked, 'You don't like the Labiche boys?'

She had given a laugh, lips parting, revealing the softness of her mouth and caught him looking.

'No,' she had answered, cutting short her laugh. 'And I fear you already are becoming as emboldened as they are . . . Monsieur . . . Monsieur . . . ?'

'Moran . . . Monsieur Moran . . . from Ireland!'

'Oh, the Irish!' she had replied, again laughing. 'That explains it – the charming, adventuring Irish.' Then she had stopped walking. 'My father was Irish . . . Murphy . . . but I kept my Creole name – Toucoutou . . . Kizzie Toucoutou.' Oxy couldn't have blamed her, the name ringing around in his head. Toucoutou, Kizzie Toucoutou. How exotic, how full of rhythm . . . full of . . . just like this whole place.

'Kizzie . . .Toucoutou,' he said aloud. 'My pleasure to meet you.'

Then she had taken the basket from his startled hand and turned to the right, up a side street. He had waited, knowing she would turn. That was her way, this Kizzie Toucoutou. She did – half turn, called over her shoulder, 'Maybe we could talk more of Ireland and you could carry my basket, Irishman.'

151

Languidly then, as if in no hurry anywhere, Kizzie Toucoutou had disappeared further along the alleyway. Like the sun going down on a Delta night, washing the world with its reds and purples, its yellows and browns.

She had never said where or when, but the next day and the next, he had waited near the markets. He had known she was playing with him, trying to take the edge off some of that Irish charm, as she called it.

On the third day she came.

Jewel, the young Congolese slave, had been sold. Now, damaged goods, the sixteen-year-old attracted a much lesser price than the eight hundred dollars she once fetched.

After that, Patrick observed, Emeritus Labiche fell back in with the old tradition of going to the levee. The reinstatement of this practice attracted no more comment, than had its previous abandonment.

'A conspiracy . . . language used to conceal rather than reveal,' was Oxy's view.

Patrick wondered at Jewel's fate . . . and asked Emmeline.

'Father keeps all such troublesome estate business from our eyes and ears. Apart from the house slaves, Mother leaves everything to him. He is such a wonderful father, ever attendant to his duties toward us. If Jewel, distracted girl that she was, finds a home as caring, and a master as kind, she will do well.'

'It doesn't disturb you?' he asked her.

'Disturb me, Patrick?' she reacted, with surprise. 'It is our way of life, what we are. Lamarr says it is unproductive to discuss what is immutable. The "peculiar institution" – as you Northerners call it – was not instituted by us. It was here before us and, no doubt, shall remain long after us.'

Patrick started to say something but she smiled and put her finger to his lips.

'Don't! I fear you are becoming tiresome, Patrick. You haven't yet admired my new walking outfit from Marseilles!'

she chided. 'Mr Moran seems to lack no such taste for finery, equally complimenting my *chemisette* and my pagodas!'

'It's a conundrum,' Oxy said to him. 'You love her . . . and they are a Christian-hearted people, treating their slaves with charity and justice. Yet the thought of the girl Jewel and the dog troubles you.'

'And still . . .' Patrick replied, 'we are ready to fight to uphold their institution – this human bondage.'

'No, Patrick, we are ready to fight for a republic. For democracy, to uphold freedom, and the right to self-determination,' Oxy corrected.

'What about self-determination for Jewel and Cicero . . . and all the rest?' Patrick argued back.

'More importantly . . . what about self-determination for ourselves . . . for the Irish in America?' Oxy countered.

'That will come too,' Patrick replied. 'As it will come for the blacks. In the process of which the Irish will fight the blacks – and you and I, Oxy Moran, will fight the Irish.'

'One war at a time, I say,' Oxy Moran answered.

And Patrick left the last word on war to his friend.

THIRTY-ONE

Then the word came. Spread like wildfire along the bayous, swamps and levees.

Louisiana had seceded from the union of States.

If the news sent a shiver through the great plantations along the Mississippi, it was one of excitement and pride. Not a shiver of fear at impending war.

'At last! At last!' Emeritus Labiche pronounced. 'We are ready to take our place among the nations of the earth. No longer will we be under the Yankee yoke. Make no mistake . . .' he addressed Stephen, recently returned from Richmond, who had joined Patrick and Oxy on a trip to Versailles, 'this war, if it comes, will be a War of Northern Aggression!'

Then, still in defiant mode, Emeritus Labiche further addressed his guests. 'I have heard, my young friends, that the Irish in the North are enlisting in their droves. Selling out to the Anglo-Saxon aggressors against their Southern cousins,' he levelled at them, in accusatory tones.

'Some will go to the North, some with the South,' Stephen responded. 'It is all a matter of geography over ideology . . . where one lives.' Stephen's answer cut little favour with his host.

'The Celtic races should stand together,' the Creole planter explained, with barely-tempered patience. 'It is a folly to think that fighting on the side of the aggressor will make the Irish any more "white" in the eyes of the North. The same folly that a perceived "freedom" will make the Africans any more equal in the South.'

He stood up before them, moving to where his hunting rifle lay cradled on the wall.

'Blood is good for soil and when the fields are red, true freedom will flourish!' He seized the gun, patting its black metal. 'The Tenth Amendment to the Constitution guarantees the rights of individual States over a Federal system. What else does a State's rights consist of if not the issues of commerce, taxation – and our property?'

With that Emeritus Labiche brandished the weapon, salute-like, above his head – as if to the Almighty. 'I pray that this Southern rifle may bring tears from many a Northern mother before this thing is over,' he said chillingly.

The guests of the house retired to bed that evening, heads aflamed with the wrongdoings of the North and the ringing tones of Emmeline and Cordelia's final duet of the evening.

God Save the South!

THIRTY-TWO

Despite the turmoil of the secession in the January of 1861, nothing was going to stop New Orleans from teasing every last spring of frolic and fun from Mardi Gras, the Fat Tuesday of 18 February.

Oxy, glad to be back from the bayous and levees and to see his Kizzie again, reckoned that 'It might be the last time we'll be kicking our heels up for a while – unless in a shroud.'

And Mardi Gras was a riot of high-kicking heels and tapping toes. Sound and colour merged into one kaleidoscope of merry-making and feasting. For Ash Wednesday, the day following Fat Tuesday, signalled the start of the Lenten season of fasting, abstinence, sackcloth and ashes. And no dancing.

As they lay together for the first time into the ash-streaked dawn, Oxy Moran stroked his Kizzie's honeyed skin.

She whispered something to him, raised her face above his.

And then gave him her fondest kisses.

THIRTY-THREE

Le Petit Versailles was as ever splendid inside as out, its
rococo revival furnishings floridly reinterpreting the court of
Louis XV. Armoires – a matching pair, decorated with
pineapple motifs; a black-lacquered *Bureau de Dame*, set in
the bowers of a deep bay window fringed on the outside with
vine. At the end of the room, above the bleu-turquin stone
mantel, hung a large mirror with a porcelain-gilt surround
and delicate mother-of-pearl edging. This mirror, slightly con-
caved, gave those present a sense of there being also present,
an identical group of people to themselves. A gathering,
which continuously aped their movements – and 'somewhat
disturbingly so,' Oxy observed.

Both Patrick and Oxy realised it would be one of their few
last visits to this splendid place, so often home to them in
recent times.

The house had an air of impregnability, as if war could not
touch this place. That it was impervious to war. Above it.

Patrick now looked about the room where they sat. The
magnificent six-holdered pewter chandelier hung from a ceiling
of asymmetrical patterns of scrollwork and shellwork: crabs,
crayfish and crustaceans – *les fruits de Mississippi*. The ceiling
was the river, which brought bounty to the table beneath.

The table itself was of sixteen-setting proportions and

157

carved of solid mahogany. On its richly-hued surface, silverware sparkled, face downwards to reduce wear. Thus also, the Labiche coat of arms, finely etched onto the gleaming underside of each piece, was upturned to face the guest. Over the table was suspended a large shoofly fan, attached to a plaited cord of crimson and gold. Discreetly standing behind Patrick, a young slave boy, decorous in matching colours of gold-trimmed crimson, waited to pull the rope, which opened the fan, which shooed the flies.

And there were yet other intriguing inventions to deal with the tender vicissitudes of Southern life. A duo of flytraps of intaglio-design cut-glass sat innocuously at an even distance from each end of the table. These were filled with equal measures of molasses and sticky, sugar-laden poison. The molasses with which to entice and entrap, and the poison to eliminate these uninvited guests from the Labiche table.

Window draperies puddled the floor. 'No cutting of one's cloth to more modest measure here,' Oxy quietly observed to Patrick.

Rosewood and tulipwood tables were arranged along the walls of the room. These, interspaced by gondola chairs and a pair of high-backed Hitchcock chairs 'from New England, but beautiful,' Lucretia Labiche explained, in their defence.

A dual coffee table cum serving tray, now bore to the table cherubic syllabub, heavy with mantling cream and syrup-of-peach liqueurs.

Oxy enquired about the pineapple motif on the tray.

'The pineapple is a symbol of Southern hospitality, Mr Moran,' Lucretia Labiche answered. 'But beware should ever you find one at the base of your bed!' She left the warning hanging there, suspended above them.

'A pineapple is a double edged fruit so to speak . . . like a sword,' Emmeline chimed. 'On the one hand hospitality . . . on the other hand, one at your bed means you have over-extended that hospitality. Oh, but it never happens with gentlemen!' Emmeline was quick to qualify her explanation.

'But the very beds themselves are made of pineapple?' Oxy offered, somewhat mischievously, causing Cordelia to titter briefly beneath the tips of her fingers.

Her father continued the explanation. 'Hospitality is something that is not an end in itself – a notion of the Northern neo-Christians. Here in the South, people – our cousins – travel great and treacherous journeys to visit each other. So, here in Louisiana, no hog is not fattened, no juicy morsel left unpicked. Visiting is what binds the family, the community, the South itself! And for our glorious South no effort is too great, no welcome too lavish!'

Both Oxy and Patrick concurred wholeheartedly and said so, encouraging their host to give further vent to his favourite subject, the South . . . and its superior culture.

Oxy flashed a quick smile at Patrick and both slightly reclined in their seats to hear the 'Sermon from the Mouth', as Oxy ungraciously referred to these passionate monologues from their host.

They were not to be disappointed.

'Low-born, East Coast Americans have always threatened our culture, laughed at our houses and refused to speak our language. Now . . .' Emeritus Labiche seized his sword and flashed it in the air. Without a flaw in the arc of its flight, their host sliced in two an unsuspecting pineapple held quakingly on a tray in the attendant slave's hands.

'Till the spoilers be defeated and the Lord's work completed,' he said triumphantly, as the juice of the fruit dripped from his blade. 'And neither will Southern hospitality be found wanting, even for our foes. Let them advance a hostile foot upon our soil, and we will welcome them with bloody hands and hospitable graves.'

THIRTY-FOUR

Everywhere, now that Louisiana had seceded, secession badges – a pelican-shaped button within a field of ribbons – appeared. Symbol of Louisiana, the pelican, it was said, would tear at its own flesh rather than see its young starve.

Emmeline, for her part, sported the Bonnie Blue Flag on her bosom. With a blue field and a single white star, the Bonnie Blue Flag had gained popularity through a rousing song of the same name. 'Oh, if only I were a man, so I could fight!' Emmeline sighed in exasperation to Patrick on more than one occasion.

Stephen had left this visit to the Labiches prematurely to ride to see the swordmaker, Griswald. He was also to be fitted for a new, double-breasted, frock-coat . . . in Confederate grey.

'War is inevitable,' he had told them, prior to leaving. 'Secession has come in too quickly for the North to ignore it.'

First it had been South Carolina, declaring by unanimous vote five days before Christmas 1860 that 'the Union existing between South Carolina and other States is hereby dissolved'.

The state of Mississippi followed suit, ringing in the New Year by announcing secession on 9 January. Next day brought Florida, the following day Alabama, and Georgia on 19

January. Then it was Louisiana's turn and on 1 February the Lone Star State of Texas left the Union.

That Virginia, Arkansas, Tennessee, North Carolina, Missouri and Kentucky did not join with the 'secesh' States until later, mattered little. By then, as Oxy put it, 'The die was well and truly cast.'

At 4.30 a.m., on 12 April 1861, General Beauregard's Confederates fired for thirty hours on the Federal Government munitions dump at Fort Sumter in the Bay of Charleston, South Carolina. Peppered it with ball and grape, until the Union garrison surrendered.

The war between the States had commenced.

THIRTY-FIVE

'I want you and Oxy to be my sergeants,' Stephen Joyce announced to Patrick, when they had later rejoined him in New Orleans. He, himself, had been given the rank of Captain of Infantry. A rank it seemed to Patrick which had disappointed Stephen, when he announced it to them saying, 'I have put conscience above career.'

Now he had given them their ranks. Next came their duties. It was an exciting time, an adventure as good as any, Patrick reckoned.

'Patrick, you have such an unswerving eye, you will be with my sharpshooters. And you, Oxy, so swift and nimble, you shall be colour-sergeant and proudly bear the flag of your adopted State.'

At the onset of Fall, all three rode to Versailles to make their goodbyes. It was a melancholy ride, little spoken between them, and Stephen wondering if he had chosen wisely for his two young comrades. Patrick, Ellen's son, would be safe enough back from the front of the fray. Under the protection of some hardwood tree or behind some grassy knoll. Still, the other side would have its sharpshooters too.

He worried about Oxy. The slender youth was agile as a cat – ideal to be at the head of infantry. With his likewise agile tongue, he would whip and lash his front line forward. But in battle, the colours, and colour bearers, were a prime target for enemy marksmen. Still, if the lad were quick and not lacking in bravery, it would be difficult to fix sights on him.

Looking at Patrick, Stephen again wondered about Ellen? What had happened to her life? Where had she fled – and why?

The truth about their affair had not been revealed – of that he was sure. Patrick had made no mention of it. Should he now tell the boy? In case one or other, or both of them, failed to return from the tides of war on which they were now thrown.

He decided that now was not the time. Patrick's heart would have its own heaviness with which to contend. That of leaving Emmeline.

THIRTY-SIX

All along the River Road, the looming war brought an intense excitement. The Mississippi itself was frantic with craft of every proportion, skiffing and scudding its waters with a new urgency. The river, an avenue of commerce to the Northern States on one side and to New Orleans and the Gulf on the other, was now also a territory to be defended.

As they passed the great plantations, once ceded to the French for defending the bayous and swamps against the English, Patrick wondered about the future of the great houses? Now, again there would be armies. Huge cannons and ships – floating arsenals to pepper the curving staircases; to cripple the Doric pillars and to blast the high-glassed Belvederes to the high heavens.

Garçonièrres, pigeonairres alike, would be target practice before the real work began; that of levelling the aristocratic uppityness of families such as the DuPlantiers, the Delarousses . . . and the Labiches. The ladies, Patrick worried, what would happen to the ladies?

'If they are gentlemen and I fear they are not, they will not sully Southern womanhood by laying one Yankee finger upon us,' Emmeline had defiantly told Patrick when he voiced his fears. 'Otherwise we will throw ourselves to the river.'

'That will never come to pass, dear Emmy,' he promised.

'I, Captain Joyce and Mr Moran will defend the South to the last drop of blood. God and right are with us. The Yankees have no such right.'

Later, they had what seemed like a victory banquet, so fine a feast it was and attended by toasts to the South and to the *Fleurs du Sud* – the Flowers of the South – its virtuous womanhood. Patrick wondered if, even through war, a house like this would lose its magnificent banquets. He thought not, unless the South lost, and the slaves were freed. The wealth was vast. Sugar would still be sold. Commerce would still flourish – even in war.

A large company of cousins and relatives had drawn in, some having travelled for days, for soon Emeritus, Lamarr and Lovelace would depart for New Orleans. From there to the clammy climes of Virginia 'where no French is spoken,' Lamarr had declared contemptuously, 'but where most of the fighting will be done.'

'To fair Virginia, to defend our Confederate capital, Richmond and to assault the Union seat of arrogance – Washington,' Emeritus Labiche stoutly chorused.

Music was called for. 'Dear, cheery little cousin Constance' – as Emmeline referred to her out of hearing – coyly obliged with 'The Minstrel Boy', which she informed them, 'will be instantly recognisable to the Irish gentlemen.'

Indeed it barely was, Cousin Constance bringing such an insipidness to Moore's dashing marching tune, that Oxy immediately re-christened it 'The Mincing Boy'.

There were calls for 'Cousin Emmeline' to sing. At which exhortation she and Cordelia took possession of the duet stool with welcome alacrity. Thus, in one swoop, relieving both Cousin Constance . . . and her audience.

Patrick looked at Oxy, wondering if his friend would sing on this last night. Oxy never had up to now shown the slightest inclination to repeat what Patrick had once heard on the Pontchartrain. Nor did he now, declining his head against Patrick's unasked question. Patrick put it down to a natural

165

shyness. Not that Oxy couldn't hold his own against either of those now about to sing.

With Cordelia sweetly accompanying her – and providing seconds to Emmeline's clear soprano – the beautiful Scottish melody of 'Annie Laurie' melted all hearts from thoughts of war. The ovation was as prolonged as it was emotive, with encores instantly arising.

After a polite whisper with her accompanist, Emmeline announced she would sing a newly-learned piece, also by the Irish melodist Thomas Moore, 'which,' as she delicately observed, 'expresses the heart's cry at this parting hour, better than can any words.'

She looked briefly at Patrick before composing herself.

> 'Has sorrow thy young days shaded,
> As clouds o'er the morning fleet?
> Too fast have those young days faded,
> That, even in sorrow, were sweet?
> Does Time with his cold wing wither,
> Each feeling that once was dear?
> Then, child of misfortune, come hither,
> I'll weep with thee, tear for tear.'

Emmeline sang as if indeed her own heart had withered with thoughts of impending doom. Lamarr, Lovelace, her dear father and protector . . . and him, Patrick, so desolately in love.

And for Patrick it was as if the veil of the years had been lifted. He remembered his own sisters. He had written twice – the letters returned unopened. Now his heart pined for bygone days. Mary, beautiful red-haired Mary. How her fingers would float over the piano notes. And Louisa, his adopted sister, reaching into every heart with that final piece on their piano, Bach's Largo in F Minor. He had never forgotten the name nor the melody, dropping slowly from Louisa's fair hand, closing a door softly. Like Emmeline now was.

'If thus the young hours have fleeted,
When sorrow itself looked bright,
If thus the fair hope had cheated,
That led thee along so light.
If thus the cold world now wither,
Each feeling that once was dear,
Then, child of misfortune, come hither,
And I'll weep with thee tear for tear.'

Patrick thought his heart would shatter. Had to slip outside before she had finished singing. The song, as he perceived it, was a lament for the once life of a great house, for all that they had known here. An age of innocence, an age of timelessness. Her voice filtered out to him in the Louisiana night, floated to meet the fragrant, scented air of a disappearing world.

Soon she came looking for him, no sign of Queen in attendance.

'Thank you!' he said. 'It shall be the vision and the sweet sound of you. My brightest day that will bear me through the darkest night.'

'Oh Patrick, it is so wretched! Such a wretched war that takes you away! But I am the less afflicted by such thoughts, when I consider how glorious you will be for us all . . . for me,' she said, shyly.

'Emmeline!' he began, not knowing what to say.

Unusually, she interrupted him. 'Here . . . !' she said. 'Bring it safely home to me – unstained and unbloodied?' Into his hand she pressed a tiny, white lace glove. Affixed to it with the tenderest of stitches, a small paper heart.

'It is a sweetheart's glove,' she said, looking away. 'The first I have made . . . it may not be so perfect.'

He held fast onto her hand. 'Oh, but it is, dearest Emmeline! It is! I shall treasure it always and pray that you may never have to make another.'

167

'Oh, Patrick!' she cried, and like a trembling dove flew to him, frenetic beating heart in her breast. 'I shall never, never, make another!' she sobbed. 'If it were not to dishonour you, I would beg you not to go. Even though, in doing so, you would think so little of me, as to never love me.'

In the long months ahead each word torn from her now would be a saviour to him. A reason to stay alive. He waited to let her continue.

'We are losing everyone we love so dearly,' she wept. 'Father, dear, dear Father who is always there for us all. Constant as the river itself. My loving brothers, so dashing and so brave. Mr Joyce and Mr Moran, too – oh, I shall miss his laughter and his shy smile. And you, dearest Patrick . . . but . . .' she said, brightening up, 'when we are all free . . .' She let the words ebb away as if the wished-for might evaporate with the wishing.

'It *will* be a short war,' he comforted, sure of himself. 'When the North feels the steel of our resolution they will fall back from their oppression.'

'That is what Mother says,' she answered, some of her old resoluteness returning, 'and that we ladies must be strong for our valiant heroes, showing no doubt, no fear. Promise me you will return!' She paused, thinking of the burden of duty he must bear. 'Promise me!' she entreated.

And he kissed her and promised that he would.

'Before magnolia time again.'

THIRTY-SEVEN

Confederate Army, Virginia, 1862

'Your father was a soldier,' Stephen Joyce said to Patrick. 'Not a uniformed soldier like you, but a soldier nonetheless. He died fighting the oppression of a foreign Crown.'

He paused. 'I was his commanding officer.'

'So history repeats itself,' Patrick answered. 'Perhaps fortune will favour me more than it did my father.'

'I brought you this,' Stephen said, ignoring the younger man's barb. 'The hours before battle are long. This may shorten them!'

Patrick took the book of poems. '*Love Elegies* . . . John Donne?' he questioned.

'Yes,' Stephen answered. 'A priest-poet. He could see deeply into the human heart and questioned all metaphysical things. He will provoke your mind.'

'Thank you!' Patrick said, some vague familiarity that he couldn't place, niggling at him. 'I shall treasure it.'

For Stephen the familiarity of the exchange was shot through with an intensity that melted away the years. It was the self-same book he had given to Patrick's mother. She had given it back, wanting *his* copy, the one from which he had read to her. They had exchanged the books like vows, sealing their love in the eternity of verse. He wanted the boy to have it – something of her – a talisman to keep him safe. Stephen was aware of how intently Patrick now watched him. Though of a different colour to Ellen's, the boy's eyes had the self-same set – direct, uncovering, drinking in what you said – and what you did not say. He bid Patrick a good night.

When Patrick returned to the tent, Oxy was already under the covers but not yet asleep. Thinking of his Kizzie, Patrick imagined. Just as he himself was of Emmeline.

'Oxy,' he asked quietly, 'are you afraid?'

'Of course I am . . . but if a fellow could get enough sleep, he could then be speeding ahead of those slow-coach Yankee bullets.'

Patrick laughed. Oxy could take the sting out of anything with his sharp wit. Even death.

Then he wrote to Emmeline, the words tumbling unmanageably onto the page. He had not seen her since they had left before Christmas. It was different now, the pomp of their leaving Louisiana, the bands pumping out their 'oom-pah-pahs', the banners, the ladies' fondly-scented handkerchiefs, fluttering them away to glory. They had been trained, roughly enough trained, Patrick thought, in the taking of orders, marching and the use of their weapons. It was enough, he supposed, to kill . . . or be killed. Now, in the early spring of 1862, they would be put to the test. Now they were in the heart of it all. Virginia, its state capital Richmond, also the Confederate capital. Its roads and rivers within striking distance of the other capital, Washington.

The letter to Emmeline was short, Patrick afraid he would reveal his fears to her. Now he must concentrate on the next morning's battle.

Tomorrow he would train his eye on men he never knew. Shoot them dead . . . or be shot dead by them.

It was a restless night but blessedly brief. Reveille sounded at 4.30 a.m.

170

Before they broke camp, Father O'Grady, the chaplain, a robust and bearded Irishman addressed them. 'Men! This is your first battle. Do not fear it. Put on the whole armour of Good. Your cause is just and you must be clear of mind, ready now before the throne of God, to die rather than forsake the cause . . . Trust . . . Obedience . . . Faith. Trust . . . Obedience . . . Faith,' he repeated. 'For the honour of your country and for Christ as Saviour, the true soldier is prepared to die in the path of duty even if it leads to the very mouth of the cannon. 'Remember,' he reminded them yet again. 'Trust . . . Obedience . . . Faith.'

'Twaddling Theology,' was what Oxy called it.

THIRTY-EIGHT

Louisiana Infantry
Army of Northern Virginia
near Richmond, Virginia
12th April 1862

Dearest Emmeline,

It seems a thousand miles since I left Le Petit Versailles and a thousand days since I left you. Each mile and each day I draw away from you is a burden but each such day draws us closer to the task at hand. Through it all I have the picture of you before me – pleasant days filled with magnolia and evenings full with music. It is my hope to return at the earliest opportunity to such happy hours.

Captain Joyce has proven to be a steady choice for the men. He sends his kindest of regards and to Madame Labiche. Oxy, too, asks to be remembered to you and Cordelia.

What news of your father and brothers? Write and tell me all and of your sweet self.

My warmest affections to your mother and sister. It is a trying time for good ladies to whom the reins of responsibility have been passed.

Ever affectionately yours,
Patrick O'Malley

THIRTY-NINE

Louisiana Boys
Army of Northern Virginia
Via Richmond, Virginia
12th April 1862

My darling Kizzie,
Already I am missing you, your silken purse, your
sheltered cove.

Here, I am one of the boys, a 'Johnny Reb'.

The only fear is in being wounded. Death is not a
fear – I will be dust to dust like the rest. But hospital
and the Protestant doctors! They dislike to touch us
Irish anyway! What of a perverted Papist like me?

But I should not talk like this when all my thoughts
are of you . . . and your fond breasts and steaming
nights in New Orleans. And you, sweet Kizzie, tossing
and turning to the heat with no soothing hand or
cooling lips.

Patrick asks me about 'my Kizzie' in the same way
he talks about 'his Emmeline'. He is forever writing to
her, of the days of splendour . . . and the magnolias
. . . and music . . . and the lips he has not yet kissed.
I am polite, agree with him, without revealing too

174

much of days of a thousand kisses . . . and lips –
unspoken of. I think he would be shocked to learn
how gloriously free I have been to taste whole joys in
you. And now I lay to sleep and think on them.
Write and write and write.
Your darling Johnny Reb,
Oxy

FORTY

Dear Mr O'Malley,

Your much sought-for letter received amidst great excitement. Cousin Constance was visiting and I trust you did not mind my reading to her the parts not intimate to you and I. She and Cordelia so begged me.

The gardens miss you and the magnolias – and other flowers too!

Of Father and my dear brothers there is no news yet. Perhaps they, like you, are marching, marching. Mother has taken the reins of running Versailles very admirably and to the surprise of all has succeeded wonderfully, following father's written instructions. She has some trouble with Cupid, who so impudently spoke that 'the Mistress could never be her Master'. Mother, to her credit, did not fail in administering the required remedy to the girl. She has now accepted that Mother is both Mistress and Master.

Cordelia enquires after you and Mr Joyce and Mr Moran.

We ladies send our affections to you all, who are our gallant protectors.

I am endeavouring to knit. It is tiresome but we hear reports that our army is short on socks.

I shall await hearing from you every day.

Emmy

Patrick, marvelling at the postal service, was in his element. The men spent much of their free time writing letters to loved ones. It was their lifeline to a previous life, a world once known – loved-ones, now framed in larger, more longed-for relief by the twin magnifiers of time and distance. But it was a retreating world – it retreating from them, they retreating even further from it.

A letter from home halted that retreat, reversed it momentarily. He wondered if, as war proceeded, railroad tracks ripped from the ground, deliveries intercepted, the old safe world would even further retreat.

For now, though, he was grateful. Grateful that the old world – the world of Emmeline, the girl he loved – had been delivered to his hand.

FORTY-ONE

Bourbon Street
New Orleans
Confederate States of America
17th April 1862

My darling Rebel,
    Your letter excited such thoughts in me; I
immediately went to my room. There, it being a hot
day, I unshifted all clothing and stood naked at my
window to catch the breeze of Bourbon Street, while
again I read your letter. Then lay on my pillow,
putting your soft words to my body, imagining the
slender hand pressed against the page now pressed to
me. Now I lie on it but it is flat, unmounded – no
Oxy Moran!
    A page is such a flimsy imposter.
    On the street I hear the cries calling up to me . . .
    'Watermelon! Watermelon! Red to the rind! Juss eat
the melon and pree . . . serve the rind.'
    And the vendors, 'Belles calas! . . . Belles calas!
Rice fritters! Rice fritters! Tou chou! Tou chou! Tou
chou! All hot! All hot! All hot!'
    And I am remembering. Eating the sounds . . . and

178

remembering. And I have a present for you . . . and within it a secret.

Do not think of me in this state . . . you will be unfit for marching!

Your best-kept secret,

Kizzie . . . tou chou, tou . . .

P.S. Today I printed out a prayer in my best hand and pinned it in the church, that the pestilence might fall on the Yankees as a sign from God of His intention to save New Orleans.

P.P.S. God and I are at odds. I thought Him merciful. That He would not send us General Butler and yellow fever at the same time!

FORTY-TWO

Patrick saw the Bluecoat pitch forward and fall.

It seemed he only needed to point his gun. Not even squeeze the trigger and they would fall. As if he hadn't shot them, just aimed the intent at them. He marvelled at the sighting scope on his rifle. It made a sharpshooter invincible. Giving the enemy nowhere to hide.

Just as if the Yankee was stood in front of him. Waiting.

Patrick could not decide how to choose to which of the enemy he would send his singing bullet. An awkward movement which attracted his attention; an upright runner; or one crouching too low, trying to escape his notice. Whatever notion took him at the time. *He* was the arbiter of death . . . and its dispenser.

He always tried for the heart. To make it a quick dispatch. Sometimes, unwittingly, another Yankee stood up and took the shot, sometimes a jerk of the body over uneven ground, an angle of flight changed and he would miss the heart, shatter a shoulder instead, or a man's throat.

The words of Emeritus Labiche drummed through his head: 'I pray that this Southern rifle may bring tears from many a Northern mother before this thing is over!' Emmeline's father would be proud of him. Patrick was exhilarated, brimming with the destruction he was wreaking, stopping only when his barrel, hot from death, burned his hand and he could no longer hold it. Then, he would fall to the ground at the base of the tree on which he was leaning his musket. Then the whining minié balls of the enemy would harmlessly thud into the tree bark. They, too, had their sharpshooters but *he* was untouchable. Now, with his barrel cooled, he was ready again.

'The colour bearers,' Stephen had instructed. 'Lower the colours and you will lower morale.'

He must not think so much on everything, he reminded himself. Only concentrate on the job at hand. A fresh wave of Federals pushed forward, Stars and Stripes to the fore. Patrick tried to swing his rifle around but the fork of the tree where he rested his musket was narrow and would not allow it. Casting all caution to the wind he shinned the tree to the next level. 'Thwack.' A minié ball struck his knapsack, another so close he thought the hair on his forehead singed. He collapsed down to earth again and slowly edged upwards along the trunk of the tree.

A boy, carrying the flag of his country, entered Patrick's vision. For a moment Patrick hesitated, then pulled the trigger. He saw the staff of the Union rise upwards like a prayer, slowly somersault on itself and then fall, banner downwards into the Confederate mud of Virginia. A great cheer went up from the Louisianians but before it had subsided, the enemy banner was again aloft. Once more he sighted the bearer. This time a slow moving, red-faced infantryman – a family man. He could not think of that, Patrick told himself and, letting his sight drift momentarily, mistakenly sent a bullet to the man's head, instead of his heart.

Then, thinking of Oxy, Patrick scanned for his own flag. He rammed his cheek against the sweaty stock of the gun, closed one eye and rotated the sights through the Confederate lines. With what relief he spotted Oxy, somewhat adrift from the colour party, struggling to get back to his small band of men. Patrick relaxed, dropped to his knees, exhausted from the noise and the heat and the feverish excitement of the kill.

Then it was all over, a Rebel charge had repelled the Union troops, who 'skedaddled, tails between their legs all the way back to Boston,' Oxy reckoned.

Stephen who, from his big white charger, had led his command gallantly praised them both. Oxy, 'for our colours never once being soiled' and Patrick for his 'unerring eye for Yankees.'

FORTY-THREE

Louisiana Infantry
Army of Northern Virginia
near Richmond, Virginia
3rd May 1862

Dearest Emmeline,

Thank you for yours of the twenty first inst.

It is perfectly all right for you to reveal portions of my letter to Cordelia and your cousin. I know you are discreet beyond virtue.

We had our first engagement and Captain Joyce said I have an unerring eye for Yankees. Indeed we sent them skedaddling northwards.

This war will be a short season and we shall soon return victorious to New Orleans. Will you come there? No matter what size the gathering you will stand out – like the morning star over the Mississippi. Hurry the day when I will see your dancing eyes and hear the sweet notes of your voice. My respects to Cordelia and your mother. War changes all things when even ladies are forced to be the steering hand.

Captain Joyce and Mr Moran, as ever, convey cordial wishes to all the ladies.

Please write again soon and tell me of your father and dear brothers.

Your ever affectionate,

Patrick O'Malley

Later, after he had sealed the letter, Patrick withdrew the book from his knapsack, leafed through it. *Love Elegies and Holy Sonnets*. His mind ever occupied by thoughts of Emmeline, he was drawn to the former. A page oft-opened it seemed, presented itself.

> Twice or thrice had I lov'd thee,
> Before I knew thy face or name;

It was the feeling Emmeline had stirred in him. He read the full poem. Then re-read it again, whispering the words. Sending them South to the vast wetlands and the magnolia blossoms of Louisiana.

Then he wrote it out word for word in a new letter to Emmeline. But he would save this one, send it after the first letter. Surprise her with the poem.

FORTY-FOUR

Camp life seemed to revolve completely around two things: Food – and how there was never enough of it; Time – and how there was always too much of it.

Initially, time – like last year's snow – evaporated in the thrill of the great adventure on which they were all embarking. The new grey uniforms, the rations, the guns, bayonets and all the accoutrements of war occupied their minds and their time. Then too there was a getting-to-know one's fellow soldiers – a motley crew of swamp diggers, shopkeepers, bakers and butchers; Germans, Poles, French, Creoles, a wayward Welshman or two . . . and the Irish. The latter came from the four provinces of Ireland and the fifth province – America, both north and south. Fighting for as many different reasons as there were fingers on their hands.

'Adventure' . . . 'Money' . . . 'To "see the elephant".'

'For the Republic and agin' the Nativists.'

'To keep the niggers down south!'

'To raise an army when this war is over and take British Canada.'

'The New England girls is too uppity – the Dixie girls more fun.'

Or even, 'I just "jined" up.'

*

185

In Patrick's own group along with Oxy and himself was an O'Toole from Oranmore in County Galway, who quickly earned the sobriquet of 'Orator', and with good cause. For as he himself said, 'At forty paces I could talk the hind leg off Lincoln's jackass, without Abe himself or the poor beast ever knowing it.'

'Recruited in Ireland – a gun put in me hand when they got me to America' was how he 'was jined up!'

The Orator had a view on everything: the war; its real causes; how it could be won – if they'd only listen to him. Generals who had gout had not escaped his rheumy eye and the Orator could even recount how the alligator was once native to Ireland and brought over to America by Saint Brendan from the Allihies in Kerry, hence the origins of the first part of its name.

Then there was 'Mother of Sorrows' from Dublin's Liberties, 'christened as a child by the name of Mick Liddy!' No sentence escaped Mick Liddy's lips but it invoked God's Mother at some stage before it was finished.

'If the Mother of Sorrows looked down on us now what would she think? All this killin'. I'm killed meself too – the humidity is killin' me – not a breath. An' as well, I'm soaked through with that drizzly mist – it's very wettin'. An' if I put on me oilskins the backs of me trousers gets soaked on account o' the drops of rain. O' course I'm not thinkin' straight – I should've stayed in the tent . . . but on a day like this with the smell o' the wet on the canvas and them Germans steamin' beside me, I'm scuppered altogether on account of the air an' I won't sit down in a tent neither, on account of I get *agoraphobia* an' I have to get outside again, in the air. It's a terrible thing – that *agoraphobia*.'

The Germans – Himmel and Gimmel – brothers fresh off the boat from 'Lutherland' as Mother of Sorrows called it, hadn't two words of English to rub together. Fine buxom lads they were, 'corn-fed like Virginia chickens, with heads like batterin' rams on them,' the Orator said.

'Great men to have at the gates of Washington!'

FORTY-FIVE

When Patrick could get clear of them without attracting too much comment from the Orator or Mother of Sorrows about the Creole girls, he would again read the book that Stephen had gifted them. Now he pulled the book from his knapsack. He had not heard from Emmeline in response to the poem he had sent but was sure it would be acceptable to her, convey his deepest feelings. Now he read 'To His Mistress Going to Bed'.

> Licence my roving hands, and let them go,
> Behind, before, above, between, below,
> Oh my America, my new found land

This one he wouldn't be sending to Emmeline. He showed it to Oxy. 'Donne didn't put a tooth in it. Can you imagine sending such-like to a lady?'

'I can,' Oxy answered him and asked permission to transcribe it for sending to Kizzie.

FORTY-SIX

Louisiana Boys
Army of Northern Virginia
24th April

My darling girl,
    You are a bold letter writer.
    Imagine if General Butler, thinking you are a spy,
should open it – it would surely unhorse him!
    I go into the tall woods to read your letters. Press
against a firm bark so I should not faint. It is impossible
to read you in company – and have such thoughts.
    Your gift I held to my face – the silken foulard that
touched you . . . the last lingering of your scent . . .
the secret within its folds. Now, beneath my grey-
trousered garb it gilds my skin, as it once did yours. I
am a soldier in silk! I hear the cries of the heaving
street as you write them . . . and mixed with them
your cries . . . like the cry of the heaving sea.
    This from Patrick's book (I do not think he sends
such lines to Miss Emmeline).

    Full nakedness, all joys are due to thee.
    As souls unbodied, bodies unclothed must be,

189

To taste whole joys . . .

Tomorrow, clothed we fight the Northerners. I am exhilarated by love and ready to shoot them!

Write and write and tell me of your innermost thoughts . . . and deeds.

Your darling Johnny Reb,

P.S. When watermelons get ripe send one in a letter.

FORTY-SEVEN

New Orleans, May 1862

Kizzie Toucoutou, like all the other women of New Orleans, was outraged.

General Benjamin F. Butler, the Yankee-appointed Governor of New Orleans, had announced himself and his new appointment forcefully. Firstly, by hanging a local man for desecrating the Union flag. The General had then set about confiscating the property of those citizens who refused to swear allegiance to that foreign flag, as Kizzie and New Orleanians at large regarded it.

Now, with General Order No 28, he had moved against Southern women.

As the officers and soldiers of the United States have been subjected to repeated insults from the women calling themselves ladies of New Orleans, it is ordered that hereafter when any female by word, gesture, or movement insult or show contempt for any officer or soldier of the United States she shall be regarded and held liable to be treated as a woman of the town, plying her avocation.

General Benjamin Butler

For Kizzie it was a move too far.

Butler indeed was a Beast, the name well merited. To call her and the other loyal women of the South 'women of the town plying their avocation', could only come from the lips of a man whose country had 'no gentlemen – just beasts in uniform,' she wrote to Oxy.

Kizzie was not going to take it lying down. To have Butler or his low seed, name her as a street woman. She would bide her time.

Word quickly spread through the French Quarter of an enterprising potter who was now selling chamberpots complete with General Butler's portrait on the base of the bowl. Trade was brisk for the new chamberpots, and Kizzie had to queue along with other women eager to 'baptise the Beast into a good Christian gentleman!'

Amusement ran high as, unknown to General Butler, Kizzie and the women were more loyal to the Confederate cause than even he suspected. The ever pragmatic Southern ladies were contributing to the front-line effort in more ways than by taking up their needles. The urine with which they would baptise Butler was also used as a raw ingredient from which to distil nitre for the manufacture of Confederate gunpowder.

'We piss on the Yankees in every way now!' a laughing woman in front of Kizzie, who had just collected her chamberpot, said with glee.

Kizzie's intent went further than that.

FORTY-EIGHT

My darling Oxy,

You will be proud of me.

Today, I was every bit as good a Johnny Reb as you are against the invading Yankees who have taken New Orleans, sacked our beautiful jewel and insulted its womenfolk. We do not talk to the Yankees as do the plantation 'ladies', saying the Yankees are 'so-called gentlemen'. We cross the street from their presence – it has an offensive odour. We spit at their arrogance. Now Beast Butler, their General, has made an order that any woman of New Orleans who insults his men is to be named a common streetwalker and can thus be imprisoned.

'*Soudard!*' I say to Butler and his 'men.'

Beneath my window today were six Northerners, loud-talking and of vulgar appearance. So, in keeping with our tradition of hospitality, I gave them that in which they were of most need – a good wash – with the full contents of my *pot de chambre*!

I am awaiting the knock that will summon me from here. Whomever that unfortunate Yankee be, captain or corporal, I will spit him with my *petit* dagger.

But when are you returning to me, *mon petit coeur d'artichaut*? Every day the pit of your absence grows deeper, the yawning ache wider, until now all is unstoppable pain. My mouth grows weary from no sweet kisses. My eyes grow dim with no light of passion. My ears, once alive to every stirring of your breath, are filled only with the sound of your no-voice. My skin, each pore, each soft and secret place, once moist with *sève d'amour*, is now an unquenchable thirst and I fear I shall be consumed by some insatiable fire. What if you should take an ignorant bullet – it deprive me of the pyramid of desire you have built up in me?

What then?

I could not live with such burnings. I would return to the Pontchartrain. Walk far out into its cooling waters. Sing its wild song – forever.

Oh, my Johnny Reb, I am *désolée* without you . . . *désolée* . . . *désolée*.

Je t'aime,
Kizzie

New Orleans
Confederate States of America
3rd June 1862

My darling O,
  You are my Omega, the last of all my desires, my
Ox, my fiery paradox. I miss you like the bayou
misses the moon, like the Mississippi its delta. I say
merde to war. What has it to do with me that you
have trousers, a flag and a *baionnette* of cold steel? I
am Kizzie Toucoutou . . . Tou chou! Tou chou! Tou
choucoutou . . . ! All hot . . . ! All hot . . . ! All hot!
  I am octoroon, only one-eighth not human – yet
still not worth dying for. War is *très terrible*. Men,
foolish things, substitute it for their *flèches de
l'Amour*, their 'little generals'!
  What is war to do with us women? I am so
frightened for you, my sweet O! My watermelon . . .
my *belles calas*! Love alone is worth dying for. War is
nothing – a *pistache*, a *praline*, a sugared almond.
Today I was angry at war, but not at you. You I love
. . . like a little pig loves mud. If only you had wings,
like a little pig, to fly to me.
  Your Konstant . . .
  K

P.S I am ripening the watermelon . . . 'til it is red to
the rind, for my O.

195

FORTY-NINE

The more Patrick read the poems of John Donne the more something began to form in his mind. As if the mystery of the poems was slowly unlocking itself to him. What finally sprung the lock was a long, longed-for letter from Emmeline.

'Mother manages things well with some small help from Cordelia and me – and letters from Father on how to conduct matters.

   In the evenings, I bring your most recent letter and place it beside me on the piano . . .'

Piano . . . ! Patrick had stopped, re-read the line. The piano . . . ! 'Place it . . . on the piano . . . !' he said aloud.

But it was a book . . . not a letter, on a piano! A similar volume to this book once left on a piano by his mother.

All night he lay awake turning over in his mind the poems he had read. And what of Stephen's motivation in giving him the book? Patrick sifted through the events leading to the disappearance of his mother.

Her parting letter. The words were stamped on his memory. 'I must leave your lives . . . and I pray forgiveness for the ruin I have brought upon them.'

What if the 'ruin' was not the business ruin, as they had

imagined, for which she had so abjectly blamed herself? He had often thought it not a strong enough reason for the finality of her leaving. Lavelle had argued with him that the strain on her mind would have produced such drastic action, illogical to all save herself!

What if the 'ruin' was of a different, darker nature? Of a nature that, if revealed, would indeed bring ruin – and shame – upon her family?

The thought that his mother had had an illicit affair with Stephen now began to take root in Patrick's mind. The same Stephen Joyce, first his father's comrade-in-arms and then Lavelle's compatriot. Finally, his mother's lover.

It had to be Stephen. It was all so simple, so clear . . . so maddeningly clear. The book in his possession was his mother's. Stephen must have had some meeting with her since her disappearance – and all this time he had kept silence.

Angrily, book in hand, Patrick went to Stephen's tent. He would have it out with the man now before tomorrow's skirmish.

'Is this book related to my mother?' Patrick demanded, brandishing it at his commanding officer.

'Yes, it is, Patrick!' Stephen Joyce answered, no hint of surprise in his voice. 'I thought you would have discovered the truth sooner!'

'You and she were lovers behind Lavelle's back?' the younger man accused.

'Yes, Patrick, and I am sorry for that deception,' his captain answered.

'Sorry?' Patrick fired back at him. 'You've kept up the pretence all this time – New Orleans, Versailles, here in battle! You know where she is, you've seen her – the book!' Patrick charged, shaking the proof, before the other man's face.

'No, I haven't, Patrick!' Stephen answered strongly. 'We have had no contact since . . . since before. I am as much concerned as to her whereabouts as you are. This is not her book. There is another copy which she still holds, which once was mine.'

'How can I believe you, Stephen?' Patrick challenged.

'It is true . . . by the honour of the South it is true.'

He went on to tell Patrick how, recognising their transgression, he and Ellen had decided to never meet again – 'More sorrowed than I had ever previously known.'

Patrick said nothing, a look of utmost derision masking his face.

'On the eve of tomorrow's battle, Patrick, I ask your forgiveness. I have dishonoured you all, not least your mother's good name.'

'Live with it, Stephen . . . and die with it!' Patrick retorted angrily. The betrayer would get no easy forgiveness from him.

Back in his own tent, he failed to find sleep.

So, he was right about her. Stephen had made a full confession. He didn't blame the man entirely. It wasn't the first time his mother had betrayed them.

She had left them as children, with their father not cold in the grave. Fled to America. Found herself a 'fancy man' – Lavelle – before coming back for them. Then, cuckolded Lavelle for Stephen Joyce. God knows in what corner of America she now was with her latest 'beau'.

She was alive, of that Patrick was sure. Oh, yes – and he and Lavelle like fools traipsing every hill and hollow looking for her. Lavelle, like a father to him in the end. He wondered if by now Lavelle knew her story?

'He's better off deluded,' Patrick muttered to himself, knowing that Lavelle would criss-cross America to find her.

When his first furlough came up, Patrick would seek out Lavelle, tell him.

He would not immediately go south.

Emmeline would understand.

FIFTY

Out of the corner of his eye Patrick saw Stephen's big white, rear on its haunches. He turned his head fully to see the red patch spread out over the stretched white coat of the animal. Then horse and rider collapsed. Nearby, a bluecoated infantry sergeant who had fired the shot also saw the Rebel captain go down.

Patrick, reading the sergeant's mind, followed him with his sights as the Yankee moved through the fray towards Stephen. His captain was somewhere on the ground but Patrick could see only the kicking frenzy of the dying horse. Then, deliberately, he turned his musket away from the unfolding scene, seeking instead his original target, Union colour bearers. He spoke out loud his sharpshooter's instructions – Stephen Joyce's instructions.

'The colour bearers – bring down the flag!'

Beyond that Patrick had no other duty to Stephen Joyce.

Now, in his sights, Patrick had found the flag of the enemy. He dropped his aim down along the flagstaff to the hands which so ferociously gripped the Northern banner. Then, he followed the line of the arm to the curve of the man's shoulder, slightly adjusting his aim the eight inches or so to the cavity of the colour bearer's chest. A pressure on the trigger and the flag carrier would fall.

Afterwards Patrick couldn't reason it out. Why he had relented. Turned instead back to the writhing horse and the Bluecoat sergeant, bayonet raised for a fallen Secesh captain. Patrick had fired before he knew it. Didn't much care if his aim was true. The Yankee's mouth was opened wide in the killing yell, as he gathered himself to deliver Stephen Joyce of this earth. Mesmerised, Patrick watched, his bullet drawn by the curdling sound, until it tore the man's mouth apart – transforming the death-dealing yell into a muffled cry. Then Patrick put the big white out of its misery.

In the respite after battle Stephen came to him.

'You saved my life, Patrick – I am in your debt . . .' He paused before asking the question . . . 'It must have been hard?'

'It was,' Patrick answered.

His captain made no reply but turning to go, turned back.

'When I was down . . . facing my Maker, my last thoughts were not of salvation but of your mother. Without right or hope have I loved her . . . since you were a boy.'

FIFTY-ONE

When, after the battle, they had returned to camp, the normally easy-to-hear chirpiness of Oxy was noticeably missing. Immediately Patrick was concerned. He searched the camp and, not finding him, had gone back to the site of the day's encounter. Many from both sides sought out the dead and dying. Some, for darker reasons than charity for their souls and a decent burial. But for boots, items of clothing and the contents of cumbersome knapsacks.

Stretcher bearers, blood-soaked doctors and priests abounded – and bonneted nuns. But of Oxy there was no sign. Bodies of the near dead were piled high on stretchers and carts, like great bloodied hams from a slaughter house. North, South . . . it didn't matter now, all lumped together, sinew to sinew, bone to bone, brothers in blood. Now that the mutilation of each other had ceased, the limbless young men were no longer soldiers. No longer bringers of death – now just close to it. Mortal after all.

Patrick prayed that Oxy had been taken to hospital – even a Union one. If Oxy were dead he would have been left on the bloodstained field to be buried by his own side. But while the dead were collected each by their Confederate and Union comrades, the wounded sometimes were not and went to the hospitals of the enemy.

And the wounded in their death-hour,
Speak of their loved ones' woes,
Nearer drew each other,
Till they were no longer foes.

The song 'After the Battle', a morbid favourite of the
futility of war and the commonality of man, ran through
Patrick's head. If Oxy were still alive he could even now be
among their foes. If so Patrick would likely never see his
friend again until this dread war was over.

But at least there would be hope.

At roll call the following morning a pall of death hung over
the camp. The Yankees had exacted a fierce toll. Where once
there were fully-fleshed lines of hardened campaigners and
eager boys all wanting to see action, now those who remained
stood together like rows of gapped hedges.

'Gimmel von Bingen?' the sergeant called.

'Ja!' Von Bingen the elder stepped forward.

'Himmel von Bingen?' elicited no such movement in the
ranks. 'Himmel von Bingen?' The sergeant called louder. These
damn Germans didn't even know their own names.

Then a voice rose, soft, faraway as the Fatherland, 'Himmel
isht not here – mein brüder isht gone.'

The silences grew shorter then, after each missing name.
Such were their diminished numbers that the sergeant now
called each name but once, then drew a line through it.

One other name Patrick knew would not be answered
was . . .

'Oxy Moran?'

Now, today, Patrick listened as the sergeant's voice droned
on, beaten down by the grim litany which he was reciting.

'Moran, Oxy?' Silence.

'O'Hagan, Patrick?' Silence.

202

'O'Sullivan, Michael?' Silence.

'Polanski, Wrad . . .' The sergeant struggled with the name. 'Polanski?' Silence.

'Roberts, Nathan?' Silence.

'Stroud, Elias?' Silence,

'Tibbetts, Hiram?' Silence.

'Zwaieur, Hans Christian?' Silence.

Of the hundred and three who went into battle that morning less than forty answered.

'This war'll be the death of us yet,' Mick Liddy later complained. 'We'll be all kilt before we get home . . . on account of the lice . . . big as buck rabbits . . . Oh, Mother o' Divine Sorrows, they're after 'atin' the arse o' me!'

'Knock them off with your hand, Mick – sure you're not a child!' Orator O'Toole advised, casting his eyes up to heaven, then across at Patrick.

'I can't knock 'em off on account they'll fall down the leg o' me trousers and into me boots . . . and get in between me toes, and then how will I keep up with yis wid all this marchin'?' the lice-ridden Dublinman asked.

'Well, what if they go for your goolies, Mick?' The Orator couldn't resist it.

'For the love o' the Mother o' Sorrows, Orator, don't be sayin' that! It's no laughin' matter and amn't I after losin' that horse comb I got from the Germans for getting them outta me hair. It's a shockin' awful place to live in this America. Ever'thin' 'atin' you all the time.'

'Aye, America . . . and this shockin' awful war that's 'atin' *it* . . . and all that's in it,' Patrick said savagely, mimicking the man . . . and remembering the roll call.

FIFTY-TWO

Three days later Oxy was marched into camp in chains, a heavy block of wood hanging from his neck.

'A deserter. The Irish . . . always skedaddlin' home.' The word ran through camp like wildfire.

'Oxy . . . !' Patrick said, when he reached his disgraced friend. 'What happened?'

Oxy, bending under the weight of the block which hung from him, struggled to look up at Patrick. 'I just couldn't bear it any longer without Kizzie. I'm sorry . . .' he replied, downcasting his eyes again.

He looked so dejected, so unlikely a soldier to send out to battle, with his fair skin and his soft, troubled eyes. But then there were many like him . . . and who didn't desert.

Patrick was highly concerned. With the amount of recent desertions, the Confederate army, already outnumbered, was still haemorrhaging numbers. It was a serious problem, Patrick knew . . . demanding a serious remedy.

Death.

He had to act quickly, enlist the aid of the chaplain, Father O'Grady . . . and their captain, Stephen.

Patrick went first to Stephen.

Immediately he entered his presence, Patrick could see that Stephen was angry. 'Sergeant Moran has not just disgraced himself, Patrick, but his regiment, his flag . . . and the whole Irish nation!' was the captain's response to the question still yet in Patrick's mind. He asked it anyway.

'Stephen . . . Oxy was foolhardy . . . in love. He didn't go over to the other side, like many. He has been a brave soldier in every battle, shirking no danger in carrying the flag. Will you plead clemency . . . imprisonment . . . but not the ultimate sanction?'

Stephen paced up and down in front of him, hands clasped behind his back, thinking. For Patrick, it held out some hope. He turned to Patrick then, looking solidly at him, the dark spot under his eye, unforgiving. He spoke. 'There are many in love, Patrick . . . many married and with family. It is for those we love, we fight. It is for the freedom of love and of family that we put duty first . . . and push aside all thoughts of love . . . for the time when we are at war. Only by this sacrifice will we have a lasting victory for love.'

He paused at some thought, before continuing. 'Love and sacrifice have long been constant bedfellows,' he said sombrely, then drew himself out of whatever reverie he had entered. Stood square in front of Patrick.

'It's out of my hands now, Patrick – it's higher up! The generals must put a stop to this!' was the cold comfort Patrick finally received.

And the generals wasted no time.

Within weeks, the court martial followed. Oxy was found guilty of desertion from duty and a sentence of execution by firing squad was handed down.

Patrick was frantic with apprehension at what must now follow. With Stephen's permission, he rode to Richmond with Father O'Grady, seeking a suspension of the death penalty. The general was polite, short of time. He had 'a war to run,' he brusquely told them but he would listen to their appeal.

By means of a compromise Father O'Grady suggested that,

'A fearful punishment be administered on Mr Moran . . . but less than the absolute one.'

They left, the general's ominous words still ringing in their ears, 'This is war, gentlemen. Many will want to turn their backs on it, seek the comfort of home and family. Already the Union troops outnumber us. We must send a clear message to would-be deserters.'

It was almost an echo of what Stephen had told Patrick. Yet Father O'Grady held out some faint hope, something about the 'Gruffness of generals and the goodness of God.'

Patrick wondered how God's goodness would fare with this particular general.

They had not long to wait. Within a week the killing letter came. Their threadbare hopes had not been sustained.

Sergeant Oxy Moran, stripped of all honour, would, as determined, face a firing squad of his former comrades . . . and be shot dead by them.

To his horror, Patrick – as a sharpshooter – was one of those selected to carry out the fatal duty.

The night before the appointed day, Oxy, having been granted a final request, sent for Patrick.

When Patrick arrived at the small but sturdy wooden structure which held him, Oxy was sitting there, still in leg-irons, rocking himself gently and singing a love song to his Creole lass. He continued, unaware of Patrick it seemed, until he had sung out the whole song. The same one he had sung that time two short years back when they had seen the Pontchartrain for the first time, stood together on its wondrous shores. Who was to have known then what life would hold for them . . . or death?

'So fare thee well my Creole girl,
I never will see you no more,
But I'll ne'er forget your kindness,

In the cottage by the shore;
And at each social gathering,
A flowing glass I'll raise,
And I'll drink a health to my Creole girl,
And the lakes of Pontchartrain.'

His song over Oxy just sat there, still rocking himself, the sping of life already gone from him.

'Oxy . . .' Patrick said gently. 'Is there any message . . . anything?'

Oxy looked at his friend, that strange smile crossing his face. He did not seem dejected by the thought of death. Resignation to it, Patrick thought, or something more . . . in that smile . . . a relief. In a different circumstance, Patrick might even have considered his friend's face to hold a certain serenity . . . a happiness. It puzzled him. Now Oxy was quietly instructing him regarding his last wishes . . . what Patrick must do. He listened attentively as Oxy spoke.

'Write to Kizzie . . . that I died . . . the Bonnie Blue Flag proudly aloft, her name on my lips and forever in my heart.' He stopped, looked closely into Patrick's face. 'She is the most perfect of human creatures. To have loved her, even briefly, was my highest point on this earth. I bring her with me in the final moment.'

He drew back a little then.

'Write also to my father back home . . . I was always a disappointment to him . . . the last of seven girls . . . he always wanted a boy. But he will be proud now that I have fought for my country . . . for America. He loved America. It was ever a vision in his mind. "A great place for young men," he always said. I suppose it is. Patrick?' Oxy reflected. 'It will be hard on my mother, so send prayers along with my love. It is always hard on mothers . . . always.'

'I will, Oxy . . . I will . . . everything you ask, Oxy . . . and . . .' Patrick hesitated but there was no way now of avoiding it. 'They've ordered . . . me . . .'

207

'Yes, I know, dear Patrick. I know . . .' Oxy interrupted. 'The sentry told me . . . but I am not unhappy and you must do your duty. You are a true shot and a true friend . . . so despatch me quickly. Aim for the heart . . . here . . .' Oxy said, taking Patrick's hand, putting it over his heart, holding it there, making sure that Patrick felt the full roundness. Nevertheless, it took Patrick a moment to realise the implication of what was happening. Of what Oxy was doing, what his friend was now telling him, face again close to his.

'Now you know . . . at last!'

As the full import of this startling revelation hit him, Patrick instinctively withdrew his hand from Oxy's breast.

Oxy let it go, smiling that smile at him. 'It's all right, Patrick, you couldn't have known – much less accepted it.' Then he laughed. 'You should see your face now, Patrick O'Malley! I suppose I owe you an explanation . . . and an apology.'

Patrick was truly shocked. He had never suspected. Oxy's gentleness, the strange smile, fairness of complexion, his privacy about his person. It all made sense now. Final sense, in these final hours of his life.

The stories, the vague stories about his childhood, his father . . . Oxy being the long-hoped-for son. How he had been so cleverly . . . and so cruelly named. A contradiction – an oxymoron – this boy-girl! His secret revealed only to his one true love, Kizzie Toucoutou. Part of Patrick recoiled from such a notion that the girl, forced to live out a man's role, should at last have found happiness, with another woman. His mind fought to come to terms with the notion of what supreme happiness it must have been for Oxy to have deserted, to be prepared to die to reach his Kizzie, at last fulfilled.

Patrick's thoughts were a jumble of images, remembrances. Oxy had been such a firm and true friend. But Oxy as a youth, a man. Not as a girl, a woman. How could he not have seen it, sensed it? All had changed. Changed terribly in this, Oxy's last day on earth. Oxy – his friend. Everything had changed but nothing had changed.

He took Oxy's hands. 'Everything is as it always was, Oxy,' he said. 'And always will be.'

'Thank you, Patrick.' Then Oxy, in that old earnest way, pressed on Patrick, 'You're not to tell them, Stephen, the others. Promise me! I don't wish to be spared because of what I am – it would ruin everything. I always only wanted to be a good soldier, make Kizzie proud.'

'I promise you, dear friend,' Patrick replied and he sat holding her hands as the young woman, bereft of all hope of ever seeing her Kizzie, spoke again of her Creole girl on the shores of the Pontchartrain.

Far, far from the cruel shamrock shore that had shaped her life.

Then sent her to America to die.

The following morning Oxy was taken to a clearing in the camp. All were summoned and gathered round in a square with one end vacant for the condemned man. The marching bands struck a drum-laden dirge as Oxy was led out. The charge was read and the musket of each of the twelve-strong firing squad loaded by the sergeant. One musket, as per tradition, received no ball. Patrick prayed he wouldn't be the one; he wanted a ball to speedily take Oxy out of the miserable half-life his friend had known.

Then it was time. Rifle to shoulder. Patrick levelled his line of sight at the place where Oxy had placed his hand the previous day.

'Make ready!'

Patrick tried not to imagine how his bullet would shatter the soft breast, the beating heart beneath. In his mind instead, Oxy's smile . . . that strange, radiant smile.

'Aim!'

Patrick held his breath, focusing his mind on the white square of cloth over Oxy's heart, which was their target. His aim would be true . . . like a true friend. At the 'Fire!'

command, Oliver Xavier Moran smiled at the world and held out her chest like a true man and soldier should. For a moment, Patrick imagined Oxy and Kizzie in their last tender embrace before his bullet sped home through the perfectly formed breast, stilling all life in the trembling heart.

Patrick closed his eyes hard against his rifle as Oxy fell backwards into the open coffin over which the girl had been straddled.

Within moments it was all over.

Then he, along with the rest of the assembled troops, dispersed back to their various camps, the marching bands each now striking a merry tune to lift the spirits of the men for war.

Stephen had consoled with him over Oxy but Patrick, grim with his own thoughts, had no time for such words.

Immediately, he wrote to Kizzie, telling her how nobly had Oxy carried the standard of the South and upheld the honour of Southern womanhood in all his actions. How, in his dying moments he had spoken only of his love for her, departing this earth, her name formed on his lips.

Then he wrote to Oxy's father, of how his 'son' had ennobled the name of Ireland in answering the call for freedom, how he was a son of whom any father could be proud. To each he sent a lock of Oxy's hair and to Kizzie the fine silk handkerchief into which she had embroidered a delicate kiss in the form of the letter X.

Then Patrick wrote telling Emmeline and expressing his own fears that he, too, might not see her again.

FIFTY-THREE

'It's a shockin' awful thing, Patrick,' Mother of Sorrows said. 'A shockin' awful thing to see one cut down in the flower of youth. That poor boy would be better off if he'd never set foot outside of the *ould dart*. Mixin' with them quarter-grained *hoc-troons* is not a good thing for an Irishman: not a good thing for a young innocent Irish fella. An' then him havin' such a quare name. Oxy . . . what were the parents thinkin' at all? Ah, he was a shockin' nice lad. God rest him. A shockin' nice lad. You'll miss him – an' you havin' to be the one to put a bullet in him. I wouldn't a' liked that at all meself. An' then not knowing whether I got the loaded gun or what. Lyin' awake thinking about it, not gettin' any sleep. That *insombia* is not a good thing for a battle. But then too much sleep can make you slow. You could collect a bullet bein' slow. Maybe cash in your chips. What would you say, Patrick?'

Patrick wished Mother of Sorrows would just be quiet. The man could put talk out of fashion he had so much of it. Patrick himself was still in shock over Oxy's death – and the revelations leading up to it. He was also grappling with his own mixed emotions – his loyalty towards Lavelle; his once hero-worship of Stephen; and a bitterness towards his mother – and indeed for her being the cause of this very flux in his emotions.

211

Love was a dangerous and debilitating thing that it could exact such strange and punishing behaviour from human beings. There was Stephen and Lavelle whose lives his mother had burdened with such trouble. Yet they both loved her. She herself must have loved both of them . . . after her own kind of fashion.

Patrick couldn't fathom it. Emmeline was the sole object of his affections and would continue to be so. That he could entertain a notion of simultaneously loving someone else was beyond his comprehension, repulsive to him. Love was singular in its affection and then absolute in its singularity. To be 'in love' with one person *ipso facto* meant not to be in love with everyone, or anyone, else. The two were mutually exclusive. Then Emeritus Labiche, did he 'love' the young slave girl, Jewel? Yet he had branded her with an iron. Or did duty over-rule love? What then of Lucretia Labiche – her husband in every other respect dutiful to her? Duty did not exclude love nor did it include it. It was superior to love. Yet from where did duty itself derive – if not from love?

And Oxy and Kizzie? Who was to say that this was a lesser love because it was between two women? To ease his mind Patrick read from Donne's *Holy Sonnets*. 'Death be not proud . . . One short sleep past, we wake eternally, And death shall be no more, Death thou shalt die.'

Life and death he concluded, were much more simple concepts with which to grapple than love.

And more certain.

FIFTY-FOUR

The next day's fighting was the fiercest yet.

Stephen had exhorted his men to engage at close quarters. 'The bullet is foolish: the bayonet alone is wise.'

And so the Louisianians had foolhardily braved fusillade and cannonade alike in an attempt to rout the Yankees with steel. From his vantage point in the woods, Patrick observed the carnage exacted on his comrades.

At dusk the fighting stopped. From sheer exhaustion, Patrick thought. The exhaustion that sets on the soul from physical slaughter.

'Men were not made for this,' Orator O'Toole had concluded the previous night, as they chipped their teeth on biscuits and blackened them with coffee that 'you could trot a mouse on'.

'This is a rich man's war and a poor man's fight,' the Orator opined. 'All about cotton and commerce – neither of which will fatten our pockets. What do poor ignorant men like us want with killing poor ignorant men like them?'

'The Orator is right . . . that's what!' Mother of Sorrows joined in.

'Half o' the time I'm for shootin' them poor misguided Yankees an' half the time I'm sorry for them . . . I'm for them shootin' me! They're not Yankees neither, any more than we're Johnny Rebs. They're Micks and Paddies just like us – reddenin' the dust of Virginny. An' tomorrow again we'll be killin' our own . . . an' our own killin' us! Is it any wonder that our Mother in Heaven is a Mother o' Sorrows?'

Now, after today's savage encounter, Mother of Sorrows had not returned. Patrick and the Orator searched for him with lanterns but returned unsuccessfully. Before first light they went again, the pale moon declining, the morning star, Lucifer, rising.

They found him supported by a tree, his stomach shot through by a cannonball, worms already feasting in the open cavity. He stood there, as always, talking.

'Oh, lads, what took ye so long? The pain was shockin' at first but the Mother o' Sorrows looked down on me an' sent the worms,' he said, a ghoulish grin on his face. 'An' the little feckers eat the pain . . . God forgive me for cursin' – an' I goin' directly to meet Him! Look at them! Will ye look at them . . . havin' the time o' their lives, jigglin' an' wrigglin' . . . an' gorgin' themselves on Mick Liddy's vittles!'

'Mick!' Patrick said, 'we'll carry you back.'

But Mother of Sorrows put his hand out in front of him. 'No point in that, lads – sure it's only on account o' the ball I got that's holdin' me up, stuck to the back o' this tree, an' the lice only 'atin' the arse o' me. Everythin' in this damn country 'atin' a person. If it's not them *allygators* down in the swamps, it's the lice an' the greybacks . . . an' these slimy little bastards swimmin' round me stomach. But Mick Liddy, the Pride o' the Liberties, will have the last say on them yet. Oh, Mother o' Sorrows forgive me!' he said, casting his eyes to heaven.

Then, from his stomach he scooped out a handful of maggots. He shook them violently in his fist, goading them.

'Go on, ye little bastards – if ye're any good, go on an' *ate* me! Or Mick Liddy'll bite the bollix off o' ye.'

And with that he stuffed the maggots into his mouth and

214

viciously started to chew on them. Swallowing them back down into the place from where they had just come.

'Holy St Jesus . . . !' Orator O'Toole exclaimed 'Did you . . . ?'

Then another handful followed the first . . . and another until the chewing stopped and the mad delight faded from Mick Liddy's eyes.

Patrick, his stomach churning, had already sought refuge behind the tree to which the man had been impaled by the cannonball.

'Oh, Sweet Divine Jesus . . .' the Orator began, for once stymied for words. He blessed himself frantically.

'God help us all with this terrible war!'

FIFTY-FIVE

The day after they buried Mother of Sorrows, Patrick received a letter from Emmeline. She had obviously not received his concerning Oxy. Her letter greatly revived him.

While there was a general restlessness on the plantation with the slaves openly saying 'Lincoln is a comin',' her mother seemed to have found a new lease of life.

> Mother rises at six and tends to all things as if a man. Why she even gave a whipping to one of the kitchen boys who had overstepped his position.
>
> Father is expected soon. The *Picayune* reports regularly of his gallantry and dash. Always at the head of his troops – not like some other rear-guard generals.

Patrick read on.

> We have not received direct news from Lamarr and Lovelace for some time, but likewise believe them to be gallant in the saddle. Life here is incomplete without them. Sisters do miss loving brothers. And what of you, dearest Patrick . . . and the gallant Mr Joyce and Mr Moran? Every day, I am walking to my trees watching

for the first green bud to sprout, knowing that soon the blossoms must come . . . and you with them.

Daily too, I pray to the Lord who watches over all, to watch over you during this great unpleasantness.

Your ever-faithful and ever-waiting

Emmy

P.S. My glove, with its heart . . . is it yet unstained?

Three days later Patrick received another letter, edged in black. Recognising the handwriting, he unceremoniously tore it open.

Le Petit Versailles

Confederate State of Louisiana

25th June 1862

My dear Mr O'Malley,

I have the most terrible of news to bring you. I could not bear to send it earlier. My dearest, dearest Lamarr and my lovely Lovelace have been borne home as corpses.

It is too much.

Father, wounded though not sorely, accompanied the remains. Oh, it grieves me to say the word 'remains' after all they have been to me. Everything loving brothers could be. Showering their sister with sweet, sweet kisses. Nor did they, ever once, neglect their duty when vexatious times crossed our paths. Only caresses to a dear sister's forehead. It greatly wounded Mother, her baby boys taken on the tide of battle. Father said they were to the fore of every charge and died gloriously for the South and their sisters' honour.

There were two carriages with six plumed horses. To the front of each a brother's horse, riderless now with only dear Lamarr's and Lovelace's boots in the stirrups. But reversed as is the custom. Mother was magnificent despite her mourning weeds – a steadfast support to Father, who held his bearing throughout. The slaves set up a great wailing of grief that 'the young massas be comin' home no mo'!'

I cannot imagine how life will be now, without their daring – and the expeditions we undertook with them. I know that you and Captain Joyce and Mr Moran will be greatly, greatly grieved by this news. Two Yankee officers in the vicinity who also heard the news called to pay their kind respects to Mother. The slaves were greatly excited upon seeing them. Gentlemen both, they conducted themselves with all decorum in the presence of ladies. They begged permission to call again at a more convenient time and Mother assented.

I pray for you, dear Mr O'Malley, that the Lord may shield you in battle.

My mind is a blank and I cannot write further. I hope my letter has not left you too distraught.

As Ever,

Yours,

Emmy

He replied immediately, wishing he could be with her to offer even the smallest of consolations. For her to be the subject of two such losses was beyond all that he could imagine. He bore the news with heavy grief – such good comrades, such gallant soldiers, such brothers to loved sisters. That they died so gloriously in such a just cause, Patrick wrote, would, he hoped, be a comfort to their mother.

The clocks would now be stopped in the great house, the rooms draped in lavender, the mirrors in black to ward off evil spirits. Twin curls of hair – one turned east, one west – Patrick remembered, would be taken from Lovelace and Lamarr, framed forever in grieving oak.

Le Petit Versailles would be one giant mausoleum.

FIFTY-SIX

A week later, Patrick received yet another letter from Emmeline, enclosing a cutting from a New Orleans newspaper, the *Picayune*. First, he read the letter.

Le Petit Versailles
Confederate State of Louisiana
1st July 1862

Dear Mr O'Malley,

I am in receipt of your disturbing news regarding Mr Moran. The true circumstances were reported in New Orleans (enclosed) with details of another sad case – a woman from the French Quarter, of Mr Moran's acquaintance it seems. It is all such a regrettable affair, Mother says. That some should so dishonour us all, while others make the ultimate sacrifice for our freedom. Poor Cordelia no longer speaks of him. Not to dwell on such disagreeable matters, I am happy to relate that Father has already returned to the front and Mother once again amazes us all. She is ever occupied from morning to night cutting patterns for shirts and dresses for the domestic slaves. She regularly visits the fields and the Sugar

219

House and consults (when necessary only) with Mr Clinch on the state of the crop. Mr Clinch, it seems, resents Mother's growing knowledge.

Permissions for marriages among the slaves and new names for their many offspring take up more time. Cupid, the troublesome one, has recently produced a fine strong son. He will do well in the fields one day when this distasteful business is over and the Yankees skedaddle homewards to think again about setting foot where they do not belong, or are not welcome. Cupid, being unhusbanded, as they often are, Mother had then to find her a likely candidate, none of the blacks claiming responsibility for the girl's predicament. These domestic matters Mother keeps until evening time when the fieldwork is done. By midnight she is exhausted.

It is hard work being a man.

The Yankee officers, who are unlike the bulk of their race, have again visited and comfort us greatly in our continuing grief. One, a Captain Garnett, is from New England, the other is of higher rank, a Lieutenant Frothingham. For Yankees they are pleasant company and make only solicitous remarks of our well-being . . . and, indeed of Father's.

Mother often enquires as to Captain Joyce when I am writing to you. Please do make mention to him.

Finally, a solitary white glove here enquires as to the state of her sister glove – and if she will be returning soon?

As ever,
Emmy

With mounting apprehension at what he would find within it, Patrick then took hold of the newspaper article.

A Sad Case

The body of a young female not of high colour, was taken by boatmen from the waters of Lake Pontchartrain on Tuesday last. She is believed to be one Kizzie Toucoutou missing from the French Quarter of the town. The girl, a *femme de couleur libre*, was seen by observers to walk out from the shores of the lake into its deepest waters – and singing. Further intelligence reports her to have conducted a friendship with a Sgt O. Moran of the Louisiana infantry. A native of the Old Country, the same recently faced the ultimate judgement, for deserting his fellow countrymen in the hour of battle.

Patrick stared at the paper. He was desolate, fearing his letter had been the pre-emptor of Kizzie's death. She would have been heartbroken at the news of Oxy . . . but to . . . Patrick couldn't comprehend. He re-read the article, searching out any veiled reference to Oxy's true identity. There was none that he could fathom. At least Oxy was spared that. Patrick hoped beyond hope that the *Picayune*, or its reportage, would not find its way across the ocean to a struggling townland in Roscommon. Devastate it yet further with the news of Oxy's desertion . . . and his love for a dark-skinned woman of New Orleans.

He then read Emmeline's letter again. This time he observed her concerns, or lack of, for the tragedy of Oxy's and Kizzie's lives more evidently on the page.

As quickly, he forgave her. She, still grieving so over her beloved brothers.

FIFTY-SEVEN

Louisiana Infantry
Army of Northern Virginia
Near Richmond, Virginia
12th July 1862

My dearest Emmy,

I am sorry that, at this time of grieving, my news of Mr Moran so disturbed you and caused an upset to your mother and Cordelia.

I did not know of the Lake Pontchartrain tragedy. At Mr Moran's last request I had written to Miss Toucoutou. Despite what the papers report Mr Moran was a brave soldier. He led his colour group valiantly into many a hazardous breach with no thought to his own safety. The ultimate sanction was a harsh example to those entertaining similar thoughts. This he faced with undaunted courage, forgiving me my part, by duty, in the final act to his life.

Indeed, dearest Emmy, thoughts of you and when again I might see you sometimes bring me to think of throwing aside my gun. However, I could never put love above duty, only consider it.

It is a consoling thought that your foreign visitors

display only civility and solicitude, being in the company of such ladies as are found at Versailles.

As to your solitary glove – there is here another, close to my heart, ever-pining to be reunified with yours.

Yours faithfully,

Patrick O'Malley

P.S. Captain Joyce sends all compliments to your mother as always.

FIFTY-EIGHT

Le Petit Versailles
Confederate State of Louisiana
19th July 1862

Dear Mr O'Malley,
Your letter unsettled me so, that you would ever
even consider putting your affections for me above
those of duty to your country. My country and I are
inseparable. Mother says that this is the reason our
brave boys go to battle – to preserve inviolate our
beautiful South and the honour of Southern ladies.
There is not one without the other.

'Love' would not be love (of the higher order) were
you to yield to such thoughts. A lady could not
encourage such a debasing of love's virtues. Nor
could she entertain a gentleman – for he would cease
to be one – who would present such a jaded offering.
(Such as might appeal to those personages in New
Orleans whom General Butler declares no longer
'ladies'!)

But this is not to chide you – for you are ever the
object of all my affections. I know that you, like my
brave Lamarr and Lovelace would make the final

224

sacrifice if called upon – in the name of those you love and who love you dearly.

As always,

Emmy

P.S. Mother sends respects to Captain Joyce.

LAVELLE

FIFTY-NINE

Irish Brigade, Army of the Potomac, Virginia, 1862

Lavelle looked every bit the part. Every bit the part of the
beau idéal of a soldier in his Union-blue uniform. The breeches
came up a bit short on the ankle, for his full height of six
feet and one inch. But he was pleased how the jacket stretched
comfortably over his broad-shouldered frame.

The kepi – the French military cap with the horizontal
peak, which would keep the sun from his sharpshooter's eyes
– sat square on Lavelle's head, accentuating the raw-boned
structure of his face. The eyes themselves gave nothing away.
Would fix on a thing, take it all in . . . work it all out . . .
and then move on. From under his fighting cap, a sheaf of
wheaten-coloured hair swept back over a firm but not unkind
forehead.

He checked his kit issue, calling aloud each item in turn.

'2 flannel overshirts . . . present and correct!

2 woollen undershirts . . . present and correct!

1 pair white cotton drawers . . . present . . . not correct!

One pair?' he queried to himself and laughed.

'One pair of white cotton drawers absent without leave!

2 pairs cotton socks . . . present!

2 pairs woollen socks . . . present!

2 coloured handkerchiefs . . . present!
2 pairs stout shoes . . . present!
2 towels . . . present!
1 blanket . . .' He paused, examining the article.
'1 blanket . . . with hole in middle, present!
1 blanket for cover . . . present!
1 broad brown hat . . . present!
1 lb. Castile soap . . . present!
2 lb. bar rough soap . . . present!' It is either going to be a short war, he thought, or else a dirty one!
'1 belt knife . . . present!
Thimble . . . present!
Housewife . . . present . . . and ready for duty.'

He laughed again, checking off the two large needles, spool of stout linen thread, beeswax, buttons and a paper of pins, all in a buckskin bag, which constituted the 'Housewife', as it was known.

'Housewife . . . present . . . in all but human form!' he said, still laughing at the idea of it.

'1 overcoat . . . present!
1 painted canvas cloth, 7 feet 4 inches long by 5 feet wide . . . present!'

He clicked to attention and saluted the kit laid out before him.

'All present and correct, sir, Sergeant Lavelle! Apart from a missing pair of drawers.'

A man would need a second pair, with all that marching to be done. He'd see the quartermaster about that. Otherwise it was all there and the knapsack in which to carry it.

He checked his gun and his sharpshooter's spectacles. Amber-coloured to increase contrast when spotting a target, the periphery frosted to create a pin-hole effect in the centre for greater accuracy. Not that he always needed to use them when shooting the enemy.

He picked up his rifle, balanced it in his hand.

Three months now he'd been with the Irish Brigade in the

Army of the Potomac, named after the river that flowed through Washington – the Northern capital.

Lavelle was proud to be with the Irish Brigade. The Brigade's three regiments – the 63rd, 69th and 88th New York Volunteers – had been mainly formed from that city's teeming refugees who had fled Ireland's Great Famine of the 1840s. Lavelle smiled to himself. These same Irish now fighting for Lincoln had ensured Lincoln's loss of New York City in the 1860 elections. No more than Lavelle himself the Irish did not want in power an abolitionist Republican Party who would bring the slaves north to take their lowly-paid jobs. When war broke out however, the Irish answered the call of their powerful countrymen in America including the charismatic Democrat, Thomas Francis Meagher, to 'fight for freedom'. A call they were well used to answering in their own country. Their view was that the lowly Irish would 'up' themselves in the eyes of their adopted country – if they fought, and more especially died, for it.

In spring 1862, the non-Irish 29th Massachusetts Regiment had been joined with the Irish Brigade to bring it to the required strength of four regiments.

Three bloody months.

Lavelle felt good today.

Ready for Rebs.

SIXTY

'We're fightin' to become *white*, not to free the slaves,' Lavelle said, to the small cluster of Union Irish who listened. 'If we cannot live equally as Americans, we will at least die our way into Yankee hearts.'

The Irish Brigade had of late been involved in some of the fiercest fighting of the campaign and many familiar faces were no longer seen at campfire gatherings.

'The piccaninnies of Alabama are better housed and better fed than are the free peasants of Ireland, in Boston,' said the Little Bishop, as the speaker was known in New York's Hell's Kitchen, from where he had been recruited – or 'salvaged', as he himself described it.

His rightful name was MacEneaspey . . . Benedict MacEneaspey. All six feet seven inches of him, from the Connemara coast. Until some wag with a smattering of Irish had broadcast it over the Kitchen, what the English translation of his name meant – *mac an easpaigh* – son of a Bishop! But the Little Bishop had had the last laugh. Waited for the right night. Sent him, who mocked him, to eternity, a baling hook in his gut. Word was that the Little Bishop's tormentor was closer to the truth than anyone in the Kitchen dare mention. He then 'enlisted' in the Union army to escape arrest, the local constabulary glad to have him fighting the Rebs instead of them. His name had followed him and indeed, the Little Bishop could pulpit talk as good as any prince of the Church. Particularly with stories of his earlier life.

Like, how when he was 'full-grown' to his present height, he had left for America, and how each of his six sisters in turn 'had leaned down to me and kissed me on *top* of my head!'

Now the Little Bishop poured forth his latest homily.

'In this war the Green fall equally with the Blue and the Grey. Irish blood reddens the plains of America – not for any other freedom – but that the cotton kings of Boston may spend nights as well as days in their counting houses.'

And so it was, Lavelle thought. The Little Bishop had it right.

'Why indeed are we fighting?' Lavelle later asked of himself. 'Killing our brothers? Good honest men from the bare hills of Connaught and the fertile plains of Tipperary.'

He fanned the newspaper out in front of him, the *Pilot* – Boston's Catholic newspaper. 'And stamped with the imprimatur of His Lordship, the Archbishop,' Lavelle announced to no one in particular.

He commenced reading: 'What has the African done for America? What great or even decent work has his head conceived, or his hands executed? We pity his condition, but it is unjust to put him in the balance with the white labourer. To white toil, this nation owes everything; but to black, nothing.'

There it was in black and white – from the Holy Roman Catholic Church itself. It was the Irish who had built America, not the blacks.

Later on Lavelle showed the *Pilot* to the Little Bishop, commenting that, 'The British Crown has stirred up the South for its own ends. Therefore, the Irish *must* fight, if for no other reason but to protect our second country – America – and our first – Ireland – against the Crown. Not one Irishman in a hundred has joined with the Union to liberate the slaves, but Lincoln and his warmongers have now seized on

233

"freedom", "democracy" and "emancipation" with which to justify seizing the riches of the South. Lincoln has betrayed us. No true Irishman should ever vote for him.'

'No true Irishman ever will,' the Little Bishop affirmed. 'But for now we have to pacify those Rebs. Especially our own fightin' for the Rebs,' he said, looking down at his hands. Hands as big as Virginia hams. 'Pat them on their astrayed heads and send them home safe to their mammies.'

The big man laughed, bringing his hands together in a thunderclap.

Lavelle would more have feared a 'pat on the head' from the Little Bishop as the full blast of a Confederate cannon at close range.

'The Irish Rebs will need ladders to get at you, Bishop!' Lavelle said. 'Unless any of those sisters of yours have started producing!'

He ducked the swing that he knew would come his way and headed towards his tent with the sound of the big man's laughter still ringing in his ears.

As he lay awake, Lavelle realised how weary he had become of the banter of war, and the newspaper columnists so safe in their cities. Throw in the lot of the 'champagne' generals, Yankees and Rebs alike, and even the 'gallant fighting Irish'. He was weary of the whole lot of them. Weary of war itself.

What alone sustained him now was the faint hope of, after the war, still finding Ellen.

Until that time he would, tomorrow, and all the tomorrows after that go out again.

Killing.

SIXTY-ONE

'Lavelle!' his captain shouted at him above the din of battle. 'Already we have lost a captain of cavalry, a colour sergeant and two soldiers of rank to that Rebel sharpshooter. Find that soldier and dispense God's mercy upon him.'

Lavelle stripped away from the main line of the regiment out to its right flank. Finding a sunken hollow he flung himself into its protection and waited.

He did not watch the enemy's line but his own – the colour party. He would know the signs. So many times had his own rifle occasioned the same death-signs on the other side. The flag would pitch forward, its bearer jerk as if struck by some invisible force.

A step or two.

Fall.

He had not long to wait. He saw the young Union standard bearer twist in flight, the staff spun from his hand, him hitting the ground before it. Lavelle's eye formed an angle between the line at which the boy had been running and the beginning of the arc through which his body had twisted.

It gave him a bearing.

The sniping fire was to the right of the battlefield. A thicket of trees on the Rebel side. It was this he now watched.

A movement almost escaped him. Then it was gone.

Lavelle narrowed his range of search, slid his gun forward over the edge of the bunker . . . and waited.

Again movement. Again almost imperceptible.

Lavelle trained his sights in time to see a rifle, arm and shoulder withdraw into the shrouding foliage.

Then stillness.

Lavelle's gun never wavered from the spot. The Rebel sharp-shooter was good. Not too anxious for the kill – picking his time and his target well. Then was content.

If Lavelle took a chance, fired now and missed it would put his own life at risk.

He held his breath.

Patience, stillness. These were the watchwords of sharp-shooters. Those, who were strict in their observance, lived. All others died.

He waited and waited, the prickling damp rising on the back of his neck . . . his brow . . . beneath his armpits. Soon it was in his nostrils, the stale smell of uncertainty. His most basic instinct told him to get out of there, preparing him for flight.

But flight would be death.

Movement of any kind would be death.

At last Lavelle saw the gun snake out again, a grey-clad arm snuggling it. Lavelle spread himself on the ground, demanding greater purchase, and nudged his rifle a hair's breadth to the right.

It was enough to give him away.

The leaves of the tree shook vigorously, the sniper's gun turning anxiously in Lavelle's direction.

Now it would be the faster of the two.

The steeliness of nerve.

Whichever of them could keep the trembling to a min-imum.

Momentarily Lavelle glimpsed the grey of the Rebel uni-form, the dark head.

'Now!' he ordered and his rifle spoke.

He couldn't remember squeezing its trigger but felt the kick against his shoulder. Blinking at the sting of sweat in his eyes, his vision blurred, Lavelle did not see the body fall. Only in its aftermath the shaking of the sprung-back branches.

It had been touch and go. The Reb or himself.

Too close.

Now, he must be cautious. Maybe the Reb had slid down the tree? Was even now waiting for him to show himself?

Lavelle did not move, not even to cuff the sweat from his forehead.

He lay there, the paralysis of near-death on him.

A hand shook his shoulder, returning him startled, to life.

He swivelled his gun.

'Lavelle! Lavelle! It's all right, it's over for today!' The voice, blurred in blue before him, said, 'We lost many . . . so did they . . . but the sharpshooter is gone. Dead or fled.'

'I think I got him, Captain!' Lavelle said, raising himself from the ground. 'In the tree . . . over there.'

'Well if you did, Sergeant Lavelle, you should go find him, pay honour to that gallant fellow who caused so much calamity and is now himself fallen.'

Lavelle moved across the battlefield, deserted of all now save the daily spectre of the bayonet-gashed and the bullet-gored, their estranged blood mingling freely together. The Gatherers – those who came to save the wounded and bury the dead – had not arrived yet. As Lavelle passed among the stricken and strewn, some died, shouting a curse on God and man. Others, more resigned to their fate, fearfully whimpered their way out of this vale of tears. What little water he had he pressed to lips seared with the final thirst. Blue or Grey, it mattered not to him.

Eventually he reached the thicket of trees.

Everywhere were bodies fresh from the fields of New England and the streets of New Orleans.

Then one body, face down in the bleeding grass.

Lavelle knew it was the enemy sharpshooter. Something about the way in which he lay, as if not dead but merely fallen from grace.

He reached down, and catching the soldier by the shoulder jerked the body towards him.

The man groaned. Was not yet dead.

As Lavelle turned him, his stricken foe, seeing his assassin, clenched the killing hand.

'Lavelle!' he gasped. 'It's you . . . Lavelle!'

SIXTY-TWO

'Patrick!' Lavelle cried, recognising him. 'Oh my God, Patrick, it was you! In the tree . . . the dark head . . .'

Lavelle fell to his knees at the enormity of what he had done.

Feverishly, he cradled Patrick. Rubbing his pallid face. As if that alone could restore life to it.

'Oh, Patrick! Patrick! What have I done? What have I done?' Lavelle called hopelessly.

Patrick lay limp against him, unanswering.

'God's curse on America! On the East and West of it, and the accursed North and South of it!' Lavelle railed, unable, in any other way, to express the unplumbed depths of grief to which he was now sent.

He felt Patrick stiffen, and try to raise himself up.

Lavelle pressed the last of the water to his lips.

'Lavelle . . . Emmy . . . the glove . . . sweetheart's glove,' Patrick got out with great difficulty, in vain trying to open the stained buttons of his tunic.

Lavelle took his hand, set it tenderly aside, then gingerly unfastened the grey uniform. Inside was a sticky mass . . . then something else.

Lavelle withdrew the book . . . its pages edged with blood. Instantly, he recognised it.

'The *Love Elegies?*' he said disbelievingly, imagining that Patrick had at last found Ellen. 'Ellen! Ellen! Your mother, Patrick, where is she?'

'Glove . . . back . . . Emmy . . . magnolias . . .' was all the boy answered.

Lavelle tried to revive him. Slapped his face. Shook him. But to no avail.

'Patrick! Patrick! Don't go! . . . No . . . not yet! . . . I'll get . . . Oh God, Patrick, I'm sorry . . . I didn't . . .'

Lavelle kept talking, openly weeping, frantic that he should be doing something . . . anything. He tried to shout for help but the only sound he could produce was a strangled whisper.

Then spasmodic firing broke out in his direction. Some last hurrah – from which side, he didn't know.

He tried to lift Patrick's body but was forced to stop as the firing came nearer. He laid the boy gently down, crossed his arms, and drew close his eyes. He said a prayer over his stepson, touched his forehead in a final act and then made for the Union lines in a stumbling zig-zagging run. His mind was numbed, criss-crossed with conflicting prayers.

Petition, that he yet might find Ellen alive. Contrition for killing her son. Hope and despair.

When at last he reached his own lines, Lavelle just lay there, the book in his grasp. The Little Bishop and others found him, carried him to the tent, revived him with water.

When he had recovered he told them to leave him, and thumbed open the book. In it were letters inserted next to various poems and a snow-white glove to which a snow-white heart had been stitched. Miraculously, the glove was unsoiled by the stains that had seeped onto some of the poems, mapping out clusters of words like blood-red countries.

He would keep the glove safe . . . bring it to the boy's sweetheart. That was Patrick's dying wish. The least he could do.

Lavelle fought to keep the awfulness of what he had done from his mind. Ellen, Ellen, he had to think of her. Find her now more than ever.

The letters, the letters . . . They would have something of her.

He fumbled one open. It was headed . . . *Le Petit Versailles, Confederate State of Louisiana.*

He leafed through it. Then another and another after that. Looking for a sign . . . anything . . . the words of longing in them, crimson elegies to a bloodied cause.

But of Ellen there was no word. Only of Patrick and of Emmy, the girl he loved . . . and 'magnolia time'.

SIXTY-THREE

Accompanied by Father O'Grady, the tall figure of Stephen Joyce edged its way through the sprawling jigsaw of corpses.

He had to find Patrick. He had sworn in his own mind to protect him; restore some honour to the whole sorry mess he had brought upon the boy and his mother. Purposely he had put him with the sharpshooters, to keep him out of direct fire. But now Patrick had not returned.

Stephen knew that the boy reviled him, as much for not telling him about the affair with his mother, as for the affair itself. During their time in New Orleans, he could not bring himself to do it, especially as Patrick and Emmeline had eyes only for each other since first they met. He could not ruin that for the boy. Pour cold water on the fires of young love. Emeritus Labiche – welcoming and all as he might be – would do that.

Patrick, though of right age, holding the right religion and of sound education, did not have the most important, the only, qualification by which to gain a plantation daughter's hand. Patrick was not a gentleman. Nor had he a gentleman's means.

Patrick was . . . *sans richesse, sans ressources* – without riches and without resources. Incapable of providing a continuation

242

of the privileged lifestyle which Emeritus Labiche not only expected for his daughters but demanded.

The outcome of the present skirmish aside, the *inviolata* of Southern womanhood would not be blemished by an unsuitable marriage.

Patrick would weaken the family – and the family would not be weakened. Nothing had been said, nor would be said now, with the boy off to war. Who knew what might happen? He could die a hero and Emmeline – poor little Emmeline – could weep, wear widow's weeds if she wanted to, and remember her gallant soldier boy. Daddy and Mammy Labiche would nod sagely.

Not a word need ever be spoken. Labiche tears would dry and everything remain in its accorded place.

However, none of that was any of Stephen Joyce's concern just now. He must find Ellen O'Malley's son.

'There are so many fallen, Father!' he remarked to the chaplain, 'and only the Union hospital to which to take them.'

'The good Sisters care not the colour of their uniform,' Father O'Grady replied. 'To them the soldiers are all stateless. Children only of God's Kingdom and in need of His refining grace.'

'Pray that we find him, Father . . . and find him alive!' Stephen said, he himself becoming more forlorn of that hope, his brows grim with worry.

As bodysnatchers under darkness they went casting their lanterns into the hideous-faced, the half-faced . . . and those who had no faces.

The priest spotted Patrick first. Quickly he ran and knelt beside the boy, reaching down a life-seeking hand, then shaking his head. 'He is still warm – but barely so. I am afraid he has gone to God, Captain Joyce.' The priest began to administer the last rites to Patrick but Stephen interrupted him, unable to concede that the boy was yet dead. 'I have seen the surgeons bring the dead back to life with the use of ether,' he argued. 'Maybe there is yet a chance, if we are quick!'

With Father O'Grady's white handkerchief aloft, they approached a group gathering bodies – a priest of the Union and some soldiers.

'Gentlemen, could you spare space in your hearts, and on your cart, for an enemy, mortally wounded?' Father O'Grady asked.

The other priest and the soldiers agreed.

With a barn door for a stretcher, they heaped Patrick on to it, along with three other bodies, and made for the converted shoolhouse that constituted the Union hospital.

Despite his earlier insistence, Stephen now feared their journey would be a wasted one. There had been no stir from Patrick, only the creeping dampness over his body. They would be turning around again, he knew, bringing him back to his own side – for burial.

As the queue waiting admittance inched forward, Father O'Grady sensed the loss of hope in Stephen.

'We've come this far, Captain. Let us trust in the healing hands of Providence.'

But it was not the healing hands of Providence which received Patrick O'Malley's body. It was the stricken hands of his mother.

ELLEN

SIXTY-FOUR

Union Army Field Hospital, Virginia, July 1862

'It's Patrick, Mother! It's Patrick!' Louisa shouted from the doorway, above the noise and bustle.

Ellen, not sure she heard, raised her head from where she was at the far end of the hospital and saw Louisa's stricken look. A terrible fear overtaking her, Ellen dropped the bandages she was holding and started to run, looking for Mary as she did so.

'Patrick?' her voice mumbled. 'Patrick . . . here?'

How? Why? How badly was he wounded? She thanked God they were all here to look after him.

She saw Mary already ahead at the door, helping Louisa carry Patrick in.

Yes, it was him. Her long-lost son – found at last. He had on a grey Confederate uniform but she'd know him any-where. That face, the dark head.

There was a priest beside him muttering prayers. Why was the priest . . . ?

Then something seized her. Some uncontrollable thing. A restraining vice from which she could not break free. Her legs seemed not to move.

Holding her back from what lay ahead instead of pro-pelling her towards it.

She saw the priest raise his head solemnly towards her. Then the tall soldier in Confederate uniform beside the priest turn, his face aghast at the sight of her, telling her everything.

'Oh my God, Stephen? Stephen Joyce?' she gasped, disbelievingly.

And then she knew.

Silence descending.

Everyone turning to look at her. The priest, Stephen, Mary . . . Louisa.

'Oooh no! Oooh no!' she screamed. 'Pa-trick! Pa-trick! Oh God! no!' She reached them, bursting through the protective wall around her son.

She looked at Patrick, her beautiful boy, Patrick. Stretched there. Dark curls falling on his quiet forehead, the grey tunic, red-rusted with his blood. Frantically, she tore it open, his shirt reddening her hands, seeing the neat bore of the bullet. Feverishly, she sent her index finger to probe for it. Withdrew it, as if to reverse the process.

'Mary – ammonia!' she shouted. 'Louisa the probe! I need the probe!'

They stood looking at her.

'Mary . . . !' she began again . . . could they not hear . . . ? 'Louisa . . . ?' She turned to Louisa, the hopelessness in her voice reflecting the hopelessness in their faces.

'Ellen . . . Ellen,' a voice said gently. It was Stephen Joyce, arms enfolding her from behind, staying her own frantic hands. 'Ellen! Ellen . . . he's gone! Patrick's gone!'

Something about the way he said it caused her not to resist.

She stood there, immobilised, then staring at Patrick, her hands still on his breast, the priest droning in and out of her consciousness. Mary lifting her hands from Patrick, helping her find his frozen hand, locking their hands together. Louisa buttoning back Patrick's shirt, his tunic. Mary with a white cloth damping the clay from his hair, soothing his forehead where he had fallen. The priest still intoning in the strange Latin tongue of a foreign God. Stephen, behind her, half holding, half supporting her. Dr Sawyer fading backwards out of her vision. To see to others who had some chance at life, she supposed. Else pronounce them dead. Everybody doing what they should be doing.

Except her.

Now Stephen whispering to her. 'He was a brave soldier Ellen – the bravest.'

It didn't even register with her as to how Stephen knew, why he was together here with Patrick now. How, after years of separation, he was again back in her life. So fatally back.

'Lavelle?' she heard herself whisper. 'Is Lavelle dead too?'

Stephen paused. 'Patrick was the last to see Lavelle. They searched for you. Then, Lavelle went west, Patrick south – where I met him!'

He paused again.

'To where did *you* go, Ellen?'

His question hung somewhere in the ammonia-scented space before her, detached from them both, unanswered.

She pushed back his arms.

'I wish to be alone with my son,' they heard her say.

The others carried Patrick's body then into the operating room, set him on a trestle and left. She sat there, watched with Patrick, among the dead; the three or four others carted in with him, slumped together in the final slumber. Death was the normal inhabitant here; she, the living, the transgressor. She lay her head upon him, her red hair streaming across his red breast, like a sheltering flag. Her arm outstretched to his head, tenderly settled his boyish curls, tracing with her fingers the line of his forehead, the dark pools of his eyes. Her touch lingered a moment along the furrow beneath his nose. She remembering that that alone of his features he had inherited from her.

Then, in murmuring tones she traced out his life with her. The green valley days in Ireland . . . the prayers learnt at her knee . . . later, the blackened days of blight, their flight to America . . . Lavelle. Ah, Lavelle . . . if Lavelle were here now he would be heartbroken. But Stephen, Stephen Joyce

. . . here now to witness Patrick's death. Stephen always at Death. Death and desertion. She asked Patrick if, now at the right hand of God, he would at last forgive her – be her strength. Look down on her.

Outside, Mary, Louisa and the others waited.

The wounded, their own woes put aside, mourned for her. Then they heard her song, in the old tongue. A *suantraí* – sleepsong.

Her voice trailed away, no longer able to express the inexpressible. So she sat half lain across him. Silence now her only voice.

'Lay down your head and I'll sing you a lullaby,
Back to the years of Loo-li-ly-lay,
And I'll sing you to sleep, sing you tomorrow,
Bless you with love for the road that you go.

'May there always be angels to watch over you,
To guide you each step of the way;
To guard you and keep you, safe from all harm,
Loo-li-loo-li-ly-lay.

'May you bring love and may you bring happiness,
Be loved in return, to the end of your days;
Now fall off to sleep, I'm not meaning to keep you,
I'll just sit for a while and sing Loo-li-ly-lay.'

Her voice trailed away, no longer able to express the inexpressible. So she sat half lain across him. Silence now her only voice.

When Ellen emerged, one dark lock of Patrick's hair circled her finger. She stopped in front of Stephen and looked up at him.

'Thank you,' she said. 'I know you sheltered him as a father would.'

He held her close to him a moment, then gently took her by the arm, leading her outside.

'He was your son – how could I not?' Stephen at last answered. 'And yet I didn't shelter him enough.'

She touched his hand. 'For those in this war, there *is* no shelter. I see it hour by hour, day by day. But tell me about him . . . Patrick . . . when he was a man?' she asked, knowing that there might only be these few moments in which to learn of her dead son.

And he told her. All of it. New Orleans . . . Oxy . . . the bayous . . . Emmeline.

Even the book.

'Patrick knew?' she asked.

'Yes!' he answered simply.

'You wanted him to know, Stephen.' She stated more than asked.

He nodded. 'I wanted him to know that I have loved you since he was a boy . . . and to ask his forgiveness for dishonouring you.'

'You never dishonoured me, Stephen. Dishonour has its own harbour – within.'

'What will you do now, Ellen?'

'I will stay. Be with Mary and Louisa. Do my work, as God directs. And you?'

'I will return to my men, do my duty. If I could find Lavelle, I would ask his forgiveness.'

'As would I,' she answered. 'If you should find him first . . . send him safe to me, Stephen.'

'I will,' he replied.

'Will you be safe yourself . . . returning?'

'Yes, thank you. Father O'Grady has God's countersign – the pickets will let us through.'

He began to say something . . . 'Ellen . . .'

'Stephen!' she said. 'Don't. Let the unsaid remain unsaid.'

She held his arms for a moment then turned to go. Remembering something, she turned back to him.

'Patrick's letters from his sweetheart . . . and the book . . . I would like to have them.'

He looked at her, at first not understanding that she did not already have them. Had not found them on his body.

'He always kept them both about his person – even in battle,' Stephen answered.

'Then they must have been stolen,' she replied, strangely comforted at how Patrick had kept her book next to the sweetheart letters of his Emmeline.

Stephen looked at her, hair wild about her, face streaked with the tears she had wept. He had loved her since sixteen years ago when he had first set eyes on her, her beauty the talk of Connemara. From Maamtrasna to the Killary fjord at Leenane, all the way back to the Sky Road at Clifden. It was seven years since he had last seen her but the memory of her love had since burned in him like molten metal.

She had lost little in the intervening years. Little of that strength of purpose, that way of carrying herself, even now burdened with grief. She was not as splendidly beautiful as then, but her true beauty – of the spirit which she had always possessed – had not faded but nurtured itself, gracing her years into age. That she had mellowed was without doubt. Her eyes, stricken as they were, told him. The tempestuousness of character was absent, that element of fire – so long a fateful trait – she had muted, sublimated.

That he still loved her she knew. Of that he was certain. He had been on the point of saying something of this but she had stopped him. Nor would it have been appropriate. Of her own feelings towards him, he did not engage in such thought at this time. Any intrusion, even by thought, into her sorrowing state, would be unworthy.

She was looking at him now, the green eyes fixed on him quizzically, waiting for him.

'I'm sorry, Ellen,' he said, a bit flustered at having been caught thinking of her.

She said nothing, smiled – a wan, painful smile. Before he

had time to think about it, he had embraced her, held her shivering body tightly to him. 'I am so sorry about Patrick, Ellen. So, so sorry . . . and for everything.'

She held him a moment, stretched to kiss his cheek and said in a soft voice, 'I know, Stephen . . . thank you . . . you're a good man . . . and try as it may not, my heart is glad to see you.'

He left then. And she stood and waited. Watched him and the priest go back to the far side.

Back inside, Mary and Louisa awaited her.

When she came in they went to her, each silent with her own grief. In the cradle of her arms, she brought them with her to where Patrick lay. Took out her white oak beads and prayed the Rosary over him.

Then arrangements had to be made

If she wished it, Stephen had offered, Patrick could be buried at Richmond with his comrades, rather than here next to the battlefield. She thought about it. Here would be a scrawl on a shabbily erected cross to mark those fallen, then tumbled into a trench, perhaps with hundreds. Here he would be close to her for the moment, but indistinguishable. In Richmond, at least, she could mark his spot, give him an identity. It be there for all time, that he had lived . . . and died.

SIXTY-FIVE

In the days following Patrick's death, Ellen was turmoiled beyond any previous grief. Thoughts, tears, terrible questions, crowded each other in unending sequence, crushing all impulse for living. Mary and Louisa tried to force her to rest; Dr Sawyer, solicitous for her state, brought morphine. Both she resisted, knowing somewhere deep down that if she succumbed to any outside influence, passed over control for her functioning, that she would cease to function and be a drain on all their resources.

She continued to do her rounds, comforting, healing, assisting Dr Sawyer. Those who were there when Patrick had been brought to her at first avoided any contact with her. Unable to express to her what she had so often expressed to them. With the new admissions it was different. Their needs so pressing, many so close to their own demise that all thought was blocked, save of loved ones back home and their own flimsy mortality. Out of their fear and pain they called to her for comfort but the others would whisper roughly to the new patients, of how 'the woman had tended her own son's corpse'. Then, those, even at death's door themselves would shrink from any further demand upon her.

She came to marvel at Mary and Louisa, how they respected her wishes, sublimating their own natural instinct to shepherd her through those awful days. Only at night kneeling down together with her to pray for Patrick. Occasionally a slipped word from one of them, betraying her own internal struggle with the inexpressible.

'God wills this contest – permits it for some wise purpose,' was Mary's supreme act of Faith. Quietly said, quietly left there. In those dark days Mary came to be their rock, their font of all wisdom.

Louisa too was stoic in her steadfastness . . . but at times would suddenly disappear. Neither Ellen nor Mary ever asked her, understanding her flawed humanity, along with their own. Loving Louisa the more for it.

And the days came and went in one unending cycle of suffering and hope; misery and joy; and of unending goodbyes. Now, more than ever in each of the wounded she dealt with, Ellen saw Patrick – some mother's son . . . her son.

SIXTY-SIX

'*Gaudeamus igitur. Iuvenes dum sumus* – Let us be happy while we are young.'

In Latin, Herr Heidelberg barrelled out the thirteenth-century student drinking song, as he marched up and down the row of beds.

The cheery Rhinelander was back under their care again. Ellen smiled, glad to see him. They had patched him up previously, sent him out – and now he was back. This time not seriously injured but more emboldened. Now a real hero. Twice injured.

He grabbed her around the waist. She knew the others encouraged him about how 'the *Irische Frau* petter likes *de sauerkraut* den de spud!'

'Now ve valzer,' he said as he kept singing, this time something about 'The Fatherland most beautiful'.

The men clapped and shouted. Despite their professed aversion to 'Dutchmen'. Herr Heidelberg, with his larger-than-life good humour was, to a man, universally liked.

'*Frau* Ellen, you dance *mit* me!' they now called out, mimicking this broth of a man who was tearing the heart out of her, with his erratic swinging-about. Eventually he finished grinding out the '*Vaterland*' song and put her down.

'I vill not forget you in *Der Vaterland, Frau* Ellen, *danke,*

danke,' he got out in one gasp. When the war was won, he would go home, see his mountain, the Königsstuhl, and his river, the Neckar.

She bade him well, the road to Heidelberg be short before him and to 'Keep up the dancing!'

He drew himself up, portered out his chest, clicked his heels and saluted her.

When next Ellen saw him, a Confederate cannon had torn a hole as big as his fist through that great-barrelled chest.

Herr Heidelberg would not rest under the ledge of the Königsstuhl, nor hear the murmuring Neckar flow. It would be a pit in Virginia – in Virginia's bottomless pit.

She resolved not to let his last resting place be unmarked and so fashioned a St Brigid's Cross out of some reeds.

His death had affected her more than most. He reminded her of Roberteen, a neighbour's son who had once taken a shine to her back in the old days. A simpleton of a boy but devoted to her. Now, this simple boy-in-a-man's uniform had wanted only to sing and dance with her, like she was some fresh-faced *Fräulein*. Wanted, with such undisguised glee, to go back home to see his river and his mountain.

This war was wearying her – its relentless savagery, its unremitting death-dealing. Day after day, night after night, it was the same. Was there ever to be an end to it, so they could all go home? Or did every last one who strapped on a sword, or shouldered a musket, have to die? Until only one was left standing – and he the victor? But of what – a land of no young men, neither North nor South? A land of widows and mothers and sweethearts made barren by war.

America would become a country of old women. Revert to being an unpopulated wilderness. Unless . . . the slaves, the blacks with no souls, but liberated by the destruction, made it rich again. And that, she knew, would depend, on whatever the last soldier standing would be – North . . . or South?

SIXTY-SEVEN

Before the fog had lifted, the skies had already filled with the agonised cries of the dying. Enough alive though, and moving, to give the misty field a singular crawling effect. As the mist rose further, Ellen wondered how they would cope? July had been a wicked month.

She started out, searching for those who had not yet gone beyond help. She tried to avoid stepping on the bodies, but it was impossible. You could walk on the dead in any direction a half-mile without a foot touching the ground. She stumbled, fell against a stiffening corpse, her face but inches removed from socketless eyes and a mouthless face. Once, a voice seemed to come from such a hideous wound that she stared stupidly at the mouth of the great gaping hole, only to realise the strangled sound came from beneath the lifeless body. Then would she struggle to separate the dead from the living. Many times she failed, the bodies so masticated together by cannon fire as to render separation fatal to the living portion. Here and there a peach tree rained down its soft pink petals, the flowers changing to blood-red where they fell on open wounds. Drawing new colour from ebbing life.

In vain she searched their faces – where faces remained. Praying she would not find Lavelle. Guilty, at the selfishness of her thought. A wagon came. She helped them heap it up, and watched as it cranked away through the mist – a cranking, creaking abattoir. One stiff arm, raised above the rest, swayed with the roll of the wagon. Involuntarily, she raised her hand to wave back, then closed her palm. She watched the wagon recede, the defiant arm still raised, its dead owner appealing to Heaven for vengeance.

She felt someone beside her. A Union soldier dragging a lifeless leg back towards his own side. 'Victory has no charms, Sister . . . no charms!' the anonymous soldier said. 'But he who does not see the Hand of God in this is blind!'

Later that night as she knelt in prayer, Ellen wondered hard and long about the Hand of God.

SIXTY-EIGHT

The one thing Dr Sawyer could not fault the Sisters on was their absolute dedication to the wounded.

A 'Society Sister', as Dr Sawyer called those others who infrequently came to minister to the men, and generally at that, only the handsome ones – arrived one day in a flurry of fuss and feathers. Mary, unregarding of the flim-flam which accompanied the woman – a local doctor's wife – brought her to the nearest bed. It contained a young soldier recently admitted with a macerated face and who still bore the stench of his wounds.

Mary addressed him. 'Mr Addison, you have a kind lady visitor who will tend to you a while.'

The young man turned to face his Lady Bountiful. She, upon seeing the decayed state of his face, immediately drew down her fan between herself and the offending sight.

'Oh, Sister, could we not turn to some other poor soul. Less . . . you know, Sister?' she asked, in the soldier's hearing.

Dr Sawyer overheard Mary's reply. 'Whatsoever you do to the least of mine you do also to me.'

To her credit, he observed that the lady remained awhile with the man, her gaze averted.

It was not the way with the Sisters. All were equal in their eyes. North and South, damaged and whole. Generals

260

and the lowest foot-soldier, Protestant or Catholic. If only they weren't always so damned busy trying to save souls as well as bodies. He supposed that was their *raison d'être*. What he did out of duty to country, they did out of duty to God. They had no side and it granted them a moral superiority which, if forced to, they used like a velvet-covered battering ram. The Sisters never flinched that higher duty – even when faced with the dreaded smallpox. The lay nurses, even the good ones, would not venture near smallpox victims. The Sisters and the Lavelle woman were the very opposite. They, he observed, would not venture away from any poor soul needing help. Smallpoxed or not.

Dr Sawyer wondered about the Lavelle woman?

The two nuns were her children: the quiet one, Sister Mary, her birth child; the other one, Sister Veronica, or Louisa as the woman called her, who would cross swords with the Devil, an adopted child.

The Lavelle woman had been seeking her husband and son. One, she thought with the Union, the other Confederate. With the two nuns, she would scour the battlefield after every encounter, painstakingly examining each body, or what remained of it. Each fresh intake arriving at the hospital, she would run to, searching the faces for any sign of recognition. Dr Sawyer had long ago imagined them dead – but *she* had never given up hope. Now with her son found, delivered to her as a corpse, hope had been dashed from her. Now, with even more desperate fervour, she sought her husband.

Already hundreds of thousands had fallen from minié ball and cannon; many more from disease. It would be a miracle if she found him alive. Dr Sawyer hoped she yet would.

A strange case the three of them – no care for the gentility of their looks or attire. Their garments, like his own, festooned with the blood of the two score of men he had amputated that morning, she and her daughters holding steady the atrophied limbs for the bite of his surgeon's saw.

He tensed himself as Louisa approached him. 'Cross swords with the Devil,' he whispered under his breath, awaiting the opening thrust.

SIXTY-NINE

'Men need guns, not basins and beds!' Dr Sawyer answered his matron bluntly.

'It is ridiculous!' Louisa stormed. 'Two basins for dressing the wounds of three hundred men . . . the better of which has a hole in the bottom stuffed with rags! We are reduced to using the tin cups from which we eat and drink for bandage wetting. It won't do! It just won't do, Doctor!'

'Sister! The Quartermaster-General will not divert funds from buck and ball to wash-hand basins!' Dr Sawyer replied, explaining how 'My nights, when not in here, are futilely spent in writing letters of request to General Headquarters for more supplies for the wounded. I fear my words are falling on deaf ears,' he said, with an air of resignation. 'Very deaf ears.'

'Then I myself will go to General Headquarters,' Louisa declared.

Dr Sawyer smiled. He relished the idea of the sparks that would fly between the General, any General, of whatever reputation, and the young Irish nun bristling before him.

'Of course . . . if you must, Sister,' he said, disguising his delight. 'I'll send a guard to accompany you.'

'I must . . . but I have no need of protection,' Louisa replied firmly. 'The Archangel of God will be my guide and protector.'

'Well, Madame?' General Bickerdyke, in truculent humour, barely raised his head to acknowledge Louisa's presence.

She didn't speak. Waited till he looked up at her.

'Well?' he demanded, angered by her silence. 'Devil got your tongue?'

He had a war to run and who did they deem themselves to be. These fanatics in strange garb who were swarming the hospitals, baptising on every side?

Louisa didn't flinch, stood there, hands clasped in front of her.

'We have a growing army of sick and wounded and . . .'

'Rebels, mostly, I'll warrant!' the general unceremoniously interrupted.

'Rebels or Federals, Catholic or Protestant, drummer boy or general, I do not ask. They are not soldiers when they come to us – simply suffering fellow creatures. Our work begins when yours is done. Yours the carnage, ours the binding up of wounds!'

General Bickerdyke sat back, set down his nib and studied her. He had heard much of the 'Sisters', mostly Irish and with no husbands. Who, when they took charge of them, ran the hospitals with sabre-like precision.

'What do you do with all your beggings, Sister?' he asked in an accusatory manner.

'Some day you may know, General!' Louisa answered and turned to go.

'Stay!' he ordered. 'You're Irish?'

'I'm human!' she answered, 'and so too, could you be . . . General!'

He flushed slightly but she did not break stare with him. Brusquely then, he pulled out a piece of vellum and scratched the date at its head.

'Well, go on then, Madame . . . spell out your needs but don't come bothering me further!'

So she listed her demands while the general scribbled furiously. He kept his eyes down as he struggled to keep pace with her and so, did not catch the smile that lighted hers.

'Flour . . . Ice . . . Coffee . . . Cups . . . Basins . . .' She paused, thinking what would Dr Sawyer say now?

The general, thinking she had finished, made to flourish his name and rank at the bottom of Louisa's list of 'beggings'.

'. . . And beef! All at the usual commissary prices,' she added, almost beneath his hearing.

He snorted in disbelief. By all that was holy, she had temerity, this Lucifer bonnet!

'. . . And beef!' he exhaled, '*all* at commissary prices? By jove! There . . . !'

He held out the paper to her. 'Good for three months at army terms – a reduction of one-third on market prices,' he said with the smirk of a smile, and added, 'But you already know that, Madame!'

'Indeed I do . . . sir!' Louisa answered and took the paper from him. She studied it, a frown coming on her face.

'What now?' he exploded.

'Oh!' she said, smiling at him. 'Thank you kindly, General, but I almost forgot . . . to ease the pain of the wounded . . . a couple of jiggers of whiskey . . . sir.'

A month later he was wheeled in, delirious with pain, his right shoulder shell-torn, wanting only to die. She assisted at the amputation, and then nursed him for weeks through a tortuous recovery, which often pendulumed between life and death.

When he first regained consciousness, she was leant over him, dabbing his temple with ice-cold water.

'It's you!' he said, as if still haunted by delirium.

'Yes, General,' she answered, laughing.

'. . . And is this the begging ice?' he asked.

A month on, after he was released, Louisa received an envelope. In it a cheque for two thousand dollars.

'For the beggings,' was all the accompanying note said.

SEVENTY

'Smallpox!'

The word ran like contagion through the hospital.

Dr Sawyer summoned Louisa. 'Sister, we have two cases in those admitted today. Their wounds are otherwise light which, in many respects, is an unfortunate circumstance.' He looked hard at her. 'But they are *our* boys. How can you safely accommodate them?'

Louisa understood what he was saying. To bring smallpox into an already overcrowded hospital was to invite in catastrophe. The disease, highly contagious, would spread like fire among the weak and the infirm.

'They will be as wheat before the reaper,' the doctor said, echoing her thoughts. Isolation was called for, but where?

'*I* will take responsibility for them, Doctor,' Louisa answered. 'We will accommodate them in our own quarters away from the mass of the patients. Sister Mary and I will improvise.'

The doctor left it to her.

She told Mary and Ellen of her decision. 'Mary and I will sleep on the floor next your bed, Mother – for all the sleep we ever manage. We will take turns to watch the men. The lay nurses will not want contact with them and who is to blame them? They have their families to protect.'

'No, Louisa!' It was Mary. 'They will be in *my* care. You have the administration of the hospital to see to – and you, Mother, cannot risk infection, you work so close with the doctor.'

What Mary said made sense – that she and Ellen were both more valuable to the overall function of the hospital than she was. Still, Ellen was uneasy about Mary's plan. She wanted to share the risk, halve the risk, of Mary contracting the disease.

In the ward the men were in consternation until word went around that the two poxed soldiers would be cared for, away from the general body of patients, by Sister Mary.

On hearing the news, one Pennsylvanian – a rough old Dutchman – caught Mary by the hem of her habit, as she passed.

'Sister! Sister! Listen to me!' he wheezed at her. 'Do not protract your visit with them, for fear you carry the contagion back to others.' And he yanked at the folds of her habit to emphasise the gravity of his message.

Mary waited until he let go, said nothing, and then went on her way to prepare the room.

SEVENTY-ONE

'Foreign Devils!'

The insult was thrown at Mary by the younger of the two with smallpox when first she came to tend them. It did not bother her. The young man from 'up New England way', as she subsequently found out, had probably never seen a nun before. To many like him, dark stories about nuns and nunneries had been told as a child. Just as you would tell stories of ghosts or pookahs, she knew, to frighten young listeners into obedience, or staying in bed once put there!

New Englanders, those from her own state, Massachusetts, were the most prejudicial.

To Abner Seaborn, nuns were aberrations. Foreign devils in strange garb. He repeated the well-worn quote to her that nuns were 'Mournful prisoners in their convent doomed by unhappy love affairs to lives of sinful indolence.'

'The Puritan Streak', Louisa dismissed it as, fed by lurid novels such as Maria Monk's *Awful Disclosures of the Hôtel Dieu Nunnery in Montreal,* in whose pages could be found stories of infants born to devilish Romish liaisons between priests and nuns. The infants would then be murdered and buried in convent basements. The myths perpetuated by this novel – published a quarter of a century earlier – and many since – still lived on.

The young man spoke again to Mary, 'I'm a Christian man and I don't hold with no Romish practices. I know all about them!'

'What do you know about them?' Mary asked patiently.

'I heard a good and holy man – the Reverend Lyman Beecher – preach that, "The Catholic Church holds now in darkness and bondage nearly half the civilised world. It is the most skilful, powerful, dreadful system of corruption to those who yield to it, and of slavery and debasement to those who live under it." And it frightened me so, that I remembered the Reverend's words by heart,' Abner Seaborn said, proudly.

'Oh!' was Mary's only reply, not that she thought her own Church lived out the Christian teachings as Christ would have wanted, anymore than did the Reverend Beecher think it. She wondered what the Lord would say on Judgement Day about the Catholic Church's silence on another kind of bondage? That which bound one person in servility to another. Or the Church's abetting of it by deeming the black people to 'have no souls'?

'If they have no souls as the Church says, then how could they ever be saved?' she had wondered to Louisa.

'Oh, they *have* souls but misguided ones,' Louisa had argued, 'they need to hear the word of God.'

'But if the only word of God they hear is that they are less than human and bound to be bound, then how will they ever listen to it?'

'This war will change all that,' Louisa answered. 'The war is the word of God speaking. When the black people are freed, they will fall to their knees in thanksgiving.'

Mary thought the war more the word of Mammon speaking, than the word of God.

Whatever about souls, and those without, and the word of Mammon, Abner Seaborn had fever. The smallpox had seemed to over-run him quickly. Even so, when she tried to open his shirt, dampen his fire with the cold poultice, he slung her hands away.

'Begone, Lucifer!' he shouted at her. 'You ain't gittin' my Christian soul!' And he called on all the biblical demon-slayers he could muster to defend it from the 'Winged Whore' who had come to seize him.

Mary waited, until his rantings tired him. First, she mopped his brow, dampening his eyes until they closed, then dapped the raging pulse in his neck, all the while whispering to him, 'Hush now, little Abner Seaborn – you've a big voice for a little man.' Then she opened his shirt and daubed his boy's hairless chest. 'But you're a brave little man to be out here fighting this big man's war.'

She shouldered him over, starting with his back. He *was* only a child, maybe fifteen, she thought. He should still have been running around a New England farm, getting into mischief, being scolded by a loving mother. A fall, bruised knees, would yield an embrace. Arms around his small boy's shoulders, the miscreant safely folded into forgiving skirts.

She looked at those shoulders now, too slight for a gun, and covered with angry pustules. Gingerly, she applied the poultice – bread-soda – all she could get. It had warmed in her hands from contact with him. She dipped it into the small billycan of water – the best ration doctor would allow. Its temperature was barely less than that of the poultice. Still, she wasted not a drop in the wringing out of it.

He murmured something.

'There now, little fellow! There now!' Mary answered, as she re-applied the sodden bread-soda, wondering what good it would do.

'Your God is my God – your devils, mine too!' She prayed over him for a speedy deliverance to the archangels and martyrs he had earlier summoned against her. Then she resettled the shirt on his back.

'He won't come out of it, Sister . . . will he?' the other man, a Sergeant Doherty, asked.

'I don't suppose he will, Sergeant,' she said, seeing his eyes fix on her answer.

'How are *you?*' she asked.

'I'd be better entirely if I was out there, charging a Rebel breastworks, taking a sight o' them with me when I go, than malingerin' in here!' he said defiantly.

She laughed. 'That you would, Sergeant Doherty, but you're staying put here.'

'But . . . !' he started to argue.

'No buts,' she said firmly. 'And I hold rank here!'

Afterwards, she wrung out the poultice as best she could. She would need it again. Provident in all things, the water Mary also kept. Water, even used water, was better than none.

SEVENTY-TWO

Abner Seaborn did not recover, nor did he make his peace with 'the devil in the Lucifer Bonnet'. Mary stayed with him to the end, desperately trying to soothe his demons of disease and distrust, with water and words.

'Tell the bees, Mother! Tell the bees!' he called, clutching her, mistaking her for another.

'I will, Abner, I will, son,' she answered in character, not knowing what he meant.

The sergeant knew. 'It's an old New England custom. To tell the bees when someone dies. They drape the hives in black.' He paused a moment. 'Every darn hive in New England must be draped by now – and in old Ireland too!'

Now, Mother Seaborn's hives would be added to those thousands already draped.

He had not expired as gently as Mary had hoped. Rather did all his bodily functions collapse at once. Like a tree, cracked and felled by a raging fire.

Afterwards they took his body, covered it with lime to kill the contagion.

By then Mary was running a fever.

SEVENTY-THREE

Ellen was in a panic. 'Mary . . . not Mary!' she said to Louisa. 'We must do something . . . Otherwise . . .' She didn't finish the sentence, couldn't admit her fear out loud that Mary must soon follow Abner Seaborn unless they could arrest the disease taking hold.

Serum, she needed serum. In vain she enquired of Dr Sawyer.

'I will go anywhere – walk night and day to get it. Only tell me where!' she pleaded.

'I cannot, Mrs Lavelle,' he replied. 'I simply don't know. Maybe at Richmond – Chimborazo – one of the other hospitals. The Surgeon-General dispenses what small supply of crusts he gets.'

'Crusts?' she queried.

'Yes . . . crusts!' he answered again. 'They take the scabs of the pox from those already infected and use them as an antidote.'

'But where does he get the crusts?'

'I don't know,' Dr Sawyer responded. 'Nobody enquires too much.' He paused . . . 'There are stories.'

'Tell me, Doctor! Tell me!' she demanded. 'My child is dying . . . and you would let her die rather than betray some military confidence.'

*

274

She found Dr Licoix.

Ten miles she had trudged. Dr Sawyer had not told her much. Enough so she could track down the dapper doctor with the gruff moustache. It was oversized for his mouth, so that you could not see his upper lip move when he spoke. As if the sound came out of some pink burrow, thatched with hair.

He was cautious of her at first. Who was she? Who had sent her? What did she know?

She convinced him that her errand was one of mercy only, for her own daughter. That she was not employed by any agency to spy on him or his work – and swore herself to secrecy, if he would only help her.

Dr Licoix would – but for a price.

'I have the money,' she said.

It was a strange set-up. For a doctor, he was well off the beaten track. A tumbledown shack with weathered fences and a garden patch where something must once have grown. There was no sign, nothing to signify the occupant was a practitioner of medicine.

At a distance apart from the house by some fifty yards or so, stood two other shanty-type shacks. These were almost secluded from view by a draping copse of mixed bushes. Aloft from one of them floated a white flag. Her heart lifted – a hospital. Within it what she most desperately needed for Mary – the smallpox antidote.

Dr Licoix seemed in no hurry. Said not a word as he set off towards these buildings. The mahogany medicine case, carried in his right hand, caused his upper body to tilt slightly to the right. With his left hand he fumbled in his pocket, as if checking that he hadn't forgotten something. She followed him in silence across the divide between the house and the hospital.

As they approached she could hear rising murmurings of sound from within the two buildings. Not until they were through the clearing and almost there did she notice the pad-locked doors.

The back of Dr Licoix, labouring under his load, moved ahead of her. Nothing she could discern in his tilted gait, suggested that this was anything other than usual. Unease at the whole situation gripped her – the house, its condition, the hospital buildings in front of her – the little lop-sided doctor with the too big moustache.

Ellen steeled herself for whatever might come. She was here for Mary. That was all that mattered. Already had she witnessed what harsh horrors war – 'humanity stripped away from itself' – could confront her with.

'Roll up your sleeve!' Dr Licoix ordered the young negro boy.

The child, eight, maybe nine years old, did as he was told. Not once, not twice, but six times the needle punctured the boy's arm, drawing tears from his eyes.

'Now, the other arm . . . quickly!' the doctor barked, jabbing the needle into the bottle which held the cow-serum.

Fearfully the boy obeyed.

'Hurry up, boy, I've others to do!' the man said, startling the child even further. Dr Licoix reached over, impatiently ripping the flimsy homespun from the boy's shoulder, forcing him to cower away.

'Now, see what you've caused!' the physician said angrily. 'Extend your arm to me. Now!'

As he administered six further vaccinations to the boy's shaking arm. Dr Licoix raised a mottled eyebrow and looked about the small cabin.

Runaways . . . contrabands of war these, their children, forfeit. It was a brilliant idea, this, his Crust Farm. It saved hundreds of lives, maybe thousands of soldiers, who might die from the smallpox were it not for his crusts.

Ellen, aghast, stood back from it all in the farthest corner of the room. At first she had started to speak, say something about what was happening before her very eyes.

'Silence!' he barked at her, without looking up from the

task at hand. 'You came to me, Madame . . . and now you must be quiet . . . not interfere with Science.'

And so she had crouched back like a crippled thing, unable to intervene, reasoning that this scene would have been played out, had she been there or not.

But to be here . . . to witness it.

'Next!' Dr Licoix ordered from beneath his moustache, ignoring her presence, musing still on his own brilliance.

'Next,' was a tousle-headed girl.

He mussed her hair playfully. 'Now, li'l Maybelline, you show those wet-eyed boys the sterner stuff you little piccaninny girls are made of,' he coaxed.

Li'l Maybelline, all of six years old and bright as a button nodded her head. 'Yas'n, suh, Doctor,' the child said, her eyes downcast, not looking at the boys, nor him.

When he had finished with the fifteen or so children, he smiled, waved, and with a 'See y'all in two weeks!' beckoned Ellen to follow him, padlocking the door behind them, as she did. With a similar key – and no explanation – he unlocked the door to the adjacent cabin. As previously, the children, all black, withdrew into a corner away from him.

Again he smiled. 'Come, come, children, who's your friend?' he began. 'Who brings you nice things?'

He put his hand into his pocket and held it there. At that the children surged forward, arms outstretched. He grabbed one of the arms.

'No! No! No . . . ! Wait . . . ! Let's see what surprises you have for me first,' he teased.

The boy whose arm he had seized tried to withdraw it.

'Oh no, Jason! Fair Jason – you cannot desert the ship. For in your possession you have the Golden Fleece.'

Ellen waited in fascinated horror for what would happen next.

Gingerly Dr Licoix lifted the sleeve of the boy's shirt. 'Excellent, Jason! Excellent!' the doctor purred, well pleased with what he saw. 'A host of golden fleeces . . . and you, Jason, shall have your reward when we have removed them.'

It had been two weeks since he had infected the boy with the cow-serum and now the six scabs had perfectly formed, and were ready for harvesting. Ellen watched as Dr Licoix opened his operating case, its corners edged in protective brass. The maroon lining with the American Eagle design was in dull contrast to the glittering array of instruments displayed. Ellen recognised the implements of the surgeons' trade: the Herstein Capital Blade Saw, with its interchangeable blade for the larger bones of arms and legs; there too the ebony-handled chainsaw for bones inaccessible to the blade saw; then, the eel-like staves of solid German silver for locating calcific deposits in the urinary bladder. She wondered if – and where – he used them. Imagined he must.

Dr Licoix delayed, waiting for the boy's eyes to settle on the neatly stacked set of surgical scalpels.

Maybe the boy would be a doctor one day . . . maybe!

If only he was white.

Jason was a bright boy, Dr Licoix knew.

From amongst the assorted sizes and shapes, he selected a scalpel. One with a long ivory handle and the shortest blade.

'This won't hurt, Jason, you know that! We can't damage the harvest you've so carefully grown.' With that, the man gently cut away from the boy's flesh the crust containing the cultivated smallpox scab. Before completely severing it, he safely secured the valuable crust in the grip of a dissecting forceps, used normally for holding tissue during operations. Now, like an artist, he completed the procedure. The boy felt nothing. Only a slight nip as the crust came finally away from its donor.

Carefully the harvester placed his yield on a piece of tin-foil sheeting. In silence, deftly and beautifully, he removed each of the other five crusts from the boy's arm.

'Now, the other arm, Jason!' Dr Licoix said, benevolently. 'Then you get your reward.'

The boy hesitated.

'Now that didn't hurt, did it, Jason? I never nicked you the once,' the doctor soothed, feigning some hurt.

Still the boy made no move to roll up his other sleeve.

'Do it, Jason!' the doctor said, still smiling – but at the thatch of his mouth only, Ellen noticed.

Slowly the boy drew the shirtsleeve up along his arm.

'So that's it!' Dr Licoix's mien changed when he saw not six scabs . . . but four.

'You've lost them! God damn you, you've lost them!' he roared at the frightened child. Violently, he whipped the boy's arm towards him, careful not to dislodge the four remaining cultivars.

'I should have known that entreating don't work with nigger whelps. Now I gotta teach you!'

With that the man savagely scalpelled the scabs still intact on the boy's arm, taking with them slivers of skin. The boy screamed with pain, until the physician cast him aside, throwing some bandaging linen after him. 'Fix yourself up! I'll need that arm again!'

'Stop it! Stop it!' Ellen shouted, running to the boy. 'It's horrible! All too horrible!'

She busied herself with bandaging the boy's arm while Dr Licoix addressed the frightened children as a whole, admonishing them vehemently. 'I've told you young niggers about fightin' and rough-housin' . . . but you won't listen! You just won't listen!'

Ellen, when she had fixed the boy and comforted him, stood close now to Dr Licoix, holding the children's arms. By assisting him, she could at least make sure he was careful.

On he worked, reaping his grim harvest, berating them, and piling his crusts, like poxed manna into the protective sanctuary of his tinfoiled chalice.

At length the reaper, his harvest gathered, nodded to Ellen that they were leaving. She had not the hypocrisy of heart to say anything to them. Only to get away from this place.

At the door Dr Licoix turned to face his 'harvesters'. All

hope in their faces dashed at what they knew was coming.

'The crop was poor, the labourers found wanting. The Good Master rewards only those servants who are just and fruitful. Now do your dance!' he ordered.

Ellen watched as the fearful children gathered in a circle. Slowly at first they began to move. Awkward in front of the white mistress who came with their captor. Then, grotesquely they began to bob and sway, making strange bird-like motions with their heads and arms.

'It's their smallpox dance,' Dr Licoix explained. 'They do it – all those itching and scratching motions to ward off the coming of the Smallpox God.' He laughed. 'That's the little black savages for you.'

Ellen grabbed the door handle, flinging open her escape from this wretched place, and ran out. Behind her, Dr Licoix calmly locked the door on his unworthy servants, leaving them dancing to a more fearsome master still – the Smallpox God.

Outside, he released his grip on the crumbled chocolate he had held in his pocket. He had been tempted to throw them a fistful. But that would have rewarded their erroneous ways. And how would they ever learn if he displayed weakness through unearned kindness?

He mentally counted the smallpox crusts he had harvested from the eleven children in his 'farm'. One hundred and thirty-two he should have had for a full crop. That Jason had cost him two. So too, that older, full-blooded girl with the blue-black skin. That girl would be trouble when she grew older still. Three of the younger girls had picked off a crust apiece. Scratching themselves, he guessed. Seven lost in all. One hundred and twenty-five he had left, at five dollars a piece from the Surgeon-General, because of the shortage.

One hand grasping the mahogany case with its valuable crop, and Ellen at a distance behind him, Dr Licoix jauntily made his way back to his house.

Feeling the stickiness in his other hand he removed it from

his pocket. This damn weather . . . too hot by far. He examined his smudge-stained fingers and smiled. Then, as he went, he licked them clean, savouring the melted chocolate, well satisfied with the day's pickings.

Ellen couldn't wait to get away from the place, from him. He stopped by the rickety railing, hand outstretched, offering her a bruised piece of chocolate. Seemed unoffended when she refused.

'Twenty dollars!' he said.

She fumbled for the money and thrust it at him. He pocketed it away from the chocolate, opened his cache of crusts and singled out two for her. With what she had just witnessed, she hadn't the heart to argue the price with him.

'Mind it well, Madame Lavelle!' he counselled. Then, nodding backwards towards the place from which they had come, added, 'The supply is not inexhaustible.'

She snatched the life-saving hosts from him, wrapped them in her kerchief and ran down the road towards where Mary lay waiting.

SEVENTY-FOUR

Ellen held Mary's arm as Louisa made the tiny incisions. Louisa then applied one of the scabs, gouging it into the cuts on her sister's arm.

'You must have this protection, Mary,' Ellen said. 'The contagion spreads.'

'The Lord will protect me,' was Mary's answer.

'The Lord protects those who protect themselves,' Louisa added matter-of-factly.

Mary falling ill with smallpox was Ellen's worst fear realised. In vain had she and Louisa tried to get Mary to share the burden of care. In the end they recognised that it presented no second thought for Mary. It was 'in His name'. Risk to self was not even a consideration. To deny Mary that, would have been to inflict indignity on her vocation, worse than any mortal ailment could ever do. Now Ellen assumed that same mantle of care for her sole surviving child, as Mary had so often done for others.

She forbade Louisa to intervene. 'My life is of little consequence. Your life, Louisa, as matron of this hospital, is of great consequence,' Ellen said firmly.

At first, Mary had brushed off the notion that she had contracted the disease. 'I am flushed from overwork, that is all, Mother!' she had answered, when Ellen had previously raised the question with her.

But that night Mary herself knew. Her temples throbbed, her body bathed itself in perspiration. 'If it is Thy will,' she prayed, already reconciled to whatever might come.

Later, Ellen heard her stifle a moan – Mary not wishing to disturb them. Taking her night-light she ran to Mary and put her hand to the girl's forehead.

'Oh my child! My poor child! You're raging with fever!'

'It will pass, Mother – just a night fever. Go back to bed,' Mary insisted.

Ellen ran for water, waking Louisa. 'It's Mary!' was all she said.

Then she mopped Mary's forehead and neck, while Louisa fetched a fan, left behind by a society lady of Richmond.

'Move her to under the window – the night breeze,' Louisa said, already at the bedhead. Together they lifted Mary's cot.

Outside the pale Virginian moon hung there, witness to their feverish efforts to curtail the rise in Mary's temperature.

Eventually, it seemed to stabilise. Ellen wondered for how long? She ordered Louisa to bed. 'I will stay with Mary – your work is with many.'

She sat stroking all that remained of Mary's hair, the beautiful golden-red tresses, long-shorn. A mark of Magdalen modesty. Ellen recalled the hundred strokes she once lovingly administered to Mary and the others each Sunday before Mass. Back when they were small. Then, down they'd all go, over the mountain-pass road to the little thatched church at Finny. Alongside the church, the Finny river, would gurgle its way happily between the two lakes, the Mask and Lough Nafooey. Each vying in grandeur with the other.

'Mother, you should not be here!' Mary's voice drew her back.

Ellen let her hand rest on Mary's brow.

'Oh, but I should, Mary. Too long I wasn't here!'

Mary did not remonstrate with her.

'Then pray with me – the Holy Rosary,' she asked. '– Our Saviour's Resurrection from Death. Whatever our suffering, it is of little consequence compared with His.'

Quietly then, the moon giving them its light, they tolled out the Five Glorious Mysteries, with their implicit desire for Heaven and eternal happiness.

Resurrection from the Dead
Ascension into Heaven
Coming of the Holy Ghost
Assumption of the Blessed Virgin into Heaven
Crowning of the Blessed Virgin

Into the daylight Ellen sat with Mary, Louisa appearing frequently, the same question always on her lips.

'How is she?'

And the same answer, when Ellen would tell her, 'No worse.'

Dr Sawyer came to her bringing some whiskey and quinine, 'For when the pain comes.'

Mary refused all such medication. 'I want to be with you and Louisa, not ginned up to the gills,' she weakly laughed.

Then, the fever revived itself more virulently than before. Ellen worked furiously to quell its worst ravages, and alarmed, sent for Louisa. In turn they tried to wet her lips, first with the quinine, then with the whiskey. Mary resisted so strongly that they desisted, fearing to usurp all of her remaining strength.

Throughout the next day – punctured by all the normal sounds of war – Ellen sat with her child.

The blister-like vesicles on Mary's face she lanced and drained, in an attempt to decrease the irritation. But the clear vesicles turned into ugly pustules, pockmarking Mary's beautiful face.

'Sulphuric ointment might help – if we had some,' Dr Sawyer advised.

Ellen hurried the ten miles there and back through both sides of the conflict to the nearest hospital to get some. Religiously she applied the sulphuric plasters, cementing them against Mary's skin to keep out the noxious air. For each of the pustules that Ellen masked it seemed another erupted as quickly to replace it. Then she noted more severely inflamed lesions with hard, everted edges. Different from those already there, these were of a copperhued colour, and rapidly spreading over Mary's body.

Immediately, Ellen summoned Dr Sawyer, pointing out these new foul-surfaced lesions.

Shubael Sawyer examined Mary, recognising something, his face darkening.

'Doctor . . . what is it?' Ellen asked, riven with panic at what the doctor's face clearly told. There was some complication. She knew it!

He caught her arm, quickly propelling her away from Mary, only stopping when out of earshot.

'Tell me, Doctor . . . tell me . . . whatever it is!' Ellen pleaded.

'Mrs Lavelle,' he said, in a grave voice, still holding her arm. 'Sister Mary . . . your child . . . Mary has contracted Syphilis!'

She looked at him – it was a mistake – he was wrong – Mary – impossible!

'The crust . . .' Dr Sawyer explained. 'It must have come from an infected donor. Many soldiers of both sides . . .' He let the words trail off, averted his eyes from hers. 'That by which we sought to cure her has . . .' Again he left the sentence unfinished.

'What chance has she now'? Ellen asked, not letting go of him, feeling that same sensation she felt when first they brought Patrick to her.

'Less . . . although the latter infection is of itself not fatal, her constitution has already been seriously weakened by the former. I have no words with which to idly comfort you, Mrs

Lavelle,' the doctor continued. 'That this should be visited on such as Sister Mary is beyond human comprehension – and the gods do openly weep.'

Presently he returned with an amber bottle. **Mercury,** *the label read.* **Pilulae Opii with morphine USA Medical Purveying Dept., Astoria.**

'It will ease things for Sister Mary,' was all Dr Sawyer said, handing Ellen the bottle.

She was distraught. Mary, her child, her last remaining child, her vessel of purity, to be stricken by syphilis – the soldier's disease. How could it be? How could anything be so cruel? Any God? And she herself had brought the diseased crust to Mary. Not trusted in the healing goodness of the Almighty but rather wanted to interpose herself between Mary and her God. Had wanted of her own accord to be Mary's saviour. And now . . . ! Consumed with her own grief at what she had been complicit in, it took some time before Ellen's thoughts returned to Dr Licoix and his farm – the source of Mary's infection.

'Oh, my God!' she cried out. 'The children! The children – it's one of the children!'

Then she remembered the older girl, the beautiful blue-black girl. It had to be her. Her not more than a child – and with the soldier's disease. She couldn't dwell on it – how the girl-child . . . but she resolved there and then, when Mary's sickness subsided, to return to Dr Licoix's hellish place and smash open its prison doors. Free the children. But what would she then do with them?

Her mind, agitated by everything that had happened, raced ahead to this new problem. She couldn't let them run loose in the rampaging countryside. They would be captured again, shot . . . or worse.

The beautiful blue-black girl leapt into her mind again. The hospital would take them – maybe – in Richmond? If she brought them South they would likely end up again enslaved. North they would become contrabands of war. And the girl at least needed treatment. She heard Mary whimper and for now put all such thoughts of the black children out of her mind.

Often, Mary would call out for Ellen, or Louisa.

The dead were on her lips as much as the living. Her father, Michael and Patrick.

Each fond name was an arrow to Ellen's heart – the grief of remembrance now bound up with the grief of what lay ahead.

Then, in moments of lucidity, Mary would pray, always pray. The New Testament: 'Let not this cup pass from me.' Or the Old: 'Naked came I out of my mother's womb, and naked shall I return thither.'

Or, her favourite prayer – to the Mother of God. 'Hail Mary, full of Grace . . . Holy Mary . . . Pray for us sinners now, And at the hour of our death. Amen.'

Once, when Ellen could no longer hold open her eyes, she laid her head beside Mary's. She had not intended sleep, only rest. When she awoke, Mary was caressing her head as one might a child. At this, Ellen could no longer contain her composure in front of Mary and broke down, the tears flooding her cheeks unashamedly.

'Oh, Mary, my love!' she sobbed uncontrollably 'I'm going to lose you – lose you so soon – I just can't bear it any more!'

'Sshh now, *a Mhamaí*!' Mary replied, still stroking Ellen's head, calling her by the old-tongue Mother-word.

'We will never be lost to each other – you know that,' Mary said in the softest of voices. She stopped the stroking a moment, thinking of something. '*A Mhamaí* . . . remember how you once scolded me for calling you that – for using Irish – on the ship, when we first came to America?'

Beneath Mary's hand, Ellen nodded.

'You said we should leave behind the old tongue now that we were going to a new land – to America.' Mary paused, gave a little laugh. 'Strange, how some things you can't leave behind, no matter how hard you try? Anyway . . .' she continued, 'I prefer it in the Irish. *A Mhamaí*! . . . it's gentler – more like mothers really are.'

287

Ellen wiped her eyes. Mary always had a little parable – would never openly chide her for anything.

'You are so wise, Mary,' Ellen said, sitting up. 'Where did you get it all from?'

'From you and all that went before you,' Mary answered simply.

'Mary . . . I'm sorry for all the . . .' Ellen began, but Mary reached over, putting a finger to her mother's lips, silencing her.

'We are all vessels of clay waiting to be broken. God has long ago forgiven you as I have . . . and long before you asked. Now, no more of this – will you sing to me?'

And Mary lay back, closing her eyes, waiting.

Ellen started, an old infant-dandling song. One she would often lilt out to Mary, dandling her on her knees. Every so often bouncing her into the air at the start of each new round of the tune, Mary shouting with glee, wanting her to do it again, and again . . .

She felt Mary squeeze her hand with the shared remembering, the song soothing both listener and singer alike, binding them together, expressing some unspoken thing between them

Then a softer, tenderer song – Moore. His melodies had found their way even over here, to America. This one written for the young Sarah Curran, engaged to be married to the executed patriot, Robert Emmet.

Rebellions, revolutions, executions – it was the song of mankind – and of Stephen Joyce, Ellen thought. Where was Stephen now in what battle, she wondered?

She felt Mary stir, started singing.

'Has sorrow thy young days shaded,
As clouds o'er the morning fleet?
Too fast have those young days faded,
That, even in sorrow, were sweet?
Does Time with his cold wing wither,

288

Each feeling that once was dear?
Then, child of misfortune, come hither,
I'll weep with thee, tear for tear.'

Somewhere, not far off, the cannons of war boomed, death
withering its way on their cold wings.

And those, newly-withered of limb, would tonight have
only themselves to sing to sleep. Maybe 'The Last Rose of
Summer', another of Moore's love songs and popular with
the soldiers. Strange, how they had to come to America to
learn them. The songs, as it were, following after the people.
It was not the music Ellen had previously known, the songs
of mountain, river and stream. Moore's music was the music
of cities, like Dublin and London, for the drawing rooms of
fine gentlemen and their ladies. But here, in America, his
songs had become the sorrowing songs of soldiers on both
sides.

Now she sang Moore's song for Mary.

> ''Tis the last rose of summer
> Left blooming alone,
> All her lovely companions,
> Are faded and gone . . .
>
> 'Since the lovely are sleeping,
> Go, sleep thou with them.
>
> 'When true hearts lie wither'd
> And fond ones are flown,
> Oh! Who would inhabit
> This bleak world alone?'

She never felt Mary slip away – just a cooling of her hand.
Thinking her temperature had once again abated Ellen kept
singing to her, song after song after song.

'She's gone, Mother. Mary's gone!'

289

Louisa had entered the room, stood listening as Ellen sang her elegy to her last remaining child. Now she had lost every single one of them.

Louisa, too, was filled with the unutterable grief of Mary's death. She put her arms around Ellen's neck, resting her head on her mother's, as Ellen, lost somewhere in the song, still sang to her dead child. Next to her God, Louisa recognised, she loved this remarkable woman more than anything else on this forsaken earth.

'She's gone, Mother,' Louisa repeated, kissing Ellen tenderly. 'Our Mary is gone.'

They sat a while with Mary, prayed with her. Then Ellen caught Louisa's hand.

'She is not going in the lime-pit, Louisa. Mary is not going to be eaten by lime.'

Ellen had seen that before, back in Ireland, at the workhouse. Those dead by famine, moulded by lime into a monstrous and unidentifiable mound. Like a great black sun, the mound rising crescent-like against the workhouse wall, where the lime had eaten both flesh and bone. And the stench, Ellen had never forgotten the stench.

They took Mary. Stole her away into the night. Away, to the far side of the trees.

In a gladed spot, Louisa stopped.

'Here, where it is green and sheltered, we could gently lay her back to the earth,' Louisa said.

'No, Louisa!' Ellen answered. 'Mary will not go into a shallow grave, to be picked at by hogs and the prying of soldiers' bayonets.'

She explained no further, nor did Louisa ask. At the edge of the copse, Ellen motioned Louisa to set down Mary's body. Louisa then sat on the ground, Mary's head in her lap, waiting. She watched as Ellen gathered some dry brushwood, set it into the broad-based fork of a low-lying tree.

Her mother was building a funeral pyre – like the pagans

of old – committing Mary's body to the moon and the stars.

Louisa looked upwards – the Handle of the Plough. That's where Ellen had told them her own parents were, tilling the great wastelands of the sky. Harvesting the heavens to give light to the earth.

Ellen set some leafy boughs above the brushwood. Soft for Mary's last sleep. Louisa looked at the ravaged face of her sister. Ravaged but possessing such serenity, such peace. Mary had no earthly attachments. She was here in this world only to be the instrument of Him who had created her. Disease, death, rejection, humiliation – all human frailty held no fear for Mary. Everything was His plan. Life led to death. Death led back to Him – to everlasting life.

Louisa whispered aloud the words she had heard her sister so often say, 'Grains of sand in the desert, Grains of time in an eternity, Inconsequential yet unique.'

Mary was that . . . unique.

Then Ellen was ready.

Between them they lifted Mary's slight body, raising it above their shoulders. Slowly, they bore her aloft, procession-like, approaching the burial platform. Louisa gently lowered Mary's head and shoulders onto the fronded bier. Inch by inch then, stepping backwards, delivering forward the remains of her sister, while Ellen supported Mary's legs. Then, from the other side of the tree-fork, Louisa settled Mary deeper into the pyre, Ellen assisting her from the opposite side.

They never spoke, except in prayer. Louisa led the Litany of the Dead, Ellen responding.

'From all wrath'

'Good Lord deliver them'

'From the strictness of thy justice'

'Good Lord deliver them'

'From the gnawing worm of conscience'

'Good Lord deliver them'

'From the weeping and gnashing of teeth'

'Good Lord deliver them'

'From eternal anguish'
'Good Lord deliver them'
'That thou wouldst deliver the faithful departed from the penalties of sin'
'We beseech thee to hear us'
When they had finished the monotonous chant Ellen took from her pocket the white oak Rosary which Mary had given to her. Entwined it then through her child's fingers, the crucifix upright facing Mary. Carefully, Ellen undid Mary's bonnet and with small surgical scissors, took a snip of her child's hair. Reverently, she placed the hair into some bandaging linen, folding it over and over, like some liturgical rite, before re-fixing Mary's headdress.

Louisa watched Ellen whisper something into Mary's ear . . . some last intimacy between them. Finally, Ellen kissed her child's forehead, then her eyes and lips. Anointing her, Louisa thought. As Ellen turned away her hand found Mary's, held it briefly, bidding it a last farewell. *'Slán abhaile, a stoirín!'* Louisa heard the final blessing. 'Go safely home, ashore!'

Ellen moved back, waiting.

Louisa then paid her last respects, touching her sister, talking to her as if she were still there.

Then it was time.

Ellen struck the Lucifer match. It flared in the gloom, catching her face for a moment.

Louisa watched her, started the De Profundis, the great prayer of the soul seeking its God.

> *'De Profundis a clamavi ad te Domine!'*
> 'Out of the depths I cry unto you, O Lord!'

Ellen set the fizzling match against the hem of Mary's habit, held it there, watching the dark brown heat-spot expand until it took flame, edging slowly into Mary's shroud. Then it spread, ever-widening its orb, licking now at the tinder-dry wood.

'Domine exaudi vocem meam fiant.'
'O, Lord hear my voice.'

Ellen stood riveted to the spot, watching the flame, as if it were a thing apart, had its own beauty and would not, in moments, devour her darling girl.

Louisa ran to her, caught her by the shoulders.

'Mother! Mother – stand back!'

Then Louisa felt what, at first she thought was a trembling, deep within her mother's body. Then the low rumbling grew slowly more distinct. Out of the depths of Ellen's being it rose. Up through her body until, in her throat, it held a moment, transforming itself from movement into sound.

Louisa continued to hold Ellen, trying to quell the trembling. It was her mother's own De Profundis, her soul crying out for deliverance.

When it did find release, what passed her mother's lips was no prayer. It was savage, primeval. It came from long before the prophets and the priests. From a time when woman was a beast of the forests – hunting, killing, being killed.

The fearsome keening bruted itself out of Ellen's body, from her eyes, her ears, her nostrils, the savage mouth. She threw back her head, arms raised, fingers extended towards the flames, shaking off Louisa's embrace.

'*Och . . . ! Occh . . . ! Oochh . . . !*' The sound came like some strangulated thing fighting for breath. *Ooooochón! Ochón! Ochóóóón!* Each push of the sound rising the note. Distorting it. Flinging it far above the trees and the heavens, her grief pouring over all. Wave after wave of it, rising and falling – as though a knife, repeatedly plunged and withdrawn. Louisa stood back, the flames lighting the Heavens, consuming their beautiful Mary. Ellen continued her lament, singing now in the language she always had . . . once.

'*Is briste mo chroí, is uaigneach mo shlí* . . .
Broken is my heart, desolate my life . . .

. . . Don't leave me alive here, behind
With my darling stretched out before me.'

And she cursed God. Cursed the famine that had sent them
here to this land. Cursed the unGodly war that had cost her
her son, and now her daughter.

'Curse be upon me for my sin! Curse be on the mother
who sees her children die!'

Louisa did not notice Ellen withdraw the curved surgical
scissors from her pocket and then open its gleaming jaws.
When she did observe it in her mother's hand, its intent at
first escaped her.

As if in another dimension of time, Louisa saw Ellen bare
her left shoulder. Then slowly, inexorably, she dug the curved
blade into the flesh of her shoulder and dragged it downwards over her breast. Three times, she inflicted the mark
upon herself, no outward pain visible. As if flesh and sinew
and life itself had already been deadened.

When finished, calmly she returned the surgical implement
to her pocket, wiping its blade with her finger. Then she
pulled up the shoulder of her dress, covering the gashed limb.

Only then did the sound come again.

Ochón . . . . *an Gorta Mór! Och, Ochón* . . . . . .
. . . *Americeá! Ochón! Och Ochón* . . . . *An Bás!*

'Famine', 'America', 'Death' itself, she lamented.

When she was spent, Louisa went to her.

Drew her down to the ground.

Sat with her into the dying night. She muttering as a child
might, mostly making no sense – only their names.

'Mary . . . Patrick . . . Michael . . . Lavelle.'

Then she would change the order around. 'Michael . . .
Mary . . .' as if to try to make meaning of it. Every so often
she would raise her head, look at Louisa, mouth something

. . . reach out a desolate finger . . . withdraw it again before touching her . . . start up some old *suantraí* – a sleepsong for children.

The day edged in on them, greying the ashes of Mary's funeral pyre. No last glow left with which to comfort them. Only the blackened stump of the tree, ribboned with ash.

'Dust to dust . . . ashes to ashes . . .' Ellen said, nothing left in her now. Not even grief. She remained on the ground while Louisa rose and went to the tree. There, Louisa gathered within her hand some of the remains of her sister's bodily life. Safely then, she knotted the handful of ashes within her handkerchief. Next she trailed her fingers through the remaining ashes, finding what she expected – the metal crucifix. She wiped it clean in the folds of her habit, kissed her crucified Saviour and put Him in her pocket. Her own grief Louisa joined with His suffering. Nor did she pass any judgement on Ellen, for the ritual in which they had both participated.

Her mother would need healing now. As much as any of the other poor wretches with whom they daily dealt.

Even, if she would not admit to it. Or ask for it.

SEVENTY-FIVE

'There's work to be done . . .' Ellen said after a while, to Louisa. 'Others . . .'

In silence they walked together back from the grove where they had made their last partings with Mary.

At the hospital Dr Sawyer was waiting.

'Mrs Lavelle! Sister! I am sorry, deeply sorry. Sister Mary will be sadly missed.'

Ellen nodded, turned into the ward. The men fell silent at her presence, bowing their heads, averting their eyes. Some, who could raise an arm, crossed themselves. This was her second to be taken – in as many months.

It was Sergeant Doherty who broke the pall of silence. Came to her. Went down on both knees before her.

'She took my place, ma'am. She knew it but she didn't care!'

She lifted him to his feet, put a hand to his forehead.

'Mary will be happy, Sergeant.'

'Because of her I can leave here tomorrow – God rest her! God rest her!' he said awkwardly and retreated to his bunk.

Gradually, she moved among them, receiving their condolences, offering comfort and hope in return. Mary had touched so many of these men's lives even those of a different faith. Some couldn't understand why the 'quiet Sister', had had such an effect on them, much less express it. Just knew that she did, that Sister Mary was 'different – not like the rest of us', a seasoned campaigner said to Ellen, adding that 'Some good did come out of this war, with the likes of Sister Mary.'

Ellen prayed for the strength to get through that first day. She did not ask for the ache within her to be stilled, only that somewhere she find the will to deny pity to herself. Pity did not heal, it sucked up the spirit, kept a person looking in on themselves when the whole world needed her to be looking out. So, she would do what she always did – a bandage here, a shot of morphine there. Hold a hand, lend an ear to the dying. Go on dispensing the necessities of life and death to those who needed it . . . needed it in a seemingly unending stream.

That night, as always, she knelt and prayed. Offered up the events of the day – 'All my prayers, works and sufferings, for all the intentions of thy Divine Heart.' It was fervent, devout. She had long-learned, through self-abnegation to sublimate her human wants to that of a higher will than hers. Even so, as she clambered into bed, her body shivered with loss.

She clenched the threadbare blanket in an effort to still herself. She prayed until she thought prayer would numb her. But she was not numbed. Only bereft beyond prayer's reach.

At first she tried to console herself with the thought that, all through her saintly life, death and death alone had been Mary's only desire. But she could not even take comfort that now Mary would be re-united with Patrick . . . take care of him. Together forever in Paradise eternal.

It was no use.

Nothing was of any use now.

She fought with all the capacity of will at her command, pulling the blanket above her head, as if to shut out grief.

The breath began to catch in her chest. Thinking it was the confined space, the lack of air, she threw off the blanket and lay there, unable to stop the breathing; every pore in her body lathering her with grief.

When Mary's name finally burst forth, it came not just from her lips but from the unstoppable trembling in her legs, her twisted gut, her mutilated breasts. It came from the great cavernous hole which inhabited her.

Louisa, still on duty heard it; the men heard it. More fierce than the shriek of any artillery, more piercing than steel through flesh – it silenced all, the sound curdling its way to the innards and the unfathomable places where terror lives.

'Mar . . . eeeeeee!'

Louisa ran to her, swept Ellen into her arms. Cradled her mother through the deep, deep night.

Ellen slept late, and awoke, wondering if it was all a terrible nightmare.

Louisa had returned to the ward.

Before Ellen had time to gather her thoughts, she had been summoned by Dr Sawyer to assist at an amputation.

It was a half-leg, from the knee – nothing too serious. After that a hand crushed like a flatiron by a collapsed cannon; a gangrened arm to be taken; and a mortally wounded flag bearer for whom all she could do was whisper the Act of Contrition into his soundless ear.

She often wondered about that – whispering the act of sorrow to those unable, or perhaps unwilling to hear it? Did it do any good?

The Church taught that though the body might be in the terminal state, the subconscious mind might register the words, giving them some silent assent. Thus by seeking forgiveness and resolving to sin no more, the soul might be spared eternal banishment.

Those who wreaked such havoc on the young men of America by putting guns into innocent hands had, she thought, a much greater need for forgiveness than the likes of the dead boy in her arms, to whom she now whispered it.

After that the day slipped into the ordinary day it had always been. A cry of pain, a call for relief, a bed to be turned down, its occupant departed for this world or the next. 'Water!' A letter to be read or written or a comforting word occasioned by the message sent or received.

That day, of all days, she felt she had physically aged. That day she knew she would not remain any longer. Even if it meant leaving Louisa.

First, though, she had to deal with the matter of Dr Licoix.

The following day, and before she had time to talk with Louisa, and just a few short hours after he had bade them goodbye, Ellen heard that Sergeant Doherty had got his wish. Taken half a dozen with him when he was downed going over the top of a Rebel breastworks.

Finally, she spoke with Louisa, revealing to her the source of Dr Licoix's deadly crusts and her part in their procurement.

Louisa took her mother's hands. 'You did then what you had to – I would not have done less. Now we must put right the wrong,' was Louisa's only comment.

They embraced, flawed, fallible, each needing that forgiveness of touch that prayer alone could not grant.

They left by nightfall, a flat-faced axe, which Louisa had conjured up from somewhere, hidden in the concealing folds of her nun's habit.

Ellen, wondering if she could find the way again, asked light of the nourishing stars. To be creeping by night in the cauldron of war was to invite being shot – by either side, both being fearful of surprise attacks.

Hours it took them to find the place. It was all in darkness, eerie by moonlight. Past Dr Licoix's house they crept to the wooded area where the 'hospitals' stood.

Ellen put her face to the door.

'Jason!' she whispered. 'Jason!'

At first there was no reply and she feared that Licoix, seeing her reaction when she first visited had spirited them away. But no. On a further call she heard stirrings from within.

'Jason!' she called . . . louder. She heard feet coming to the door.

'It's the woman . . .' she said, describing herself, 'come to free you. Don't be afraid.'

Then the patter of more feet, whispered talk. Silence.

'I'm going to break the door and get you out – so stand back! Don't be frightened!' she repeated to them.

At the door to the other cabin Louisa enacted the same scene. They would have to be quick, let each group of children know what was happening so that they didn't panic and disappear through the fields.

Then, Ellen raised the axe, fiercely striking the door handle. Three blows it took before the lock gave way. Immediately a great shout – fear mixed with uncertainty – arose. She handed the axe to Louisa and pushed in the door. Frightened, the children stood crushed together in a far corner. Ellen spotted the older girl and was relieved to see that she had not noticeably failed since last she had seen her.

'Sshh, children!' she said. 'We are going to get you safely away from this awful place.'

They looked at her disbelievingly, this white woman, who had but some days previously assisted in their suffering. Ellen heard Louisa crash the other door with the axe.

'See!' she said. 'Everybody is going to be free. Now stay together!'

She got them outside in time to see the rest of the children dash wildly from the other cabin, terrified as if the very Devil himself was after them. Screaming at the strange sight of Louisa and her axe.

'The Smallpox God! The Smallpox God is comin' to git us!' they cried in alarm.

Eventually, and with much coaxing, all the children were rounded up. Even then they crowded around Ellen for safety. Louisa had considered removing her winged headdress, thinking that it might calm them somewhat. Almost immediately, she had reconsidered her idea. Her closely-cropped head, might, she thought, cause even more terror among the children. For a moment her thoughts lingered on Jared Prudhomme. As briefly, Louisa dismissed them again with a silent 'Grant eternal rest to his soul and may perpetual light shine upon him.'

Although there was much commotion, there didn't seem to be any movement from within the doctor's rickety house. Licoix was not there.

They counted the children, twenty-two in all, less than Ellen had remembered. She did not dwell on what dark reasons might have caused the disparity of numbers. The girl she made a point of going to, bending down beside her, stroking her wrists.

'What's your name, child?' she asked, gently.

'Delta!' the child answered. 'Cos of where I was born.'

'It's a beautiful name, like you are – Delta,' she said.

'And do you know how old you are?'

'I'm not sure, ma'am – thirteen – but I could be twelve,' the child answered, large ebony-hued eyes fixed on Ellen's red hair.

'Would you like to touch it?' Ellen asked, seeing the child's fixation with it.

Shyly, the girl lowered her eyes and said, 'Uh-uh.'

Then Ellen took the child's hand and placed it on her head, moving it through the thick tresses.

'You have beautiful hair too, Delta. May I touch it?' Ellen asked, but the child backed away, taking her hand from Ellen's head as she did so. 'It's all right, Delta – you've been hurt and by white folk, like me – I understand.'

On the way back, Ellen noticed that the girl, despite her earlier reticence kept close by. Watching like some wounded animal for danger on every side and an escape route through which she could bolt.

Dr Sawyer could scarce believe his eyes when next morning he found twenty-two little 'piccaninnies' asleep on the floor with Ellen and Louisa keeping watch over them. Louisa, he noticed, sat with the head of an axe visible from underneath the hem of her habit.

He sighed as he approached the two women. 'Why am I not surprised any more?' he asked resignedly, eyes fixed on Ellen.

She started to say something, some explanation.

'Don't!' Dr Sawyer, hand upraised, stopped her. 'It is impossible for them to stay here. From whence they came, I will not ask.'

'I think you know, Dr Sawyer – or at least have guessed,' Ellen said, unflinchingly.

'And what a story it would make with the reporters,' Louisa added. 'Lincoln, the Liberator of the Negro, harvesting the scabs of their children.'

'What these children need now is some rest, food and medical care,' Ellen said, lifting up the sleeve of one of the sleeping children. '. . . And this young lady needs more urgent care . . .' she continued, 'for there, Doctor, lies the innocent source of Mary's disease.'

Dr Sawyer winced at her words, visibly paling.

'I will assist you,' Ellen continued. 'Matron here . . .' she said, referring to Louisa, 'has other business . . . with the Surgeon-General.'

Dr Sawyer smiled a pitying smile for the Surgeon-General.

Three days later Louisa returned, two orderlies in tow, with much needed medications and supplies.

'And news!' she beamed. 'The Surgeon-General, of his own accord, offered to have the children escorted northwards, whenever they are ready to leave here. There they will receive fostering until the war is done. Thereafter, every effort will be made to reunite them with their families.'

Ellen was greatly relieved. Later she asked Louisa if it had been difficult with the Surgeon-General.

Louisa laughed.

'Mother, it was an unfair contest. The Surgeon-General had only Mr Lincoln on his side . . . I had God on mine!'

SEVENTY-SIX

A week after Mary's death, Ellen decided to leave.

Mary's death was her epiphany.

God could ask no more of her. Nor would she give it.

Mary had freed her of debt to God. Mary and Patrick both.

Somewhere in the distance gunfire cracked and the killing began again. She must find Lavelle – go and find him. Not wait here until he was stretchered into her, like Patrick. Or she stumble over him in the blood-laden, after-mist of battle, a note pinned to his breast so that he could be named and claimed. She did not want to claim him in death. Death was forever, an eternity of remorse that she hadn't found him in time.

She bade goodbye to the children, hugged each of them, the girl Delta wanting to come with her.

She took her leave of the men, every single one of them. They stood, those who could and cheered her. The remainder raised what crutch or good limb they had left, in a farewell salute.

'The Union has two million men they say and the Confederates, a million,' Dr Sawyer told her as he handed her the note. 'It is an impossible task.'

She knew it was.

'Life itself is an impossible task, Doctor,' she replied and thanked him for the note that would garner her safe passage – she hoped.

'South is it, Mother?' Louisa asked.

'Oh, I don't know, Louisa! I think so. I have enquired of every Northern soldier who has passed under our care and there is no word of him, even amongst the Irish. He must, after all, have gone South . . . with Patrick.'

Louisa saw her falter.

'Are you sure you're strong enough?' Louisa started to ask and regretted it, almost immediately.

'I have never been strong enough,' her adoptive mother said, no reproach for Louisa in her voice – only for herself.

'I will storm Heaven mercilessly that you find him . . . and for your safe return,' Louisa said, embracing her.

Ellen held her tightly, instinctively caressing her in a slow circular motion, as if to a child. 'Flesh of my flesh, bone of my bone,' she whispered into Louisa's headdress.

They parted, all spoken and unspoken between them.

Louisa watched her from the doorway.

It was her way . . . journeying . . . a task . . . an over-coming. It was a curse, a cross on her back. Her mother atrophied when still . . . facing herself.

Louisa watched Ellen's back reach the edge of the trees. Already had her hand raised when the traveller's footsteps stopped and Ellen turned. Just a backward look, no sound, no hand. Then, as quickly, her mother turned on her path and disappeared from view.

Louisa waited, the hand that blessed the traveller still raised, some song from her childhood murmuring up inside her, that the tinker-folk had. Some prayer to the moon, the bright jewel of the night, to light the traveller's way.

She whispered 'Amen', lowered her hand, looking for a moment to where the trees had swallowed Ellen. Then went in to the cries of the anguished.

'. . . To the tainted and needy, five senses restore . . . give song to our voices, sight to our eyes . . .'

'Mother . . . !' a poor soul beseeched Louisa, his face where it had half been shot away replaced by a thin layer of cork.

'Mother, put your hand to the good side before I go . . .' he pleaded.

She moved towards the man – another voice shouting.

'Aw shut-up, cork face, for Christ's sake!'

She sat beside the man, put her hand on his fevered forehead, inadvertently touching the lifeless material. Damp it was, with his own sweat, giving some false semblance of mottled life.

He seized her hand with both his own, holding it there, in case she removed the soothing touch, before he went.

'Ah thank you, Mother – God's grace on you!' the man with the cork face said.

She sat thinking of Ellen, her own mother, until the grip on her arm gave a frightened clasp in the final clutching.

SEVENTY-SEVEN

If she had looked behind her, had seen Louisa standing there, Ellen knew she would falter, retrace her steps and go back to her last remaining constant in the world. Louisa was her *anam chara*, her 'soul-friend'. Keeper of things that went beyond words, beyond any kinship. Louisa likewise, would understand why she didn't look back. Louisa was the light of the moon ahead of her, the sheltering stars, the guiding wind at her back. They were two sides of the same coin . . . maybe even the same side. She would go to the ends of the world for Louisa, and Louisa for her. Now she must go to the ends of the Confederacy – the slave states – to find Lavelle.

She prayed for safe passage and to travel hopefully.

As ever her prayers ended with Mary. She asked Heaven's newest angel to keep her spirit strong and true. Mary, inviolate, the most beautiful among tainted humanity. Taken, poxed out of life by the most vile, the most hideous of diseases. Mary, touched by the Divine, scarred by the sordid. The Magdalen sin – Ellen's sin – she had brought to her own child. Her own complicity in Dr Licoix's evil deeds had been responsible. She had known it to be wrong, inhumane, the children to be harvested thus, like some infected crops. She had gone against her own nature – and nature had exacted its price.

And now . . . ? Now she must find Lavelle. Why? She questioned herself, as if necessary to ask after all this time. Guilt . . . so that he would absolve her? Vanity . . . that he still would love her? Everything she touched, it seemed, turned to dust, rancid dust. What if she also brought destruction to Lavelle in order to fulfil her own wayward needs? If she became to him the *bean sí* – the *banshee* – harbinger of death . . . the death messenger?

Now, she was filled with self-doubt. She should have stayed with the men . . . put them first, not herself. What of Louisa? She too had suffered grievously, lost a brother in Patrick, a beloved sister in Mary? Now she, the only mother Louisa could ever remember, was leaving.

Lavelle! Lavelle! She must keep him fixed in her mind. He would know what was best, what suited.

Lavelle always knew what was right, even when she had argued against him, used her superior intellect.

There were truths, basic truths. These could be argued away by slight of tongue, by intellect, but they could never be denied. Lavelle had truth – he knew things – even when she, by dint of argument, convinced him otherwise. Truth existed of its own accord, it didn't need explaining. Sometimes she wished she were closer to how she once had been. Rooted in the old safe ways; barefooted, clenching the sure earth, living the meagre life. The hungry years were the best. Then she was selfless, no thought for her own gain. A story at the hearth, a handed-down tune on the fiddle of a winter's night. The snipe diving at dusk – *mionnán aerach* – little goat of the air – the wind bleating through its wings; the cuckoo-infested valley in May; a look – a loving cup passed frugally. How far she had come – America, land of plenty, the New World. What did it all mean? And young boys who couldn't scratch their names, killing each other like savages, dreaming of glory . . . and liberty? And an imagined America filled with false dawns.

If only she were a philosopher, she could work it all out.

Pull the pieces together. She thought she had . . . many times. Only to have it all fall in on top of her again.

But Lavelle would know. Lavelle knew the ordinary of life. Lavelle would be her Saviour.

LAVELLE

SEVENTY-EIGHT

Union Army, Virginia, 1862

Lavelle knew that by going South his life would be at risk. It didn't matter. He had grown so tired of war. The endless tramping, the skin-and-bone rations; the hollow talk of glory; and the faint promise of a quick victory over the Rebels receding more and more into the never-never land of political wishfulness.

And he was tired of killing . . . sick of lying in the long grass, flat on his belly like some venomous serpent, spitting out death to some mother's son . . . like Patrick.

How now could he face Ellen if he ever found her?

Wherever she had gone, whatever imagined wrong she thought she had done them, nothing could compare with this. Her son . . . the light of her eyes . . . the reincarnation of her first husband, Michael. And he, Lavelle, now her husband, had taken that son away from her. Lain in a hollow, singled him out, and shot him down from a tree like some wild animal.

He took out the blood-edged book he had found on Patrick. Lavelle was convinced it was Ellen's, and that she had given it as a present to Patrick on account of this Emmeline. Lavelle wondered how Patrick had so successfully tracked down his mother after all this time when he himself had failed to do so?

He had assumed Patrick would have long abandoned all notion of continuing to search for Ellen. The boy had not been as forgiving of her disappearance as he had.

Patrick must have changed his mind after he had gone South. But what had Ellen been doing in the Deep South?

He himself, at one stage, had declared he would join with the South.

Ellen had chided him for this. She had argued that 'freedom' was a principle which over-rode Lavelle's arguments about the blacks who, when freed, would swarm northwards like locusts to take Irish jobs, in the process, making the Irish the 'new blacks'.

She had been having none of it.

In time he'd had to admit that, as in many things, she was right. Ultimately he had declared for 'freedom' and the North.

Now, remorsefully, Lavelle thought, if he had *not* listened to her, and instead gone South, Patrick would be still alive.

But he had chosen to stay North for another, more pressing, reason. To find her, thinking she would stay in the burgeoning East Coast cities.

Yet again he had been thwarted. *She* had gone South. Now it was where *he* must go to reach her. Break her heart with the news of Patrick.

SEVENTY-NINE

Armed with a three-month furlough and a letter from General Meagher himself, Lavelle faced towards the 'secesh' State of Louisiana.

The letter would provide him with safe passage through Union lines. Then he would have to destroy it. Take his chances on the return journey. Emmeline's letters to Patrick would gain him safe conduct through Confederate lines. He was on a mission of mercy, bringing news of a gallant sweetheart's glorious death for the South. His three-month furlough should, he hoped, allow sufficient time to visit Emmeline . . . and find Ellen.

Once having found her, he would happily return to the battlefield until his term of duty expired. Safe at last, in the knowledge, that she would be waiting for him.

EIGHTY

Labiche Plantation, Louisiana

The hound with the ice-blue eyes surveyed Lavelle. The man
on the end of the dog's leash spoke in a voice used to asking
questions, not answering them.

'What's your business, mister?' it demanded thickly.

'Is this the Labiche Plantation?' Lavelle ignored the man's
question.

'Who's asking?' the man returned. Then, for Lavelle's benefit addressed the hound. 'It's all right, Beauty, Bayard Clinch
got this boy covered.'

The dog pricked up its ears, causing a ripple of muscle
across the grey-spotted, mahogany-coloured neck.

'Lavelle is my name and I'm seeking Miss Emmeline. I have
some solemn news.' Lavelle decided to stop the game. 'I am
Patrick O'Malley's stepfather!'

Bayard Clinch and the dog eyed him with equal suspicion.
Eventually the man spoke.

'Wait here!' he ordered. 'I'll go see in the house,' and with
that turned on his heel.

'House?' Lavelle exclaimed to himself, surveying the un-
restrained splendour of Le Petit Versailles. Here was a land
and a world as different from anything he'd ever seen in his

other travels. It was a *foreign* land, this Louisiana. People looked different, spoke different, even when in English, not French, which he observed was widely used. No wonder they regarded the North as usurpers and invaders. And the plantation houses? All were palaces, the like of which he'd only heard about in fables and fairytales. Little wonder the South would fight to hold what they had. He wondered what would happen to these gilded mansions when the North came South? Down along the Mississippi in iron-clad gunboats, bristling with plantation-pounding artillery? The slaves, too, once freed, would want to raze to the ground these fabulous and monstrous symbols of oppression. The wealth of which, stone upon stone, had been built on their backs.

Lavelle hoped the houses would be left to stand.

A reminder.

The man with the hound did not re-appear. To his surprise a well-fitted-out negro appeared in the man's stead.

'Mistress will see you now, suh!' the man said, pleasantly.

Lavelle didn't know why he was surprised. Some notion at the back of his head that they would all be in leg-irons and chains . . . with that cowed and hunted look. This man, Lavelle observed, was both, as to manner and bearing, the superior of many of the raggle-taggle band of soldiers now fighting to free him! Neither did the burly slave exhibit any sign of want or hunger.

'Benevolent paternalism,' he remembered Stephen Joyce once calling the South's institution of slaveholding.

Lavelle had travelled weeks to get here. Weeks of avoiding both armies and the trials of an inhospitable climate and terrain. Now, as he awaited the mistress of the Labiche Plantation, he was filled with both hope and apprehension. Hope that, finally, he was on the verge of being reunited with his beloved Ellen. Apprehension, at the prospect of telling her – and the young Miss Labiche – the awful thing he had wrought upon their lives.

Lucretia Labiche arrived, decorous in black, but businesslike and with a capable set of mouth. The younger woman with her, Lavelle guessed, was Emmeline. Fair and fragrant and displaying a delicate reserve. Younger than her maturity implied, Lavelle thought.

He was welcomed in true Southern fashion, Madame Labiche not hearing of anything until the temporal needs of one who had travelled so far, had been fully attended upon.

Lavelle wanted to get on with the burdensome news he bore.

'I am afraid, Madame Labiche, Miss Emmeline, that I come laden with sorrowful news . . .' he began. Emmeline gave a little start but the older woman's immediate glance caused the girl to hold her reserve.

'I . . . I am Patrick's stepfather,' Lavelle continued. Their eyes never left him, knowing what must come next. 'He is, was . . . my son . . . and . . . he has fallen . . . gallantly fallen in battle.' He heard the little thrum rise in Emmeline's throat and he continued more quickly. 'I was with him before he expired . . . and his last words were of you, Miss Emmeline. He put me under a promise to bring you this.'

Lavelle unwrapped the snow-white sweetheart glove and handed it to the girl.

'He wanted you to have it . . . "before magnolia time", he said.'

Emmeline solemnly took the glove from Lavelle, gazed on it a moment then placed it to her bosom, holding it there like a prayer.

She must be no more than sixteen, Lavelle thought. Yet, like some untouchable thing, inwardly riven with grief, outwardly displaying no emotion. It struck him that with their menfolk gone to war the women here were now forced to step into their shoes, and therefore display all the emotions of the missing gender. He broke the moment, addressing the girl.

'Your letters, Miss Emmeline – he carried them on his person.'

316

Lavelle withdrew from his pocket the crimson-edged avowals of love. Madame Labiche made a slight motion of her head and the waiting young female slave presented a salver to Lavelle on which he placed Emmeline's letters. Instead of bringing the letters to Emmeline, the slave girl placed the salver on a discreet corner table.

'And what news of the gallant Mr Joyce?' Lucretia Labiche enquired, passing on from the moment.

'Mr Joyce . . . ? Mr Stephen Joyce . . . here?' Lavelle was taken by surprise.

'Yes, Mr Lavelle, many times with your son,' Madame Labiche explained patiently.

'They went to fight the cause together – what news of him?'

Lavelle had not been prepared for this turn of events. In confusion, he replied, 'Of Mr Joyce I know nothing . . . I . . .' Lavelle began.

'But you *served* together?' – it was Emmeline.

'Miss Emmeline . . . Madame Labiche . . . I have a confession to make,' Lavelle began, wanting to put matters to right. 'Although I am Patrick's stepfather, I have not seen him for some years, nor Mr Joyce for even longer. I did not know Patrick had come South, or Mr Joyce for that matter. I had gone west . . .'

'To search for Patrick's mother?' Emmeline Labiche interrupted.

'Yes . . . ?' Lavelle answered quizzically. 'Is she also here in the South?'

'Of your wife, Mr Lavelle, I cannot enlighten you except as to Patrick's disappointment at her . . . folly,' the young woman said coldly.

Lavelle was perplexed. He thought Ellen to have been here in the South with Patrick. But if she were in the South, she had not been here. Nor did it seem clear from the girl's answer that Patrick had seen her. But he must have. The book . . . how was the book to be explained?

317

'This book, Miss Emmeline, have you seen it before?' Lavelle asked, rising and going with the book to Emmeline, before Madame Labiche could motion the slave girl to intervene.

'No, Mr Lavelle, I have not – and it is in such a disagreeable condition,' Emmeline said, disdain in her voice. 'But do go on with the main story,' she instructed.

'When I returned from the western States, I joined the Northern cause . . .' Lavelle began.

'Cause? Northern *cause*? There *is* no Northern cause, Mr Lavelle.'

It was Lucretia Labiche, anger streaming from her towards him. 'Unless, you call the genocidal oppression of a flourishing society a *cause*.'

'Please, let me finish, Madame Labiche!' Lavelle interjected. 'I am sorry if my looseness of speech has caused you offence.' He paused momentarily, before correcting his earlier statement. 'I joined the Union army and was dispatched to the front as a marksman.'

'Oh . . . !'

Lavelle heard the intake of Emmeline's breath. And then the moment he was dreading.

'It was you . . . *you* killed him!' she said, getting to her feet, the full horror of it dawning on her face, all reserve now unreserved. 'You murdered your own son!'

EIGHTY-ONE

Lavelle had grown to hate the smell of sugar. It was every-where around him: in the air . . . in his clothes and hair . . . in his nostrils . . . his eyes . . . his mouth. The whole surface of his skin felt as though a thin layer of suffocating molasses had been spread all over it.

'Food, Yankee soldier.' The girl who had come into the Sugar House put the plate of mush between his hands and feet, laughed and skipped away to a safe distance. 'How you goin' free us poor niggers now?

'Massa gonna string you high as soon as he comes back.'

With this comforting thought the girl laughed even more.

At the door she turned smilingly to say, 'Now don't go nowhere, Yankee, you hear!'

Lavelle didn't quite see the funny side to his predicament that the girl obviously saw. He had carried out Patrick's dying wish. Now, here he was an enemy soldier, shackled hand and foot like a slave, in the sickly sweet Sugar House of a southern plantation.

The Labiche woman had called Clinch and the dog. Two of the blacks he and the rest of the North wanted to set free, had manacled him. If he wasn't strung up by the 'massa' he faced another just as dire possibility – a desertion charge for breaking his furlough.

Three days now he had been held prisoner in the sugar house. Sugar and cotton – and the control of it – at the bottom of this whole sorry mess. Young men like Patrick . . . told to go and fight for it. A gun jammed into their hands. And the glory of America rammed down their throats.

Some, hardly old enough to dress themselves without a mother's helping hand. Lavelle had seen them – nine, ten, twelve, thirteen years of age. Skin soft as a baby's bottom, ripped open by shells big as themselves. Or, like unripened watermelon sliced into slivers before an enemy bayonet. Most of them only trying to get a few dollars to send to mothers who now would not want the use of it. Only their darlings to be back home again.

Mothers would struggle to tell themselves how important it was that their babies had fought and died, and to banish any thought of ripped-out stomachs or worms and flesh-picking birds. Nor the hot broiling sun, scorching and stenching their longing-to-be-held babes-in-arms.

Oh no, none of that! Only 'defending the flag', when they should be wiping their arses with it.

Flags, marching songs, countries – all bullshit!

Then would come the cold-comfort letters from Lincoln in Washington or Davis in Richmond . . . both in their grand White Houses. All worded the same. 'The great sacrifice your son has made . . .' and 'freedom'. It would make a man puke.

The two Presidents didn't know one piece of cannon fodder from the next and didn't give a fuck either! Would stand up after fine dinners, and wipe away the crumbs from their lips with fine linen. Then, in the company of fine ladies, speak bravely and dreamily of Liberty and the Constitution. Dab away a crocodile tear or two for 'our gallant boys at the front' and light a foreign cigar with which to comfort themselves.

And then at the table around them, applauding the Presidents for keeping the war going, those men who made the rifles and the cannons and grew fat on war. Oh, *they* would be free all right . . . their money safely made.

Lavelle was reminded of other men, those little *slieveens* who, like carrion, arrived before the battle hour, pushing cards into the shitting-themselves hands of young men. So that, when cut down and cut in half, the self-same cards would be found on their young bodies. Commerce done.

O'Shea and Sons: Coffins, Undertakings, Professional Embalmers

Lavelle once had one pressed into his own hand before battle. He had flung it at the scavengers and cursed them – the Irish feeding off the dead of their own country.

War was such a business and a profitable one. The more killing, the better. The gout-ridden generals, who could scarce mount a horse, would bask in the reflected glory of the blood of their men. And ladies like Madame Labiche and Miss Emmeline – and all the vapid ladies of Richmond and Boston – would be fascinated and hearts-a-fluttering at stories of gallantry by generals *at table*. Some of whom had never led a charge, or strayed within range of a careless bullet.

Lavelle was angry. Angry at the waste of it all . . . the hypocrisy of it all. Angry at himself . . . angry at Ellen.

And that was not all. Some other great foreboding now hung over him, like that damnable sugar vapour.

His mind had begun to put together the puzzle regarding Ellen. Much as Lavelle wanted answers, so equally did he fear them.

He kicked away the plate the girl had brought. Cupid she had said her name was. Cupid! From where did they get such foolish names?

He went back over the events of Ellen's leaving, the fact that out of all else she had taken the book. It must have been of great significance for her – these *Love Elegies and Holy Sonnets*. Somehow, then, her book had wound up with Patrick.

It was becoming increasingly clear from his visit here, that

321

it was unlikely to have been Ellen who had given the book to Patrick: the girl, Emmeline, had seemed to say as much. If it had not been Ellen then the boy had received it from someone else . . . Stephen Joyce!

It had some meaning.

Was it Stephen's own book? If so, why this of all books for Patrick?

Lavelle's emotions fought against the unerring conclusion towards which his mind was leading him. If it were not Stephen's own book, then it was Ellen's . . . and *she* had given it to Stephen. *And since the time she had deserted them in Boston!*

The book was the connection between her, Stephen and Patrick. The truth at last was beginning to manifest itself. Ellen's disappearance was linked with Stephen Joyce.

EIGHTY-TWO

The following day the slave girl returned. She came up close to Lavelle, but not too close. Threw the corn-slop or whatever it was, down in front of him.

'You's getting thin, Yankee – thin as a chicken's shin! Be no good t'Lincoln now!' she said coquettishly, hand on hip, baiting him.

'Well, go tell your friends, Cupid, that Lincoln is coming,' he said crossly to her. 'But if I tell Massa Lincoln that you let one of his boys stay locked up here, the President of the United States is not going to be too friendly!'

The girl looked at him, working out the import of the message. He was trouble for sure, this Yankee, but he was one of Massa Lincoln's soldiers, and they all hoped Lincoln was coming for them. She stopped her taunting and ran out. Lavelle knew that tonight, word would be passed along the cabins below the oak alley.

Clinch and the dog came to see him next. The overseer led the animal right up over him. Let the beast sniff his face, make that low purring sound like a great cat. But it was the Catahoula's eyes that were the most frightening. So close now to Lavelle's own. Large and at odds with the dog's colouring. Like icebergs, with the sky and the sea inside them. Now, Lavelle recognised, at this nearness not the same. One, ice-blue, the other ice-green. Lavelle imagined them fired with fierce light, all seeing in the dark . . . capable of freezing their hapless prey.

'Beauty sure likes you, Paddy Yank – likes you a lot!' Bayard Clinch nodded, knowingly.

'Got a good sniff of you too, in case those darkies get any ideas of giving you *French Leave*. Ha! Ha!' he laughed. '*French Leave*! C'mon, Beauty, there's a honey. Now you kiss your new Yankee friend goodnight!'

EIGHTY-THREE

After Clinch and the dog had left, Lavelle again turned over in his mind the question of the book. There was something he was still missing.

He tried to recall when first he had seen it. Slowly, it had come back to him – the piano, at No 29 Pleasant Street. Ellen had liked to hear Louisa and Mary play. Bach . . . Bach . . . and more Bach!

She had been so delighted, like a child, when the piano arrived, filling up the little room, even though she herself couldn't play. She could have learned if she'd put her mind to it he knew. Could sing like a blackbird but she was happy to listen, to lose herself in the joy of what they could play.

That was it!

She had been listening to one of them play . . . put the book down . . . been distracted and left it there. He remembered the conversation with Stephen about it – the fact that a clergyman had written erotic love-poems. What had prompted the conversation was that, on some previous occasion, he had seen the self-same book with Stephen. When he had made an innocent enquiry about the book she, surprisingly, had said she found the book in Montreal. Not at her favourite Boston haunt, The Old Corner Bookstore.

Montreal . . . the place where everything pertaining to their business seemed to have gone wrong. He remembered her returning from one such journey. Him at the station sweeping her up, twirling her around and later that girlish giddyness still on her, refusing him her lips but surrendering all else.

Had Stephen Joyce been to Montreal? The man travelled widely, lecturing on Ireland – its distress – to all who would listen. He would find Stephen – ask him.

Even though the thing now clawing at his insides had already told him the answer.

He stopped – alert now. All thoughts of Ellen momentarily banished. Somebody was at the door of the Sugar House. His bluff with the slave girl had worked. If the slaves could get him out he'd worry later about Beauty.

The door unlatched, creaked slightly. He wondered how they'd managed to spirit the key away from the house or from Clinch?

A figure rustled through the gloom. It was Emmeline!

Skirts raised, she tiptoed towards him.

'Emmeline!' he started. She put her finger to her lips and, kneeling beside him, un-padlocked his chains.

'I cannot forgive you, Mr Lavelle, for what you have done. But neither can I have your life on my hands. That would dishonour him whom I loved. So, I must disobey what would be my own dear Father's most earnest desire – to hang you!'

Lavelle didn't know what to say.

The girl continued. 'However, if you do re-enter the conflict for the North, then I pray that the gallant Mr Joyce, who has gone so bravely to defend the South, will one day shoot you dead!'

Then she was gone, shimmering like silk back into the gloom.

EIGHTY-FOUR

Now that Lavelle no longer had Emmeline's letters, he was in trouble. They had been his passport through the South.

With them in hand, to all intents and purposes he was a Confederate soldier, charged with the task of bearing sad news of a comrade to a grieving sweetheart. A man of serviceable age without such evidence, if accosted, would be classed either a deserter or a spy.

Emmeline had left him only the *Love Elegies*, a small parcel of food and some Confederate money to see him by. The girl had taken it upon herself to free him but not with the blessing of the plantation's mistress. He would, therefore, be pursued. Not just by Bayard Clinch and his hound but by any Confederate party which might call at Le Petit Versailles seeking provisions. In light of this probability, he decided he would keep to the swamps until well clear of the plantations.

The swamps of Louisiana, Lavelle soon discovered were a place unto themselves. There was more swamp than Louisiana, it seemed, and they looked different and sounded different from anything he had ever previously experienced. Hoots and trills and cackling calls of every description, mixed with squawks and screeches and spiralling sweetsong.

Then the silences. Oppressive and so heavy they pounded the eardrums. The waiting-silences, as Lavelle thought of them. Swamplife waiting to dart or to dive, or to swallow or snatch a smaller inhabitant.

Then the whole cacophony of sound would start up again . . . in celebration of life . . . or death. Lavelle, in the middle of it all, didn't know which.

He heard nothing. The thump of the body against his own caught him completely unawares. Knocking him face down, breathless, on the mud bank. Then, strong thighs were astride him, a ham of a hand gripping the hasp of his neck, bruising his face into the mud. The heel of the ham-hand then squashed him further down, for emphasis.

'I shuh don't want kill you.'

A runaway.

'I'm a Yankee – on the run too!' Lavelle managed to get out. The grip loosened for a second. Then tightened again.

'Don' trus' no white folk fo' nuthin'!'

'Listen!' Lavelle squeezed out, the vice-like grip even further mashing his face downwards. 'Why would I be out here if I wasn't on the run?'

The grip again loosened. Lavelle turned his face upwards, recognising the runaway. It was the burly house-slave, who had first ushered him into the presence of the Labiches. Behind him, in the shelter of a tree, stood Cupid, the girl who had brought him food. Lavelle looked from one to the other. The two looked at each other. The girl spoke, keeping her eyes averted, telling him that she and 'Easy Money', as she called her companion, had been planning to get him out of Versailles. Instead, finding him gone, had decided it was a good thing because 'Clinch an' his dog'd be huntin' you . . . an' pay no 'tenshun to us!'

Easy Money let Lavelle go. He got up and dusted himself down.

'So that was it! You were going to free me as a distraction – bait for the dog – while you two made off?'

He laughed at the two of them, now sheepish before him. 'Well, now – you've made a right dog's dinner of it because that hound is going to come high-tailing it right here after me and eat your black hides,' he said loudly at them and set off on his way. He hadn't gone ten paces when they were behind him. He stopped and turned. Cupid confronted him, telling him she and Easy Money were going to Virginia too, to join Lincoln's men. 'So Mistah Yankee – you go your way to Virginny an' we go ours . . . but they's both the same way!' and she stood, saucy as you like, challenging him to defy her.

What would they be like, Lavelle thought, when millions of them got free? There'd be no gainsaying them then. He shrugged, turned and trekked off again, them jabbering at each other and plashing through the water behind him.

'Join with Lincoln's men, be damned!' he said to himself.

That night, as they made shelter they heard it. In the distance – maybe a mile away. High above all the other sounds. High and lonesome and calling them. The blood-baying cry of Beauty.

The effect was to halt all movement, muffle all sound.

'It's the dog!' Easy Money said, in a kind of awed reverence. 'May the Good Lord save us this night.'

Much and all as they had tramped through miles of water to shake off pursuit, it had been to no avail. Bayard Clinch and his Beauty seemed to have a line to them like a homing arrow. They'd never out-smart nor out-run the beast.

Neither Easy Money nor the girl had a weapon. Likewise Lavelle. Before leaving the Sugar House he had searched for something that might suffice as a makeshift weapon. All he had found was a slender steel rod of about two feet long, broken off from what looked like a large ladling spoon. He had grabbed it, hoping that, at worst, it might help him spear a sluggish swamp fish or a scuttling, soft-shelled crab. Now, it was all that lay between them and a return to captivity. Or worse.

First, Easy Money secured a short and jagged stump of cypress branch. The length of cord that circled Cupid's shift at the waist became the tie that bound Lavelle's steel rod and the wood together into a makeshift spear.

The thrashing sound of man and dog came closer.

Easy Money and Cupid lay flat on the ground. Lavelle covered them with branches already gathered. They were safer there than up a tree, where if the dog found them they would be trapped – and Catahoulas could climb. At least on the ground, if Lavelle killed the dog or . . . He shuddered at the alternative, even distracted it, they had some chance of escape. Some.

Lavelle moved off a distance, staying in the open. For the plan to work the dog had to see him as well as scent him. With eyes like that, Lavelle was sure the dog had darkness vision.

Then came the night-renting howl, silencing all else.

Lavelle held his stance, shouted and then started to run. From somewhere behind he heard the yell of the stalker, 'That's him! Go get him, Beauty!'

Lavelle ran as fast as heaven and earth would allow, away from where the two petrified slaves hid. The baying had stopped. He could not hear the great Spanish war-dog. Now he would have to rely on instinct to do what he must do. Then, from behind, he heard the splashing sound, the spring-bound haunches and great striding forelegs scarcely touching land or water in their eagerness to get to him.

Lavelle, his fleeing back to the dog, felt fatally exposed. His every instinct was to stop, turn and face his destroyer.

But he needed the dog to be hurtling forward, in full flight, when it attacked. Now, it seemed as if the very earth beneath Lavelle's feet trembled with the bounding mass of muscle and bone in his wake. He prayed he wouldn't stumble, fall flat on his face, the dog land on his back, tear out his neck.

Lavelle listened, trying to sense the moment. The silence that would signal the second when the dog would leave the swamp in one mighty bound; sail above the ground towards him like some flying hell-hound.

Then at once everything seemed to stop – the noise, the pounding paws. The swamp silence descended. The killing moment had arrived.

Clear as the knell of death, Lavelle heard it. The low purr in the throat. The sound he had heard the day Clinch had let the brute slather all over him.

He stopped. Turned. Dropped to one knee and rammed the spear-base into the soft underbelly of the swamp, its point at a forward angle. At the same moment the dark and speckled cloud in the air hurtled towards him. Would the makeshift spear hold?

For an instant Lavelle thought he had mis-timed his turn, that the sheer savagery of the dog's killing leap would cause it to overshoot his timid spear.

Then, as if his whole body had been hit by a twenty-six-pound ball at close range, Lavelle was bowled backwards, the cypress branch ramming against his groin, the agony causing him to lose his grip of it. He landed on his back, the dog half over his face, its hind legs clawing for purchase, the stench of its smell overpowering. Then the sound that rose out from its belly, suffocating him. Going down his throat into his own body, hideously howling within him.

He had sprung the trap, impaled the beast. But it was far from dead.

Lavelle struggled to get out from under the dog and onto his feet.

But as he did, so did Beauty.

331

The steel rod had pierced the animal through so that either end protruded, the beast's chest and back both bleeding profusely. Undeterred, the Catahoula immediately came at him, the object of its hate, as if nothing else – not even its own existence – mattered. In vain Lavelle tried to fight it off but its strength sent him backwards, off the mudbank and into the green-slimed water.

He went under the water, the weight of the dog submerging him, its face eerily lit above his. Eyes blazing at him through the gurgling water, jaws opening in slow swirling motions trying to get at him.

Lavelle's own mouth and nose were suffused with swamp slime. He couldn't move the dog and he couldn't breathe. As he struggled for air it seemed the watery haze now forming in his head would drown him. The giant jaws would be denied their purpose as nature had intended – that of tearing him limb from limb. Instead his lungs would fill with comforting, green, swamp water.

It all seemed absurdly comic.

Images swam before him – the dead Patrick . . . radiant . . . borne up on angel's wings; Ellen . . . laughing . . . mouth wide open . . . head back . . . nostrils flared; Stephen, his rifle pointed at Lavelle – and then the shot. Oh, Christ, he felt the shot!

Then the girl was pulling him from the water.

'C'mon Yankee, don' die on us two niggers yet!' And she was laughing at him, their 'saviour', Clinch's gun on the bank beside her.

Lavelle turned, looking for the dog. It was on its back beneath the water, paws at half-mast, the great gaping hole of the shotgun blast in its side. He peered down closer just to make sure. Thought he saw the ice-blue light fade, finally flicker and leave the great hound's eyes – like burnt out coals – empty of all fire.

'The dog wuz only actin' nat'rilly,' Cupid said, still laughing at him.

EIGHTY-FIVE

Lavelle mused on the irony of things.

The blacks whom he was supposed to save, as Cupid had so smartly reminded him, had saved *his* skin. While Easy Money had been struggling with Clinch – breaking the overseer's neck – the girl quick-thinking, had grabbed the gun and chased after Lavelle and the Catahoula. But for her, Lavelle knew, he'd be long gone. She'd saved him for sure and she only a slip of a girl. *Fleurs du Sud* – Flowers of the South. Black flowers as well as white.

As they trekked on Lavelle wondered about it all. Not so much about the war itself and the men who fought it, but the women. It was the women, both North and South, whose lives would most be changed.

Back at the Labiche's – the place seemed to tick over like clockwork, all overseen by the stately-named Lucretia. Previously, Lavelle had heard it said that the old planter stock liked to keep their Southern belles on the mantelpiece – so they could throw sugar at them! A Southern woman of a certain class could have neither her virtue sullied nor her hands soiled and slave society had helped perpetuate this high-mindedness. Now, the war had changed everything. Women had been catapulted into the public sphere – forced to manage the huge sugar and cotton enterprises, and work from first light to last. The mighty plantations could not be let slide under just because the Lord and Master was to war.

Lavelle wondered how it would be when these Lords and Masters returned from battlefront to home front? Would the women who had stepped into the breach to 'run the South' ever step back out again and into the long shadow of their former patriarchal protectors?

As always, every thought Lavelle had, returned at some stage to the woman he so enduringly loved. Ellen had long been a woman before her time – stepped over the threshold and out of the domestic circle. He had never sought to stop her. Maybe if he hadn't countenanced her being so much in the public sphere, the boundaries of home life would have prevented her from stepping outside her marriage too. Not that all the evidence of such betrayal was present. And doubt – Lavelle wanted doubt. Would welcome doubt . . . was clutching at it but deep down he knew. Knew she had betrayed him.

She had betrayed him and Stephen Joyce had betrayed him. Then everything it seemed had come tumbling down. She had exiled herself because of the shame it would bring on them – on the girls. An adulteress for a mother would have been a fruitful cause for the expulsion of Louisa and Mary from the Magdalen Convent.

To some extent Lavelle could understand the demons that drove her: the suffering in her previous life; her will to make America work for them. That driving restlessness of spirit which she possessed. He knew too, that when the first fires of passion with Stephen had died in her, she would have become so utterly disillusioned with herself . . . go to any extreme to gain redemption.

He vowed that wherever she was he would find her. He had already forgiven her in his heart.

Stephen Joyce he could not forgive.

ELLEN

EIGHTY-SIX

Virginia, August 1862

At the end of the first day of her journey, Ellen had no idea
as to where she was. Apart from that she was lost.

She had decided to make her own way to Richmond, board
a train there to take her South as far as the war and damaged tracks would allow.

She had generally borne east. That much she knew. Kept
out of the path of all military, lest they think her a spy.

At first gotten a lift on a farm-wagon, along roads rutted
by armies and their cannons. The land was beautiful, the
gentle plains, the forests of beech and birch and black tupelo.
Everywhere wildflowers – lowland laurel and flowering dog-
wood, the State emblem. She would cross first the James river,
then the Appomattox, then on through the Piedmont region
to Richmond, capital of Virginia.

Virginia, named after Elizabeth I of England – the Virgin
Queen.

Then, towards evening, the horse appeared. Stood waiting
for her . . . riderless . . . beautiful . . . pale by moonlight.

She approached it cautiously, fearing it would flee. But like
a deliverance from some other world it allowed her to talk
to it, run her hand along its flecked forehead . . . and mount

its back. It whinnied when she clamped her knees to its flanks and then set off at a leisurely canter, until it brought her to the old man.

'Something told me I'd have a visitor tonight,' was the greeting from the thrown-back door of his cabin. 'Come in, lady, supper's on the fire,' he said with no more ado.

Quince was his name. 'Abel's my Christian name – but that's a kind of unfortunate name to be kitted with, so folks just call me Quince. And I don't want to know nothing 'bout you, miss . . . nothing at all. Long ago gave up on being curious 'bout people.'

Quince sat her down, gave her a bowl of some corn and meat stew and a chunk of sourdough bread for 'swabbin'' the stew.

He was old, well into his seventies, she guessed. His eyes seemed to be half closed all the time – as if asleep or thinking. Above them snow-clad eyebrows stretched to the edge of his face . . . and then some. The remainder of his face was creased with age and an expression that told of an inherent understanding of frail humanity – some indelible kindness there. He shuffled when he walked – a tracker over uneven ground, uncertain of the next step.

Ellen didn't know why but she sensed he played at seeming older than he was, more decrepit than the fertile mind he possessed – betrayed when later they talked.

'We come into the world with longing and we go out of the world with longing. It is the only fixed emotion,' he began. 'Night longs for the day, day longs for night. The sea longs for the shore, a flower for the light. The heart hungers for love, the soul for God. It is in every step, every breath, and every glance of an eye. Longing is never-ending,' Quince said matter of factly, as if he knew her life, the hooded eyes taking in its effect on her.

'And what of war?' she asked.

'War? War fulfils a longing – to kill,' he answered. 'A longing to explore our darkest nature, to put us on a footing

338

with God, power over death. But it is a false longing. For no man who kills another, whatever the imagined cause, will ever be free of it. He becomes dead to himself, but . . .' he added, almost sorrowfully, '. . . I think I would do it.'

'You would?' she asked, surprised by his answer and wondered if he had.

He smiled at her. 'Have you not yet learned, Miss Ellie, that reason is only skin deep. It is our emotions that drive us . . . protect us . . . betray us – not reason.'

Again, she felt as if he was talking directly to her – as if he knew. It bothered her. Was her true nature writ so large upon her face that this old man could see it?

'Consider it,' he said, 'the great minds, the philosophers of old, whose wisdom has been sent down through the ages. Put a sword in their hands. Clad them in blue or grey, with the mad generals shouting at them to kill or be killed. He paused. 'What would happen, Miss Ellie?'

'They would refuse the sword in the first instance,' she answered, 'because of the intellect.'

He never said 'yea' or 'nay' to her, only gave her one more conundrum on which to dwell. 'It is another interesting proposition,' he said, scrutinising her intently, 'the battle between reason and original sin.'

That night, sleep would not come easy. Her mind wrestled with all that the old man had said. She wondered from where it was he got his wisdom. Day after day out here in the backwoods of America with his peach orchard and sucking his empty pipe. Why didn't *his* like ever end up in the White House at Washington, or the Confederate White House in Richmond?

She had asked him.

'I'm not good with words,' he replied, 'not good with the big city words. The things I know, I know. Nothing fancy, plain as that old peach tree. The buds come, the peach grows. I pluck 'em. I eat 'em. Next year they grows again. That's all I know. Can't explain it better than that! Peaches get eat. Sure they do . . . and people too.'

Her own thoughts were anything but 'plain as the old peach tree'. Half of her wondered what on earth she was doing here, journeying to the ends of the earth? What did she expect to find there? The girl, Emmeline – Patrick's sweetheart? And what then? Stephen had told her that Lavelle was not in Louisiana. He didn't know where her husband was. Nor, it seemed, had Patrick known. Nobody knew. Lavelle had disappeared, or was dead. This last thought she utterly disbelieved without fully knowing why. He was somewhere in this Great War. She just knew it. But on which side? Some said that in excess of a quarter of a million Irish were in uniform on both sides, the bulk with the North. She was unsure as to where Lavelle's allegiance would finally lie. He was passionate about 'freedoms' – whether now it was the 'republican' freedom of the South or the 'greater' freedom of the Union of States, she could not be sure. That Patrick's, dear Patrick's sympathies had lain with the South she was not surprised at. Stephen's she could not have guessed.

Finding Lavelle seemed an impossibility. She wondered if perhaps he too was still searching for her? At this stage, with the passage of years, it seemed a doubtful endeavour. She could not expect a love to be still so enduring. After how she had defiled it.

She got up, went to the window. The moon, bright-grandeured, splayed over the land, seeming to soak up the singing sound of Quince's stream, so that the song-notes rippled upwards into the brimming light. She turned to see the peach orchard. Thought of the old man's words again. Life was plain and simple – if you kept it that way. As she watched, a peach, heavy on the bough and blushed with life, dropped. The fruit, ripe to its core, fell like the moon, yellowing its way to Earth.

It decided her. That and the state flag Quince had given her. Pointing out to her the figure of Virtue, dressed as a

woman warrior. The state motto *Perseverando* – by perse-
vering. Again she thought Quince could see into her soul.
Virtuous she might not be but she could at least live out the
other call of Virginia – and persevere. She would not go back.
Reason would be put aside and she would continue South.
At least meet Patrick's Emmeline.

In the morning Quince bade her goodbye, gave her a sunburst of peaches to bring with her, smiling while telling her,
'The peach alone is wise.' Then pointed her on the way.

'Ah, Richmond, sad, sad, Richmond. It is another land,'
he echoed after her.

She gave the silvery grey its head, pondering the miles with
all the old man had said.

EIGHTY-SEVEN

Trains always made her reflect on life, and as Ellen left Richmond behind all the events of the previous weeks seemed to evaporate, be back there in some other geography. Freeing her mind.

Her story was not yet finished. That was how she saw it. And she had to see it out to the very end. Whatever that ending, whatever the twists and turns. Whether her story had already been written, she just finding her way through it as she went, she didn't know.

It was the old question for her. Once upon a time *she* thought she was the writer, the puppeteer of her own destiny. Then, she had thought the opposite. Surrendered herself and her every thought, word and action to the higher power. Now she wanted to take back that power to herself. It was to be yet another new epiphany.

She had always sought it, the always further off land of self. Was love, she wondered, the greatest transcender to that land, or the greatest pretender? At any rate, she now followed its uncertain path, as the train plunged her southwards, transcending her into that other America – Dixie. What she could do there in Dixie – if anything – she was unsure.

She snuggled into the corner between the window and the seat back, her mind afflicted by all that she had lost . . . and thoughts of Louisa and Lavelle – all that still remained to be lost.

EIGHTY-EIGHT

Labiche Plantation, Louisiana

Ellen took in the woman addressing her.

She had arrived at Le Petit Versailles, the previous day, already exhausted from the steaming Southern climate. Even at night, she had noted, when darkness came, it still did not yield any respite from the draining humidity of the air. Exhaustion, or no, the splendour – the vastness – of the house occupied by this woman, was such that Ellen regained all her energies on first sight of it. Her immediate thought being, what a fine hospital it would make, with its different rooms for surgery, recovery, sleeping quarters, storage and a well-fitted kitchen.

Madame Labiche, when Ellen had introduced herself as 'Patrick O'Malley's mother', had welcomed her with true if somewhat reserved Southern fashion. The woman then would hear of nothing but only to bid one of the black slaves, to take Ellen, to have her bathed and fed and rested. They would talk in the morning.

Ellen had slept late . . . and been left undisturbed.

Madame Labiche, it appeared had been absorbed by urgent plantation business, until almost evening time.

Ellen listened as the woman told her of Patrick.

'Your son, Patrick,' Madame Labiche began, 'first came to us as a guest of the gallant Captain Joyce – a gentleman and a true friend to this house, and more latterly a loyal defender of our Republic.' The plantation mistress sucked in her breath, narrowing further the purse of her lips. 'Often they were accompanied by a companion of your son's – the unfortunate Mr Moran.'

'Why unfortunate?' Ellen asked.

'My husband and I never thought Mr Moran to be fully qualified as a gentleman . . . and indeed we were proven correct,' Lucretia Labiche replied. 'Mr Moran traded his country's flag . . . for a . . . *tignon*!'

'I don't understand,' Ellen interjected.

'A *tignon*, Mrs Lavelle . . .' Madame Labiche said tartly as if her guest should know, '. . . a *tignon* is a headdress, worn by white "ladies" – though General Butler would not call them so. White "ladies",' she re-emphasised, 'of high colour who are to be found in New Orleans. However, the deserter received his just deserts and the Pontchartrain claimed the temptress – we shall not mention her name.' There the matter rested.

'Poor Oxy,' Ellen thought to herself, 'to America to claim a deserter's bullet.'

Ellen had so many questions to put to the impenetrable Madame Labiche but doubted if she would receive any further enlightenment on matters Madame deemed *rested*. So she asked no question, wanting the other woman to proceed, which Madame Labiche commenced to do.

'Your son corresponded briefly with us. He was a friend to my own two boys, Lamarr and Lovelace.' She reclined her head almost imperceptibly towards the black-draped mirror.

'Oh, Madame Labiche, I am sorry . . .' Ellen said, moving towards her, but the woman raised her fan, the slight but considered movement blocking any intimacy.

'They will not have died in vain, if the tyranny of the North is broken, as broken it shall be,' Lucretia Labiche said, apparently unmoved by the memory of her loss. 'We were then surprised, within the past few weeks, by your husband, who arrived here, hands bloodied by the death of your son . . . *and* in the service of the Yankee interlopers. Your paths must have crossed!'

So matter of factly did the woman speak – each topic of equal weight with the next – that the import of what she was saying was almost lost on her listener.

'Lavelle . . . ?' Ellen began. 'Patrick . . . ?' She raised her voice as the incredulity of what she was hearing, sank in. 'What are you saying?' Ellen demanded of the woman. 'What are you saying . . . that Lavelle was here . . . my husband? That my husband killed my son Patrick?' She got up, went and stood in front of the woman, scrutinising her face, demanding some sense of her.

'You have said it, Mrs Lavelle. There is no other way in which to put it.'

'Oh my God – how – can't you just tell me . . . instead of all this?' Ellen beseeched.

'It was an accident, Mrs Lavelle – an unfortunate accident of war. That your husband and son were both sharpshooters – but on opposite sides . . .' Madame Labiche let it hang there.

Ellen was in a state of shock. How could Madame Lebiche possibly have known that it was Lavelle's bullet that had delivered her dead son to her? What must have been the chances of such an event? Out of all who fought on either side? Though she had heard stories of brother killing brother, even . . . father and son. It was a sign . . . a further cruel punishment, like Mary.

She was aware of the woman watching her, evaluating her conflicting emotions. 'An accident of war,' Ellen said, barely audibly. 'An accident of war?' Then, louder to the woman. 'But there are no accidents of war, Madame Labiche. All war is intentional. War does not just happen of its own accord. People . . . men . . . *go* to war. Your sons, your husband; my

345

son, my husband. They are sent by other husbands and sons
. . . and they *go*.' Ellen said, in a state of detached reverie.
The woman approached her, said nothing, just touched her
arm and withdrew. It was, Ellen knew, a journey of a thousand miles for Lucretia Lebiche.

'Thank you!' Ellen said softly.

Noiselessly the slave girl appeared with peppermint-
flavoured water. It helped revive Ellen.

'How did Lavelle know to come here?' Ellen asked, after
a moment, the answer not really mattering. Only that he had
been. Had been and had scarcely gone again, before she had
arrived.

'The letters,' Madame Labiche replied.

'Letters?' Ellen queried.

'Yes, letters. Mr Lavelle found them in your son's possession . . . with a book.'

Ellen started. So it *was* Lavelle who had taken the book,
Stephen's book – her book.

'The letters were kind responses from Emmeline to a soldier at the battlefront – slightly misguided . . . open to mis-
interpretation,' the woman answered, for once without Ellen's
asking.

'Can I see them?' Ellen asked, desperate to have something
of Patrick, some understanding of his state.

'They were returned to the possession of this house . . .
and destroyed.'

'And the book?'

'The book? Oh, the book was Mr Lavelle's own – not the
property of the house – the poems, if they could be called
such, of the Reverend Mr Donne! Your husband took it when
he escaped our custody.'

'Escaped *custody*?' Ellen asked, again uncertain of what
she was being told.

'He was an enemy soldier, we imprisoned him in the Sugar
House – the slaves freed him. *Your* husband, Mrs Lavelle,
has cost me my overseer, Mr Clinch, who pursued him, and

Beauty, the plantation's hound – neither of whom have returned. Now *I* must be both overseer as well as master of the plantation.'

There was no hint of self-pity in how Lucretia Labiche spoke, only the pragmatism of the day-to-day truth the woman grappled with, untainted, or so it appeared, by any defeating emotions.

Ellen needed time to think, to be on her own. She excused herself and retired. As she lay in the opulent splendour of Le Petit Versailles, Ellen wondered if hers was the bed in which Patrick had lain, or the ill-fated Oxy or even Stephen? She hoped it was Patrick's and turned her head into the comforting whiteness of the pillow. Patrick had been here, Oxy too and Stephen – then Lavelle. All of them drawn here, and now her. The house was the magnet. She wondered at the name Le Petit Versailles – Little Versailles – wondering too, at the lifestyles lived in the muddy South, which aspired to those lived in the great palace of the French monarchy – before the Revolution? At least the Labiche arrogance hadn't stretched so far as to call it by its original name or, worse again, 'Le Grande Versailles'.

Again and again, her mind returned to Lavelle . . . and Patrick. She wrestled with the awful tragedy of it all. Lavelle her husband, Patrick her son. How could it have been? What chance out of all the speeding bullets between North and South? But that was it . . . it had not been chance . . . it had been ordained. Had it also been ordained that they had spoken before Patrick had died . . . that Lavelle should discover his terrible deed? He, also, be punished, forever to live with Patrick's blood on his hands – as well as her desertion. She drove her head into the pillow, willing it to have been Patrick's; her tears seeping into its fine fabric. Fabric soft as skin.

The next morning, Madame Labiche offered some insights into southern living – and southern women – to Ellen.

'I am afraid, Mrs Lavelle, us plantation mistresses have, undeservedly, been made into the stuff of legend . . .' Madame Labiche explained over a breakfast table, heavily laden with fruits, hams, cheeses and pigeons' eggs delicately stuffed with a sage and parsley concoction. '. . . and by none more so than the Northern novelists,' she continued. 'To them we are symbols of the South – its *haute grandeur*, its undeserved wealth, its *grande dame* lifestyle. We are but porcelain dolls in flouncy dresses, decorative and much admired but of no earthly use.' Madame Labiche laughed. It was the first time Ellen had heard her do so. 'If Monsieur Labiche were to hear me talk thus . . .' She let the sentence trail off and started a new one.

'Do you know I can bleed a hog as good as any man?' she proclaimed. 'Accompany me and you'll see – if your Yankee stomach is not too delicate,' she challenged.

'I am no Yankee' Ellen retorted. 'I am Irish and a nurse. I serve equally the fallen of both sides . . . and the sights of blood hold no fear for me.'

Madame Labiche smiled and summoned one of the slaves. 'Cicero, our Irish visitor wants to see how we southern ladies fend for ourselves. Go fetch a hog and an axe,' she ordered.

The slave nodded and left but already the mistress of Le Petit Versailles was reaching under her pretty cream crinoline dress and removing the hoop which bouffanted it out from her body on all sides.

Cicero returned with a sturdy axe and the trio made their way to the hog pen and cornered a well-padded hog. The slave neck-wrestled it out of the pen, the hog's squeals attracting some of the other slaves.

'Hold it steady, Cicero!' Lucretia Labiche ordered as the slave pinned down the struggling hog.

Ellen continued to gape in amazement as the mistress of the house swung her axe to and fro, resisting its inertia, building it up towards its full axis. Then Madame Labiche brought the blunt head of the axe four square down on the skull of her victim. The stunning blow seemed to shudder

348

through the ground towards Ellen. Calmly, the woman put aside the axe and then drew a knife from the folds of her dress and slit the nut-brown throat of the animal. At this a cheer went up from the onlookers. She then manhandled the animal over to a largish, shallow container and straddled the hog's hindquarters, pulling its head backwards towards her so that its lifeblood gurgled downwards into the large, receiving bucket. A procession of four slaves then carried the lifeless hog to a waiting cauldron of scalding water over which a wooden frame had been erected. The hog was hoisted on the frame, pulley-style, then lowered into the water to scald the bristling hairs from its body. When again it was hoisted free, Lucretia Labiche was ready to dismember it.

During the process, she stopped, turned, then proffered the large knife she held towards Ellen. They all watched her, this white woman from the North. Steadily, Ellen took the knife from the woman, stood in her place and began to further dissect the animal. Slowly but with assured hands, she worked, conscious of the silence, all eyes watching, to see the Yankee fail . . . the knife slip, she gash herself. Gradually, then, the sound arose again, small, unconnected sounds at first. Then more sounds, connecting to those already made, until it became a chorus of assent . . . and then a clapping from the assembled slaves. Only then did Lucretia Labiche come to her, take Ellen's knife hand in hers and hold it aloft in the air. The still warm hog's blood on the knife trickled down over its handle, onto their hands and wrists, like some ancient ritual.

'Now we are sisters,' the woman said to Ellen. 'Sisters in blood.'

Later, at supper, a succulent loin of pork, scalded head intact, was served. Ellen paused a moment considering the dish. It was not today's victim. The one she had seen Madame Labiche skin and bleed, and from which she herself had carved cuts for curing that would some day appear at this table.

349

Madame Labiche smiled at her guest. '*Bon appetit, Madame Lavelle!*'

Ellen, her own plain dress, bloodstained from the earlier activities and now sent to the 'boiling kitchen', wore one of Lucretia Labiche's many evening dresses. 'Emerald green . . . for your eyes . . . and your country, Madame Lavelle,' was how the woman had put it. From 'the Silk Road, in China' had the fine silk been journeyed, when Ellen enquired as to its origins. The equally fine lace that fringed it, from 'Provence, the south eastern region of France' Madame Labiche told her. Indeed it was almost a perfect fit for Ellen, they being of similar height and proportions. 'Now you are in every sense the perfection of a plantation mistress,' Lucretia complimented her.

Ellen accepted the compliment but was annoyed with herself for allowing the woman to witness her slight hesitation over the pork dish.

It was hard to like her table companion in the conventional sense. Lucretia Labiche was cold, imperious, arrogant, capable of cruelty . . . but she was capable, very capable. Ellen had never met anyone quite like, the relic-like Madame Labiche. Yet, the woman had suffered much – lost both of her sons to the war, her husband still fighting, still at risk. Added to these troubles, she had the house, the burdensome plantation, the slaves – and the impending fall of it all to contend with. Ellen wondered what a woman like Lucretia would do if everything dissolved around her, if the slaves were freed, the house plundered, seized as spoils of war? Some of the slaves – the house slaves, closer to the family – might remain loyal. Not many, Ellen thought. She was on the point of raising this question when word arrived that Mr Latrobe – 'The factor . . .' Madame Labiche explained hastily to Ellen. 'A money-lender,' she added impatiently at Ellen's puzzlement.

'Come and you will see!'

EIGHTY-NINE

Ellen watched as Latrobe the factor shook his head. A straight-backed man of medium proportions and moderate years, he had large doleful eyes protected by gold-rimmed eyeglasses. 'He has a weakness of facial character, disguised by a careful beard,' Madame Labiche had earlier confided to Ellen. Now, the factor gave a mannered but very definite refusal to Madame Labiche.

'Madame Labiche, how many years have I factored large sums to your husband for the prosperous advancement of Versailles?' He extended his hand slowly, in supplication for her understanding.

'Many years, Monsieur Latrobe . . . but then there was no risk . . .' the plantation mistress began.

'Ah, Madame Labiche . . . !' the factor interrupted, with a smile. '. . . for those who lend against the future there is always risk . . . though we endeavour to mitigate it. Now . . .' he continued, '. . . the great houses are falling, the slaves runaways, or waiting for deliverance from the pretender president, Lincoln.'

'But the South *will* prevail, Monsieur Latrobe – it must!' Lucretia Labiche argued.

'Madame Labiche, were it only so,' Latrobe answered. 'But pragmatism must temper loyalty . . . even loyalty to the South.

351

It would be derelict of me to advance an old friend such large sums as would plunge you into penury. As the Emperor Caesar once said, "The house is fallen, the beaten men come into their own". And it is true, the "house" of the South is fallen. Besides . . . where ever again will be the likes of your dear husband, gone now gallantly to defend us, to restore order once more?'

Ellen could resist silence no longer. 'Mr Latrobe!' she interrupted. 'Look around you! Do you see a fallen house? Madame Labiche has by her own hand performed a miracle here. *She* is the new South. The old thinking will be swept away with the war.'

The factor raised a whimsical eyebrow above the rim of his glasses, took them off and inspected them, ignoring Ellen.

She continued, unheeding of his condescension. 'Madame Labiche's plan is a good plan – to buy slaves from the houses now closing. When the war ends and the country is united, sugar will once again be king!' She surprised herself at how authoritative she sounded.

'The slaves will leave and go North,' he answered, cleaning his spectacles.

'No, they will stay!' Madame Labiche answered. 'It is my plan to set them free . . . to pay them for their labour . . . enter the new thinking.'

'But, Madame Labiche, there's the rub if I might say so . . . paid labour will not pay for all this!' The factor raised his hand towards the splendour of the house behind them. 'The *new thinking* – as you call it – will attest that plantations such as these were built on the backs of black labour . . . *free* black labour. But black labour is no longer *free*, when freed.'

'Then, if necessary, I will live in a cabin, like them,' Madame Labiche answered, stonily.

At this the factor's face blanched. For a moment concern flitted across his face, then it was gone. He replaced his glasses with great deliberation, thoughtfully pushing the centre-rim back over the bridge of his nose. 'Then I am sure you shall,' he said, inclining forward in a half-bow. 'It is always a pleasure to conduct business with such ladies,' and he concluded the conversation, betraying not even a hint of anything other than the decorum which he had long practised.

When he had left, Ellen caught the other woman's hands. 'The Latrobes of the world will quickly enough disappear,' she said, thinking of a Northern victory.

'I doubt it!' Madame Labiche answered. 'Or if they do, they will be replaced by their Yankee counterparts. The slaves may well be liberated, us women . . . never!'

The plantation mistress then showed Ellen into the Mill and the Purgery – a hundred feet in length, fifty feet in breadth.

'It was not sugar alone that was made here . . .' she said, '. . . but history! The Jesuits brought sugar to New Orleans one hundred years ago from the tropics of New Guinea. So it is a holy tradition. But the Jesuit chemists failed. Sugarcane needs fourteen months of hot sunshine to reach maturity. Here, in Louisiana, we have only eight before the weather begins to cool. 'Here the cane never reaches full maturity . . .' she paused, as if reflecting on something else of life. 'But the cool, dry weather of early Fall produces an artificial maturity. This is accelerated by light frosts that slow the growth, and increase the sucrose levels in the juice. But if we have freezing temperatures during harvesting destroy the sucrose content and the juice will no longer crystallise. Crystallisation is the art, the divine intervention. The West Indians . . . there!' She pointed at a group of slaves for Ellen to understand. 'They are masters of the art. The Congolese slaves from Africa, less so.'

Ellen was fascinated by it all, the history and geography of the divine art of making sugar.

Lucretia Labiche continued her story while, in the next

353

month or so, this friendly frost is welcome it is the killing frost of late October, we must race against. If it comes while the cane still stands . . . then we are all dead.'

NINETY

'The river is our road,' Madame Labiche told her as she and Ellen walked under the great awnings of the house down towards the Mississippi. 'It is our great nourisher.'

Ellen could understand the respect in which the giant river was held, by those whose lands it nourished, and whose produce it whisked to the far ends of the world. The levees the human fortresses were built against a Mississippi which, if angered, could flood the low-lying plantation lands. Built by the Labiches, and completed when Emeritus, the woman's husband was a boy.

'The levees and the Labiches are synonymous – they are our safeguards,' Lucretia told her. 'Monsieur Labiche would, every evening after dinner, leave whatever guests were at table and go to the levee.' Madame Labiche scarcely paused in the telling. 'It is an old sacred tradition of the Labiche men, under whose protection we fall.'

'Do you go to the levee, Lucretia?' Ellen asked.

'Good Heavens, no! No! It is for the head of the household to do such a thing. A lady would never make for such a public display of duty!'

As if in answer, the following evening the Mississippi raised its levels, swelling over the Labiche levee. Little damage was done, some of the gardens momentarily floundering under

Big Muddy's waters. It caused excitement among the slaves – 'Big River risin'! Big River is risin'!' they chanted.

Though the house itself was untouched, Madame Labiche considered the breaching of the levee to be an ominous sign. 'Had Monsieur Labiche been here and not fighting the Northern traitors, this would never have happened,' she said, as if blaming her own faulty stewardship of the levee. 'It is a portent, Madame Lavelle, a bad portent!'

It was a portent for Ellen too. That she should leave, continue her search. That Patrick, Lavelle and Stephen had all been here previously had provided some bond, some strange attraction within her for this splendid place. She wondered if the bringing down of these great houses and all they stood for was what this war was all about? A jealous envy thinly disguised in the cloths of 'equality' and 'freedom'? A grasping kind of jealousy. Wanting first to subdue the soul of the South, then possess its riches.

She bade goodbye to Madame Labiche and thanked her for her hospitality. The mistress had ordered that a carriage take her back to New Orleans from whence she would travel northwards.

As she left, Ellen turned to look backwards. Lucretia Labiche stood framed by the majestic structure of Versailles, no hand raised, her angular frame diminishing as the distance grew between them. Like some garden detail, unmoving, its place forever determined.

The journey to New Orleans gave Ellen time to recollect her thoughts. Patrick had been here – often with both Stephen Joyce and Oxy Moran. Stephen would easily have been accepted into such society with his airish ways. Patrick had met and fallen in love with Emmeline, now sent for safety with her sister to a convent – whereabouts unrevealed by Madame Labiche. It was a doomed love, Ellen knew, a mismatch of unequals. At least Patrick would have had no sense of this, she imagined, would have gone into battle with hope in his heart. He and Oxy had gone under Stephen's command with the Louisiana infantry. Lavelle, having found, what he mistakenly imagined was her book, and Emmeline's letters, had then arrived, thinking Ellen to have been there at some stage with Patrick.

Lavelle would then, from his visit, have learned of Stephen Joyce. Maybe by now have puzzled out that the book was not indeed Patrick's but Stephen's. The question would then arise as to why he had given it to Patrick. Then Lavelle would remember. Her disappearance . . . all of it would now fit together in his mind.

He would try to find the Louisianians, find Stephen. Exact revenge on her once lover. She quailed at the thought.

She must prevent any retribution, further losses. Get back to the battlefields . . . must first find the Louisianians. Then she would find Stephen . . . and Lavelle.

NINETY-ONE

Antietam, Maryland, September 1862

Lavelle spoke to the picket. 'Any of our lads on the other side?'

The man, rough-faced from duty, answered him thickly, the nervousness of the coming battle in his voice. 'A fair few I think, can't you hear them singing?'

Lavelle listened and heard the familiar tones of 'The Last Rose of Summer' come from the enemy lines across the river.

The Irish always sang before battle. Now, at last, he was back amongst them. Back with the Irish Brigade – the trip northwards uneventful after Clinch and the dog. Easy Money and the girl had slipped away one night. Gone on the Underground Railroad – the secret means by which sympathisers helped spirit runaway slaves to the North

'All our wars are merry, all our songs are sad,' he muttered to the jittery picket. He brought his hand to his mouth, waited for a gap in the song . . . and shouted back the next line.

He heard silence, a break and then "Tis the last rose of summer left blooming alone . . .'

The singing from the rebel camp stopped, waiting. Lavelle, again made a horn shape with his hands and sang out loudly

358

the rejoining line 'All her lovely companions are faded and gone.'

Then silence followed by a shout – 'Is that you, Paddy Yankee?'

'It is, Paddy Reb.' Lavelle called back. He heard the laughter then, already knowing the next question.

'Are you the Irish Brigade?'

'Yes!' Lavelle answered. 'And you?'

'We're the Irish Brigade too!' the enemy soldier roared back, and Lavelle could hear the laughter rise higher. 'The *real* one!' the voice continued, amid more loud merriment.

'What county man are you?' Lavelle shouted back.

'Mayo . . . and Galway and the whole thirty-two counties together!' the unknown soldier returned, to the continuing merriment of the 'real' Irish Brigade.

'And yourself, Yankee, what strange parts sent you over here – to the losing side?'

'Mayo, too, God help us!' Lavelle answered, the *craic* now attracting the Irish of both sides. The Irish, always looking for *craic*, wherever it could be found. Even with the enemy.

And so it went, Lavelle, the Yankee Mayoman and the Johnny Reb Mayoman, shouting over and back the river, establishing a commonality of ties and background; if not of current allegiance.

'Meet in the middle – and bring letters!' the other voice shouted. 'And we'll sing a few songs for the old times.'

'Tell your pickets not to plug us!' Lavelle shouted back.

He went back to the camp and rounded up the Little Bishop and a few of the others, telling them, 'There's a good crew of Irish fighting men across the river, who want to sing us a few songs.'

They brought some coffee, a few plugs of tobacco . . . and the letters from home. As they passed the jittery pickets Lavelle warned them to 'Keep your guns pointed at the Heavens and let no Irish shoot Irish this evening. Tomorrow will bring what it will bring.'

Then Lavelle and his small contingent in blue waded out into the water, the river being shallow enough, never more than waist high. From the far side they could see a slightly larger band in grey uniform do the same.

At first both groups were tentative, eying each other up from a distance but when they got close enough, all relaxed and Lavelle called, 'Who's the Mayoman here?'

'I am,' a fair-haired lad called back. 'John Brady from Bohola.'

At this the others let up chanting yelps.

'Bohola! Bohola! God help us Bohola!'

John Brady from Bohola, reminded Lavelle of himself, twenty years back. Young, fair-haired, and eager for adventure, but still longing for any link with home. The Little Bishop, higher above the river's surface than most, thought the two groups should fight each other then 'with water instead of guns – and whichever side's the winner, wins the whole damn war . . . and we can all go home!'

This idea was greeted with cheers all round and a general mêlée of splashing and roughhousing ensued between the 'enemies' for a few minutes. The result was declared 'A victory for Ireland!'

But more serious business was called for. 'The very reason this summit meeting of the common soldier of North and South, was convened in the first place,' the Little Bishop declared.

Then the trading began.

Though it was more than an exchange of gifts – an expression of friendship, of understanding that they were to each other only 'the enemy' because of circumstance, or geography . . . or colour of uniform. Tobacco was swapped for coffee; a rusty penknife for a mostly intact 'housewife'; Southern hardtack for Northern hardtack.

'It's all the same louse-infected stuff anyway,' an O'Mahony from Kerry lilted in that singsong way.

Lavelle gave young Brady a chunk of chocolate he had

been saving. The youngster's eyes lit up and then, his hand ready to take it, declined the offer.

'What's the matter, lad, don't you like it?' Lavelle asked, puzzled at the boy's reluctance.

'No, it's not that . . .' the boy answered, '. . . but I have nothing to give back . . . only the letter from home . . . and I wanted to keep that . . . but I could read it!' he added brightly, thinking of a solution.

'It's okay, son!' Lavelle said, pushing the chocolate at him. 'Here take it and welcome.' The lad took the chocolate, eying it with delight, feeling its milky texture with his finger. 'I'll keep it till after tomorrow,' he said. 'When we're all tired from fightin'.' Then he took out his letter. 'Four thousand miles this came to me,' he said, holding it up with a kind of reverence.

'Three,' the Little Bishop interjected. 'Sure isn't Mayo the very next parish across the Atlantic from America; if it came from Dublin it'd be the four all right – but from Bohola it's three.'

John Brady from Bohola waited until the laughter had subsided and then began reading. 'It's from my mother,' he said simply.

'My dearest and youngest son John, Your Uncle Pat brought your welcome letter to us. We were all glad to get it and read it at the hearth, everybody taking turn who could read: your father, Uncle Pat, your sister Kate and Mrs McGlade and Father Dermody, who read it like you were here reading it yourself.

'It grieved me that you were finding America such a hard country to be in . . . and the fierce fighting there over the black people. God keep you safe and out of harm and maybe you'll come again when the fighting is finished at last. We thank you for the dollars sent.'

This last part the boy hurried over. Not to have his mother embarrassed in front of the men, talking about 'money from America'. Now he continued more slowly, drinking in the words with his eyes, his face alight with the fond memories they evoked.

'Your father is working hard again this year in the wet and the damp but the potatoes got put down in the low field and they will be successful again this year with God's help. The fine weather comes somedays and I go out in the fields and in my mind see you running and playing with the village lads and sitting, looking out across the sky towards America. The Durkan lad went last week. They had a great American wake for him and two of the Costello girls a *whileen* before that. The whole place is going bare with the young people scattered to America and over to England as well. Though I think America is better for Irish people even with the war. The young are left behind here, right enough, but haven't much for themselves here and are causing trouble going at night to landlords' houses. But then it comes back on them when the peelers come after them and they are up before the Assizes.

'Your sister Kate is seventeen now and is waiting to go over to you. It would break your father's heart and little Jimmy's. To tell no lie, I would find it hard to lose another of ye to America but I wouldn't stand in her way. As long as she was careful.

'Poor Annie Diskin passed away after Christmas – went to her reward – and the frosty days took another few from the valley as well. January is a hard month on poor people.

We are all doing fine here and enjoying the springtime. The hawthorn is in full bloom along every hedge and the cuckoo is above on the *moneen* this year again. Singing her song all down the valley. I don't think America is a place as good as this – if it wasn't for the work. I hope you find a nice girl over there to be your companion in life. A nice, good Irish girl, from back home. I wouldn't be well pleased if you were mixing with any of them black ladies, that I hear tell some of the Irish boys from Galway and the cities is mixing with. Stick with your own, John, that's my dearest wish and not be with those black ladies who are causing such trouble for ye all now with this fighting. Write soon, my dearest young son . . . and may God protect you in all you do.

Your dearest Mother and all at home.'

As John Brady gazed lovingly at the last lines of his mother's letter, Lavelle looked around at the men, waist-high in America. All were silent, some looking down into the eddying waters, seeing Ireland there. Others looked to the sky, their thoughts winging the thousands of miles to the sights and sounds of an Irish spring day. Lavelle's own thoughts travelled the miles, resting on the imagined place from where his Ellen had first come out of Ireland: its hanging valleys, its bristling lakes, its sheltering hills. Could she ever be back there now he wondered . . . back among the hawthorn flowers and the cuckoo-call?

Then John Brady, from Bohola, County Mayo, carefully folded away his mother's letter. They thanked him – it was as if his mother had written to them all . . . those who, so infrequently, got letters from the homeland . . . and those who got none.

'Your mother has a fine way of writing about her,' Lavelle said, looking far beyond the lad. 'You should go back to see her when this business here is put behind us.'

'I will surely,' John Brady said.

Then another of the Rebs – a McGillicuddy from the Reeks of Kerry – called for a 'Song for old Ireland!' and he led off into Moore's rousing march – 'The Minstrel Boy'. Soon they were all joined with him.

> 'The Minstrel Boy to the war is gone.
> In the ranks of death you'll find him.
> His father's sword he has girded on
> And his wild harp slung behind him.'

Next, it was a song much favoured by the Irish Brigade . . . both camps.

363

'Here Scots and Poles, Italians, Gauls,
With native emblems tricked;
There Teuton Corps, who fought before,
Für Freiheit und für Licht;
While round the flag the Irish,
Like a human rampart go;
They found Cead Míle Fáilte here –
They'll give it to the foe.'

They bade their goodbyes then. A jibe or two: 'We'll wallop you Yankees with saucepans!' or 'We'll skedaddle you Rebs all the way back to Mayo!' and wished each other well in battle, sorry that they were on opposite sides Then they had 'one more for the road' – 'Or the river,' quipped the Little Bishop – and John Brady again started up 'The Last Rose of Summer' most-beloved song of the Irish North and South. They sang a verse standing together, arms clasped around each other's shoulders. Then gradually they drifted away from each other, no word spoken, back towards their own camps, dividing the song, each group bringing it back to its own side.

When true hearts lie wither'd,
And fond ones are flown,
Oh! Who would inhabit,
This bleak world alone.

Back at their own camp on the Northern side, Lavelle and the others sat to dry themselves by the campfire. No one spoke of the encounter from which they had returned but it filled every mind.

'Democracy is at stake,' declared the Little Bishop. 'That's why we're fighting . . . isn't it? If the aristocratic monarchism of the South prevails against the democracy of the slave – then where will we be? Struggling Old World nationalists like us Irish – *niggers-turned-inside-out* – 'cos that's how they see us – will have no chance. We've got out from under one Crown back home . . .' The Little Bishop drew breath and like all good preachers, kept them waiting, '. . . but, make no mistake about it, there's a Crown in the South too, the big sugar men and the monarchs of the Cotton Kingdom.'

The Little Bishop was right, Lavelle knew. 'What's at stake for sure is the safety and welfare of our adopted country and its Constitution,' Lavelle added, unsure of what the future held for the niggers-turned-inside-out, once three million proper niggers swarmed out of the South.

'Couldn't put it better myself,' the Little Bishop chimed in. 'For this country to prosper there has to be no North, no South, no East, no West but the whole Union – and if it takes a war to achieve that, then who better to see to it than the Irish!'

'Here! Here!' the Irish chorused . . . sending the Little Bishop into further flight.

'Isn't war, with all its gilded fascination, such a splendid game – a splendid game?' The Little Bishop sat back, arms folded. That'd give them something to chew on . . . to send home in their 'letters-from-the-front'.

'Before this "splendid game" is over . . .' a fresh voice interrupted, '. . . there'll be many an Irish cottage and many a home on the Rhine . . . and many a Welsh village, steeped in sorrow.'

The speaker was Evan Williams, tall and stout-throated, from the Valleys of the Rhondda.

His intervention was met with silence. All were waiting for the Little Bishop to come back.

'Listen up, *bach* . . . !' the big man began, '. . . us Irish have a fight on here tomorrow and we don't want any of that old Welsh guff about the Valleys and that Mother o'Jaysus place you hail from.' This drew a loud cheer. You couldn't whack the Little Bishop for whacking the Welsh, or anybody else, for that matter.

Lavelle did not join in.

'Ah, sweet Llanfairpwllgwyngyll!' Evan Williams said quietly, ignoring them all; walking into their midst, drawing out the words of his home place like a song. They knew then he would sing and when Evan Williams sang, all others listened, even bishops.

> 'A dyro'th law, Myfanwy dirion,
> I ddim and dwend y gair "Ffarwél".

> 'Give me your hand, gentle Myfanwy,
> If only to utter the word "Farewell".'

All fell silent then on the night before battle. Somehow, the young man's song with its *Hiraeth* – its *longing* for homeland, for what might have been – was all of their songs and the *yr hen iaith* – the ancient language of Wales – their common tongue.

Lavelle understood it – the *Hiraeth* – the longing. Everyone had it. Always there, waiting to be called up, by some song . . . or remembrance . . . or fear. Then, like a great army, it would sweep over the body leaving it defenceless of reason, immobilised. Lavelle's *hiraeth* was always the same – Ellen O'Malley. She was his green Rhondda valley – his Myfanwy.

That night, as he crawled under his rough blanket and anxious of the morning, he wished he could sing like Evan Williams.

In the morning General Meagher gave them a rousing address: 'The Irish Soldier – His History and Present Duty to the American Republic'.

'It's more geography than history!' the Little Bishop whispered to Lavelle, being as the speech followed the Irish soldier from Bolivia to Venezuela and from the Andes to the Orinoco. Then, the General swung the far-flung hero back to France. To Blenheim and Fontenoy, where Irish dragoons had borne away the enemy flag.

'Remember Fontenoy!' Meagher's voice rang out.

'Remember Fontenoy? As if any of them had ever heard of it in the first place.

'The general talks a good battle . . .' Lavelle said to the Little Bishop, '. . . even if he doesn't always attend them.'

The flags of the Irish Brigade fluttered on every side of Thomas Francis Meagher. Flags with guidons of the richest silk all executed in Tiffany's best. The general's hand swept towards them, embracing them, sanctifying them. 'These colours are the gift of fair women to brave men. Think of those who presented them. Die if necessary but never surrender.'

Lavelle wondered if half of those listening knew for what it was they would be dying. Apart from the exhortation to do so, by one of their own. To Lavelle, the *grande-hautered* Irish voice – so differently toned from that of the common fighting man; the Tiffany-fashioned flags; the Irish Brigade itself, all seemed to be just part of 'the splendid game'. The game which sent them out to die, while prancing-horsed generals with flowery brogues hung at the fringes and collected the plaudits – but not the buck and ball.

'I wonder, Lavelle . . .' the Little Bishop slid in, '. . . would the general have given the same rigmarole of a speech if he had joined with the South, as he had first planned – until the North gave him a better commission . . . and a brigadeful of fools?'

'Probably,' Lavelle answered.

Then they fell into line. Marched to meet the enemy – the Irish of the South.

When, in the aftermath of the day's battle Lavelle found him, Evan Williams was sitting, his back to a tree.

'I stopped a minié ball with my name on it,' he said with a little laugh.

367

Lavelle ripped open the Welshman's undershirt. The small wound above the breastplate hardly looked significant.

'We'll get you out of here, lad!' Lavelle said.

'No, don't move me but I want you to take this – it's from the mines.' He opened his hand, revealing a small glinting piece of anthracite. 'Myfanwy gave it to me – she said it would warm the cockles of my heart, here in America. And there's a letter too. Send it to her for me.'

'I will, I promise,' Lavelle answered.

Then the lad closed his eyes, and thought of greener days and more welcoming valleys than America could offer.

> '*A dyro'th law, Myfanwy dirion* . . .
> Give me your hand, gentle Myfanwy,
> If only to utter the word "Farewell".'

He sang in a voice released of this world's *hiraeth*. Calling across the blood-spilt plains to the fertile valleys of Wales.

Later, Lavelle put the piece of coal and the letter into a large envelope and addressed it.

> Myfanwy Thomas,
> Llanfairpwllgwyngyll,
> Wales.

There would be no more a welcome in the valleys for when young Evan Williams returned home again to Wales. Only the longing his letter would bring.

Later, when sleep would not come, Lavelle thought more about the Welshman's letter, along with a myriad of other thoughts which paraded before him. Elusive thoughts he could not catch, nor mould into any sort of sense. In the distance he heard the Southern pickets call out to each other. Then he went outside and saw the smoke of Southern fires weave into the night, hang there like incense over a prayer and be gone. It was like his thoughts. They were there, real, but escaping from him into the sky where they disappeared.

In that moment he resolved to write to Ellen. It was not that he feared the coming battle. No unusual dread of not returning. He had conquered that a long time ago – if ever it had been a factor for him. But, some day, he thought sanguinely, a Rebel bullet *would* find him. And if it did he wanted her to know, know he had searched and searched . . . forgiven her. Know darker things, how he had taken her beloved son out of this life . . . needed her forgiveness. She was still alive – somewhere out there – and whatever her deed, she was more to him than life itself.

Lavelle arose early the following morning. It was bright autumnal weather. He began the letter, read what he had written, scratched it out, then began again. Again he stopped; looked across the river to where the Confederate army were bivouacked, and determinedly started writing once more. This time he did not consider what his pen might say, only that it spoke for him.

The Irish Brigade
Army of the Potomac
Maryland
September, 1862

Dearest Ellen,

Lest I should be unable to write to you again, I feel impelled to send a few lines that may fall under your eye when I am no more. I have no misgivings about, or lack of confidence in the cause in which I am engaged. And my courage does not halt or falter. I know how American civilisation now leans upon the triumph of the government and how great a debt we owe to those who went before us through the blood and suffering of the Revolution. And I am willing, perfectly willing, to lay down all my joys in this life to maintain government and to pay that debt.

Ellen, my love for you is deathless. It seems to bind me with mighty cables that nothing but Omnipotence can break. And my love of country comes over me like a strong wind and bears me irresistibly with all those chains to tomorrow's battlefield. A memory of all the blissful moments I have enjoyed with you come crowding over me and I feel most deeply grateful to God and you that I have enjoyed them for as long. If we do not meet again, dear Ellen, never forget how much I loved you. Nor that when my last breath escapes me on the battlefield it will whisper your name. Forgive me my many faults and the many pains I have caused you. How thoughtless, how foolish I have sometimes been. How much you must have felt compelled to bear before life drove you from me.

And now, I have brought to you, my most grievous, deepest wound of all. It was this hand, which now addresses you, that so cruelly deprived you of that most beloved of sons, Patrick. Nor do I seek absolution in the knowledge that I could never intentionally harm him whom I loved as my own. But, oh Ellen, if the dead can come back to this earth and flit unseen around those they love we will both always be with you on the brightest day and the darkest night. Always, always, and when the soft breeze fans your cheek it shall be my breath, or the cool air your throbbing temples, it shall be my spirit passing by.

If you mourn, do not mourn me dead. Think I am gone and wait for me. For we shall meet again.

Your Loving Husband

He paused. Did not even read it through, then signed the name by which she had always called him – Lavelle.

He felt relieved. It was all there. He fanned the pages in

370

the morning air, relief growing into satisfaction. He had done it. Set down his life on the scrawled pages. Concentrated it into the one true thing that gave it meaning – his love for her.

Carefully he folded the parchment into three and ran the heel of his hand along the creases, flattening them. Having inserted the letter into its carrier, Lavelle then sealed the envelope with hot candle wax using his thumb to press home the seal. He smiled feeling the sting of the hot wax.

On the front he wrote only *Ellen Lavelle, formerly O'Malley.*

The twin names caused him to pause, think back on the history revealed within each name.

How much and how little.

NINETY-TWO

Confederate Camp, Bunker Hill, Virginia, October 1862

While Ellen knew that Stephen Joyce fought under the Louisiana flag, she had no notion of where he now might be. The war had raged far and wide from the Shenandoah Valley to the coast of the Atlantic Ocean. Troops were dispersed, dislocated, dispatched, it seemed to wherever the whim of the generals decreed.

She had been back a month now from Louisiana. Glad to be re-united with Louisa and her work again. Nothing much had changed in her absence.

Louisa was saddened beyond words at the news of Lavelle and Patrick.

'Oh, poor Lavelle,' she grieved. 'Poor, poor Lavelle – you must find him now Mother . . . give him your forgiveness.'

What enquiries she now made of those Confederates who fell under her care, yielded no more news of Stephen Joyce than did her similar enquiries of Lavelle.

'Ma'am!' one veteran of a dozen dogfights told her. 'There's towards half a million Irish out there fighting this war and fighting each other. From New York to New Orleans and every hitching post in between – and some of 'em straight off the emigrant ships. They never stood a day in America except to fight for her.'

Then one day her luck changed. Overhearing a newly admitted casualty tell another about 'those Louisiana Tigers', she immediately quizzed the youth. 'More like devils than tigers – don't fear nothing,' he told her. 'Only yellin' like they was crazed with hooch. They was cut to shreds at Antietam.' They'd crossed back into Virginia he said and she'd find them 'in Bunker Hill Camp, if you go quickly. They don't set down anywhere too long – these swamp devils.'

Twice she was stopped by Union soldiers and warned of the hazards of marauding Rebels. Then, beyond the Union lines, Southern pickets stopped her. At first they tried to turn her back as a Northern spy until she explained that her son had fought and died for the Southern cause. She was then escorted the remainder of the way to Captain Joyce's tent. That he was both surprised and delighted to see her, Stephen Joyce made no secret of.

He looked tired, his gaunt features even more so, Ellen thought, fatigued by the grinding everyday normality of leading men to their death.

'I thought I should never see you again,' he said, coming warmly to greet her.

'Nor I you,' she answered. 'But it seems that the circles of life . . . and death . . .' She stopped, thinking of Patrick, '. . . inextricably bind us.'

He smiled at her, took her hand. 'If only that were true, dear Ellen . . . if only it were true.'

'It is!' she said simply. 'Despite all that has passed, all that I have aspired to be and not to be, the past cannot be erased. It is why I am here.'

He looked at her. 'The passage of time has not erased my imaginings of you, Ellen, although I sense you are less truculent now!' He laughed.

'Stephen, be serious!' she scolded and then 'It was Lavelle who shot Patrick – he did not know it,' she began, taking his arm to stay him. Then she told him the whole story – the missing book, Lavelle going South, her own journey South after Patrick's death. She stopped, letting it all sink in with him.

When eventually Stephen spoke, he was grave in tone. 'Then Lavelle will have guessed everything,' he said, looking intently into her face.

'Perhaps not . . . but he may well have.'

Stephen was silent, considering her answer a while. 'Through all of this, you and Lavelle have not spoken?' he then asked.

'No – and I must find him, Stephen – tell him.'

He nodded. 'If war throws up even one truth, then it will have had some merit.'

'I pray he has not discovered it for himself,' Ellen said, tightening the grip on his hand. 'Or he will come searching for you, Stephen,' she added, concerned for them both.

He looked at her. 'If he does then no harm will come to him at my hand – and if reason prevail on his part I will direct him safely to you.'

She thanked him.

He bade her stay a little longer, ordered some refreshment for her and for a while they sat, patching together the inter-vening years of their lives, since last they had seen each other. Her own life she relegated to being, for the most part, of little importance.

He enquired of Mary and she told him. They sat in silence for a moment, his presence a comfort to her.

'There's only you and Louisa now. How strange the fates that sent her to you,' he remarked, thinking how much had been taken from her.

'Louisa is a gift from Heaven . . . and I am ever fearful that Heaven will ask her back of me.'

'You have lost enough, Ellen,' he said with compassion. 'Heaven will not, could not, ask more of you.'

'My sin was great . . . and far-reaching,' she said simply, casting no blame on him, only on herself. 'The atonement must match the wrong. Only then comes forgiveness.'

He did not answer her directly. Instead saying, 'There is a great gathering of armies in this place. Men who know not each other, who have never spoken, and who have never heard of the far countries and places from where each other comes. Yet daily they . . . we . . . kill each other. If there had been even one hundredth of the forgiveness between North and South that you have sought in your life, then this corroding carnage of war would have been spared all who now participate in it. You must forgive yourself, Ellen. You are human, fallible, flawed like the rest of humanity. Perfection is denied us. Forgive yourself.'

It was the Stephen she knew – and loved. Full of passion for whatever cause possessed him, Ireland, freedom, love, forgiveness . . . her. She stood to go, tenderly kissed him on the cheek, below the dark spot. Neither said anything until he called for a sentry to see her safely to the lines.

Once, she paused, looked behind her but he had not remained to see her leave. Him fearing it might be his last sight of her; wanting to preserve the memory of her being there with him, the farewell kiss, rather than the slow lingering view of her leaving. She disappearing away from him.

NINETY-THREE

Irish Brigade, Fredericksburg, Virginia, December 1862

Lavelle looked towards the town.

Fredericksburg. A burning town . . . the Rappahannock river between them and it . . . glaced ice and mud everywhere . . . and the Confederate cannon lined up waiting for them. 'Peace on earth, my arse,' he said into the fog and the damp. 'What a place to be, with Christmas only two weeks away.'

Earlier in the day, he with others had slaughtered hundreds of bullocks, enough for three days' rations. Rounded them up in a field and shot them down like traitors. That's all they seemed to be shooting these days – bullocks.

Lavelle thought they were in disarray. The previous month President Lincoln had sacked the Union Army's commander, General George McClellan. 'Little Mac', as the men called him, due to his diminutive stature, had dillied and dallied after Antietam, always looking for more men, more resources, before he would pursue the Confederate Army, under Lee. To Lavelle's mind, the superior sized Army of the Potomac had 'let the Rebs think we're afraid of them, given them courage.'

Now under this new commander, General Burnside, the advantage had again been lost. Lavelle, and all the men, knew that Fredericksburg could have been taken three weeks ago in November, but Burnside had delayed everything, wanting pontoon bridges built, when they could have waded the river, caught Lee before he was ready. Now Lee had been allowed valuable time to construct new defences, earthworks rising higher and higher on the heights overlooking the town. The boys of the Irish Brigade were worried, preferring 'Fightin' rather than friggin' around in the mud'. Lavelle too, felt some foreboding at Burnside's new plan to attack the Confederate cannon frontally. He spoke to Father Corby, the Brigade's chaplain.

'Our generals are going to lead the men in front of those guns, which we have stood back and admired the Rebs placing unhindered before us these past three weeks.'

'Do not trouble yourself,' the priest told him. 'Your generals know better than that.'

Now the Union generals had bombarded the town, raining down tons of iron on it like some dastardly manna; the flames rising high above the stricken streets, like the star of Christmas, leading the Northern enemies to capture it. The next day, 12 December, Lavelle along with the 1200 men of the Irish Brigade, marched into Fredericksburg. That night Lavelle hunted down a piece of board, upon which to sleep, the mud oozing up around its sides each time he restlessly turned.

The Saturday morning was misty, damp, bone-piercing cold. General Meagher addressed them, reminding them in his highly-charged manner that the eyes of America were upon them. The flags of the three New York regiments of the Brigade had been so tattered by gunshot, they had been sent homewards for repair. But so the enemy would know it was the Irish Brigade, General Meagher had had distributed to each man a sprig of green boxwood to be worn in their caps.

The new green flag of the 28th Massachussetts Infantry, with harp, sunburst and a garland of shamrocks was unfurled. ''Faugh a Ballagh' the legend scrolled across it said – 'Clear the Way . . . for the Irish!' the men shouted.

Lavelle and the 28th marched south through the town, towards the Rebel artillery on Marye's Heights.

As they went Rebel shells peppered the sky about them. Lavelle saw many Negro women, run with their children from the ruins of houses, in chaos and fear not knowing which way to go for safety. As he watched one barefooted and aged woman, carrying a basket and with three children clinging to her, passed close by him. He heard the hiss of the shell, shouted at her but was too late. She was cut literally in half. Two of the children were likewise killed by the missile. He broke rank, ran to where they lay, gathered up the surviving child and threw the both of them to the ground until the danger had passed.

As he arose, the child, a little girl of about six years, kicked and screamed against him. While he struggled with her, he was approached by a well-dressed, elderly man and woman. But it was not to render assistance they came. The man addressed him in an aggressive manner . . .

'I am a minister of the gospel . . . and you Yankees have burned us out of house and home. Take me to your commanding officer. I demand that restitution is made . . . the people of the North must now give me the living they have deprived me of here. You must take us with you – and damn you all to Hell!'

Lavelle, well used as he was to camp life, was shocked at the level of profanity the minister continued to level at him and his indifference to the blood of the old negro and the two children at their feet. He thrust the young girl into the protesting parson's arms and levelled his gun at him. 'If I am damned to Hell, your reverence, you'll be there before me!' The man shrank back, his wife beginning to intervene. Lavelle pointed the rifle closer at the man's head. 'Now, fulfil your duty and take care of this child . . . and but for her you'd be dead by now.' The woman bustled her husband and the child away from Lavelle . . . and he shouted after them, 'I'll be back when this thing is over.'

378

He had to run to rejoin his regiment.

The men of the Irish Brigade crossed a small canal, eventually coming to rest before a hill. Beyond the hill was the enemy.

Silence.

The waiting for the command.

'Fix bayonets!'

Now silence was broken. The men shouted and cheered with the exhilaration of that order. It would be close and bloody Lavelle knew. Today he could not lie in the long grass awaiting his moment. He clinked his bayonet into place, the air ringing with steel on steel, the music of war. Lavelle felt his blood run cold at the sound. They were not first in but he watched as the bayonets in the hands of those before them glistened in the sun, advancing into battle like a huge serpent of blue and steel. Then they heard the terrible fusillade of the Confederate guns . . . and it never stopped.

A second wave of Union soldiers was sent forward, and the Irish Brigade moved up to fill their places. An equal fate met this second attack. Lavelle could feel the sweat rise on him, cold as the rifle he carried.

Then it was 'Irish Brigade, advance!' followed by 'Forward double-quick!' Then they were running, rushing up the hill, wildly cheering, as if chasing some hunted prey. When he saw before them the Sunken Road, the stone wall running alongside it, Lavelle knew the prey was them. Behind the stone wall waited a thousand rifles, it seemed. In front of the wall lay the Union dead, heaped upon heap upon heap.

It was madness.

They were as lame ducks, having to climb, stumble over their own dead, be picked off like flies. The impetus of the others carried Lavelle forward in some kind of murderous delirium, some releasing death-wish. Was this how it all would end? Now, charged with a wild terror and an equally unfettered bloodlust, he didn't care . . . would take with him as many Rebs as he could. From somewhere behind the wall he heard an Irish voice. 'Oh, Christ, what a pity – it's the Irish . . . Meagher's boys.' Then Cobb's Georgia Brigade, many of them immigrant Irish themselves, opened fire on their fellow countrymen.

Around him, Lavelle saw his comrades mowed down like grass before a reaper. But still he went forward, crouched as best he could, the bayonet useless before him, no enemy with which to engage. Men were blown off their feet by the sheer volume of fire. About him minié ball after minié ball whizzed.

Lavelle flung himself on his back between two corpses, using his blanket roll as a further shield. As he did he felt the bullets thud into the bodies. He lay there a moment, turned quickly, picked a target head and shoulders framed above the stone wall and fired. He saw the grey tunic slump away from the wall, only to be replaced by another. He lay low again, reloading on his back and repeated the manoeuvre. He saw that Rebel fall. 'Get down!' he shouted to those around him. 'On your backs!' It was their only chance – to seek the shelter of the corpses raised like barricades around them. Many followed his example, at last providing some sort of response to the Rebel fusillade. A response Lavelle grimly noted only afforded them by the dead bodies of their comrades.

The gaps now in those who followed them into the Sunken Road were so great but still the men of the Irish Brigade poured forward to fill them. Then, rising above the shells and the scream of battle, Lavelle heard a strange sound. He raised his head. The din of battle abated and before his eyes he saw Rebels standing up from their posts, cheering and applauding the fearlessness and bravery of their Irish foes.

It was a brief interlude, of some deep-down humanity, amidst the terrible slaughter. Soon however the carnage resumed and Lavelle, and those few who had survived with him, were trapped. They could neither move forwards nor backwards without attracting the attention of the enemy.

Now out of ammunition, Lavelle was forced to raid the cartridges of those around him who had no further need of them.

He lay there then, practised in a sharpshooter's stillness, ignoring the blood of comrades, which seeped from their bodies and coagulated on his.

When the fire eventually slackened about dusk, Lavelle crawled on his hands and stomach over his dead and dying comrades. His blanket roll, when he shook it out later, let fall fourteen Rebel bullets.

The following morning, Lavelle learned the full cost of the battle for Marye's Heights. Of the 1200 men of the Irish Brigade who had gone into battle, more than 500 were killed, wounded or missing; those from Massachusetts, making up a third of that number. The Union army had suffered an unforgettable defeat at the hands of Robert E Lee's Confederates. 'That's the end of the Brigade now,' the Little Bishop said sorrowfully. Lavelle was glad to see the big man had survived.

'Well if it is, Bishop, I won't be sorry. The Union army doesn't deserve us. It was a death trap we were sent to . . . bayonets against firing squads,' he said in disgust.

'And where was the man who sent us in – our gallant leader – I never saw him after the speeches and the damned boxwood sprig?' Lavelle angrily tore at the green emblem, still miraculously attached to his kepi. He threw it from him, trampling it into the muddy ground.

General Meagher, they later learned, had mysteriously 'retired' from battle at an early stage.

NINETY-FOUR

Gettysburg, Pennsylvania, 1st July 1863

'Gettysburg will not be forgotten,' Dr Sawyer said to Ellen. 'For all the wrong reasons.'

Ellen's heart quailed at the thought. They had been despatched out of Virginia and here to Pennsylvania, to establish a field hospital. Word had come that the two great armies were massing, with great quantities of men, towards this sleepy little town of Gettysburg. A sleepy little town of the North – but on the road to Washington for the South.

The war had gone on relentlessly into its third year. Their work of caring and nursing had gone on relentlessly. Everything seemed so relentless, so unyielding, so unforgiving. Though the fighting may have stopped over the worst of the winter, those wounded by it had no such relief. Nor those who tended them. Ellen along with Louisa had hardly had time to bless herself over the Christmas, though for many months now they had a succession of well-meaning lay nurses. Ever since Mary.

Lavelle and Stephen, wherever they were, had probably dispersed to winter camp somewhere. Until the New Year spring started the killing all over again.

Now this Gettysburg. Ellen was filled with a foreboding

about this place. Dr Sawyer, Louisa, herself – they all seemed to feel it.

'When will it all end?' she beseeched of Louisa.

She had seen so many of her countrymen – bog-ignorant boys, mostly – perish in this American war. There seemed to be such an obscene supply of young men, not just the Irish, but Americans, Germans, Poles, English, Scots, Welsh – the whole world. All wide-eyed for glory, all spewn out of the emigrant ships, the sweatshops of New York, and the swamplands, coalmines and prairies of this vast land.

Today's fighting had been fearsome and when it had been quelled, Ellen would again go out.

Again, now she would go out. As once she had gleaned the stricken fields of Ireland for the odd potato bypassed by blight, now did she glean the stricken fields of America, for the many blighted by this cruel war.

She went with Louisa, the air still burning of shell and shot, of grape and canister. Ellen, by now, well knew the terminology of death. Nothing of war afflicted her anymore. Not the nitre-scented odiousness. Not the full-scented richness of men's blood, dampening the receiving earth.

She stopped, kneeling here and there dispensing comfort where comfort often was to no avail. Everywhere the cry for 'Water! Water!' as if the blood-soaked earth had run dry of it. Those with some hope, she directed the litter bearers towards. And even this mercy itself inflicted more pain, as broken limbs became separated from their last sinewed attachment to the body.

By a farmyard she came upon a body, in Confederate grey. Pinned to it a scrap of paper. *Here lies the body of Pvt. Willie Mitchel, son of Irish patriot John Mitchel.* She knelt, pushed back the hair from the young man's face. She wondered who it was had left the note? Like her, all would have known of his father, John Mitchel. The outspoken critic of the Crown back in Ireland had been, like his then comrade, General Meagher, exiled to Van Diemen's Land. Mitchel, she had

383

heard, was now with the Confederate press in Richmond. The men, once comrades in a common cause, now supported opposite causes.

She said a prayer over the young Irish Rebel – and moved on, fearing what more of them she would find.

Blue and Grey alike called to her or, silenced by shock, and shell-shattered mouths, held out a hand in the last hope. All she touched, held briefly, prayed over and moved on. To some she was 'Sister!' To others, blinded by buck and ball, she was the womanly scent of home.

'Mother!' they called, in the fever of the dying. She answered to each, 'Yes, son . . . I am here.'

Others pressed letters upon her, an heirloom, a pledge locket, or a lover's parting gift. If she bent too near, some grasped at her clothing – pulling her face to their mouths, whispering some final confession – seeking her absolution. 'The Lord has forgiven you!' she said, each time with unwavering conviction.

An Irish boy in Confederate dress, scarce fourteen winters asked of her: 'Are you from the Old Country?' When she answered he said, 'It's a long way off. Close my eyes now so that I may see it.'

She cradled his sweet face, gently putting her fingers to his eyes, shuttering out the terrible world he was leaving. Before she had withdrawn her hand, he had already gone.

The litter bearers came back to stretcher yet another load to the hospital. Now that the fighting had stopped, they lifted, carried and dragged the wounded from both armies. Others, scavenging the dead and wounded, unceremoniously upended their bodies, reefing boots, trousers and jackets, from comrade and foe alike. She did not castigate them as once she did. The flimsy mantles of this world were of little use in the next . . . and might prolong another life, however briefly. On she went, scavenging what little life she could find. In the failing light she toiled. Behind, to her left, she saw Louisa.

Everywhere she looked it was the same. As if it were

Judgement Day and a wrathful God had smitten down all of mankind. Not even one worthy of salvation.

She prayed that one great battle would end it all, uncaring of who the victor might be. Death was the only victor now. Death would die only when they were all dead . . . all the young men dead.

She thought of Patrick, her beautiful dead Patrick. Estranged from her in life, now estranged from her in death. As all here were estranged. For there were no last farewells, no tender kisses. No asking forgiveness for old slights, hurts, betrayals. At the end of the first day of Gettysburg, she was exhausted, in spirit as well as in body. Never before had Ellen witnessed such carnage, such a 'laying waste of human life', as Louisa described it. This Pennsylvanian crossroads seemed the very axis of war, so great the armies of troops that had gathered here. Somewhere among them, Stephen and Lavelle.

Tonight she would pray for them. Tomorrow go out again. Hoping against hope she would not be too late.

NINETY-FIVE

Gettysburg, 2nd July 1863

Lavelle fell to his knees.

There was something about this day. Apart from the heat.

Around him, every man of the Irish Brigade also fell to kneeling, their heads bowed down. They had been woken at three-thirty and on the move since four-thirty that morning, marching along the Taneytown Road, from Round Tops, three miles south of Gettysburg. Lavelle and the men had been grateful to be able to lay down their heads on the Northern soil of Pennsylvania, for the previous night's rest. For the month of June they had tramped and trampled across the Rebel territories of Virginia and Maryland chasing Robert E Lee, the Confederate general. Some days it had been fifteen or eighteen miles. On 29 June it had been thirty-four.

Lavelle was ragged and tired and like all the men he was unsure of the new general – Meade – who only a week previously had replaced General Hooker at the head of the Union army. Hooker had been blamed for the loss at Chancellorsville in May. It was the Brigade's first engagement of the new battle year – their last since the slaughter at Fredericksburg, before Christmas.

General Meagher had also gone in May. Tendered his

resignation, piqued over not getting his way to raise more recruits for his sadly-depleted Brigade. No longer having a Brigade to 'general' as the general saw it. But Lavelle was happy with the new Commander of the Irish Brigade – Colonel Kelly, from Castlehackett in County Galway. Not flamboyant like Meagher, a decent man, well respected and calm under fire. Came out in 1850, after the Famine Lavelle had heard.

But what were all the generals up to? The armies had been assembled here all morning. Now it was almost noon and nothing much had happened. Everybody waiting. For what, Lavelle wondered? He remonstrated with himself. What was the hurry either?

Soon enough they would be at battle; the uniforms in which they now knelt, their 'grave clothes'. He tightened his grip on his single-shot Enfield rifle, tried not to think about it. Focused his attention instead on the chaplain to the Irish Brigade, Father Corby, who stood atop a boulder in front of the two massed armies.

Never before had Lavelle felt such an apprehension as he felt today. And there was no cause.

Word had come down that the Army of the Potomac, under Meade had over 90,000 troops and three hundred and fifty cannon. The Rebels, under General Lee had but 75,000 troops, and less than three hundred cannon – and were greatly out-numbered. Victory would be with the Union. Though wor-ryingly, yesterday had seen Lee's army win the day and take many prisoners.

Lavelle looked at the countryside around him. Both armies amassed in a great blue and grey arc, on the ridges surrounding this insignificant Pennsylvanian town, Gettysburg.

Cemetery Ridge lay between them and the Rebels, Cemetery Hill to their right. Lavelle pondered the names; Cemetery Ridge, Devil's Den, the Wheatfield, the Peach Orchard. The names all seemed at odds with each other – simple and colourful farm-country names and dark, death-conjuring names.

This battle would reflect that contrast. Would be both the brightest day and the darkest night.

He thought of his letter to Ellen, felt for it in his tunic. Shivered.

Father Corby, hatless, receding hairline and long dark beard, like some prophet of old, held one hand outstretched, the other placed solemnly on his breast. He wore his long cassock to the ground. Around his neck was draped a purple confessional stole. The little priest, raised up on his rock, reminded all – Papish, Presbyterian, Protestant, and Jew alike, of their sacred duty as soldiers, the nobility of their cause. To drive the message home he cautioned how, 'The Catholic Church refuses Christian burial to the soldier who turns his back upon the foe or deserts his flag.'

He then proposed to give a general absolution of all their sins, prior to battle, provided the men embraced the first opportunity of confessing them afterwards.

Lavelle prayed for courage and made a sincere Act of Contrition, as the roar of battle resounded from nearby Little Round Top. He felt edgy. 'O my God . . . heartily sorry . . .' The words seemed to come in little pent-up gushes. '. . . firmly resolve . . . never more to offend Thee . . . amend my life.'

Father Corby then extended his hand towards the multitude of men and pronounced in Latin the words that would purge their souls of all sin. Thus allowing them swift passage to eternal life, should they fall that day, and be taken from this mortal one.

'*Dominus noster Jesus Christus vos absolvat, et ego auctoritate ipsius, vos absolvo ab vinculo excommunicationis et interdicti, in quantum possum . . .*'

The general absolution from sin was for all, whether North or South whether present or not. For all about to appear before their Maker that Gettysburg day.

'*Et vos indigetis, deinde, ego absolvo vos a peccatis vestris . . .*'

Lavelle blessed himself at the '. . . *in nomine Patris, et Filii, et Spiritus Sancti.*' The priest's absolution had resigned him to whatever fate now lay in store. The monotonic ageless-ness of the Latin, strangely calming.

'*Amen!*'

'Load! Fix bayonets!' At the word of command, Lavelle was already on his feet and moving out quickly. He needed to pick his spot. From where, he could oversee the battle. Wreak more damage on the enemy.

A mile away on Seminary Ridge the massed forces of the Army of Northern Virginia waited. Amongst them, Stephen Joyce – champing for battle. Asking his God, not for deliv-erance . . . but for victory.

NINETY-SIX

'You must be prepared for the worst, Mother!' Louisa said
to her. 'As I must . . . that we may never find Lavelle.' *In
this world*, she had almost ended with.

'He must be here,' Ellen replied. 'He must be . . . I can
sense it!'

Louisa sat on the bed beside her mother. 'I know how you
have sought him, sought to confess to him,' she said tenderly.
'Went on an arduous journey South.'

'Yes, Louisa,' Ellen answered. 'But I knew then it would
lead me to him . . . as I know now that he is here – with
the army of the North. I can't explain it better – I just know.'

'Well,' Louisa said slowly, 'if Lavelle *has* gone to seek
Stephen Joyce, he may not have re-joined – anything might
have happened. You must be prepared for God's will in these
matters.'

'You, Louisa, are trying to protect me from further grief.
Thank you . . . but what is there left of grief to grieve?' Ellen
asked. 'I have no grief left.'

Louisa nodded. Whatever her own pain at the loss of her
adoptive sister and brother – it was as nothing when set
against Ellen's. Now there was only the two of them. The
'good' had been taken to their reward; she and Ellen left
behind to hunger and thirst on this unyielding earth. She

wondered if it would have been better to have never gone to half Moon Place with Mary. Never to have found their mother. How she had since suffered. Still craved Lavelle's forgiveness, trawling this America-land to find him. That was her way. No matter what penance had been exacted of her. Or what sacramental absolution the all-loving God had extended, it would never be enough. It had to be Lavelle who would forgive her.

'There are so many of the Union troops here – close to a hundred thousand they say – that he must be here,' Ellen said, as if reading Louisa's thoughts. 'And the South, too, has mustered its tens of thousands, therefore Stephen is also here. I *will* find Lavelle before this Gettysburg thing is done . . . and pray that I find him, before he finds Stephen.'

Word had come of the extraordinary scene gathering before the small, bearded chaplain of the Union Irish – Father Corby.

Ellen and Louisa had gone out, stood atop a high place. Below, like some Biblical scene, stood the priest on a rock, before him on every side, Blue and Grey, foot and horse, standing in silence.

Ellen knelt with Louisa as Father Corby sent his absolutions for all past sin over the silent hordes, North and South – believers and non-believers. She crossed herself, offering her own contrition for past wrongs, as the priest's voice rang out – '*Ego absolvo vos a peccatis vestris.*'

It was the most peaceful, most beautiful moment of this whole war. Here, gathered hundreds of thousands of souls, making peace with their Maker, accepting of whatever fate lay ahead.

'What a miraculous thing it would be, if the Lord would only send a sign to all here gathered,' Ellen said to Louisa. 'Turn them away from each other . . . ?'

'Yes, Mother – if He only would,' Louisa answered. 'Sometimes I am lost for understanding.'

Ellen surveyed the might of Meade's Army of the Potomac.

Even to her unpractised eye it seemed to vastly outnumber Lee's Confederates. But this would be no quick victory. No skirmish and retreat, living to fight another day. This would be long and bloody, many battles within the one great battle. She prayed that both Stephen and Lavelle would be spared all battles, particularly today's.

On every side now the fighting flags affronted the heavens, demanding allegiance of those who massed behind them, even unto death itself. Her eye picked out the colourful silks, lovingly embroidered by wife and mother and sister alike. It was then that she saw it – the green and gold catching her attention. Excitedly, she pointed it out to Louisa. 'See . . . it's the Irish! Lavelle, Lavelle will be with them!' she said, the words coming in little nervous bursts. Now she was on her feet wanting to go down through them all. Go to that flag, comb through its followers line by line, one by one, until she found him.

Louisa caught her arm. 'Mother – I'm not sure it is the flag of the Irish Brigade. Even if it were so, Lavelle may not be under its colours. He could be anywhere!'

Ellen wanted to shake off Louisa's restraining arm. Lavelle *was* there. She *did* know it – in the way in which she had always known such things.

'And what will you do, Mother, even if he is there and you do find him?' she heard Louisa ask, as the din below them increased and, absolved of all sin, the vast armies began to muster themselves for war.

'We will go out later, when it is all over,' Louisa said, shepherding her away from the cauldron below.

NINETY-SEVEN

Lavelle surveyed the might of the two armies arrayed against each other. It was indeed a glorious sight: the grey and blue formations of infantry and horse; flags flying; sun-splashed sabres; the glinting of cannon, caisson and gun.

'Every man, boy and child in America must be here,' Lavelle exclaimed to himself. A sense of tremulous excitement began to rise in him. This was what brought men to the cauldron. To be part of a great design, partake in the grandeur of war – this splendid game. Yet it was all so raw, so primitive, so savage – tribe against tribe. 'Whatever war is – we're here . . . we're it,' he said out loud, then focused on the particular task at hand. Wherever, amongst the milling thousands would he find Stephen Joyce? Slowly he rotated the long-range lens of his rifle through the Rebel ranks of the Army of Northern Virginia. Hand unsteady, his scanning of Lee's army was erratic, so that when he got to the end of the seemingly never-ending long grey line, he was forced to start again.

It was no use. There were too many of them, and they were moving – anxious for fighting, outnumbered and all, as they were. Gettysburg was the 'high tide' for the Confederacy. A decisive win here on Northern soil – and the North would be dispirited . . . the North would crumble. Lee knew that. Today there would be fierce fighting. Today would be bloody.

393

Lavelle, himself, was ready to crumble with the North. The heat, the relentless marching, the continuous bloodbath it had all become. If the Rebels won today and the North surrendered, it wouldn't have worried him too much. Not that he thought the North ever would surrender. They couldn't . . . and not while the politicians could still dupe the next draft of sitting ducks to fill up the ranks, to be next in the firing line.

One way or the other, Lavelle was going to get out after Gettysburg. He had been one of the fortunate ones. The Irish Brigade had been cut to shreds, the losses so high, it caused the Little Bishop to say that 'The Brigade lost half of Ireland while fighting for America.' Recently Lavelle had begun loosely to think that a bullet itself might be kind, finish everything off . . . be a blessed relief. Be killed, instead of killing. It was a dangerous thought. Could take hold in the mind . . . make a sharpshooter not sharp . . . but shoddy . . . and slow.

If it wasn't for her. Yet, he was no nearer to finding her – and the Gettysburg crossroads was as about as likely a place as the Horn of Africa. But Stephen Joyce he might find here. Somewhere in the midst of all this mayhem.

Sulphurous smoke rose in great billowing clouds across his line of vision, as cannons pounded the skies, in a misguided kind of industry.

He would just have to wait, be patient. He decided his most effective plan would be to follow the flags. If he could find the Louisianians, then he would perhaps find Stephen. Even when the smoke cleared, it would still be difficult. The general mêlée of close-range charges and hand-to-hand combat would also prove an obstacle to identifying anybody. But he was trained for this . . . to seek and destroy a single individual. To follow that soldier's path, be patient in the kill. Today, he would seek out no other enemy soldier but one.

Stephen Joyce.

Again and again, his face squeezed against his gun-barrel, his eye squinted to the sights, Lavelle's gaze travelled over and back, and back and over the Confederate lines. Even while he looked, great gaps appeared in their ranks, the fallen matting the fields and hedgerows like some great blight on the land. For a moment Lavelle surveyed his own side.

Equally did they fall.

Momentarily a pang of conscience assailed him. He should be killing those who were killing his comrades.

He returned to the Rebels, and waited and watched, until the blood-drenched day was in its last frightful hurrah. His whole body ached, his eyes stung with the smoke of sulphur. It had been another fruitless day of many in the past months. No Stephen Joyce.

He began to doubt that Stephen was still with the Confederacy. Maybe, like General Meagher, Stephen too, had resigned. Or been already killed.

Then a pall of smoke from another killing explosion, rose and lifted clear of its victims. From behind it like some apocalyptic vision fading into sight, Lavelle saw him. Knew him instantly. The tall angular body astride the prancing chestnut, sword in hand urging on the grey hordes in front of him.

He levelled his sharpshooter's rifle. Stephen Joyce was in his sights and well within his accuracy. One shot and the despoiler of his family would be just another Confederate casualty. No one need know the history behind the speeding bullet – the betrayal, the loss of love, the family tragedy . . . Patrick.

A further cloud of battle-smoke obscured Lavelle's target. He had waited for this moment a long time – all the pavements of Boston, the rail-splitting miles to California, and all the dog-weary miles from Louisiana . . . to Gettysburg. It had driven him onwards, sharpened his will to survive all hazards.

Now he was here.

When the smoke cleared Stephen Joyce was still there.

In an instant Lavelle changed his mind. He had to confront his once-friend, see his face. Find out about Ellen, before he killed the man.

Leaving his place of cover, Lavelle ran low, back into the right flank of his own lines. Then he saw a small band of New Yorkers push forward into the Confederate midriff. He jostled and elbowed his way forward to join with these. They had formed themselves into a small circular group – watching their flanks and their rear as well as the enemy ahead. The fighting was toe to toe, each foothold of ground fought for, with spent muskets being used as clubs.

'The bayonet alone is wise,' Lavelle said to himself, now affixing the dreaded gun-knife to his weapon. Normally he had little use of it, today he might well have. The little band of Union soldiers he was with broke through the battle-line forcing the Rebels to retreat. Lavelle was now not thirty yards from his enemy.

'Stephen Joyce!' Lavelle shouted above the din.

He saw the horseman jerk the bit, turn around to face him. Then the look of recognition; the surprise as Stephen saw his old compatriot, now in the Union Blue of the enemy.

Lavelle broke through into a clear space between them. Stephen edged the seething chestnut towards the same space.

'Lavelle . . . old comrade – you're on the wrong side!' Stephen shouted, laughingly.

Lavelle now stood in front of the edgy animal. 'No, Stephen – not I, but you fighting for bondage instead of freedom.'

Stephen looked at him – no sense of past comradeship on Lavelle's face. 'Lavelle!' he tried again. 'We may be at arms but we are brothers-in-arms!'

'We might have been . . . before this!' And Lavelle thrust the book, stained with Patrick's blood into Stephen's hand. The mounted man looked at it – a darkness coming on his brow.

'It was you who found Patrick . . . the book?' Stephen said, some darker-still realisation striking him.

'It was I, Stephen, who killed my own son,' Lavelle replied. 'What matter if mistakenly . . . from a distance . . .' His words trailed off.

Stephen looked at his old friend. The loss of Ellen, then Patrick's death, had exacted more than the toll of time and battle. Lavelle was heart-weary, his handsome face gravelled with the disillusionment of life. Stephen remembered his own promise to Ellen. 'Lavelle – I am sorry to hear that. Sorry for everything. I never meant to dishonour you. I have loved her from first I saw her, long before your time. What force it was that drew us together again, I do not know.'

'You betrayed my trust, Stephen – seduced her with fine words – not even your own!'

Without awaiting an answer, Lavelle then flung himself at Stephen, catching his tunic, unhorsing him. The other man did not resist.

'God knows I loved her, Lavelle! But I won't kill you for her. You should go to her, Lavelle!' Stephen said.

'Where is she?' Lavelle demanded.

'She is here – on the battlegrounds,' Stephen said, turning his back to walk away.

Enraged that Ellen was somewhere nearby and still with Stephen, Lavelle charged at the retreating uniform, knocking Stephen to the ground. Knowing that Lavelle had misunderstood him, Stephen called out, 'No, Lavelle! Not as you . . .'

'You'll fight! By God, Stephen, you'll fight!' Lavelle rasped at him.

Then, oblivious to the raging battle, the two men circled each other, Stephen with his Griswald-made, push dagger, Lavelle with no less a fatal blade – curved, its tip like a harpooning fork. Steel would talk with steel – till one or other was silenced.

And so it waged between them, North and South, comrade against comrade. For love . . . for country . . . for pride . . . for revenge – it mattered not now in the rage that consumed them. Nor was even survival the cause which now fuelled their ferocity. Only to bring death to the other.

The slash and thrust of the knives bloodied their faces – slicing the battle-clothes they wore. Soon they were indistinguishable – blue or grey. Nor could one best the other – deliver the mortal blow.

Then Lavelle tripped against something behind him – a dead comrade's arm – lost his footing, half stumbling backwards towards the ground. Stephen was upon him then. Held him up a moment and drew back the push dagger to drive it home.

'I am sorry, Lavelle!' Stephen said, regret momentarily staying his hand.

Lavelle felt the rush of wind that preceded the thrust. He tried to shake free of the full driving force of the blade, succeeding in sending his own curved messenger to Stephen's breast.

'It is finished!' Stephen said, withdrawing his weapon from Lavelle. Then he took his friend's face in his hands and kissed him.

Lavelle started to say something, tried to remove his own weapon from Stephen but their combined strength could no longer keep them afoot and they sank to the ground. Beside each other they lay then, on the spent battlefield.

'She is here,' Stephen said. 'Not with me but with the wounded.'

'Ellen . . . ?' Lavelle asked.

'Yes, Ellen . . . she received Patrick's body,' Stephen said.

Lavelle somehow pushed himself up to look at the man. 'Here . . . ? Ellen . . . here . . . she knows . . . about Patrick?'

Stephen Joyce nodded. 'She seeks your forgiveness, Lavelle – as do I.'

Lavelle gave a little laugh. 'Forgiveness . . . ?' He took a moment. 'I have long sought her and long forgiven her . . . as I now do you, Stephen . . .'

'You still love her . . .' Stephen stated.

'After everything . . . and before everything.' Lavelle paused . . . 'And you – Stephen?'

'No . . . ! No . . . ! It was a thing apart . . .' the Confederate captain lied. 'It has long since passed.'

Lavelle listened, the fickleness of all things swimming in his mind – friendship . . . freedom . . . forgiveness . . . love . . . mankind itself.

Here at death's door, their life-blood ripening the earth, how hard it still was for men to be free . . . about truth. Truth – the first casualty of war . . . and of life.

'Yes!' Lavelle said, accepting the untruth.

NINETY-EIGHT

That second day of Gettysburg they could not deal with the wounded who now littered the outside of the hospitals, as well as the floors, walls and every conceivable space within. That day Ellen could not quell the tears of hopelessness that arose in her.

It had always been awful, horrible – soul killing – this wanton waste of life. Yet somehow, somewhere she had found hope and strength to carry on. Hope that soon it all would be over, that peace would at last reign. Now it seemed hopeless, no end to the madness assaulting men's minds; the lust for blood seemingly unquenchable.

Still, as darkness fell, she dragged herself out again to search through the wounded, Louisa accompanying her.

Now, her senses dulled by so much death, Ellen bypassed those calling for help. Over mangled mounds of limbs she stumbled, driven on by some madness, as if the malodorous air had taken her over, impregnated her body with its evil intent.

A hand clawed at her skirt. Frantically she brushed by it, intent only on covering as much ground – and as many bodies as she could.

Now, those clad in grey did not warrant even a cursory glance. For Lavelle was not in grey – but in blue. Where she could she untangled those in blue, tugging at an arm or foot to pull them clear for inspection. Then, her eyes closed to their wounds, her ears to their cries, she half ran, half crawled to where next she might find him. Once, while tugging at a body in grey, which lay over that of one in blue, a voice from a raggle of Confederate litter-bearers shouted 'Git away from that boy!' while another said loudly, 'Damned Yankee wom-en'd have the trousers off'n you quicker than a N'Orleans whorehouse!'

She scampered away, making no rebuke, hearing them talk as she retreated. 'C'mon, pitch him up here, 'fore 'em maggots get him.' While yet another said, 'Bet he'd prefer maggots all over him than those Northern she-devils!'

Ellen, bent to examine another corpse, heard their laughter. She moved on, began whispering his name to herself. 'Lavelle! Lavelle!' As if it gave life to him, as if he were somewhere there – near her.

Then she began to say it louder over the bodies, sum-moning him from wherever among them he lay, until she was shouting it out – 'Lavelle! Lavelle!' – like the damned calling out for redemption.

Louisa, some distance behind her, struggled to keep up with her mother, fearful of whatever consequence might befall Ellen – whether she found Lavelle or not.

The dusk-light now cast its silvering hue over the giant battlefield. Low clouds of smoke or mist – she couldn't tell – eerily etched the crutched, the crippled and the corpsed, into one. Grey became blue; blue became silver-hued – changelings all, metamorphosed into each other. A Stygian field filled with shadows, awaiting angels to bear them up out of the Dantean darkness.

A voice called out for 'water!', then another.

She hesitated. Could not see them.

Then the first voice again.

She went towards it. Hurrying. Something about it. She, still calling for – Lavelle! Lavelle!

At first she thought she was mistaken. Then she heard it again. Her own name being summoned.

'Ellen! Ellen!' the faint voice called.

It must be one of her boys – from the hospital. One whom she or the others had 'made whole'. Sent out again for destruction.

Her mind was in turmoil. The men never addressed her in that manner.

She turned – saw the two bodies lumped together. Confederate grey . . . Union blue.

Ran to them.

Trembling.

Spilling the precious water from the canteen.

Then she saw him, hand outstretched to her.

'Oh, Stephen! Oh, my God, Stephen!' she cried. She fell to her knees beside him, looking for the wound.

'Lavelle! Lavelle!' he gasped into her face, his eyes frantically trying to get her to understand. His mind was altered – she could see the knife, its ornate hilt. But he was alive!

'Oh, Stephen! It's all right now! I'll get . . . !'

'No . . . No!' he said, grabbing at her arm, mouthing something. 'Lavelle!'

What was he saying?

'Lavelle?' she repeated, still wondering what Stephen meant.

Somehow he found the strength to tug harder, pull her arm around. 'Lavelle . . . there!' he gasped.

It took her a moment. She looked at the crumpled body in blue beside Stephen. Then looked back to Stephen, trying to make sense of it all.

Fearfully, she reached a hand for the half-buried face, slowly turning it towards her, into the dying light. Then she saw him – older, war-worn . . . but it was *him*.

'Lavelle . . . ! Lavelle . . . ! How? . . . Stephen? Oh, Jesus . . . ! Oh, Jesus, Mary . . . !'

She turned from one to the other. Like some wild thing. Trapped. Beyond any utterance.

'Oh God! Oh God!'

She turned Lavelle, seeing Stephen's knife beside him, talking madly to herself, the tears flooding her face, trying to swallow, fighting for breath.

He was still alive but semi-conscious.

'Louisa . . . !' she shouted – 'Oh, Sweet Jesus – Louisa!

'Lavelle! Lavelle!' she again shouted. 'Wake up! Wake up!' She slapped his face. Then harder, welting his skin.

'It's me, Lavelle! Me . . . Ellen! Oh, God, you found . . . ! I found . . . ! Wake up!' she screamed.

He made a sound. Tried to open his eyes.

'The water!' She remembered. 'The water!' Somehow, she managed to hold his head and get the canteen free of her body. She wet the tips of her fingers, shaking – trying not to waste it – but it still dripping on to his shirt.

Where was Louisa . . . anybody?

She put her fingers to his lips, moistened his eyes. Fumbled some more drops from the canteen. Repeated the anointing.

He opened his mouth. Now she forced the canteen against his lips. Then he opened his eyes, saw her.

'Ellen! Ellen . . . ! Darling Ellen!'

'Lavelle! Oh, thank God! Thank God – Louisa . . . Louisa?' she called out, the names tumbling from her lips.

Stephen! She had to give *him* water. Save the two of them!

'Stephen!' She moved over to him – got her free arm around his shoulder, pulling him into her. Propped the two of them there, her face between them. The water! Stephen was able to half-hold it to his mouth but it sluiced out over his face and hers.

Then Lavelle. He couldn't take it. She couldn't manage the two of them.

'Louisa!' Where was Louisa?

She gulped a mouthful of water, held it there. Then with her lips forced open Lavelle's mouth and expelled the water into it. The same she did for Stephen.

'Ellen . . . !' It was Lavelle . . . 'I searched . . .'

'Oh, Lavelle . . . ! I knew . . . I couldn't go back . . . after . . .' She looked at Stephen.

'Stephen . . . ! Lavelle . . . ! I brought it to this.'

She held the two of them into her.

'It was me . . . Ellen.' Lavelle's mouth moved against her breast, muffling the sound.

'It was me . . . Ellen . . . I . . . Patrick . . . I didn't . . . !'

'I know, Lavelle . . . oh, I know,' she said. 'You couldn't have known . . . there is no blame.

'No blame,' she repeated.

And she knelt between them, comforted by their nearness, as much as she sought to comfort them.

She spoke to them, 'Lavelle . . . ? Stephen . . . ?' They did not answer. Heads still bowed in silence – forgiven and forgiving her.

Behind her someone approaching . . . Louisa!

'Lavelle . . . and Stephen!' she said, without turning to face her child.

Louisa knelt beside her, releasing Ellen's arm from Lavelle, the younger woman in turn holding him, kissing his fair hair, giving thanks to God. She found Lavelle's wound. It was badly oozing blood. From some deep fold within her nun's garb, she drew a wad of bandaging. This Louisa packed hard against the wound, to stem the further flow of his blood. Praying that she wasn't already too late.

Ellen remained kneeling. 'Soil is sacred,' she whispered, absently.

Louisa watched as her mother, one arm still around Stephen, bent to the reddened earth, kissing the dark soil, in some primitive consecration. On the ground between them Louisa noticed the book. Somehow, managed to retrieve it. *Love Elegies and Holy Sonnets*. She remembered it. 'Love elegies, holy songs – one and the same,' she said aloud, 'both searching the higher ground.'

Now in the after-mist of battle, the sounds of destruction had abated.

Beyond them Ellen saw the slow line of lanterns yellowing the fields. Criss-crossing, stopping, being lowered, then being lifted again, their clanking and creaking strangely comforting against the calls for comrades, long lost to the world.

She thought of them all – the young men. All the fine young men.

From Tennessee and Germany; from New York and New Jersey; from New England to New Orleans . . . and the four green fields of Ireland. The list was endless, every one of them a mother's son – some mother's fair-haired boy.

She stood then as Louisa held them both. Then keened out her song of lamentation over the plains of Gettysburg.

Keened it out for Lavelle and for Stephen. Keened it out over the bodies of all the fine young men . . .

> 'Oh, my fair-haired boy, no more I'll see,
> You walk the meadows green,
> Or hear your song run through the field,
> Like yon mountain stream . . .

Absently she sang as if to block out the enormity of at last finding Lavelle and Stephen.

> 'If not in life we'll be as one
> Then, in death we'll be;
> And there will grow two hawthorn trees
> Above my love and me;
> And they will reach up to the sky –
> Intertwined be,
> And the hawthorn flower will bloom where lie,
> My fair-haired boy . . . and me . . .'

All around them the battlefield had gone quiet, the lanterns stilled. It would be her last song.

'Stephen is gone, Mother!' she heard Louisa say.

She knelt down again to take him from Louisa. Hold him

in the last embrace, kissing his dark head. 'Goodbye, *a stor*,' she said fondly, offering a prayer over him, not that he was ever much for prayers, she remembered.

She looked at Louisa beside her, still cradling Lavelle, caressing his forehead. Louisa – Sister Veronica, as the nuns had re-christened her – wiping the face of Jesus. Ellen reached over a hand, touching Louisa's face. She, stained with tears, looked up from holding Lavelle.

Everything had been stripped from this woman . . . stripped naked as the Cross. She was all Ellen had left now. Nothing between them. Not blood, not kith nor kin. Only a chance crossing. Nothing between them . . . but everything.

And now, Lavelle, and Stephen, both succumbed in the last sleep.

How they both did love her . . . and she them. Loved each of them in a different fashion, but truly, Louisa believed. Love, no more than hate, was not an exclusive emotion. She thought again of Jared Prudhomme . . . and her God. How the boy had almost come between them – for a while.

The night breeze caused a shiver in her. Someone walking over her grave, the old people held it to be. She looked down at Lavelle, about to unlock him from her arms – pass him to Ellen who had gently laid Stephen to rest and now waited to receive Lavelle.

Louisa felt the shiver again. She said nothing. Waited to be sure.

Then she felt it again, almost imperceptible – the shiver, not in her, but in Lavelle.

The dead come back to life.

Louisa bowed her head a moment, giving thanks. Then, looking to Ellen kneeling stricken beside her, Louisa reached out, taking her mother's hand in hers, the words trembling from her lips.

'*Níor éag sé fós!*'

'Mother – he's alive . . . !'

'Lavelle is alive!'

406

AUTHOR'S NOTES

The American Civil War commenced with the firing by Southern Confederate troops on the Union garrison at Fort Sumter, in Charleston Harbour, South Carolina, at 4.30 am, April 12th 1861. It ended on April 9th 1865 with the surrender by General Robert E. Lee to General Ulysses S. Grant at the Appomattox Courthouse, Virginia. During its four-year campaign, there were 10,000 engagements in battle. Over three million Americans fought each other, killing some 620,000 of their countrymen – two per cent of the population. An estimated 145,000 Irish immigrants fought for the Northern cause, some 40,000 for the South. Many who in Ireland shared the same Republican ideals in Ireland.

'Your soldier's heart almost stood still as he watched those sons of Erin fearlessly rush to their death. The brilliant assault on Mary's Heights of their Irish Brigade was beyond description. Why, my darling, we forgot they were fighting us, and cheer after cheer at their fearlessness went up all along our lines.'
                                                                Confederate General George Pickett

The minie ball caused ninety-four per cent of all wounds.

'I firmly believe that before many centuries more Science will be the master of man. The engines he will have invented will be beyond his strength to control. Someday science itself shall have the existence of mankind in its power and the human race commit suicide by blowing up the world.'
                                                                Henry Adams, 11th April, 1862

Lavelle's letter to Ellen is based upon Sullivan Ballou's letter to his wife Sarah written on 14th July 1861, from Washington DC. A major, 2nd Regiment, Rhode Island Volunteers, he was wounded one week later on 21st July at the battle of First Bull Run. He died on 29th July aged thirty two years. Sarah was twenty four. She never remarried and died at age eighty in 1917. They are buried next to each other at Swan Point Cemetery, Providence, Rhode Island. Ironically, Sullivan Ballou's love letter to Sarah was never mailed.

The scene where Lavelle shoots Patrick is based on an account at the battle of Malvern Hill where a Sergeant Docherty shot dead his own son, a sniper on the opposing side.

The Crust Farm scene with Dr Licoix and the negro children is based on real events

The Father Corby scene is based on various recorded accounts of the priest's dispensation of a General Absolution from sin, before the second day of the Battle of Gettysburg. A statue to Fr Corby was erected on a boulder at Gettysburg, in 1910. Some accounts indicate it is the actual boulder on which the priest once stood.

As did Oxy, women joining the armies as men was not unknown and there are at least some reported cases of 'male' soldiers actually giving birth. Other 'roses of intrigue' acted as spies for either side. Some five hundred Civil War soldiers faced firing squads or the gallows, the majority for desertion.

The description of Le Petit Versailles is based partly upon Evergreen Plantation and also Houmas House Plantation in Louisiana.

Civil War Songs

The first Civil War song was written three days after the firing on Fort Sumter. Four years later, by the time the war was over, two thousand new songs had been added to the American popular songbook. Many existing songs crossed the ocean from Ireland to America, the same songs often sung by both sides of the conflict.

Songs in the book
Readers have seemed interested in the origin of the songs, poems, prayers and sayings used throughout *The Whitest Flower* and *The Element of Fire*. These are now posted on www.brendangraham.com

Here are notes to the songs used in *The Brightest Day, the Darkest Night*.

Praise to the Earth
. . . a song written for Ellen.
Used by permission Warner Chappell Music/International Music Publications

Ochon an Gorta Mor`
An unaccompanied song in Irish in the *sean-nos* style. I had begun working on this song when coincidentally I was invited to write a piece for inclusion in the *Ceol Reoite* (Frozen Music – after Goethe's 'Architecture is frozen music') Millennium project. Composers were challenged to release the 'frozen music' in a number of Ireland's best-known Heritage sites

The gifted young *sean-nos* singer from Barna in Connemara, Roisin Elsafty invested the song with ancient life for the *Ceol Reoite* project, while what was only intended as a demo, recorded in St Kevin's Church, Glendalough, slipped un-named on to the Dervish album Spirit as the final and 'hidden' track.

Mention must also be made of Nuala Ni Chanainn's performance of it in Aistir/Voyages, a contemporary dance piece from acclaimed Swiss troupe Tanz Ensemble Cathy Sharp. Used by permission Warner Chappell Music/International Music Publications.

You Raise Me Up
Norwegian composer, Rolf Lovland and Irish violinist, Fionnuala Sherry, who together make up Secret Garden, contacted me upon reading Ellen's story in *The Whitest Flower*, and asked if I would write a lyric to a newly-written melody. The result was You Raise Me Up. It seemed fitting that the circle should be completed and the song end up back with Ellen – and so it has, as Jared Prudhomme's love song to Louisa. I am grateful to Rolf, in the first instance, for trusting me with his beautiful melody and to the many wonderful artistes the world over, who have lent life to the lyrics; most notably Brian Kennedy's emotive first recording of it with Secret Garden; and Josh Groban who so movingly brought the song to the heart of America, *buiochas mor*.
Used by permission Peermusic, Ireland; Universal Music AS, Sweden.

Sleepsong
Again, a Rolf Lovland melody. The words came when sitting by the bedside of my youngest daughter, before she left for Australia. The years just seemed to roll away, to a previous time of lullabies and sleep-songs. It then seemed an appropriate song by which Ellen could say goodbye to Patrick. First recorded by Secret Garden, featuring Saoirse, more recently Kate Ceberano has been singing it . . . in Australia!
Used by permission Universal Music AS, Sweden

The Fair-Haired Boy
I wrote this specifically to be Ellen's song . . . and it is indeed her song for each of her loves, for Patrick, her son – and for all the young men who so tragically perish in the terrible cauldron of Civil War. Of Cathy Jordan's rendition of it, I could ask nothing more.
Used by permission WarnerChappell Music/International Music Publications

Crucan na bPaiste
The melody based on a traditional tune – Cailin na Gruaige Bainne – I wrote this song for Ellen. Crucan na bPaiste – a burial place of unbaptised children – sits high in the Maamtrasna Valley, over Lough Nafooey and Lough Mask . . . and is the location of the final scene in *The Whitest Flower*. Irish singer Katie McMahon and, more recently, Scottish singer Karen Matheson have each brought to it their special gifts of lifting a song out of the ordinary in which it was written.

I Am The Sky
Some words written for my daughter's wedding, it is here Ellen's remembrance of sustaining elemental things in this area where I live.

The Lakes of Pontchartrain
Since first I heard Paul Brady's singularly fine version of this old Creole love song I, like Oxy, have wanted to go there. It also seemed fitting, when the character of Kizzie presented herself, that her doomed romance with Oxy should hasten to a conclusion on the shores of the Pontchartrain.

Myfanwy is one of the great Welsh songs of *hiraeth*, or longing. Bryn Terfel's evocation of it convinced me it had to be Evan's cry of belonging for homeland, for his love for Myfanwy, and even for life itself.

The Last Rose of Summer
In one of the many museums I visited in America, I came across a 'Top Ten' of American Civil War Songs, of which Moore's famous melody was at No.1. For centuries those who have crossed the Atlantic Ocean to America have brought their songs with them. Like the people themselves, the songs ended up divided on both sides of the conflict. This was one which brought comfort to the campfires of both North and South.

Has Sorrow Thy Young Days Shaded
Another of Moore's melodies. The moment I heard Roisin O' Reilly's singing of it, I knew it was what Ellen would sing in Mary's last moments.

Full lyrics are available on www.brendangraham.com